Life on Pleasant

Therese Dotray-Tulloch

To Timothy, Thank you for believing in me.

"Darkness cannot drive out darkness; only light can do that. Hate cannot drive out hate; only love can do that."

Martin Luther King, Jr.

"If we cannot now end our differences, at least we can help make the world safe for diversity".

John F. Kennedy

"Every moment and every event of every man's life on earth plants something in his soul."

Thomas Merton

Therese Dotray-Tulloch

Prologue

The first time I laid eyes on Mickey M. Beaulieu was in the backyard of our three-storey, stucco house on Pleasant Avenue. The plastic swimming pool in the backyard was filled nearly to the top of its twenty-four inches, and all the kids from the neighborhood were lined up outside of the chain-link fence waiting anxiously to see who would be the lucky ones to get to cool off in the only pool on the whole block. There were eight of us kids in the family at that time with one more on the way, and the pool was only so big, so Mom allowed each of us to choose just one friend to come in and swim with us.

At the time, I had two best friends to choose from. It wasn't too hard to keep track of whose turn it was to swim, Sandy's or Tessa's. Sandy was short and tan with thick black hair down to her waist.

She was quiet, sweet, and obedient to all of my wishes. Tessa was tall and pale with a huge guffawing laugh that made whatever we were doing seem that much more enjoyable. Her stringy brown hair was usually held back with a rubber band giving her a no-nonsense appearance which suited her personality. The girls always knew whose turn it was to enter the yard and swim. I never tricked them or varied the order at all, so much so that they both wouldn't have even had to turn up except that they knew that my sister Marilyn only had one best friend in the neighborhood, an only child named Lee-Lee Gauze.

Lee-Lee was sometimes forced to do boring grown-up things with her Mom and so couldn't always turn up to go for a dip. On those days, Marilyn borrowed one of my best friends to come in the yard and be her swimming-pool mate. I was happy for my friends when this happened, but it always made me feel a little bad, too, because if Sandy or Tessa came in as Marilyn's choice, then they would have to be Marilyn's friend the whole time. Marilyn was two years and one month older than me which meant she did everything better and sooner than I did. She was rather bossy, so Sandy or Tessa would start bossing me around, too.

On the day I met Mickey, I was supposed to choose Tessa. I had chosen Sandy the previous day. Lee-Lee was forced to go to Jim's Beauty Parlor the day before to sit through her mom, Gladys', haircut and perm. The good thing was that Jim had a stack of coloring books and a 64-piece box of Crayola crayons for the kids to use while their moms got their hair wound up in tiny pink curlers so tightly their faces looked all stretched out while the curlers were plastered all over their slick heads. The bad thing was that the smell of a perm stuck on you like melting bubblegum on the sidewalk on a warm summer day. Marilyn had picked Tessa as her friend while Lee-Lee colored in the foul-smelling beauty parlor. I thought Tessa had excessively enjoyed the chance to get to do everything before Sandy and me, and when we were playing 'Seven Steps', she purposely stomped on my foot on the Second Step just like Marilyn always does. I couldn't really choose Sandy again though 'cause that wouldn't be fair, and the friendship between the three of us worked because we were always fair.

As my eyes wavered between Sandy and Tessa, they suddenly alighted upon the darkest pair of brown eyes I had ever seen in all my six years. I think what struck me the most was how calm they appeared especially amongst all of the other kids' eyes which were pleading silently and trying to say without words 'come on, pick me, pick me, pick me!' Mickey's eyes were studiously curious and detached in a way that reminded me of grown-ups who really don't care about whose turn it is to sit in the front seat of the car. Every kid knows it's hugely important to the ones who otherwise have to sit in the back seat staring at the big heads in front of them, not tall enough to see over them and too short to see much out of the side windows. Mickey's dark-chocolate brown eyes stared out from his round, coffee-colored face. His black hair stood out in the crowd of pale heads like a crow perched among the blonde tassels in a cornfield.

Mickey is older in another, darker memory I have of him but not too terribly much older. He's taller yet he always was short for his age. Not little though, but stocky, strong. I remember noticing how thick his wrists looked clamped inside the handcuffs and seeing the blood on his sleeve and wondering, was it his or Dr. Olson's? His eyes were the same though, and even though Mrs. Olson was wailing and little Richard was clinging to Mickey's pant leg crying so hysterically it took two police officers to pry him off, the calm never left Mickey's eyes as they bore deeply into mine. He was not fretting nor squirming but standing completely still; his black, disheveled hair giving him a carefree, boyish look. He appeared at peace even in the midst of all the chaos.

Chapter 1

The day before I met Mickey was a hot, sticky one in the summer of 1965. I had a dishtowel tied over my eyes, and I was anxious to find out how much longer it would be before I got something to eat. Marilyn had tied the dishtowel on me. Marilyn at eight years old was tall for her age. She had dark brown hair cut in a short, pixie hairstyle, a button nose perched above a tiny mouth with cherry-colored lips. My light brown hair was longer and usually tied back in a ponytail. That day I had left the house in such a hurry, it was still loose around my shoulders.

I always let my sister blindfold me on the days we played "Let's Lunch Here". Marilyn had recently learned how to ride a bike and she always gave me rides on the back. We went so much faster than I ever could go on my trike. At lunchtime, we had gone inside and made chipwich sandwiches: white Wonder bread with creamy Skippy peanut butter and potato chips on the top of the peanut butter and then another piece of bread on top of that. We weren't allowed to leave the block, so Marilyn blindfolded me and helped me onto the back of her banana-seat bike and started biking around the block. Feeling the breeze in my hair, I held on tightly to Marilyn's waist. It felt like we were moving so fast! The cracks in the sidewalk caused us to bounce rhythmically as we rode along. After a while, Marilyn asked, "Lunch here?"

"Nope," I answered.

"Then, how about lunch here?" she asked a few minutes later. When we played 'Let's Lunch Here," we would go around and around the block for ages until I would finally thrust out my arm and enthusiastically say:"Let's lunch here!" Wherever I happened to be pointing is exactly where we would dismount, sit down, and eat our lunch. No one in the neighborhood cared, of course, if we sat on their lawn to have our picnic, and I got pretty good at knowing where we were by how fast we were coasting downhill, or by where the sidewalk wasn't smooth and we bounced over the cracks. If we stopped on the Dawson's lawn to eat, Mrs. Dawson always came outside with some freshly-baked cookies she had just made for our dessert, so we often ended up lunching there.

The Olson's lived right next door to the Dawson's. That day, Marilyn shouted out "Hey Kenny!" So I knew where we were. I pictured Kenny with his flaming red hair and his typical unhappy scowl on his freckled face. I was thinking maybe we should stop soon to enjoy some of Mrs. Dawson's cookies but I was enjoying the ride too much.

"Kenny's got company," Marilyn said, her voice sounding far away as it reached me through the cotton cloth tied over my ears. "Someone with dark hair and a big head."

After riding around the block an excessive number of times, I finally shouted "Let's lunch here!" We were on Mrs. Agneau's lawn whose house is right next to ours! Marilyn and I laughed and laughed at that but we still sat right there under the beautiful willow tree as if we were off on some exciting adventure far from home. After a while, Mrs. Agneau came outside to sit with us bringing little dishes of maple nut ice cream, something we had never had on a picnic lunch before. She wore a yellow housedress with tiny blue flower print covered by her cream-colored apron. Mrs. Agneau's silky white hair was worn long. It had a mysterious blue tint which appeared even bluer every time she came back from her appointment with Joel. Although her skin was covered with wrinkles, she still took time with her appearance and always had rose-colored cheeks and shiny red lipstick on her mouth. Mrs. Agneau had been living in the neighborhood longer than any other resident. Her house was even bigger than the Olsons. She was as down to earth as they were haughty and we loved her like a grandma.

Doc Olson lived in the big yellow house directly across the alley from ours. He was a huge man with a small voice who had participated in the delivery of most of the kids in the neighborhood. Doc had grey, greasy hair that he combed from his high forehead to the back of his head attempting to cover his thinning top. His beady eyes peered out behind glasses which were always falling down onto his bulbous nose causing him to push them back into place with his surprisingly smooth forefinger. Mrs. Olson was a tall woman but even she looked petite next to Doc. She was the only woman in the whole neighborhood who went out of the house to go to work every day. Because of this, she didn't look like my mom or the other women on our block. She always wore high-heeled pumps that made a hollow tapping sound as she walked down the concrete sidewalk to her car. She wore tight skirts and masculine blouses. Her hair was done up with so much Aqua Net hairspray that it didn't matter how windy it was outside, not a single hair of her head loosened. The Olsons had one son, Kenny. A few days earlier, we'd noticed a strange-looking bus parked in front of the Olson's large Victorian residence. Mom told us the Olsons were adopting a child. I guessed that was because Mrs. Olson was too busy going to work to take the time to let another baby grow inside of her. Besides, all those skirts she wore wouldn't be big enough for a pregnant woman to wear. She'd have to get some of the big, comfy tent dresses with large, colorful flowers scattered all over them that the rest of the women in the neighborhood wore, and she didn't seem like the kind of woman who would ever wear those.

Doc Olson's office was on Nicollet Avenue down by the Hub Shopping Center. Visiting the doctor required Mom to load all of us into our big brown station wagon for the 3-mile drive. We would sit and wait while she dragged whoever the sick patient was at the time with her in to see Doc. We weren't allowed to get out of the car while we waited, of course, but that was fine with us. We liked to watch the busy traffic on Nicollet and to analyze everyone who got off at the bus stop right in front of the doctor's office building's parking lot.

"That shriveled up old man just came from visiting his dead wife's grave at the Lakewood Cemetery," my sister Polly speculated. Polly was two years older than Marilyn and four years older than me. She had lots of different friends and was always being asked to sleep over at someone else's house. She even went all the way to California once with a friend and her family; that made her the first one of us to leave the state of Minnesota.

"And that colored man just got done with his shift shining shoes," my brother Pat answered authoritatively. Pat was just a year older than Polly. He was tall and skinny with big ears poking out on either side of his narrow face. His hazel eyes were always twinkling as he was usually up to some sort of mischief. Pat didn't want anyone to know it, but he was also the sweetest one in the whole family.

I noticed that all of the people who got off at the bus stop started walking in the same direction that the bus was going, which was towards the Hub Shopping Center. "Why don't those people just stay on the bus and get off at the Hub, that's where they're going anyway," I asked.

"That's because Minneapolis ends right here," my oldest brother, Neil answered. "If you stay on to the next block to get off at the Hub, you'd have to pay another dime. Then you'd be in the city of Richfield. It's mostly just the coloreds and Indians getting off because they don't have extra dimes sitting around in their pockets." Neil had just turned 13. He had curly brown hair, a plump, round face, and dimples on his cheeks which looked even deeper than normal every time he smiled. He smiled a lot. He had recently gotten eyeglasses which gave him a brainy sort of look. Neil took his job as the eldest boy in the family very seriously. If we ever needed any help with anything, we turned to Neil.

"Well, that's not fair," I ventured. "Why don't some of the white people sitting on the bus with extra dimes in their pockets give some to the others so they can stay on the bus, too?"

"Probably 'cause they're scared to talk to them," Neil explained.

"Scared? How come?"

"Why, mostly just because they're different. That's something you'll learn as you get older, Ginny. People like to stick to their own kind. Catholics stick with Catholics, Lutherans with Lutherans, whites with whites, coloreds with coloreds, Indians with Indians. It's easier to get along with people just like you by your side. Someone who's different from you is hard to understand and is scary even."

"I'm not scared," I declared. "That's just dumb." To prove the point, I stuck my head out the window and yelled at the colored man walking by. "Hey there, Mister, it sure is a nice day out today, isn't it? Lots better than yesterday with all of that rain!" The large man in the plaid pants I was addressing looked over at our car. He didn't answer me but he did put his hand to the jaunty-looking hat perched upon his head and acknowledged my shout with a tip of his head. "He doesn't look scared of me, neither." I sat back in my seat satisfied with myself.

The day I picked Mickey was even hotter than the day before. My brothers, sisters, and I had finished our chores as quickly as possible and were now congregating in the backyard. It was a huge, fenced in yard half covered in grass, half covered with a tarred black top, with a border garden flush against the fences on either side.

"An Injun?" Our neighbor, little Jimmy Demoray shouted. "You can't choose an Injun else'n the water in the swimming pool's gonna turn red and then we'll all turn red, too. And then we'll get kicked out of Incy and be forced to go to Agassiz and we'll all start drinkin and ..."

Jimmy's face was as red as a ripe tomato while he shouted his complaint. He had his swimsuit balled up in his tiny fist. It was apparent it hadn't been washed since he'd last swum in it and the musty smell of stale dampness was fierce.

"You shut your trap or I'll shut it for you" I hissed while shoving Jimmy out of the way. "This here boy is swimming with me today and if any of you don't like it, well, too bad, so sad!"

I couldn't look at Sandy or Tessa as I cracked open the gate for the somber little Indian to pass through. I knew well enough that their eyebrows would be shooting straight up through their scissor-cut bangs. Their mouths were probably still hanging open in surprise and indignation, too, but I knew they'd get over it just fine. They would probably end up in Tessa's backyard playing hopscotch. Before they knew it, tomorrow would be here and once again they'd be lined up outside the fence and I would surely pick Tessa to come in and swim with me. Today's indiscretion would be forgotten.

"I know who you are," I told Mickey the moment he was secure inside the yard. "You're Doc Olson's new boy." He was wearing cut-off, faded jeans with little white threads dangling on his legs. His washed out green T-shirt was too big on his undersized frame making him look even smaller. He was barefoot as were the rest of us. Thick, dark bangs fell down from his forehead above wide-set eyes with slightly upturned edges. His flat nose sat squarely in the middle of his round face.

"I know who you are, too," he replied with a crooked little grin that made the dimple in his left cheek cave in. "You're the blindfolded girl on the back of the bike."

"I'm glad you're not a baby" I grinned at Mickey.

I had assumed the Olsons had adopted a baby. But seeing Kenny Olson standing beside Mickey at the fence outside of our yard, I'd put two and two together. Kenny had never been picked to swim in our pool because he'd never come before. Kenny usually kept to himself. He was a strange, lonely boy with a mean streak. He liked to throw rocks at passing cars and shoot birds with his slingshot. Maybe he was afraid to come alone and now that he had a new brother he felt braver. Pat picked Kenny to come in and swim that day right after I picked Mickey so Kenny wouldn't feel left out. Spontaneous thoughtfulness like that was typical of Pat.

"And I'm glad to see you've got eyes behind the blindfold," Mickey answered. "Green eyes."

I pushed my straggly hair out of my eyes to size him up better. My sun burnt nose was peeling and I felt way too tall as I felt Mickey looking up at me. My legs were long and skinny; I perched on one of them while I swung the other one back and forth holding onto the fence with both hands.

"I'm Virginia Louise Ashcroft," I told Mickey. "Everyone calls me Ginny."

"I'm Mickey," He smiled a crooked grin I would soon come to know so well.

"Mickey Olson now, right?'

"No," Mickey looked uncomfortable and stared down at his feet. He began tracing the crack in the sidewalk with his big toe scraping it back and forth, back and forth.

"But I thought the Olsons adopted you. Don't you have the same last name as the folks who adopt you?" I asked.

"They're not exactly adopting me. I'm just staying with them for a while. I have my own family."

"Well, where are they? Are they staying with the Olson's too?"

"No, most of them live in South Dakota. It's in a place called Crow Creek." Mickey's eyes met mine and I saw the challenge in them. What he was saying didn't make sense to me so I persisted.

"Is that far? Why aren't you still staying with your real folks then?"

I saw Mickey staring behind me then looking as if he'd just seen a ghost. I turned around to see what it was that had scared him so and saw the back of a head crowned with shiny black hair.

"Better watch out for her," I told Mickey. "That's the old woman who's always going through everybody's garbage. Probably drunk, too, is what Neil says. Mrs. Agneau, she's the nice lady who lives right next door; she calls her Caroline and is always giving her food and clothes and stuff. I call her Crazy Caroline. People say she's a witch and will cast a spell on you if you're not careful. If I were you, I'd stay just as far away from her as possible!"

Just then, Pat pushed me from behind and shouted, "Enough of your jabbering. Let the poor boy in the pool already! Last one in's a rotten egg!" Mickey and I raced into the pool with the rest of the gang.

I didn't know it yet, but that day I met my soul mate.

Chapter 2

Before Mickey, Crazy Caroline was the first Indian I ever knew by name. We lived on the West side of Nicollet Avenue. No coloreds or Indians lived West of Nicollet. We lived on Pleasant Avenue in a neighborhood of big homes stuffed to the brims with large Catholic families. There were eight kids in our family and that was about average; Kenny Olson's family was the smallest on the block of course. I was number six in my family and the youngest of four girls. We had four brothers, too. Jane was the oldest at 14 years old. Fair-haired and beautiful, she had been taking care of the rest of us her whole life. Neil was next at 13. Full of energy and mischief, he kept the grownups on their toes. Pat, 11, was the entertainer of the family. He could make even the crotchetiest old man laugh. He made fun of all of us but no one had a kinder heart than Pat. Polly, ten, was the most social of the family and she always had a gaggle of friends around her. She was funny and game but also loyal and true. Polly was the one I always told all my secrets to. Marilyn at eight was smart and determined. I was six always trying hard to keep up with my older siblings. After me was Greg, age five. He was small for his age and seemed to spend all his time trying to make up for it. He had huge green eyes with long black lashes over a freckled, upturned nose. He was always getting into trouble and causing huge problems for the rest of us. Danny was three, our little angel. With his deep set eyes and pug nose, he acted just as sweetly as he looked. Mom and Dad weren't done yet however. When the parish priest, Father Touey, would finish baptizing the newest Ashcroft and all of the other newborn members of the church, he would always say to the proud parents, "We'll see you all back here again at next year's baptism!" The exhausted parents would smile in agreement, proud to be doing their procreative duties.

We moved into our comfortable house on Pleasant Avenue from Steven's Avenue because a freeway was being built leading from Laredo, Texas to Duluth, Minnesota. In 1956, President Eisenhower had signed the bill creating the interstate system which turned out to be one of the most successful federal programs ever. Our house had been sitting right in the path of Interstate 35. Of all the freeways stitched this way and that across the country, only I-35 bears the distinction of twice dividing into East and West versions of itself: 35East in Dallas and St. Paul, and 35West in Fort Worth and Minneapolis. Our house on Stevens was on the Minneapolis stretch of the freeway but we didn't mind leaving it as we'd long outgrown the ramshackle old home. Besides, the new house was even closer to Incarnation only 2 ½ blocks away.

Incarnation Catholic Church and School were on Pleasant Avenue, too, and at the center of our lives. Everyone in the neighborhood belonged to the parish. Weekday mornings the sidewalks would be full of kids on their way to school. Sundays entire families would be seen walking in their finest to one of the three masses offered. The corner of 38th and Pleasant was a bastion of Roman Catholicism with a spacious brick building on each corner representing her wealth and presence. There was the Grade School for First through Fourth grades on the NE corner with its surrounding playground and cafeteria in the basement. Across the street to the West was the convent, home to more than two dozen nuns still wearing the old-fashioned habits hiding everything but pale hands and faces. South of the convent across the street was the Grade School for the Fifth through Eighth grade kids. To the East was the church itself, a huge Gothic structure built 50 years earlier as a source of great pride to the Catholics in South Minneapolis. South of the church was the beautiful three-storey rectory, the home for the five priests serving Incarnation as well as a safe haven for troubled priests of the arch diocese suffering from alcoholism, a crisis of faith, or a mental breakdown. Not until years later would we understand that many of these wayward priests were actually briefly placed at Incy before another parish could be found for them when they'd had to be whisked away from their previous parish due to increasingly frequent claims of improper dealings with children.

Two blocks to the south, our house was crowded and messy in the homiest of ways. My earliest memory is one of Marilyn and me and of clothes strewn across the floor and the blanket in my crib piled up in the corner revealing stained crib sheets. The double bed next to the crib was crowded with stuffed animals almost completely covering the yellow sheets with tiny pink flowers adorning them. It's a Sunday, and Marilyn with her cropped thick, black hair began in her no-nonsense manner to dress me. Mom was busy getting the other four children ready for church. Marilyn was already demonstrating the responsibility and willingness to help she would continue to exhibit into adulthood. As she took my foot in hand and began to tug on the tiny white sock, my baby toe popped out of a little hole. Surprised, Marilyn burst out laughing causing me to giggle in response. Pulling the sock off in an effort to get it right, Marilyn once more pulled on the small anklet sock only to see that teeny little toe poke out of the hole once again. More riotous laughter followed as we shared in the spontaneous moment of childish silliness. Long minutes passed as Marilyn pulled on the sock and allowed me to poke out my little toe over and over again, each time causing hilarious laughter until finally Mom called to us: "Girls, we're going to be late for church!"

We didn't always all go to church together. Oftentimes, Mom would get up early and go to seven o'clock mass alone. She must have felt like an imposter at those masses, looking so attractive in her classic, fine dress, her shapely calves showing beneath her skirt. Sitting in the cool dark church with no children to shush beside her, it would be impossible for anyone to know what the rest of her week was really like filled as it was with unending chores from morning till night and surrounded by children. The trouble with

Mom going to mass before us was that we had to get ready for church by ourselves and we didn't always know what was considered acceptable or not to wear to church. Many's the Sunday Mom would meet us coming home from church while we were heading towards it for nine-thirty mass and she would make us turn right back around again because we were wearing the wrong thing. Usually it was me wearing one of Marilyn's outfits which were naturally way too large for me but always so much more sophisticated than the stiff little collars and short dresses I was forced to wear. After a quick change, we would have to run all the way to get to church before the Entrance Song was finished or risk getting yelled at for being late in front of the whole congregation by Father Mertz.

Dad was a convert. That is to say, he wasn't born into the Catholic Church but in order to marry Mom, he had to become one. I didn't know this for years, however, and never would have guessed it because in many ways he was an even stricter Catholic than Mom. Every year he would give up either watching TV or drinking beer during Lent. One particular year, after Pat's accident, he gave up both. Not that he ever did either to excess as far as I can remember, mostly because he never had the time. Generally while we were growing up, Dad worked two fulltime jobs to support us. Sometimes his second job was a fun one that allowed us kids to assist him. For a couple of years, he worked for a brusque man named Bob Loden installing telephone booths all over Minneapolis and St. Wayne. Bob Loden was stocky while Dad was long and lean but they were equally strong. Dad was so skinny that it hurt to sit on his lap because his knees jutted out so far. He had piercingly blue eyes and a pointy aquiline nose over thin, smiling lips. He had lengthy, slender feet and large hairy hands. Finding himself married to a Catholic and fathering an ever-increasing family, Dad stepped up and was a responsible, reliable father. He loved telling jokes. Being the head of such a large family provided him with a ready audience to listen to his funny stories. Often they were over our heads like the one with the old man reaching into his pants pocket with a hole in it and discovering a brillo pad. Mom would struggle not to laugh while she scolded Dad at the table for his off-color stories.

While the telephone booths were being installed, we thought it great fun tagging along and finding ourselves in strange parts of the city. We entertained ourselves for hours while Dad and Bob hooked up wires, poured cement, and unloaded the freshly made phone booths smelling of the same new plastic as my brand-new dolls at Christmas. The best part was testing to see if the phones worked at the end of the installation. Dad would pull out a huge handful of change from his pocket and fish around with his index finger pushing the coins this way and that until he came up with President Franklin Delano Roosevelt. "Who's on the dime?" he quizzed first. That's an easy one to remember because it's Franklin **D**elano Roosevelt and Delano starts with **d** like dime starts with a **d**. Putting the dime into the coin slot, he let me dial: 821-2312. After a few rings, mom would answer "Hello?" in her professional mom voice, not the usual way she talks to us.

"Hi, Mom. It's me!"

"Oh," her voice changed instantly back to the one I recognized. "Where's the new phone booth at?" she asked knowing immediately why it was I was calling.

"On Lake Street and Cedar," I answered, repeating what Dad was mouthing to me after he heard Mom's question.

"Okay, I'll put the hamburgers on now."

"I'm so glad its Saturday!" I told Dad as we finished sweeping out the new phone booth. Saturday meant hamburgers for dinner at our house. It was the only day of the week that we always ate the same thing: fried hamburgers with raw onion slices, tomatoes, ketchup and mustard, potato chips, and heated up cans of pork and beans.

"We'd better get a move on then, I still have one more stop to make on the way home," Dad said.

"Where's that?"

"You'll see." Dad wasn't much of a talker; instead he liked to strum his fingers on the steering wheel while driving and tap his wedding ring to the beat of the tune he was whistling. Today it was a particularly catchy tune.

"Whatcha whistling?" I asked.

"It's a tune from that new group of long-haired boys from England. It's called '*All about Loving*', er '*All My Loving*' or some such."

We pulled up in front of O'Dhoul Drugstore. I shrunk down in my seat as memories of the last time Dad and I were at O'Dhoul's flooded over me. What had happened was this: I had seen a man go up to the counter and say something real low and gruff like to the girl behind the counter. I couldn't understand what he said but evidently the girl did, because she immediately turned around and pulled one of the magazines from behind the counter and gave it to him. I thought it was funny; the cover was just brown paper as if someone had cut up a paper bag and covered the magazine with it. The man paid for it and left. I was curious to know what kind of magazine would have a brown cover on it like that.

Then it was our turn in line.

"Anything else you can think of that we need?" Dad asked. Thinking this was my chance, I said, "Oh yes, the last time we were in here I think Mom meant to get a magazine."

"Did she now?" Dad mused. "Was it Good Housekeeping?" That was a good guess because Mom read Good Housekeeping more than she read the bible. Catholics don't seem to pay much mind to studying the bible.

"Hmmm, no, I don't think so," I replied, pretending to be thinking hard. "I think she meant to get one of those from behind the counter with the brown cover." The girl behind the counter let out a yelp like a dog when someone steps on its tail.

"Really?" Dad said real thoughtful like. "Did she tell you that?"

"Well, not me, but I'm sure I heard her saying it to Polly."

"Ginny," Dad said my name slowly and drawn out. At that moment, I put down the Betty and Veronica comic book I had been perusing while trying to convince Dad to buy the magazine with the hidden cover. I knew by the tone of that one word when he said my name that I'd made a mistake. "Your mother never said anything about wanting a magazine last time she was at the store, did she?" It's always amazing to me how grownups do that. Could he read my mind? Do you not only get big ears and noses as you get older but a sixth sense, too?

"I'm pretty sure," I managed to say before Dad just looked at me and said, "Ginny," in that same, measured tone of voice.

After a long pause, I gave up. "No, Dad, she didn't."

"Alright then," he said. "Let's just settle up here and head for home."

It wasn't until we were driving home that Dad brought it up again. He explained to me that those brown-paper covered magazines had naked people in them and that they were covered so as not to offend everyone who has the better taste not to want to look at that sort of thing.

"What?!" I shouted incredulously. "Eeew, gross! That nice old man must not have known it either! He probably thought it was the Farmer's Almanac or something. Oh dear, oh dear, I sure do hope his wife doesn't get mad at him for bringing home the wrong magazine!"

Dad's soft chuckle ended the conversation which I knew he would never bring up again. You could always count on Dad that way. What was discussed in the car, stayed in the car.

The day we installed the phone booth, I remembered my previous experience at O'Doul's. "I think I'll just stay in the car."

"Suit yourself," Dad said, slamming the door loudly. At that moment, a loud squeaking noise reached my ears at the same time that I saw her, Crazy Caroline. My heart leapt in my throat as the crazy witch drew nearer. She was an Indian who had special powers that let her do all sorts of mad things. People said she was angry because of what happened to her ancestors when white people first came to the land of the Sioux Indians. Jimmy Demoray said Caroline had grabbed him once when no one was looking and pinched his arm so hard it left a bruise! I was scared of her and tried to avoid her at all costs. Her long black hair hung down heavily on her back, and her faded pink and white housedress looked grey. Although it was summer, she shuffled along the sidewalk in oversized snowmobile boots and a green army jacket.

I quickly closed my eyes before she could see me. I wasn't young enough to believe that if I couldn't see her, perhaps she couldn't see me, but I closed my eyes just the same. I waited until the sound of the grocery cart she was laboriously pushing ahead of her sounded far away in my ears. In fact, I waited until I couldn't even hear it anymore. With relief, I opened my eyes and the door in one swift movement deciding I would rather go inside O'Dhoul's and possibly be humiliated by the girl behind the counter who thought I was trying to get my Dad to buy me a dirty magazine than to confront Crazy Caroline. I didn't realize that Dad had parked a little further away from the curb than usual so in my haste, I stepped down into the street and then tripped over the curb. The next thing I knew, I was being lifted up by hands with steel grips for fingers and I turned in horror to see Crazy Caroline. She hadn't carried on down the street at all; she had merely stopped at the bus stop in front of O'Dhoul's. She cackled loudly as she held me up, the more I squirmed the tighter her fingers gripped my arms. "Let go of me!" I hollered just as she loosened her grip and I fell to the sidewalk. Without a backwards glance, I bolted right through the drugstore doors shouting "Dad, Dad!" at the top of my lungs.

"He's in the back," grinned the salesgirl with a twinkle in her eye. I saw at once that she did indeed remember me and my previous visit to the drugstore.

"Oh, thanks ever so much," I tried to say as calmly as possible even though my heart was racing so hard I was afraid it would gallop right out of my chest.

I found him at the soda counter shooting the breeze with Gerald. "Hey, Dad, Mr. Prchle," I said while hoisting myself up onto the stool next to Gerald.

"Was it too hot to wait in the car?" Dad asked"

"Mm-hmm." I murmured, trying not to look Dad in the eye so his sixth sense would kick in again. "How's Winston holding up, Mr. Prchle"?

"He's holding up like a herd of Holsteins in a hail storm," answered Gerald Prchle. Gerald used to live on a farm in Southern Minnesota where he raised dairy cows, some pigs, chickens, two sons and a daughter so his language was always sprinkled with references to his old life on the farm. Now he lived in an apartment above O'Dhoul Drug so pretty nearly every time we went to the store, Gerald would be sitting on a stool at the counter visiting with the customers. I felt sorry for him cooped up in that small apartment after living on the farm all those years. It was the same farm he'd been born on back in 1890, but Gerald said he just couldn't bear it on the farm any longer. It made him too lonesome. Gerald's wife Gloria got the cancer and died. Gerald said he just couldn't bear to be without her on the farm in the same house where they'd been so happy all the years of their marriage. He just had to leave. He gets all moist in the face when he talks about Gloria and has to take out the worn but clean red handkerchief from his back pocket and start wiping the dripping fluid from his eyes and nose. He said that he always treated his livestock with dignity because they were his livelihood and he appreciated the good life they provided for him. If an animal got ill, he wouldn't have just got rid of it and let it die somewhere else, no sirree, he would either help it to die with dignity or keep it as comfortable as possible before it was time for it to meet its maker. He said that's how he felt about Gloria. They wanted to put her in the hospital and let her die there but he said no, it was his job to take care of her. He learned how to administer the morphine so she wouldn't feel pain and he let her die right in her own bed on the place where she'd lived her life. Seems like that's just the way it should be. But I guess after that, he couldn't see the farm as a place to live life anymore but instead as a place where the woman he loved died so he left to go do the rest of his living elsewhere. His son is on the old place now, running the farm, and Gerald is living in the city for the first time in his life. Gerald still seems really lonesome living alone in an apartment. Dad says some people aren't meant to live alone and that he expects Gerald will find another woman to love soon but I can't quite picture that. Gerald is old! He has just a few pieces of straggly, grey hair that he combs over the top of his head. His wrinkled skin is mottled and he has a hard time hearing.

"Can I go visit Winston, Dad?" I asked.

"No, Ginny, you know Mom's got the burgers on already. You can visit with Winston next time."

Winston was Gerald's dog that he'd rescued from the Humane Society when he moved into the apartment. He was a huge dog that looked more like a young bear cub than a dog. The papers from the Humane Society said his name was Nazi but Gerald said that was the problem. The kind of people who would name their pet 'Nazi' was the same sort of people who would abandon the dog in the middle of winter in below zero temperatures. He took Nazi home and changed his name to Winston instead in honor of Winston Churchill. He said Churchill is one of the reasons the Nazis are no longer. Last week, Winston got his foot run over by the bus on the corner, and now Gerald says he walks with a limp just like his namesake.

"Did Winston Churchill get his leg run over by a bus, too?" I'd asked him.

"No, he did not." Gerald answered. "But Winston Churchill enjoyed his alcohol, morning, noon, and night and many times in between. He walked unsteadily on his feet on account of the tippling!" He held his thumb up to his mouth and extended his pinky pretending to drink from a bottle. Then Gerald proceeded to ask me: "What's the state capital of New York?"

"Easy, Albany," I said without even having to think on it. Everyone always thinks its New York City because everyone knows New York City is the biggest city in America, maybe even in the world. But I know its Albany because I've memorized all the capitals and Gerald knows it, too, that's why he always quizzes me.

"Easy Albany," he said. "Huh, and I always thought it was just 'Albany'." He ruffles the top of my head. Dad said it was time to go so I hopped down off of the stool.

"Bye then, Gerald, pat Winston for me." I was thinking about Mickey and how I wished he could meet Gerald's dog soon. Mickey said he loved dogs but that his family had never been able to have one on account of they moved around so much.

Dad headed to the checkout counter at the front of the store and the same girl as the brown-covered magazine incident was still there working. She took Dad's box of 2-layered Whitman's assorted chocolates and said, with a meaningful glance at me, "Will there be anything else today?"

"No, thank you," Dad said and didn't let on at all that he had any recollection whatsoever of what happened the last time we were in the store. I was pushing open the door to get outside already but then I remember Crazy Caroline so I made a point of not opening it until I was sure Dad is right behind me. He seemed to be in no hurry at all, however, as he was staring at the change the checkout girl had given him. He began to push it around in the palm of his hand. "Just a minute, young lady." he said, "You've made a little mistake here."

"Oh, I'm sorry," the checkout girl said with a worried little frown line crossing between her eyebrows. She popped open the cash register drawer again ready to find the right change to make it up to Dad.

"Seems like you've given me a little too much change back," Dad said with a smile, and he handed a few coins back to the girl.

"Thank you," the girl said with a note of surprise in her voice. I'm surprised, too, and as soon as we get out the door I said, "Dad whatdja do that for? It was her mistake. We could have used the extra change." I was thinking of the Chico Stick that I had been longing for in the candy aisle but knew better than to ask for.

"Honor is doing what's right when no one is looking," Dad said simply.

"But think about all of the times you probably haven't gotten back all the change you should have," I persisted. "This would just even things out, don't you think?"

"No, I don't," Dad said in the tone of voice that told me we were finished talking about the discrepancy of the coins and that the subject probably wouldn't ever be discussed again. I was about to ask about the Whitman's chocolate when the sight of Crazy Caroline resting on her cart on the opposite side of the street distracted me and instead, I said nothing. We drove home in silence except for the sound of Dad's ring tapping out the Beatles' song on the steering wheel of the Chevrolet.

When we pulled into the alley, I looked across the way to see if I could see Mickey over at the Olsons but all looked quiet. The smell of hamburgers frying greeted us as we entered the back door of the house straight into the kitchen. Mom was at the stove, as usual. With her back to us, you would never have known that she was pregnant again. Her diminutive frame looked petite as she scraped the frying pan. Her hair was cropped short and she was wearing a colorful blouse over stylish khaki Capri's. Dad snuck up behind her and said, "Happy Anniversary, Sweetheart!"

 Mom jumped a foot, scolding, "How could you sneak up on me like that!" but then she saw the box of chocolates Dad carried and she smiled while tilting back her head for their customary kiss hello. "You remembered!" she said happily. Mom's large hazel eyes accented the pug nose above her beautiful, voluptuous lips. "Kissable lips." Dad called them. "Now wash your hands and call the rest of the gang in to eat."

Chapter 3

The smell of cinnamon wafting up the staircase woke me. There was no pressing reason to get out of bed on this lazy summer morning, but the thought of biting into one of mom's cinnamon rolls fresh out of the oven was enticement enough. I tiptoed down the stairs knowing just which steps to avoid so as not to waken the others with the squeaking. I wanted Mom and her cinnamon rolls to myself for a while. Neal was already at the table reading a paperback but other than that, the kitchen was quiet. After I'd had my fill of the gooey, sweet pastry, Mom sent me over to the Olsons with a round cake pan overflowing with rolls she'd made for them as a way to say thank you to Doc for having so much patience with little Danny after he'd nearly gotten his heel torn off.

The day before, we had just finished playing a cricket-length game of kick the can in the alley. Growing up in the city in the early 60's, the back alley was our domain. On Pleasant Avenue out in the front of the house, that was the public side, the presentable side, the world that belonged to the adults. When we were on the sidewalks lining the street, we had to be conscious of being out in the communal eye and behaving appropriately. This is the side of the house where flowers were planted in neat little borders, red geraniums flourishing behind tiny white sweet alyssums. On the back side of the house, in the backyard and in the alley was where we kids lived from sun up till sun down and beyond, all summer long. Here we would ride our bikes up and down the alley, stopping to circle in the driveways, knowing where every little slope and bump was, where to pick up speed and where to take care. The thumping of the basketball where a sweaty-game of one on one was being battled was a sound you could practically guarantee would be heard. Games of Dodge ball, Kickball, Red Light-Green Light, and Freeze Tag were played. All of the kids in the neighborhood could join in. Age didn't matter and grownups were never needed to intercede in the rules or the fairness of the games.

We were playing 'Kick the Can', where one person is 'It' and counts to 50, s-l-o-w-l-y while everyone else finds a place to hide. The person who's 'It' goes around looking for everyone and if "It" sees you, "It" calls your name and your location out loud, like, "I see Ginny behind the Dawson's doghouse." Once you've been spotted, you're out. The game is over for you. While 'It' is roaming around looking for people, however, the challenge is to run out of your hiding place and 'kick the can' that has been placed in the middle of the alley and is the center of the perimeter around which the game is being played. If 'It' sees you running toward the can and calls your name, you're out, too. But if you get to the can before 'It' sees you, then everyone goes free!

Danny was really too little to play, but Pat defended him and talked us into letting him join the game. Danny had found an awesome place to hide, close enough to kick the can if he got the chance, but far enough away that 'It' wouldn't be too happy to venture that far to go looking. He was behind the sweet pea poles in Mrs. Trudeau's garden where he was not only completely hidden from view, but he could reach up and snack on a pea while waiting for someone to kick the can and the game to be over. The trouble was, the game carried on so long (Lee-Lee was it and she had the perfect combination of excellent hearing and fleetness of foot so whenever someone came out of hiding, she could hear them and would race back to call their name before they came anywhere near kicking the can.) that Danny fell asleep and missed out on the next three games.

He was furious he'd missed out, so Marilyn offered to give him a ride on her bike to cheer him up. Danny was thrilled and he clambered up onto the back of the bike.

All went well until Marilyn rose up out of her seat to give the bike pedal an extra-firm stomp thinking she was stuck on a stone. Instead of a rock, it was Danny's heel caught between the spokes of the rear tire that was causing the trouble, and Marilyn's clomp was so severe that Danny's heel was torn right off except for the skin at the bottom of his foot. Thank goodness the accident happened in the middle of summer and not at the beginning so the bottom of Danny's feet were already toughened up from being barefoot outside all of the time. (Sundays at church being the only time we needed to wear shoes all summer long.)

Marilyn cupped Danny's heel gently in her hands while Pat carried a bawling Danny carefully in his arms all the while making sure he didn't get too far ahead of Marilyn as they headed towards the house lest they get separated and Danny's heel drop out of Marilyn's hand. The weight of it would have more than likely caused that thin thread of skin to pull right off. After Doc Olson said he'd meet my parents at his office to stitch Danny's heel back on, my parents left Neil in charge while they jumped into the station wagon and sped off. The rest of us kids ran into the living room to turn on the T.V. to wait and see if Danny would be on the evening news. It was such a big event in the neighborhood, surely it qualified to be on T.V! We were still watching the T.V. when Mom and Dad walked in with a sleeping Danny. We hugged each other and cried sweet tears of relief that Danny had survived the accident. We were only a little disappointed that it hadn't been more serious so he might have made it onto the news.

Knocking at the Olson's back door the next morning, I accidentally-on-purpose pushed my knuckle into the frosting mom had drizzled over the warm cinnamon rolls and licked it appreciatively. Mickey opened the door with a broom in his hand. "Mom made these and says to say thank you so much to Doc for all his help with Danny." I said all in one breathe as I shoved the pan into Mickey's hand.

"Thanks! They smell great!" Mickey said as he placed them on the counter. The Olson's kitchen was always so clean and everything was always put away so that the red counter top with white swirls in it looked brand new. I tried to think what color our countertops even were with everything piled on top of them all of the time and I thought, gray or soft green?

"They taste the best now while they're still warm, so you'd better dig in." I tried not to look too longingly at the pan but hoped I would be invited to join in the sampling.

"No, I'd better not." Mickey said as he turned his back on the pan and went back to sweeping. Ever since Mickey arrived at the Olsons it seemed he always had a broom, a garden hoe, or a dishcloth in his hand. I felt bad about it, especially since the only chores we ever had to do were on Saturday mornings and then we race through them so quickly so we could get back outside to play that they only ever take us an hour or two at the most. I also felt bad because it just didn't seem right that Kenny never seemed to have to do chores.

"Where is Kenny?' I asked, pretty sure I already know the answer.

"He's upstairs, working on his model cars." Kenny had the biggest collection of model cars in the neighborhood, possibly in the whole state. The Olsons had a whole room set up for him to work on and display his models. When a new kit arrived, Kenny disappeared for weeks as he painstakingly put together the car piece by piece, first gluing, then painting the cars till they looked exactly like the real car they were modeled after except for $1/25^{th}$ of the size.

"What's he working on now?" I asked, only to be polite, while holding the dustpan so Mickey could sweep all of the crumbs from underneath the table into it.

"Ugh" Mickey grunted loudly while he reached with the broom way under the table. "It's the Dodge Monaco. When he's finished, the hood will open and everything. Then the engine can even lift out if he wants it to. It's gonna be so neat."

I studied Mickey hard while he wasn't paying attention to see if there was any hint of jealousy or anger in his response. Was he coveting Kenny's miniature Dodge? I really didn't think so. It just seemed so unfair that Mickey was always working while Kenny was always playing. Just then I heard a chorus of voices chanting "Red Rover, Red Rover send Polly right over." "Hey Mickey, wanna come play Red Rover with us?" I asked hopefully, already pretty sure what his response was going to be.

"Maybe when I finish all my chores."

"Okay, see you then. Hope you like the rolls!" I shouted over my shoulder as I was already halfway down the back stairs ready to join the rest of the kids out in the alley.

Polly was sprinting as fast as she could toward the weakest link in the line of kids holding hands. Naturally, she was running towards the littlest kid on the team. I snuck up from behind and broke through Pat and Neil's hands, the biggest kids out there, because they weren't expecting it and their hands were just loosely held together. "Hey, no fair! Nobody called you over!" Neil gave me a sharp knuckle rap on the top of my head and told me to get on the other team already.

When Mom called us in to supper that night, we told the other kids we'd be late coming back out after dinner because we had to say the rosary.

"What for?" Kenny Olson asked.

"To thank God that Danny still has two heels and to ask him to change your hair color to anything but that carroty orange color!" Pat shouted while the door slammed after him as he ran into the house.

Dinner that night was one of my favorite meals: fried chicken, mashed potatoes with gravy, and corn, plus Mom's famous pot-a-shoos for dessert. This was a treat only made on special occasions, this one being on account of Danny's accident. Pot-a-shoos are deliciously yummy little crusty ball-shaped sweets that Mom baked and then cut open to put Kemps' vanilla ice cream inside. After putting the lid back on the pot-a-shoo, she then drizzled hot, homemade fudge sauce on top. We had to take turns standing at the stove stirring the fudge sauce until all of the sugar melted and the rich, dark chocolate shined after each turn of the spoon. The taste was so good that it sparked one of those rare silences at the dinner table while we all savored the delicious taste of this rare treat. Afterwards we all went into the living room to pray the rosary.

On top of the T.V. in the living room stood Blessed Mother. She was positioned on top of one of Mom's best doilies in her sky-blue robe with her arms reaching out a little bit as if to embrace us. She had the sweetest smile on her face. Mom came in to tell us all to kneel but then realized Polly didn't have her rosary with her so we all sat back down again until Polly raced upstairs to get it. We knew from past experience that kneeling on the carpet throughout the entire rosary was murder on our knees so we didn't want to start until we absolutely had to.

Mom started by thanking God we still had Danny's heel with us and then told Him we were dedicating the rosary session to that. To his heel? I wasn't sure. We commenced with the familiar beginning: "We believe in God, the Father almighty, creator of heaven and earth." I tried to concentrate on the words like Mom said I should, but after a while my mind began to wander. I loved to study the statue of Mary and imagine her with her arms outstretched like that joining in a game of Red Rover, Red Rover with us. She looked so young and pretty with her pale skin and blue eyes. She looked strong though, too, so I thought I would like to have her on my team. Then my eyes started to wander around the room and I started to study my family.

Dad knelt on one knee only while with the other leg he rested his arm and dangled the rosary. He still had lots of thick, dark hair, clear, blue eyes, and a mustache that Mom said tickled her nose when they kissed. Actually, she said it tickled that space in between her nose and top lip but no one seemed to know what that particular part of the face was called so she just said her 'lower nose.' Dad was six feet, four inches tall. After serving in the Second World War, he missed his chance to get a college education. He married mom and then had to work at least one job to support his ever-growing family. He loved to read and was always learning about new places and things. He called himself an armchair traveler and was almost always patient and kind to all of us. I loved the sound of Dad's deep, rumbling voice repeating the words of the rosary over and over again with never the slightest variation in the recitation "Holy Mary, Mother of God, pray for us sinners now and at the hour of our death, Amen."

I remembered the time when we were staying out at the farm with Grandma and Grandpa. We were saying the rosary, and I was right next to Grandpa. He always prayed just a little bit slower than everybody else, but somehow or other he always managed to catch up with the rest of us at the end of the prayer. This drove me crazy. I was determined to figure out how he did it. He would start with the rest of us just fine: "Holy Mary, Mother of God," but already we'd start to lose him and he would get further and further behind. Luckily, when saying the rosary, the Hail Mary is repeated 53 times: ten times for every decade for five decades, plus three at the beginning just to get everyone warmed up. By about the 48th Hail Mary, I realized how he did it. Grandpa prayed away like everyone else and then he just dropped the 'at the hour of our' and simply said "pray for us sinners now at death, Amen". So smooth! Just like that he caught up with the rest of us! I was so surprised when we finished praying the rosary that time because I hadn't had to play all of my usual games to get through the seemingly endless prayers. I'd been concentrating the whole time on finding Grandpa out.

I studied Mom next. She led the rosary, of course, so she was the one who got to say, "Hail Mary, full of grace, blessed art thou amongst women and blessed is the fruit of thy womb Jesus," all by herself. I loved the way Mom closed her eyes while she prayed, gripping her hands so tightly around her shiny red rosary beads with her head tilted slightly to the right. Her voice was so loud as she prayed that Tessa Cordero once said she heard my mom praying all the way in her backyard, and she lived across the alley and down 5 houses. Mom's brown hair was kept short so that most days (excluding Sundays) she didn't have to do a thing to it other than run a comb through it. Her skin was smooth and olive-colored except for her hands which were always rough and worn. She was short, strong, and she ruled our house like a velvet hammer. Even though we were all afraid of Mom, we also knew what a softie she was. Her entire life was centered on us, her family, and we knew that she would do anything for us, to keep us safe and happy.

Mom, too, never varied the way she prayed the rosary, always highlighting the exact same words (**BLESSED** art thou among women and **BLESSED** is the fruit of thy womb Jesus.) Sometimes when I would check out where she was at holding the rosary and I knew she only had a few more Hail Mary's left, I started willing her to speed up a little, nearing the end, but she never did, praying each Hail Mary exactly as slowly and concisely at the beginning of the rosary as at the end.

It was harder to study my siblings because they were never concentrating as hard as my parents so they could usually feel right away if my eyes were upon them. They would look right back at me and nine times out of ten would do something funny like raising their eyebrows super high as if they were suddenly very surprised or puffing out their cheeks like a fish. Then I had to try real hard not to laugh out loud. One time, Pat kept crossing his eyes and then leaning to one side further and further until he was almost leaning right into Neil. . Neil didn't think it was funny at all the way Pat kept leaning into him so he kept moving further away until he was practically out in the hallway. I was struggling hard not to laugh out loud, something unheard of during the rosary. Better not to look in Pat's direction at all.

While we were still on the 4th Joyful Mystery, the doorbell rang and Doc Olson rescued us from the final mystery. "Joyful, joyful!" Pat whispered under his breath and I stifled a laugh. Mom didn't seem to notice that none of us had left the room so we got to watch as Doc slowly unraveled the bandage darkened with dried blood from around Danny's heel. The next thing we knew, we heard a loud thump. We turned to see Marilyn looking so peaceful with her eyes shut lying in the middle of the living room floor. 'Oh, ha-ha!" said Neil as he gave Marilyn a nudge with his Converse high top. She didn't even flutter an eyelash.

"Marilyn, are you alright?" Mom asked as she bent down to place her hand on Marilyn's forehead.

"It looks like she's fainted from the sight of blood. Step back everyone and let's give her some air." Doc said as he fanned Marilyn's face with the Good Housekeeping magazine he picked up from the coffee table. Fainting at the sight of blood seemed highly unlikely to me as I had a vision in my head of Marilyn carrying Danny's heel in her hands with all of the insides dangling out like a pound of thawed hamburger. She certainly wasn't doing any fainting then! Her face looked as pale as the sheets on our bed when she finally opened her sky-blue eyes and peered out at all of us from beneath her pixie bangs. When she saw all of our faces peering down at her, her skin color changed to a beet red. "You'd better not think about a career in medicine, little Missy," Doc Olson said to Marilyn unnecessarily. We all knew Marilyn was planning on becoming a lawyer just like Gregory Peck in *To Kill a Mockingbird*. "You'll be fainting and landing on top of the patients you're supposed to be caring for," Doc chortled and put his hat on as he headed for the door.

"Hey Doc," I asked. "How's Mickey, Doc?"

"Well, now, I haven't seen him all day but I believe he's the same as when I left him this morning....just fine, I'm sure." He stared at me suspiciously.

"He might be tireder than he was this morning though on account of all of the chores he had to do today, huh, Doc?" I asked. Doc Olson hesitated at the door and suddenly the entire room got very quiet. Doc's shoulders seemed to tighten underneath his shirt and he was still for a moment before he turned around and said quietly, "Oh, I don't think so. Mickey has plenty of energy!" His angry eyes glared at me.

"But I'll bet Kenny's not any tireder. No, I don't think he is, because he's been sitting up in his room all day working on his new model car, right Doc? That Kenny, he sure does enjoy all those new model cars you're always buying him. I wonder if Mickey would like to work on model cars, too, huh, doc.? Do you think Mickey might like to do that, too sometime? If he could ever get a break from chores!" Doc's eyes narrowed and his hands clenched tightly around the handle of his medical bag. He took a step towards me before stopping himself, anger emanating from him like heat.

"That's enough now, Ginny" Mom said with a catch in her voice as she placed her hands gently on my shoulders. "Doc Olson's had a long day, I'm sure, and the last thing he needs is more pestering from the likes of you. He's done a right neighborly thing stopping by to check on Danny's heel for us so let's let him get back to his own family. I'm sure Mrs. Olson has supper waiting on the table for him."

"No, actually, Mickey made supper again today; I saw it on his list of chores to do. OW!" I spat out as Mom squeezed my shoulders hard.

"Keep that heel wrapped," Doc said abruptly. "Good night then," he mumbled as he escaped into the dark night.

"Oh boy, you're in trouble now, Ginny!" Neil said at the same time that he rapped me on the top of the head with his knuckles. He was wrong, though, because all Mom said was, "We'll call you when it's bedtime, and make sure you come on the first call, not the fifth!" And we were all out the door.

Chapter 4

Doc Olson knew that Mickey would be accepted at the neighborhood schools with no questions asked. The previous year, the 1964 Civil Rights Act had finally passed. Introduced by President Kennedy and passed under President Johnson with the help of Minnesota's own Senator Hubert H. Humphrey, it outlawed racial segregation in schools, at work, and anyplace that served the general public. President Johnson wouldn't get much credit for this in our neighborhood, though. President Kennedy was considered a saint where we lived and anything good that happened in our country was all because of him. Most of the houses that I went in and out of in our neighborhood had two pictures up on the wall and a crucifix of a bloodied Jesus with a sweet look on his face in between. Those pictures were of Pope John Paul VI and President John F. Kennedy, 35th president but more importantly, the first Catholic president ever of the United States of America.

I don't remember when Kennedy was elected, but I surely do remember the day he died. Mom went around that day as if her whole world had come to an end. Her eyes were all puffy from so much crying and for the first time in my recollection she didn't care what we ate or drank all day long. The console television in the living room was on all day, too, with Walter Cronkite's comforting voice keeping us informed, right up until the final moment when he took off his thick, black glasses to wipe his eyes and announced that JKF was officially dead. For the next three days, Mom had her ironing board set up in front of the T.V. For the next few weeks we must have gone around in the best pressed clothes in the neighborhood. The mountain of clothes spilling out over the sides of the laundry basket would gradually diminish as scenes from Kennedy's growing up years played continually on the T.V; Rose Kennedy holding an angelic baby John while Joseph Kennedy grinned behind her, all those Kennedy boys playing football on the lawn at their summer cottage in Hyannis Port, Massachusetts, the wedding of beautiful Jacqueline Bouvoir to John Fitzgerald. Clothing items that were particularly wrinkled would be sprinkled with water and rolled up like cinnamon rolls and placed in the freezer. After a sufficient amount of time, the frozen mass would be painstakingly unrolled and ironed with a hot iron that would spit and steam as it was placed on our iced vestments. "The youngest man ever elected President and the youngest President to die," Walter informed us as Mom kept ironing away.

We ached for poor Jacqueline Kennedy. She looked so pretty that day in her stylish pink outfit with her customary fashionable headpiece. "That just goes to show," Mom said in between sniffles, "it doesn't matter who you are, how important you are, or how admired you are by multitudes of people. When you get up in the morning and put on your clothes, you just don't know what is gonna happen to you on any given day." Mom had to pause to take off her glasses a la Walter Cronkite and wipe her tear-filled eyes. Actually, her glasses were quite like Walter's, too, with the same thick black frame. "Just imagine Jackie that night finally changing out of that adorable pink dress after such a horrendously long day and looking at those dark red blood stains and bits of her husband's brains sticking to the fine linen. No way could she have ever seen that coming or she never would have worn that outfit." Mom put her head in both of her hands and sobbed quietly, her shoulders shuddering beneath the heavy cloak of sadness. I continued coloring in my Lady and the Tramp coloring book because I thought that was what Mom wanted me to do. Having no grey crayon, I used black with a very light hand for Tramp's coat. "Remember this, Ginny, "Mom finally said. "This is what life is, completely and totally unpredictable. It can turn a perfect frock into a bloody mess just like that!" and she snapped her fingers to complete the affect.

Every couple of weeks, I was invited over to supper at Mrs. Agneau's house. Living right next door to us, Mom always said Mrs. Agneau was the perfect neighbor. She had a house that was just as big as ours but the difference being that she lived all alone at her place. The Agneau's had one son but he lived out West in California and Mr. Agneau was dead. Mrs. Agneau had the most well-kept garden in the neighborhood. She had golden, tall cosmos, and bright, colorful zinnias standing tall behind papery bachelor buttons with sweet alyssums giving off a welcoming fragrance. All summer long she would have something fresh to eat from her vegetable garden which she was always so proud to serve me. We would have radishes when it hardly seemed as if the snow had been gone long enough for the radishes to grow, then buttery, soft lettuce and crunchy snap peas. After that there would be wax beans and zucchini and finally the sweetest little cherry tomatoes that I would love to pop into my mouth whole before chomping down fast and feeling all the insides burst out with a rush.

I was never sure why I was the only one of the whole family that was ever invited over to Mrs. Agneau's house for dinner. I'm sure part of it was because it would have been too much for her to take on the whole family at once. I was the youngest girl, so maybe she felt sorry for me, or perhaps she felt more comfortable around a younger girl rather than my sassier older sisters. It was a treat, of course, because everything always tasted so good. It was also good to stand out a bit in the family and have something set me apart from the rest. "I have to go in now and get cleaned up for supper with Mrs. Agneau." I'd say with a big sigh. It was the strangest thing, though, to be sitting in Mrs. Agneau's spotless and efficient little kitchen and see through the backdoor the boys playing an aggressive basketball game and being so close as to practically hear their deep breathing as they dribbled the ball back and forth on the well-worn tarmac. Listening to Marilyn and Lee-Lee chat while pushing their dolls in the tiny little strollers, I would marvel how I could hear every word they said as if Mrs. Agneau and I were spies eavesdropping on Russian commies. We were practically invisible to them, of course, sitting in the cool, clean kitchen and they were oblivious to our presence. At those times I would wonder how many things Mrs. Agneau had seen and heard of our escapades in the backyard. I only thought about this when I was there myself dining with Mrs. Agneau, however. Once I was free and I was the one playing Dodge ball against the outside garage wall, I never thought once of Mrs. Agneau sitting in her quiet kitchen listening in on our world.

Today, Mrs. Agneau and I were eating squash soup with White Mountain dinner rolls. Most of the soup we had at home was Campbell's from a can and that was usually chicken noodle or bean with bacon. "You sure are a good cook, Mrs. Agneau," I said truthfully as I tried not to slurp while ladling the delicious soup into my mouth.

"Thank you, dear," Mrs. Agneau replied, not realizing that she had flour on the tip of her rather large, hawk-like nose. "This was one of Mr. Agneau's favorites." I hadn't known Mr. Agneau, he died before we moved into the neighborhood but I thought he must have been a happy, fat man because every meal I ate in his old kitchen was one of his favorites. He had a lot of favorites and Mrs. Agneau knew how to make them all. One day when Mrs. Agneau was sick in bed, Mom sent over some chicken noodle soup to make her feel better and I had to carry the tray all the way up to her bedroom. Right by her bed there was a picture of Mr. & Mrs. Agneau at their son's wedding and I was astonished to see that Mr. Agneau wasn't fat by any means. In fact, I questioned whether or not it was true that he had had so many favorite meals at all because he looked like he didn't have an ounce of extra fat on his tall, lanky frame.

"Really?" I replied politely. "I can see why this was his favorite." Marilyn, Lee-Lee, Polly and Patty Delmonty were playing four-square next door and it was hard for me to concentrate on conversing with Mrs. Agneau. They were laughing so hard every time Patty bounced the ball outside the line. Her glasses always had a piece of masking tape holding them together and this must have

hindered her sight something awful. After a while, I could hear
Ethel Delmonty calling Patty in for supper, and soon Mrs. Gauze
was calling to Lee-Lee, too. Polly and Marilyn turned 4-square into
a two-square game and carried on for a while on their own. I felt so
surprised at the opportunity to witness my sisters playing so
companionably like this. I suppose if I'd been with them, I would
have been playing, too, so that I would have been a part of the
experience rather than apart from it. I had never thought 2-square
was so much fun before, not when I was right there in the middle of
it, determined not to mess up and concentrating so hard to play
well. I wondered how much of life was like this, really, too hard to
enjoy when you're the one living it. Only if you're the observer does
it take on such a magical quality. I envied Mrs. Agneau suddenly,
being able to sit here in her peaceful kitchen enjoying our games
from a distance but not having to worry about being caught by the
light during Flashlight Tag. At the same time, I felt antsy and I
didn't want to just sit quietly but wanted to be outside getting dirty,
too.

"Mrs. Agneau, do you ever feel like coming over to join in any of our
games?"

"Oh, child," Mrs. Agneau chuckled. "My game-playing days are over.
Although I do have to brag a bit and say I was not half bad at
croquet when I was your age. I was a regular whiz with the mallet,
if I do say so myself, and I loved to crack that wooden ball right
through the wicket. Indeed, those were the days." We were
munching on Mrs. Agneau's sugar cookies by now, a taste so fine the
buttery crumbles just melted in your mouth. Still, I was furtively
looking around to see if we were having some of Mrs. Agneau's
Black Cherry ice cream, too. The Schwan's delivery truck had come
through the neighborhood the previous day and Mrs. Agneau was a
regular customer with Schwan's. She always bought a carton of
their famous black-cherry ice cream and she loved it so much that it
never lasted until the next time Schwan's was delivering in the
neighborhood. "That's just fine with me," Mrs. Agneau would muse.
"I don't believe in rationing myself anymore. I did enough of that
during the war. And as poor Mr. Agneau learned, it doesn't make
much sense to hoard something for a rainy day when you might just

feel your heart giving out one day and be clutching your left arm as you fall onto the floor dead just like that. June it was, too, and Mr. Agneau still had his favorite chocolate malt ball Easter eggs in the freezer which he would only allow himself to eat once a week hoping the supply would last till the following Easter. He never did see that following Easter and I have been eating my fill of my favorite Black Cherry ice cream since." That explains how skinny Mr. A. was, I thought to myself. One malted milk ball a week?! That man was disciplined!

It didn't look we were having Black Cherry ice cream today however. Perhaps Mrs. Agneau had gotten carried away and already finished the recently purchased carton, going along with her philosophy of 'why put off till tomorrow what you can eat today.' Just then I heard a familiar squeal that turned the blood in my veins cold. I suddenly realized that all of the sounds from my backyard next door had ceased. My family was sitting down to dinner now, too, and I was happy to recall that there was a reason I was pleased not to be there. Mom was serving fried pork chops, which I do like, along with lima beans, which I don't. Mom is a stickler about us cleaning our plates. The last time we had lima beans, I got into trouble because I had discovered an amazing fact: Two-shoes liked lima beans! Or, more accurately, Two-shoes LOVED lima beans. (Two-shoes being our long-haired, mouse-loving cat). I had been surreptitiously feeding Two-shoes the lima beans off of my plate, one at a time, of course, when unbeknownst to me, Greg had dropped his spoon and clambered onto the floor to retrieve it, thus observing the complacent cat dining on my lima beans and subsequently alerting the authorities. Two-shoes was locked down the basement during dinner tonight.

"Caroline, is that you?" Mrs. Agneau called out to the backdoor screen. I felt a sickening sensation in the bottom of my stomach as I knew what was going to happen next.

"Ginny, take this out to Caroline for me, would you?" Mrs. Agneau said as she poured the leftover soup into an empty jar and wrapped the last of the rolls into a paper napkin.

"Umm, how do you know she's out there?" I asked feebly, stalling for time.

"Why, didn't you hear her cart? Of course she's out there. And you can bet your bottom dollar she's hungry, too. I would invite her in to eat but on these lovely summer nights, she has an aversion to dining inside." Mrs. Agneau prattled on as she handed me our leftovers.

Mustering up courage, I thanked Mrs. Agneau for dinner and shuffled out the back door planning to hand Caroline the soup and scram. When I started to hand over the package, however, Caroline grabbed my wrist in her viselike grip and whispered: "Where's Mickey?" Her breath was hot on my neck.

"Wh-Wh-what?" I stammered, unable to pull my arm out of her grasp.

"Where's Mickey?" she repeated, some sour smell wafting out of her clenched jaws, "How is he? Are the Olsons treating him well?" Just then we were both distracted by the sound of my backdoor slamming open and Neil shouting "I'm kickball captain and I choose Pat!" I managed to wrest my arm out of Caroline's grasp and fled to join in the game.

My heart was still racing as I lined up with the rest of them in the alley to play kickball. Why was Crazy Caroline asking about Mickey? I rubbed my wrist where she had grabbed me. Just then, I realized that Polly was complaining because the kickball teams were uneven. "I'll go get Mickey!" I volunteered. "That'll even things up."

Standing on the stoop, I peered through the screen door into the Olson's house. It was dark except for a sliver of light escaping beneath a door beyond the kitchen. Straining to listen, I heard a muffled cry from behind the door. "Mickey? Mickey, Are you alright?" I pounded on the door as I yelled. I could have sworn I heard him holler 'Help!' I grabbed the door handle and turned it this way and that but it was locked. I called again, "Hey, Mickey! Mickey! We need you for kickball, Mickey!"

Doc came through the door on the other side of the kitchen and closed it carefully behind him. His belt was undone and his shirt untucked. Calmly buckling his belt, he said, "Go away, Ginny, Mickey can't go out to play tonight," with an unsettling leer on his sweaty face. I stared at him without moving until he suddenly slammed his hands onto the table shouting, "I said, go away!"

I turned around and fled back to the alley to join in the game, my knees trembling the entire way. My heart wasn't in it, though, as I found myself worrying about Mickey all night long.

Chapter 5

The next day, I was bouncing the ball against the garage when I saw Mickey over in his yard on his hands and knees on the sidewalk with a butter knife in his hand. "Hey, Mickey, come here!" I hollered across the alley. It was a scorching hot day without a hint of a breeze, the kind where the heat just sucks the air out of your chest and you can hardly breathe even when you're standing still. No one was moving around too quickly today.

"I'll be over as soon as I finish the last two cracks," he hollered back. He was digging the dandelions out from where they grew between the cracks of the cement sidewalk, a tedious job, I knew, having done it myself a few days ago for my mom on our front sidewalk. I wondered what to say about the night before. I decided I'd let Mickey bring it up. I grabbed hold of Mickey's hands when he arrived to examine his knuckles.

"Not too bad," I said. Cutting out the weeds permanently meant using the knife to slip into the edge of the sidewalk to try to lift out the entire root of the dandelion. It was nearly impossible to do this without scraping the skin off of your knuckles over and over again as you weeded. "Wanna play?" I asked, and I handed Mickey the ball.

"You first," he said politely, so I bounced the ball against the wall. He repeated the gesture. Next, I threw the ball against the wall and clapped once before catching it again. Mickey did the same. The next time I threw it, I had to clap twice. We carried on this way, adding a clap every time, and stepping back further and further from the wall to allow time to clap, until one of us didn't fit in enough claps and then the game was finished. It was Mickey's turn to go first next, and he threw the ball against the wall and then let it bounce before catching it.

"Ugh, you know I'm not as good at this one," I complained as I took the ball from him and also let it bounce before catching it. When it seemed like Mickey wasn't going to say anything about the previous night, I finally asked him about it. He was concentrating on bouncing the ball and said something about going to bed early. I guessed he didn't want to talk about it.

We finished that game and had played many more versions of it until Mom suddenly hollered out from the backdoor, "Kids, everybody in the house. Tornado!" The message was repeated a few times to be sure everyone had heard. "Mickey, you come, too." Mom yelled. "Right now, hurry!!" I looked around then and noticed the familiar greenish hue to the sky when there were tornadoes in the air. It was suddenly still and quiet with no birds or squirrels in sight.

"Where do the birds go during a tornado?" I asked no one in particular as we headed down the basement. I always wanted to try to catch a glimpse of them flying off to safety before the storms hit but I never thought of it in time.

"The birds have basements, too, at the base of the trees, duh!" Neil said sarcastically.

We headed underneath the stairs in the basement and huddled against the inside wall, the safest place to be in a tornado. We couldn't all fit, so a few of the older kids climbed under the nearby table and sat down. Pat pulled out a deck of cards. He and Neil started playing War. "Boys, I wanted to pray the rosary," Mom said plaintively.

"Sure Ma, after we finish this game." The rest of us sighed with relief as Pat gave us all a big wink when Mom wasn't looking and we knew that the tornado warning would likely be over before they ever finished playing their never-ending game of War. If one of them had come close to losing all of his cards, the other would have sneakily made sure to lose a few rounds so that they would both have enough cards again and the game could go on continuously until it was safe enough to leave the basement.

It used to be that we all complained about having to go down the basement when it looked like tornado weather, but since the "Longest Night" we all had a healthy fear of tornadoes and we didn't say a peep about having to take precaution and come inside. On May sixth of that year, five tornadoes had swept across Minneapolis killing 13 people and injuring almost 700. It could have been so much worse, though, but the new Civil Defense Take Cover Warning Sirens had just been installed and were used for the very first time for those tornadoes.

We had all been outside playing that day when the sirens first went off. We all stood there with our hands over our ears. The sound was so loud and eerie. We couldn't hear Mom calling us to get inside and get downstairs because of the noise, and she had to run outside and start tugging on each of our arms to get us to follow her into the house. By that time, the trees were already being whipped around in huge ferocious circles, screens were being torn off of windows, shutters were slamming, and toys were being sucked up and blown across the yard like a toyshop unexpectedly come to life. Suddenly, all of the water from the swimming pool elevated and hovered a couple of feet above the pool before shooting across the fence and drenching Mrs. Agneau's vegetable garden. (Besides a few peeing accidents in the pool, the water was fine and it didn't seem to hurt Mrs. Agneau's vegetables at all. The first time I ate at her house after the storm, though, I couldn't finish all of my beans knowing that they'd been doused in Jimmy Demoray's urine.) Pat had been the last one to go into the house and he held me back for a second, and pointed. I followed his finger with my eyes and saw a large configuration of clouds starting to draw together into a very wide circle. The circle started forming slowly but gathered speed as it grew downwardly and more narrowly into the exact shape of a funnel. The tornado was black and quite beautiful as it rushed through the sky, dropping down from time to time to bounce off of the ground. Chris Shortpascher's bike flew right over us then, and Pat pushed me inside just as we heard the sound of breaking glass coming from somewhere in the neighborhood.

Except for Mrs. Trudeau's birch tree losing one entire trunk, it had been a forked tree with three equally-sized branches growing out of a base that formed a perfect chair to sit in, there was no real damage in our neighborhood. Other parts of the city weren't so lucky when the F4 tornados hit.

I was thinking about the remaining half of the birch tree and hoping that it wouldn't go the same way as its counterpart when Greg's shout brought me out of my reverie. "What is that?" he asked in a disgusted voice pointing at Mickey's arm. Mickey, who had been distractedly scratching his elbow, quickly pulled his sleeve back down and replied in a downcast voice, "Nothing."

"What?" Mom asked, taking an interest. "Let me see, Mickey."

"No, really, it's nothing," Mickey protested, but Mom had already drawn Mickey closer and was lifting up his sleeve. It suddenly got quiet underneath the stairs as we all stared at the stain of bruises on Mickey's upper arm. An ugly greenish-blue color, they were the perfect imprint of a hand, or rather of four angry fingers digging into Mickey's brown flesh.

"I said it's nothing." Mickey repeated forlornly as we all looked speechlessly on. I remembered a conversation I'd overhead about Kenny when Mickey first moved in. Mom and some of the neighborhood women were discussing how hard it would be for Kenny, who alone had been the recipient of all his parents' attention over the years, to share the love with another child and whether or not he'd accept it or be jealous, and if so, how he would vent his anger. Was this Kenny's way of expressing his unhappiness? I shuddered at the thought and felt a bad feeling in the pit of my stomach. Somehow, I couldn't imagine Kenny this angry. I pictured Doc's furious eyes glaring at me so piercingly last night, I'd felt pinned against the wall by his rage.

"Mickey, who did this to you?" Mom asked in her kindest voice. Mickey didn't say a word, he just kept his head way down so his chin nearly pressed against his chest. None of us said anything as we looked at poor Mickey's long sleeve, knowing what was hidden underneath. I finally understood why Mickey wore long-sleeved shirts even on these hottest of summer days. The realization made me want to hold on to him and never let him go back to the Olson's house again. What went on behind the walls of our neighbors' house? Why wouldn't Mickey talk about it?

"Ha-ha! Oh yeah, king beats jack and I am the king, the king of War!" Pat shouted from under the table while pumping his fist victoriously into the air, startling us all out of our melancholy.

"Good." Mom said with conviction. "Now put those cards away so we can say the rosary." We all bowed our heads as mom began, the familiar words felt comforting after such an unsettling sight. I closed my eyes and started praying fervently for Mickey, not quite sure what I was praying for, so that the bruises would go away? So he could go and get away from whoever was giving him bruises? I really didn't know, but sitting down in the basement underneath the stairs, I felt we were safe there, safe from the storm and any other evil blowing through the neighborhood.

Chapter 6

Most of the Native American Indians in Minneapolis lived on Cedar Avenue. They had long, pitch black, glossy hair and bulbous noses that were often pockmarked. I would see them from the backseat of the station wagon as we drove down Franklin Avenue where they were lingering on street corners or sitting at bus stops but our worlds never overlapped. Even after the Civil Rights Act passed and they started busing colored kids into white neighborhoods, there still weren't ever any Indians at my school. Not until years later when I was attending college and saw an Indian with a black braid as thick as an ocean liner's mooring line walking to class ahead of me did I realize I had never seen one in school before, besides Mickey.

That year, Mickey and I would both be starting at Incarnation. The glorious long days of summer were coming to an end and the start of school was just around the corner. This fact was made evident by the unusual sight of the post man surrounded by the kids of the neighborhood. As we were entering the first grade this year, we, too, got to join in the queue following Peter, the postman, around. It started around mid-August when we anticipated that the school would send out the letter listing the school supplies that students from each grade needed to purchase before coming to school. Even more importantly, the letter would tell the name of the teacher each student would be assigned to. The agony and ecstasy this information caused cannot be downplayed. We began to gather on the Bloedow's lawn, their house being on the corner and the first one Peter would come to with his navy blue postal bag slung over his shoulder. The discussion would inevitably start with someone moaning about Sister Mary of the Child Jesus and hoping to goodness not to be assigned to her classroom. "I hope I get Mr. Hanson!" Marilyn enthused. "He gives five minutes extra for recess if everyone is quiet during reading time."

Finally, Peter was spotted across the street and we all leapt up. "Hurry Peter, come on!" Jane shouted hastily. "Do you have the letters today?" "Anything in your bag from Incy?" we all bombarded him with questions.

"I may and I may not," Peter replied nonchalantly while he looked both ways crossing the street. As he sorted through his bag, he eventually withdrew a half-dozen envelopes for the Bloedow's. Even though Michael Bloedow was standing right there with all of us, Peter still opened up the black metal mailbox attached to the wall of the house to the right of the front door. "It's the law," Peter had explained to us. "The mail is federal property not to be handed over to anyone younger than 18 years of age." So at each house he would barely get the mail into the box before one of the kids of the house would already be pulling it back out again to see if the significant letter was there. Michael grabbed the stack of mail from the mailbox and one by one looked quickly at the return address and tossed the letters onto the ground, scattering them around him like petals from a flower.

"I didn't get mine today," he stated the obvious. This didn't actually deter the rest of us, however, because we didn't all receive letters on the same day, and in an inexplicable manner there was no alphabetical rhyme or reason to the order that we did receive the letters throughout the neighborhood. We continued to follow Peter up Pleasant Avenue and down Pillsbury even when he passed our house without leaving behind the critical letter. We still wanted to know which room everyone else was assigned to so that when we did get our letter, we would know right away who was in class with us. Only Matt Stidger and Brian Fogherty found out their room assignments that day. The rest of us were left with the mystery intact.

"Thanks, Peter, see you tomorrow!" we shouted as he gave us a wave without turning around and carried on across the street.

"I'll bet he hates this time of year," I mused.

"Don't be ridiculous!" Polly retorted. "This is the best time of year for him! Imagine all the rest of the year he has to walk around all by himself delivering boring bills and junk no one even cares about. At this time of year, not only does he know he's delivering letters of utmost importance, but he gets to be surrounded by us. He likes our company, I'm sure of it. Haven't you ever seen him try to hide a smile when Pat's saying something outlandish? Peter probably hates it when all of the letters from Incarnation have been delivered and no one follows him around anymore."

"Guess I hadn't thought about it that way." Polly was always noticing things like that. I sat on the porch with Two-shoes on my lap purring loudly while I scratched under her chin, on the top of her head, then behind both ears, repeating the sequence over and over again just the way she liked it, and admitted, "I hope I don't get in the same classroom as Brian. He gives me the Hebe jeebies."

"Me, too," Greg agreed. "And don't stand too close or you'll get drooled on; gross!"

"There but for the grace of God, go I," Marilyn said sagely while we all groaned.

"Seriously, if that happened to me, you'd have to shoot me. Just shoot me, right between the eyes and get it over with, quick" Greg insisted. I giggled, unable to stop myself. "Just think what his school picture is going to look like, year after year after year. Jaw hanging open, drooling, here's Brian in third grade, fourth grade, fifth grade. Good grief his drool hasn't changed a bit!"

Even Marilyn was unable to suppress a smile at that one. Two-shoes jumped off my lap and began laboriously bathing herself, licking her paw and washing herself in all of the spots where I had been scratching her. "Good grief, Toosh, I'm cleaner than you are. Why do you always have to wash yourself after I've finished petting you? You're starting to make me feel bad!"

"Feel badly," Marilyn corrected.

"That, too." I hated when she corrected my grammar like that.

Brian Fogherty and his mother had just moved into the neighborhood that summer. They used to live in a town called Stillwater but that spring the floods had washed away their home and so they were forced to move back in with Mrs. Fogherty's mother, Mrs. Jenson. We had received a lot of snow the previous winter and it had been a cold one, too. March was the coldest one on record so far, and we received the most snow since 1951. The Mississippi River forms into Lake Pepin, and there the ice cover was 3 miles wide and 20 miles long! 50 miles upstream from Minneapolis, an ice jam had risen 24 feet over the river. Then in April, spring came with a vengeance and it rained and rained and rained. Where the Minnesota River meets the Mississippi in the St. Paul bluffs, the water just kept rising and spreading to nearly a mile wide. When the rain finally stopped, the warm weather hastened the snow melt causing instant flooding downstream. It was a good time for the high school and college kids as they were let out of school on beautifully sunny spring days after being cooped up all that long, cold winter to stack sandbags on the river banks to try to suppress the flooding. Even the prisoners from Stillwater State Prison were allowed out to help. Finally, on Easter Sunday the Mississippi crested at 20.75 feet but not before hundreds had lost their homes in the flood, Brian Fogherty and his mother included.

That night after I had said my prayers and climbed into bed, Mom came upstairs and sat at the edge of my bed. "You know," she said, "I'm sure Brian could use a friend or two while he starts at a new school in a new neighborhood." Oh jeez, I thought, here it comes. Had Mom heard us talking on the porch or was this just that parental sixth sense coming into play again? "The same goes for Mickey. I'm counting on you to be kind to them, even if no one else, especially if no one else, is. Do you understand me?"

"Oh, Mom, it's a new school for me, too."

Incarnation Grade School didn't have a kindergarten, so before going to Incarnation, most of us had to go to Agassiz Public School for kindergarten first. Agassiz had been a fantastic experience for me even though I had to pretend not to like it because none of my older siblings had liked it. I only went for half a day, so that meant the mornings were still free for me to leisurely wake up and wear pajamas for half the morning, play with my little brothers, help Mom, and then have lunch with the older kids. Almost all the kids in the neighborhood came home for lunch. The lunchtimes were scattered ten minutes apart. Starting at 11:15, Mom would serve lunch to Jane first. Then ten minutes later Neil would join her, and ten minutes after that Pat would be home, and then Polly. Of course by this time, Jane had already had to start back to school because lunch was only 40 minutes long and it took at least ten minutes to get there and 10 minutes to get back.

During my kindergarten year, I left with Marilyn and Lee-Lee when it was time for them to go back to school after lunch. At first they had to walk the extra block out of their way to drop me off at Agassiz. I loved listening to their chatter as they strolled companionably ahead of me, the sidewalk not wide enough for three of us abreast; not that they would have let me walk next to them anyway, being younger and all. After a while, we decided I was old enough to walk the last two blocks by myself: I was five years old after all. But of course, Mom wasn't to know about it because to her, I was still her baby girl. Marilyn and Lee-Lee would stand on 38th and Pleasant and watch me while I ran westward, stopping to look both ways before crossing Grand Avenue, and then running the rest of the way to Harriet where Agassiz stood. I would turn back around and wave so they knew I'd gotten there safely. They looked like two tiny green dots in the distance, their plaid uniforms like fallen leaves on the sidewalk. I loved walking into Agassiz's beautiful brick building with the shiny wooden floors. Mrs. Xerxes' room was on the right.

"Good afternoon, Ginny," our teacher always said.

"Good afternoon, Mrs. Xerxes," I said as I headed straight for the miniature plastic kitchen with little plastic plates, bowls, cups, pots and pans.

Agassiz Public School had opened in 1922 and was named after Louis Agassiz, a famous naturalist who had founded the Museum of Natural History at Harvard University. Because of this, the décor tried to incorporate as much of nature and the natural world as it could. The classrooms had large windows with beautiful elm and maple trees perched outside of them.

I loved almost everything about kindergarten at Agassiz. I felt so grown up saying the Pledge of Allegiance at the beginning of class, my hand pressed proudly over my heart. "I pledge Allegiance to the flag of the United States of America, and to the republic for which it stands, one nation under God, indivizzibizzle, with liberty and justice for all."

Our eyes were all be glued reverently to the classroom flag while we recited the pledge. I adored music time, standing around in a circle doing the hokey-pokey. I worked hard during craft time gluing together Popsicle sticks to make picture frames for Christmas presents, and I loved story time, when Mrs. Xerxes would read to us from Laura Ingalls Wilder's Little House on the Prairie series, her soothing voice bringing to life the exciting events in Laura and Mary Ingalls lives in Minnesota during the 19th century. The only part I didn't like about kindergarten was when Mrs. Xerxes rang her little bell and announced: "Nap time! Boys and girls, I want you to go and get your mats and stretch them out on the floor so you can rest."

We were forced to lie down and not make a peep waiting for what seemed like forever with nothing to do but watch the second hand of the clock continue its journey around the circle of the hour. Walking to the stack of mats piled up against the wall, we each knew exactly which mat belonged to whom as we had brought them to school with us on the first day along with a box of Kleenex. It seemed like everyone else had shiny, new mats in bright exciting colors. Mine was a hand-me-down, like everything else I owned, that was not only a dingy faded orange color but it had some kind of stain on it that Pat kept apologizing for, saying sorry about the 'accident' he'd had at kindergarten on the day he drank too much milk for lunch.

I was looking forward to starting first grade at Incarnation and not having to worry about naptime anymore. Many of the kids from my kindergarten class would be heading over to Incy with me so it wasn't true that I would be a new kid like Brian Fogherty or Mickey. What I was really hoping was that Mickey and I would be in the same class.

"I can't believe my baby girl will be starting First Grade soon!" Mom's voice sounded muffled as she kissed me on the forehead and said goodnight.

Chapter 7

The night before the first day of school, Mom sent Dad out of the house with us to go to the Dairy Queen. She said the reason was to celebrate the last day of summer, but it was also because she had to be sure everyone had a clean uniform to wear to school in the morning that was washed and pressed, of course, so she had a lot of work to do. She didn't need us underfoot. Going to the Dairy Queen was a special treat. We all piled into the station wagon, into the front seats, the middle seats, and the back. Some of us got to climb in through the back window and sit in the rear seats facing out the back window. This was the favored seat because it was the farthest away from the watchful eye of the driver and we could have all sorts of fun with the people in the car following behind us. We made faces, put our feet out the window and made them move in unison, and drew our fists down in the universal signal to get truckers to honk their horns. We stopped fighting over who got to sit in the backseat after Bob Bold got sick back there after going on too many rides at Excelsior Amusement Park. He had tried to lean out the window to heave but he hadn't quite made it. It was impossible to get all of the vomit out from between the cracks, so every time the window was rolled up after that, the streaks of Bob's puke would rise up with the window. It made looking out the rear window an especially unpleasant view.

It was a perfect summer evening when we all climbed out of the car at the Dairy Queen. Although we knew there lots of ice cream choices to be had, for us there weren't. Dad went up to the window and placed an order for nine nickel cones. We always bumped into people we knew at DQ and tonight it seemed half the neighborhood was out enjoying the last of the lazy summer evenings. Lee-Lee was there with both her parents, Tessa's family was there, and so were the Olsons, Doc and the boys. Standing outside in the early evening, we made a game of eating our cones while Dad chatted with the other grownups. Round and round we'd lick around the base of the ice milk trying not to let a single drip fall onto the crispy cone. Then Greg bit off the bottom of his cone and began sucking the ice cream underneath. Danny, being too little to care about the drips, happily held onto his cone while the melting mess dripped all over his chubby little fist till it looked as if he was wearing a white, sticky glove. "Oh, Danny," Polly teased, "Guess who's going straight into the tub when we get home?"

"Take a look at that," Jane said with a toss of her stylishly coifed hair. We looked in the direction she indicated and saw Mickey with his head bowed in conversation with none other than Crazy Caroline. "What is that all about?"

"She's trying to kidnap him!" I yelped, suddenly remembering that the last time I'd seen Caroline she'd asked about Mickey. "We've got to help him!" I started heading in their direction.

"Not so fast, oh sticky one," Neil called out as he grabbed a hold of my pony tail to stop me. "That doesn't look like a kidnapping to me." Sure enough, we saw that Neil was right as Mickey was now strolling slowly back to rejoin the Olsons. "It is good to know, though, Ginny, that if there was to be a kidnapping in the neighborhood, we could count on you to stop it. Too bad the Lindbergh's didn't have someone like you around, huh?"

"Come and wash up before I let you back in the car," Dad hollered as he turned on the faucet the Dairy Queen had cleverly installed on the outside of the building as damage control. That's when I noticed that Crazy Caroline was licking on a buster bar she held in one hand as she walked away pushing her cart with the other. Turning back to look at the Olsons, I saw that Mickey no longer had his ice cream treat. I reminded myself to be sure to ask Mickey what was up with him and Crazy Caroline.

The next morning, I found myself a block away from the Dairy Queen standing in front of Incarnation School at 8 in the morning. All around me, kids were saying good-bye to their mothers and filing into the school amidst greetings and shouts of laughter. "But I feel sick, Mom," I repeated. "I'd better just go home with you, Greg and Danny". I looked at the little boys in the red wagon with such longing, knowing that their day was going to be filled with outdoor games, coloring, and freedom. I felt uncomfortable and ridiculous in Marilyn's old uniform. The green plaid wool jumper was hot, scratchy, and way too big for me as it hung below my knees. When Pete the Postman had finally delivered our school assignment letter, I learned I was to have a new nun from Nigeria as my first grade teacher. No one knew a single thing about her. Even worse, the thought of leaving Mom for the entire morning and then again after lunch was making it suddenly very hard for me not to cry.

"Ginny, I'm surprised at you!" Mom said with a small chuckle. "You've been so anxious to join your big sisters at Incy. Last year I practically had to lock you in your room to keep you from following them in the mornings! And now look at you," Mom noticed my trembling chin as I struggled not to totally shame myself by being a baby about starting first grade. I knew from experience that even all the way up to 8th grade, kids didn't forget who had cried on the first day of school back in first grade and who hadn't. Mom stooped down to be able to look me straight in the eyes, not an easy thing to do in the seventh month of her pregnancy. "Ginny, I don't know anyone who is going to enjoy first grade more than you. You are so ready to be here! You will learn reading, and arithmetic and music and the next thing you know it'll be time for lunch. Then you'll get to tell me all about your morning and I just know going back after lunch is going to be easier than this. Now, give me a kiss and get going. You don't want to be the last one in." Looking around, I realized it was already too late for that. I was the last kid in a uniform still standing outside of the school. The school bell started to clang.

"We'll miss you, Ginny," Danny said sadly as he gazed up at me and gave me a small wave. Rapidly blinking back my tears, I squared my shoulders under my overly-large uniform and walked up the stairs into the school without looking back once, knowing that if I did, I would never find the courage to step through those heavy wooden doors.

The First Grade teacher, Sr. Mary Jordan was tall, beautiful, and very black. I had never seen anyone with such dark skin before. I tried not to stare too hard. It looked like chocolate to me and I was sorely tempted to reach out to touch it. She stood at the door of our classroom and ushered me inside. After checking her clipboard, she marked my name off of her list and looked around the room for a place for me to sit. There were a few empty desks. One of them was in the front row next to Brian Fogherty. Looking up at Sister, I asked if I could sit next to Brian. The pleasure on his face as I took my seat next to him was way out of proportion to the act. I smiled back at him and looked forward to telling Mom about it at lunch. "Welcome to first grade." Sister began.

I was glad Mickey was in Sr. Mary Jordan's class, too. Right away, he missed a few days of school in September, so Mom complained to the principal that she thought the Olsons were making him stay home to work instead of allowing him to go to school. After that, he never missed more than one day of school a week. Mom also suggested that she thought it would be a good idea if Mickey could take piano lessons along with me. A sister at the convent was offering free lessons as long as the students were prepared for each lesson.

Most mornings, Mickey and I walked to school together, our feet crunching on the thick leaves covering the sidewalks from the many trees lining Pleasant Avenue. We learned to understand Sister's strange accent as well as all of the rules that came with being in the first grade. And we started taking piano lessons together.

In November, an exciting event happened in our family. The girls were cleaning up the kitchen while the boys were wrestling in the living room. We'd just finished supper. Dad came downstairs with a suitcase in his hand and said "I want you kids to pray the rosary while we're gone for the safe delivery of your new baby brother or sister, Chris." After much deliberation, they had decided the baby would be called Chris whether he was a boy or a girl; either Christopher or Christine.

"Is it time?"

"What?"

"Hurray!"

"We're gonna have a new sister, girls rule!" We all started hollering at once. Mom slowly walked downstairs holding onto the railing with one hand, her swollen belly with the other. She looked like she'd been crying. "Come on, Mary, everything will be just fine," Dad said as he put his arm around her.

"Oh, I know it will," Mom said, her big Czech nose turning redder and redder as she struggled not to cry. "It's just that I hate the hospital's rules about having to stay for five days after the baby's born."

"It'll be good for you and you know it. Otherwise these kids run you ragged. At the hospital, someone else will do the cooking and cleaning and all you'll have to do is hold and feed the newest member of our family, just as soon as Chris arrives, that is."

"No, it won't be good for me!" Mom repeated, her voice beginning to sound slightly hysterical. "It's torture, torture for me, do you hear? All I do is worry about what's happening here at home. A newborn hardly needs any attention at all: a quick feed and they're out for another long stretch. But these kids, they need so much from me! Who's going to be sure they're in bed at a decent hour, and that they have something to eat before school, and that they're not late for school, and that...ohhhhh," Mom began to moan a bit with her hands on her stomach.

"Come on, Mary, the sooner we get this little tyke born, the sooner you'll be back home again." Dad said as he left with a tearful Mom to St. Mary's Hospital. We all looked at one another in a house that suddenly seemed strange and unfamiliar without Mom's presence in it.

"Time for the rosary," Jane said in a no-nonsense voice and there wasn't a single complaint to be heard from any of us. We prayed the entire rosary with Jane leading more fervently than ever before. Besides praying for Mom, I knew I wasn't the only one praying that we girls would win the bet. At this point in our family history, we were tied. There were exactly four boys in the family and four girls. Well, actually five boys and five girls if you counted Mom and Dad. This baby being born was going to be the tie breaker, so the girls desperately wanted another girl and the boys anxiously awaited another boy. After the rosary, we put our pajamas on. Jane even let us play outside for a bit, nothing rough, just a game of horse around the basketball hoop. After a while, Mrs. Agneau called out over the fence "You kids had better get to bed. Tomorrow's a school day and I promised your mother that I'd keep an eye on you."

"Five more minutes, Mrs. Agneau, please?" Pat asked politely. "That's all the time I need to come out the winner in this game."

"He's only winning 'cause he cheats!" Neil defended himself. Mrs. Agneau stayed to watch the end of the game to be sure we turned in after that.

While we were eating the ice cream Jane was allowing us to have before bed, the phone rang. We all looked at one another excitedly for a split second of stunned silence before we jumped up and scrambled for the phone. Pat got there first but Jane insisted he let her answer the phone as Mom had left her in charge. "Hi Dad, uh-huh, oh, uh-huh, really, uh-huh, uh-huh, uh-huh. No, we're fine. Okay. Say hi to Mom for us. Bye Dad." Jane hung up the phone and didn't say a single word. We all waited with bated breath. "Right, time for bed." She said calmly. Uproar ensued as we all insisted she tell us at once what the news was. "Oh, we have another brother." She said while the boys hooted and slapped one another on their backs and congratulated each other as if they were the ones responsible for the gender of the newest member of the family.

Heading up the stairs to bed at last, Pat said to me, "What are you disappointed for? You should be glad Chris is a boy and not a girl. This way you continue being the spoiled rotten youngest girl in the family!" and he mussed up my hair with both hands while I giggled in protest.

"Spoiled, ha! With ugly old hand-me-downs to wear and dolls with missing eyes, bad hair cuts, and ink drawn all over their faces. Oh right, it's a real treat being the youngest girl in this family!" But as I settled down to sleep next to Marilyn in the room we shared with Polly, I thought about it and realized Pat was right. I knew I was special to Mom, at least, who always called me her own special baby girl. Maybe Chris being a boy wasn't such a bad thing after all.

The Friday after Chris was born, Dad was going to be late for work again as he stayed home to be sure all of the kids got off to school alright and to take Greg and Danny over to Aunt Margie's for the day until the older kids came home from school. I was still in my pajamas playing with Two-shoes, dangling a shoelace over her head until she couldn't stand it anymore. She would swat it with her big paw going instantly from sophisticated, bored cat to feisty, playful kitten. "Ginny, what are you doing? Hurry up and get dressed already or you'll be late," Dad hollered.

"Late for what?" I questioned. Two-shoes was leaping up into the air trying to catch the elusive shoelace.

"School, of course! Come on, now."

"But Dad," I explained patiently. "It's Friday."

"That's right," he said sharply, "Now hurry up or you're going to be late." The rest of the kids were already starting to filter out the door, meeting up with the other kids in the neighborhood on their way to school, too.

"But I never go to school on Fridays," I said complacently, certain that Mom had already explained this to Dad and that, with everything he had to manage while Mom was still in the hospital, he'd simply forgotten.

"That's absurd!" he retorted in the tone of voice that told me this was not going to go my way at all. "What do you mean; you never go to school on Fridays?" The surprise on his face coupled with the displeasure in his voice led me to believe that not only were Mom and I involved in something Dad knew absolutely nothing about but that it was something he heartily disapproved of, too. Mom had been hugely pregnant when I started the first grade and I had been sorely homesick for the unstructured, carefree time of my pre-school days. I don't know whether it was because she was tired of me complaining about going to school or because she appreciated my help with the two boys, but it came to pass that on Fridays, the rest of the kids would head off to school and I would stay home and spend the day with Mom and the boys. It never put me behind at school. Friday's tended to be more relaxed days at school anyway, so I kept up just fine. I loved the quiet of the neighborhood when all the rest of the kids were stuck at their desks and I was playing outside in the beautiful autumn sunshine with Greg and Danny. Obviously I wasn't going to be staying home on this particular Friday, however.

By the time I got hastily dressed and ran the two and a half blocks to school, morning prayers had already been recited and Sr. Mary Jordan was handing out our next assignment. She raised her eyebrows in surprise at my entrance as she wasn't used to seeing me at school on Fridays. "There are three items in each line," she announced. "Two of the items will be the same and one will be different. I want you to color the object in each line that doesn't match the other two items." Inside my head, I was rolling my eyes signifying boredom. We each got out our eight-pack of crayons from inside our desks and carefully started coloring.

"Be sure to stay inside the lines." Sr. Mary Jordan said with her distinct Nigerian lilt. I tried not to let my tongue slip out to the corner of my mouth which it tended to do when I was concentrating on something and not paying attention to keeping it behind my closed lips where it belonged. Sister walked slowly up and down the rows of desks peering over our shoulders at our work. Suddenly, from behind me, she said disapprovingly "Ginny, try to be more careful and color within the lines." I felt my face burn with humiliation. What? I was only doing what she had told us we should do, to first trace the outline before we start to color inside the lines. The outline of the brown bear I was coloring is what wobbled out of the line, not what I was actually coloring. I struggled not to cry as I continued coloring the inane assignment.

"Hey moron," Wayne, whom we called 'light bulb-head', said disparagingly, "your tongue's sticking out." Looking around, I saw that Mickey was absent again, and I was so lonely, I had to bite my lip to keep from crying.

Suddenly, there was a light tap on my shoulder. I turned to see a horrendous-looking naked troll with flaming orange hair exploding out of the top of his head. I jumped in fright before looking more closely and realizing that the troll's body was actually an eraser. The girl holding him out for me to use was smiling with sympathetic eyes. "Thanks!" I mouthed silently.

"You're welcome!" Lexie whispered back while I smiled gratefully at my new friend.

Chapter 8

Besides Mickey, Lexie was my closest friend at school. She was everything I wasn't. She was short, I was tall. She was prompt, I was tardy. She was an only child; I was number six of nine. She was artistic, I was athletic. She had a mom who worked outside of the home; I had a mom who worked at home. At school, I sat next to Brian on one side and Lexie on the other. Mickey sat on the other side of Lexie.

Whenever Doc Olson made Mickey do many chores to do over the week-end, I hung out with Lexie instead. Lexie loved sleeping over at my house but I would always much rather sleep over at hers. At my house, she was just one more kid in our already over-crowded bedroom. She received no special treatment, and the boys were just as likely to trip her as she walked past as to greet her. Her visits were noisy and chaotic and quite like life as usual. When I would walk Lexie home the morning after she spent the night, she would tell her mom that she had had the best time ever and that she couldn't wait to go back again! The first day I met her, Lexie's Mom told me to call her 'Stella'. Not 'Mrs.' like all the other moms were called, but 'Stella' as if she and I were friends, too. Stella always wore bright pink lipstick and shoes with heels even when she was at home. She had been born in Russia and she still spoke with a thick accent.

When it was my turn to stay overnight at Lexie's, I was careful to pack matching top and bottom pajamas. If I could find one, I put in a robe, too, because Lexie always wore one. Lexie's mom let us take all 112 of Lexie's trolls and line them up all around the pristine living room. The room looked so elegant with doilies on the end tables and porcelain figures from Germany which sat right out in the open where anyone could bump and break them. After playing with the trolls, we often had a coloring contest. The coloring contests were always fixed because Stella and I knew that Lexie always had to win. The first time that she hadn't won, she threw such a tantrum that she broke her Suzy Bake Oven and screamed and cried so much it spoiled the whole sleepover. Now Stella always gave me a little wink and a smile while pretending to judge our pictures. After much hemming and hawing, she proclaimed Lexie's picture the winner. Actually, Lexie always should have won because she was a much better artist than I was. Stella probably just hadn't wanted to hurt my feelings, initially.

Later on, we would sit in the living room to eat dinner on our own individual metal T.V. trays and actually watched T.V. during dinner! My mom would not have approved. After dinner, we played Barbie's. When we put our pajamas on and brushed our teeth, we went into Lexie's room where the covers on the twin beds were pulled back invitingly. We each had a clean glass of water sitting on the bedside table in case we got thirsty in the middle of the night. Stella came in and kissed both of our foreheads goodnight and thanked us for being such good girls. She left the door open just a crack and the house was absolutely quiet except for Lexie and I whispering our plans for our next sleepover at my house.

Lexie wouldn't talk about her Dad, so I figured she'd never actually met him, or she had and he wasn't worth talking about so I didn't bring it up. She and her Mom had different last names though so my Mom told me that meant Stella wasn't married. Stella worked as a translator. Her main job was to read everything there was to know about the sputnik program and translate it into English. *Sputnik-1* was launched on October 4th, 1957. The satellite travelled at 18,000 miles per hour, taking 96.2 minutes to complete an orbit, emitting radio signals at 20.005 and 40.002 mega hertz which were monitored by amateur radio operators throughout the world. The signals continued for 22 days until the transmitter batteries ran out on October 26th. *Sputnik 1* burned up on January 4th, 1958, as it fell from orbit reentering the earth's atmosphere, after travelling about 60 million miles."

"So what are the Russians working on now?" I asked. Stella waggled her finger with its long red nail at me.

"You know very well I am not at liberty to discuss. But," she lifted her perfectly-shaped eyebrows up and down and whispered in her Russian accent, "Americans better hurry to catch up as they are so far not winning!"

One day, Mom sent me over to Lexie's to see if Stella wanted to come to our house for Gossip Group. It was actually called Craft Night. Some of the ladies from church would meet at each other's houses once a month to work on craft pieces to sell at the parish festival in October. When it was Mom's turn to host, we would have to keep out of their hair while they worked on their knitting, quilting, and embroidery. It always seemed like they spent most of their time 'wagging their chins' as Dad would say, so we teased Mom and called it her Gossip Group instead. With Lexie and me spending so much time together, Mom wanted to be friendly to Stella, too. "Tell your mother thank you for the thinking of me, but I would not like to go." Stella replied.

"Mom never leaves the house on account of her disease," Lexie told me as she walked me back home.

"What disease does she have?" I asked, thinking of the wart people who lived in the upper duplex where Jane sometimes babysat, and how she never touched the door handles at their house without using a handkerchief on account of she didn't want to catch warts.

"She's scared to leave the house," Lexie said mildly.

"But she leaves the house every day when she goes to work," I said. Stella didn't drive; in fact she didn't even own a car. Every day that Stella had to go to work, there would be a taxi waiting in front of their house. It usually arrived just as Lexie was walking out the door for school. None of us had ever been in a taxi before so we thought it was the neatest thing ever that Stella took one twice a day.

"Yeah, but that's the only place she ever goes," Lexie continued. "And even there, she has her own office which she says looks a lot like our living room so she can kind of sort of pretend she's still at home. And she doesn't have to hardly talk to anybody else, she just spends all of her time reading in Russian and typing it out in English. The taxi picks her up and drops her off and the whole time she's in the taxi, her eyes are closed and she's concentrating on pretending she's really still at home."

I had no idea what to say to that. I tried to look at Lexie without her noticing while we walked along taking turns kicking a baseball-sized rock down the sidewalk. It occurred to me that I finally understood what Sr. Mary Jordan meant when she said to put on a pair of an Indian's moccasins if you really want to understand the Indian's life. I thought Lexie had the perfect life. She was an only child. All of her Mom's attention belonged to her all of the time. She had a neat little house, brand new toys, and no hand-me-down clothes either. And all along she was living with a woman who was scared to leave her house.

"Gee, Lex, I'm sorry," I said awkwardly.

"That's okay," Lexie said with a shrug. "It's called agora fear and it's not contagious or anything so you don't have to be afraid of catching it."

"Well, if your Mom can't come, then how about if you come and hang out in the kitchen with us, instead. There are always teeny-tiny sandwiches with no crusts on them, bars, nuts, and mints. It'll be fun." With that I took Lexie's hand in mine.

We had a great time in the kitchen that evening while the Gossip Group worked on their crafts. Chairs from the dining room had been placed around the living room to accommodate all of the ladies. The coffee table had been covered with a table cloth and snacks were placed on it; small bowls of peanuts, Chex Mix, chips, and sour cream & onion dip. The lamps were glowing brightly and the women were chattering and laughing while they worked.

Lexie and I played 'Sorry' with Marilyn and Polly for a while, and then we got out a deck of cards and played 'Crazy Eight's' and 'King's Corner'. Jane was upstairs giving the little boys baths before putting them to bed and Neil and Pat were outside playing one on one. From the living room, a sound of glass shattering was followed by silence throughout the house. We stopped playing to listen, and when we heard sobs coming from the Gossip Group, we put down our cards and crept out to investigate. Mrs. Burberry had her head in her hands and Mom was standing beside her with an arm around her heaving shoulders. Mrs. Gauze was picking up the pieces of the shattered tea cup. I ran back to get the broom and dustpan and when I returned, no one had moved at all. I realized how serious it was because Mom didn't even notice that we were there after she'd given us strict orders not to come out of the kitchen or else. I noticed that most of the women had tears in their eyes, too, and were struggling not to cry. I looked at the dishtowel Mrs. Burberry was embroidering. She had already finished the word 'Thursday' and was halfway done with a spotted puppy placed right under the day of the week. Everyone always said that Mrs. Burberry's stitching was the finest of the group, so I picked up her work and patted her back saying, "Here's your dishcloth, Mrs. Burberry. I sure do like the puppy you're working on. I'm sure this will be one of the first things to go at the Oktoberfest." That's what the annual parish festival was called. No one said a word for a moment and I looked at Mom to see if she was mad, but she looked at me kindly and nodded her head as if I should go on.

"I think it's great that you're putting the days of the week on the towels. That way, whoever buys these will remember to change cloths every day and not use the same dirty towel twice. That's how I feel about the 'Days of the week' underpants I got for Christmas last year. Most days, I wear the right day of the week when I'm supposed to, but once in a while I'll go to use the bathroom and see that I'm wearing Saturday even though I'm at school at the time. Good grief, I'll wonder, have I had these on all this time, or am I sitting here at school when I shouldn't be? Probably it's just because I was too sleepy in the morning to notice that I was putting on the wrong day of the week. The funny thing is, there are no Sunday underpants which I've always thought was really strange. Why not Sunday?" I finished lamely when I noticed that Mrs. Burberry's shoulders were beginning to shake again and I felt like I'd only made things worse. She even started to wail a little bit and then she threw her head back and started guffawing loudly. It occurred to me that the tears flowing out of her eyes now were tears of laughter. The rest of the ladies joined in, too. The next thing I knew, they were all pulling out their beautifully-embroidered handkerchiefs that they had probably purchased at last year's Oktoberfest, and they were gently dabbing at their eyes so as not to smear their mascara. I looked around the room feeling embarrassed, not sure if I had said something funny on purpose or not. Their laughter carried on for a while before Mom spoke up.

"Polly and Marilyn, will you bring in the lemon bars, please? And Ginny, get one of the boys to walk you and Lexie home now before her Mom starts to worry about her being out so late on a school night."

Lexie lived on 41st and Pleasant, one block south of us so that's why she couldn't walk home alone. It was an unwritten rule that as long as you stayed on the block you were perfectly safe, but crossing the street always required someone older to accompany you, especially once it was dark. When Pat and I got back from walking Lexie home, the Gossip Group had dispersed and the girls were helping Mom clean up. "Here, Ginny," Polly said as she threw a pair of underpants at me. "You can have that old pair of underwear of mine to wear on Sundays so I don't have to worry about you going about in nothing but your 'birthday suit' beneath your dress at church!" The kids all burst into laughter.

"Don't you pay any attention to them, Ginny." Mom said as she continued to gently wash the cups and saucers the ladies had used. They were her finest china and were only used by company. The delicate ivory-colored porcelain was outlined in gold with fragile pink and yellow flowers adorning them. And now there was minus one.

"What was wrong with Mrs. Burberry?" I grabbed a dishtowel and began drying the dishes.

"It's really horrible. For months, now, Phyllis has been saying odd little things from time to time which don't make sense but we just let pass. She has seemed a little preoccupied and forgetful, that's all. Today was the worst, though. We were talking about Becky Gordon's wedding coming up, and Marion Gordon was telling about the flowers that Becky wants to have for the bridesmaid's bouquets. She asked Phyllis how her daughter Kath had liked working with the 36th Street floral shop for her wedding. Phyllis looked at her blankly so Marion repeated the question. "Do I have a daughter?" Phyllis finally asked. We were all stunned into silence and none of us could come up with anything to say. Phyllis truly didn't even seem sad or anything at first and she repeated the question. When none of us answered, she changed the question to ask, "Do I have any children? I just can't seem to remember." I had just told her that she had five wonderful children, two sons and three daughters when she dropped her cup of tea and burst into tears." The light-hearted mood in the kitchen stilled.

"Why can't she remember that she has kids?"

"We think it must be dementia. This is just the beginning, of course. Soon it'll get so bad she won't even know her own husband," Mom wiped her eyes with the back of her wrists as her hands were all soapy from dishwater. "When you say your prayers tonight, don't forget to include Phyllis and her family."

Later, lying in bed next to Marilyn, I asked her which she would rather have, agora fear or dementia just to enjoy the moment of having her ask me what 'agora fear' was. I didn't often get the chance to know something Marilyn didn't. We talked for a while longer and then Marilyn's breathing slowed and deepened as she drifted off to sleep. My stomach was feeling queasy as I thought about how frightening it must feel to realize you're losing your memory. Who are we without memory? Memory is what makes us who we are. I lay there thinking for a long time about memories and disease. Then I squeezed my eyes shut and said a prayer. I hovered for a while in the pleasant state between being awake and asleep before finally succumbing to sleep myself.

Chapter 9

The rest of the school year flew by. On the afternoon of the last day, we all met at the Stidger's house to play 'school.' They had a huge porch with enough desks to form two rows of six desks each so that a dozen of us could pretend to be students, Matt Stidger was the imaginary teacher, and someone else got to be the principal. As we grabbed our after-school snack of peanut butter & jelly sandwiches and raced out the door, Mom shook her head and laughed saying "Nine months of school and your first afternoon free you choose to play school!"

On the way to Stidger's, we crossed the Shortpascher's lawn. "Hey, get off the lawn, or else!" a voice came from nowhere and made us jump. Snickers and laughter came from the screened in porch which was too dark to see into except to detect a variety of shapes and sizes of the many Shortpascher boys.

"Try and make us!" Greg unwisely replied. Suddenly there was an outburst of noise as chairs scraped against the floor and the front screen door flew open. We took off running and just made it inside the Stidger's front porch hastily shutting the screen door as the

Shortpaschers were shaking the door handle and making animal sounds.

"We'll get you next time, you little brats," Freddie snarled.

"Good one, pinhead!" Marilyn snapped as she swatted Greg on the back of his head. "Now we've got the Shortpaschers after us!"

What else is new, I thought to myself. Craig, Slim, Freddie, Bert, and Rita Shortpascher were the banes of our existence. Although they seemed to be close to our age, they didn't seem to go to school or at any rate not to our school. There had never been a Mr. Shortpascher as far as we knew, and Mrs. Shortpascher was mostly missing. When she was seen, she looked like she'd been run over by a truck, walked with great difficulty, and talked with a slur. The Shortpaschers didn't socialize with anyone in the neighborhood except for the Sullivans. The Sullivan's house was on the other side of ours, so the Shortpaschers and the Sullivans were always traipsing back and forth between one another's houses insulting anyone they came across on their way. Each winter, a number of bulbs would go missing from the Christmas lights Dad put around the trees in front of our house. "It's like a game to them," Dad said with no rancor in his voice. "If that's the only harm they ever commit, then that's alright with me." We knew it was the Shortpaschers and the Sullivans stealing the bulbs just for spite but there was nothing we could do about it.

The day after the last day of school, a bunch of us were following Pete the Postman around. Mom had complained again to Doc Olson about working Mickey too hard, so he was hanging out with us, too. We were anxiously looking for letters from school but not for next year's room assignments. This time we desperately awaited our final grade results. We actually weren't that interested from an academic standpoint but from a reward perspective. "I'm telling you, there's nothing in my bag from the school," Pete insisted. We followed him for a few houses but soon realized that he was right. The school couldn't possibly have put our grades in the mail to arrive the first day of vacation. We collapsed on the nearest lawn and let Pete go on with his deliveries in peace.

"That stinks," Polly proclaimed. "Now we won't get to go to Excelsior tomorrow. We'll have to wait until next week-end!"

"What's in Excelsior?" Mr. Finkelstein asked from the edge of his flowerbed. "Besides Lake Minnetonka, I mean."

It was his lawn we had collapsed on when aborting our mission to follow the postman around. Or what was left of his lawn. All of the other houses on our block had narrow little flowerbeds right in front of the house and then sweeping lawns all the way down to the sidewalk. After the sidewalk, there was another little strip of lawn just before the curb to the street. Not Benjamin Finkelstein's lawn. When he moved into the neighborhood, he immediately set about digging up almost his entire lawn and planting it with flowers, instead. Initially, the neighborhood was aghast. What a mess! How unusual! After the first year, however, when the first of the bleeding hearts started to bloom in the spring, followed by brilliant scarlet petunias, rhododendrons, irises, and splashy orange daylilies, when the fragrant phlox started to come out in force, the women of the neighborhood stopped complaining about Mr. Finkelstein. When they saw how artistically he added the heliotrope, roses, and baby's breath, they started to rave about him.

"What's in Excelsior?" Marilyn echoed incredulously. "Do you honestly mean to tell us, Mr. Finkelstein, that you've never been to the Excelsior Amusement Park?"

Excelsior Amusement Park? Hmmmm, let' see..........perhaps............mmm. That would be a 'no', can't say that I have," He continued to line the front of his garden bed with sweet alyssum.

"Poor you!"

"You don't know what you're missing!"

"The best rollercoaster ever and it goes right over the lake!" Everyone tried to explain at once.

"And gee, being as you're a lawyer and all and you had to be really smart to get into law school, you probably would have gotten tons of tickets with your report card!"

"Amusement Parks were never really my thing," Mr. Finkelstein went on.

"Even when you were a kid?"

"Especially when I was a kid," he confirmed. "I've always been afraid of heights so that knocks out half of the rides, and I get sick to my stomach on anything that goes around in a circle so that wipes out the other half. The only thing I ever really liked was the cotton candy and it seems some bully or other would always run by and grab a handful of my cotton candy and I would be left holding an empty stick." He pushed his glasses up his nose leaving a smudge of dirt across his rather large appendage.

"That doesn't sound very fun," Mickey responded worriedly, a frown creasing his forehead.

"Oh, but it will be fun for us, Mickey, don't you worry. You're going to love it at Excelsior!"

Mom said I could take Mickey along to Excelsior with us this year because the Olsons won't go. Kenny doesn't like rides. We think the real reason the Olson's don't go is because Kenny is getting such bad grades he wouldn't be able to go on hardly any rides anyway. Mickey is a much more diligent student and will likely be awarded a whole slew of tickets. Excelsior Amusement Park gives out free vouchers when you bring your report card to the park. You get four free tickets for every A you've received on your report card, three for every B, two for every C, and one for a D. As each ride is only two tickets at the most, some of the rides like the merry-go-round are only one ticket, each report card could conceivably merit 32 free tickets! Both Mickey and I were hoping to receive at least 28 tickets which is why we were following Pete the Postman around. Mickey had never even seen an amusement park before so he was feeling skeptical.

"Don't worry, Mickey," Mr. Finkelstein began and he placed a hand on Mickey's shoulder. Mickey jumped a foot and shrugged off Mr. Finkelstein's hand at the same time. Then he quickly got up and said, "Gotta go, see ya later, Ginny," as he ran off.

Mr. Finkelstein looked thoughtfully after Mickey with a hurt look on his face. He rubbed his hands on his pants and began picking up the empty sweet alyssum containers. "Don't feel bad, Mr. Finkelstein," I tried to comfort him. "Mickey probably forgot to do something on his 'job list' that Mrs. Olson gives him every day. Now that he's not in school for the summer, the list is three times as long!"

"I hope that's all it is, Ginny," Mr. Finkelstein replied, not sounding convinced. I stayed to help him in the garden for awhile but we didn't talk anymore about Mickey.

Later that morning, I knocked on Mrs. Agneau's door. "Well, hello, dear. What a pleasant surprise," she said as she opened the door for me. "Goodness gracious, what is this?" she exclaimed when she saw the armful of plants I was carrying.

"Mr. Finkelstein told me to bring you these. He says he has no more room in his garden and wondered if you would care to plant them?"

"That dear man!" Mrs. Agneau greedily handled the plants. "A pepper plant, eggplant, broccoli, and, could it be?" She picked up each of the seedlings which all looked the same to me. She knew exactly what they were. "Brussels sprouts! Oh, joy! There is nothing like fresh Brussels sprouts! I will have both you and Benjamin over in the fall when we can have fresh Brussels sprouts swimming in butter; none of this margarine business either, I tell you. My poor Mr. Agneau never enjoyed any butter believing margarine was better for him and look where that got him! He should have been enjoying butter while he was able to. Oh, there is nothing in the world like fresh Brussels sprouts doused in butter, Ginny!"

"Um, aren't those the ones that look like heads of lettuce for midgets?" I asked, trying to keep the disgust out of my voice.

Mrs. Agneau laughed. "I've never thought of it that way, dear, but I suppose you're right."

I helped Mrs. Agneau plant Mr. Finkelstein's plants in her garden. Once she got down on her knees, it was hard for her to get back up again, so I would fetch whatever she needed so she could stay put. She asked me about my last days of school and what my plans were for summer vacation. When there was a lull in the conversation, I asked: "Mrs. Agneau, what's a queer?"

"Why do you ask, dear?" Mrs. Agneau inquired. I hated when grownups answered a question with another question. It usually meant that their answer was either going to be 'no' or that they weren't going to answer the question. It could mean that Mrs. Agneau was just biding her time though and trying to decide how to answer, and I hoped that was the case now.

"Well, lots of times when Mr. Finkelstein is outside, the Shortpaschers start yelling 'queer!' They pretend they're not directly saying it to him. They'll say it to each other, like, 'Bert, stopping being a QUEER,' or they'll put it in their conversation, like, 'the weather is so QUEER today' or they'll pretend to sneeze and go, 'ah-QUEER!' really loudly. They crack themselves up whenever they do this. Mr. Finkelstein just ignores them but it's got me thinking."

"Oh, dear," Mrs. Agneau sat back onto her ankles and sighed heavily. "Why does ignorance so often reveal itself as cruelty?" she asked. I waited quietly beside her watching her face cloud over. "You may have noticed that Benjamin isn't married," She began softly. "That's alright, of course, you may think that's just his choice or that he hasn't met the right woman yet. But it may also mean that, how do I put this, that he wasn't born to love women at all, ever. I don't mean that he can't care for women, of course he can, but to love just one woman in particular in the way that your father loves your mother, well it may well be that Benjamin simply wasn't made that way. At the end of the day, that is his business and his business alone. As long as he isn't hurting anyone, it shouldn't be anyone else's business at all." As she was talking, her voice had gotten louder and louder and she almost shouted the last sentence. She gave a little chuckle then as she shook her head. "Help me up, Ginny, will you? Do you understand what I'm trying to say to you?"

"I think so," I said, helping to hoist Mrs. Agneau to her feet. "You're saying Mr. Finkelstein is 'different' and like my brother Neil said, some people don't like anything or anyone that's 'different' from them."

"That's exactly what I was trying to say, Ginny," Mrs. Agneau finished as she gathered up her gardening tools, "and it's our duty to try to convince the human race that being different is not only acceptable, but that it makes the world a better place in the end."

"Just like Mr. Finkelstein's lawn?" I supposed.

"Just exactly like that," she said enthusiastically. "Benjamin came into the neighborhood and everyone was so worried when he tore up his lawn. Now our street has been enhanced by his lovely flowers and the beauty they've added to our lives. Besides that, he is a genuinely kind man and he gives things to old ladies like me. He knows I can't afford much but he does it in such a way so as not to embarrass me." Mrs. Agneau was working her way up to a shout again. "Ooh, those Shortpaschers make me so mad I'd like to throw one of my eggplants at them, but then again I wouldn't want to waste it on them!" I laughed, picturing sweet Mrs. Agneau hurling an enormous purple eggplant right at a Shortpascher's head!

I wondered if Mickey didn't like Mr. Finkelstein because he was different. I didn't think so, though, because Mickey being an Indian made him different, too, so he ought to have known what that felt like. Besides, Mickey wasn't unkind.

The following week-end, we did get to go to Excelsior. Mickey and I cashed in our A's and spent a heavenly afternoon screaming our heads off on the rides. We shared some of our tickets with Greg and Danny because they weren't in school yet. Greg was in kindergarten at Agassiz this year, but they don't give out A's and B's. You either pass and move on to first grade, or they hold you back. While we were 300 feet off the ground on the Ferris wheel waiting for our turn to get off, I asked Mickey what he thought of Mr. Finkelstein.

"Mr. Finkelstein's alright, I guess," Mickey said while he tried to keep our chair swinging on the Ferris wheel.

"You just weren't too friendly when he put his hand on you the other day."

Mickey scowled and squirmed in the swinging Ferris wheel seat saying through gritted teeth. "I just don't like grown-ups touching me, that's all. Hey!" he suddenly shouted as a big gob of spit landed right on his arm. We looked up to see Greg and Danny in the chair above us preparing their throats ready for their next expulsion of spit. "No fair! We're the ones who GAVE you these tickets, you morons!" we shouted in indignation. And we spent the rest of the ride dodging the boys' efforts to spit on us.

Chapter 10

That May, I had gotten a new bike for my seventh birthday. It was lavender with a banana seat. It had plastic purple and white streamers that flew straight out from my handlebars when I biked fast enough. I could make them look like they were dancing in the breeze. We liked to take some of Mom's clothes pins and attach playing cards to the back spokes of the bike tires to create an awesome clicking sound. The faster we pedaled, the faster the clacking would get. Eventually, if I pedaled fast enough, the clicks would all start to run together until a terrific roar would issue from the back of the bike and I could swear I was riding a motorcycle. Up and down the alley we biked at breakneck speed. We circled the block, too, for hours, knowing exactly where every sidewalk crack, uneven pavement, and missing piece of cement was around the entire block.

I was biking up and down the alley waiting for Mickey to finish his chores and join me when a bee alighted on my wrist. Being a relatively new biker, I wasn't able to bike with one hand yet, so I couldn't remove my hand with the bee resting on it to shake it off. Nor could I remove my other hand to wave the bee away. I did the only thing I could think of to do. I began to pedal faster and faster hoping that my speed would dislodge the unwelcome freeloader. I was crying while pedaling and while my tears didn't lessen my speed, they did hinder my vision significantly. The next thing I knew, I was sailing through the air and flying right into the Shortpascher's backyard. They had a nasty little wall leading from the alley down into their backyard. Anyone else would have put up a fence for safety or extended the height of the wall to prevent accidents such as this from happening, but not the Shortpaschers. After my astonishing flight, I landed with a crash onto the Shortpaschers grass and instantly felt a stinging bite on my wrist. What?!? Not even my speed-defying fall had caused the bumblebee to get off of my wrist. I was wailing when Mrs. Shortpascher came running out of her house followed closely by Doc Olson.

After feeling for broken bones, Doc declared me fit as a fiddle and Mrs. Shortpascher told me harshly to quit my bellyaching as I wasn't even badly hurt. My howls reached higher and higher decibels as the poison from the bee sting spread throughout my arm and I felt I'd never known such pain before in my life.

"She's sayin' she got stung by a bee!" Slim Shortpascher informed them from the top of the swing set. A crowd had gathered by this point and I was hollering as to how I wanted my Mom, so Doc scooped me up in his arms and told Mrs. Shortpascher over his shoulder, "I'll be back later on." When he called through my screen door to let mom know he was coming in, the worried look on her face made me feel better instantly.

"Looks like a bee got her right here on her wrist and caused her to crash her bike," Doc told Mom as he prodded at my wrist.

"That's not what happened," I sniffled. "I was going real fast so the bee would fall off and that's why I crashed!" My arm was swelling up like a balloon and Doc had Mom put an ice cold cloth on it to slow the swelling.

"And you heard it all the way over to your place?" Mom inquired? "I can't figure out why I didn't hear it!"

It wasn't till later while I was enjoying being in the house on such a hot afternoon with the fan aimed right at me and Mom brought me my third glass of Seven-Up (for medicinal purposes) that it occurred to me that Doc hadn't explained to Mom that he hadn't been at home when I crashed my bike and that was why he'd heard me fall and she hadn't.

"Doc was at Shortpaschers?" Mom mused. "Is anyone sick over there?"

"Not that I know of," I sipped pleasurably out of my straw, a novelty we only got to have when we were sick or injured.

"Poor Mrs. Olson," Mom commiserated with a shake of her head.

I thought about this for awhile and then said, "Poor Mickey, too, cause he has to work even when Doc Olson isn't. I was waiting for him on my bike in the alley when the bee attacked me. He told me both of his parents were at work and he had to have all of his jobs finished before they got home. Now he's probably done and is biking all by his lonesome." Suddenly my arm didn't seem so bad anymore. "Mom?" I started to inquire when Mom's sixth sense kicked in and she took the cloth off of my wrist at the same time as she said, "Yes, off with you then, but take it is easy; you've had enough excitement for one day."

I proudly showed off my bee sting to Mickey. "Wow! Your skin feels so hot! Does it hurt?"

"Not as much as before. It sure does itch though," I said trying to be tough. "Doc put some cream on it that's supposed to stop if from itching. It doesn't seem to have helped though."

"When did you see Doc?" Mickey asked.

I explained how Doc was the one who carried me home and that he'd come running out of Shortpascher's house. "Must be one of them kids is sick or something."

"Must be," Mickey agreed with a doubtful look on his face.

My accident spurred sympathy from an unexpected sector which resulted in misery for my sister Marilyn and ecstasy for me. It was time for an annual event that was anticipated nearly as much as Christmas or Halloween in our neighborhood. An occasion which all extracurricular events were scheduled around, parent-teacher conferences were known to be postponed because of, and one time the Sacrament of Confession was even cancelled due to the airing of this program.

The yearly showing of the Wizard of Oz was to be broadcast on T.V. and I was invited to watch it on the only color television set in the neighborhood. Mrs. Gauze felt sufficiently guilty over my plunge off of the alley embankment to invite me over for this momentous viewing. The Gauze's house is directly across the alley from the Shortpascher's and she must have felt some territorial culpability. Watching the Wizard of Oz was always a significant occurrence but this year was to be even more incredible because up until then we had only seen the movie in black and white. Oz was a brilliant green and Dorothy's slippers a dazzling red only in our imaginations because our T.V.'s were all in black and white. Now the Gauzes had purchased a color T.V.; a perk of having the misfortune of being parents to only one offspring is the way Dad explained it to me. As soon as their gleaming new console was delivered to the Gauze's house, Marilyn had started lording it over the rest of us that she was invited to see the horse of a different color really change color in the Land of Oz while the rest of us were stuck with our imaginations. But then I was invited to the Gauze's house, too.

We spent hours acting out scenes from The Wizard of Oz in the weeks before and after the viewing. Cackles of "I'll get you, and your little dog, too!" could be heard amongst verses of "We're off to see the wizard, the wonderful wizard of Oz." We painted a yellow path up the alley and throughout the backyards and made scarecrows to stand in the gardens. We hooked arms and whispered "Lions and tigers and bears, oh my!" as we paraded around the neighborhood. Polly was taken to the hospital once after descending from a tree in a beautiful pink gown (well, a nightgown actually) wrapped in saran wrap emulating Glenda the good witch coming down in a bubble, though somehow the gentle glide to the ground turned into a wicked thump.

At last, the long-awaited night was here, and I had had the good fortune to crash my bike seriously enough near the Gauze's house to warrant a sympathy invitation to watch it in color. Marilyn tried every tactic in the book to get Mom to stop me from joining her and Lee-Lee at this momentous debut, but Mom would have none of it. I was trying my best to look grateful, excited, and humble all at once as Marilyn and I walked down the alley.

It felt strange to be the only ones outside at seven o'clock on a perfect summer's evening while all the rest of the kids were anxiously sitting in front of their television sets. How quiet the neighborhood seemed. I could see Mrs. Agneau working in her kitchen with her radio blaring some news' station and further on heard some loud orchestra music emanating from Mr. Finkelstein's house. It made me feel sad somehow as if I were witnessing the neighborhood at some future date when none of us kids would be here anymore and this is what the alley would be like: empty. Blackbirds were cawing raucously overhead as they always did whenever Two Shoes was out in the yard. Their haunting cries added a feeling of trepidation to my nostalgia and I slipped my hand into Marilyn's as we stepped silently up the walk.

"What is it?" Marilyn asked as she responded by squeezing my hand.

"Nothing," I answered. "It's just life," I looked around me and for a moment felt the earth stand still. "It's just life here on Pleasant."

"Sure, okay. Listen, if they offer us pop you can probably say yes but I wouldn't mention it to Mom," Marilyn threatened. "And if you spill anything, I will kill you, after I die of shame first." Wondering how she would kill me if she were already dead from shame, I pushed on the doorbell while simultaneously calling: "We're here!"

We gasped along with Dorothy after the tornado picked up her house, crashed it, and she first opened the door onto Oz. Seeing this scene so many times before in black and white had not done justice to how beautiful Oz looked in all of its brilliant colors. The gasp echoed around the room and we turned to see many heads peering in through the windows of the Gauze's living room to witness this epic event in living color. It looked as though over half of the neighborhood was angling for a spot to peer through the window of the Gauze's living room so see Oz in color.

The room was a bit crowded after Mrs. Gauze invited everyone in, but it was nice to share the experience. I moved over in my armchair so Mickey could sit with me, and we shared a big bowl of popcorn. I did spill just a little pop on my pajamas but not enough to get noticed. I quickly glanced at Marilyn but she was wiping her eyes, hoping no one would notice she was crying while Dorothy was saying good-bye to the scarecrow.

When Mom was tucking me in bed that night, I was telling her how blue Dorothy's dress was and how red the apples were that the mean old apple trees threw. I clarified with her that there really was no such thing as flying monkeys, right?

"Be sure to throw your pajamas down the chute in the morning so I can get that pop out before it stains," she said omnisciently as she closed the door behind her.

"There's no place like home!" I shouted after her and snuggled underneath the blankets.

Chapter 11

"I don't think we're in Kansas anymore, Toto, I mean, Chrissie," I said as I scooped Chris up off of the floor where he'd been crawling straight toward Two Shoes. The cat was lying regally on the carpet pretending sleep but the flick of her tale gave her away and I knew she was just waiting for the right moment to swat at someone. I didn't want that someone to be Chris. Going to the other side of the room, I set Chris down and he immediately took off straight for Two Shoes again, giggling with pleasure at his newfound mobility. I waited till he got close to the cat, then scooped him up again while he squealed with delight and once again set him back down on the other side of the room. Two Shoes played her part well, feigning to be oblivious to the chubby-fisted baby careening towards her. Over and over again, Chris crawled back to his quarry faster each time until he almost reached her before I would grasp him by his sturdy waist and lift him to safety, Two Shoes peering out of half-closed slits for eyes ready to attack at will.

Not wanting to miss out on the fun, Danny put aside his match box cars and joined Chris on the floor and started crawling towards the cat, too. Chris shrieked with anticipation and crawled as fast as his little legs would take him, but of course Danny got there first and

Two Shoes at last had her chance. From lethargic pet to vicious lynx in a flash, the cat leapt onto Danny's back as soon as he got too close and dug in with all four paws. Screaming in agony, Danny rolled over onto Two Shoes who dug her claws in even deeper to prevent herself from being squashed. Chris pushed himself off of his knees onto his bottom and shoved his thumb in his mouth, sucking vigorously while watching the brawl, his eyebrows creasing into a troubled frown as he perhaps empathized that it may well have been his back thus impaired and not Danny's.

"What's going on in there, Ginny?" Mom asked as the sewing machine went silent.

'Nothing," I answered as I lifted the cat onto the back of the couch where she would be safely out of reach, first ruffling up the top of her head and scolding her while simultaneously scratching under her chin. "You are such a bad kitty!" I whispered. She began to lick herself lazily as if she hadn't a clue what I was talking about. "You're okay, Danny." I said as I began to tickle him all over. He continued to wail for a moment in self-pity but soon his cries turned to gales of laughter as I continued tickling him. Chris couldn't resist so he crawled over and stuck one rigid finger into Danny's side. Danny pretended to howl with uncontrollable laughter each time Chris stuck his finger into him. Still sucking his thumb, Chris used his other hand to prod at Danny, laughing along with him, his thumb held loosely in place as he smiled around it.

Someone banged on the backdoor and I ran to get it. Rita Shortpascher stood at the door wearing what looked like one of her brother's old pair of jeans and a too-small tee shirt that probably once was white but now looked a faded grey. She had no shoes on and her unkempt, mousey brown hair covered half of her sullen-looking face. She looked to be about 6 years old but it was hard to tell with the Shortpaschers.

"Where's your Ma?" she asked bluntly. I stared back at her for a few seconds longer than necessary because the sight was such a surprise to me: a Shortpascher on my back stoop.

"Ginny, mind your manners," Mom grasped my shoulders firmly as she pulled me out of the way. "What is it dear?" she asked calmly, as if having Rita stop by was an everyday occurrence.

"My Ma's sickly, throwin' up and everything and she asked could she trouble you to come by?"

"Have you had lunch?" Mom asked by way of an answer. Rita didn't respond but just stared up at Mom. "Right then, tell your Mom I'll gather together some fixings for lunch and will bring it all right over."

As Rita walked away, Mom told me to take the boys out to the backyard and entertain them till she got back.

"It's almost suppertime, Mom, why would you offer to bring them lunch?" I asked, annoyed to be giving some of our food to the vindictive Shortpaschers. The boys were already up from their naps and Mom had already started browning the onions for the hot dish we were having for our supper.

"They're on a different schedule than we are. Besides, it's easier to accept someone bringing over some bread and lunchmeat than it is to take in a whole dinner. Go on, outside with you." I hoisted Chris on to my hip and carried him out the door while Danny and Greg followed.

The boys were busy playing with their hot wheels while Chris watched from the playpen when the older kids came running down the alley hooting and hollering and laughing out loud. Polly got to the gate first, opened it, and slammed it shut behind her. The older boys, Neil and Pat, were right on her heels.

"What are you mad at us for? We had nothing to do with it," the boys teased her. "Why are you blushing, Polly? Polly and Mattie sitting in a tree, k-i-s-s-i-n-g, first comes love, then comes marriage, then comes baby in a baby carriage!"

Polly tried to hold the gate shut so the boys couldn't get in, but soon they overpowered her. She tried to stay mad but the next thing I knew she was cracking up with laughter along with them. When we asked what was so funny, Polly forbade them from telling but I pestered them long enough till finally Polly told me herself. Apparently, while she was playing over at the Stidger's house, Matt Stidger was sitting next to Polly with a big hole in his shorts of which he was completely unaware. Polly kept stealing glances at his private parts hanging out for all to see. When Matt finally realized that he was exposing himself, all the rest of the kids had already been mindful of it, too, so he burst into tears and ran into his house.

"Big deal!" Polly tried not to laugh. "With five brothers, it's not like it's anything I haven't seen before!"

"That's not what I heard!" Pat laughed conspiratorially. "I heard Matt Stidger is hung! Like a horse! He has the 'gift' alright, is the way I heard it."

"I don't know what you're talking about!" Polly tried to look indignant but she soon dissolved into giggles again.

Mom came back from the Shortpaschers, and soon we were sitting down to dinner. Chris sat off to the side in the high chair and all ten of the rest of us crowded around the table. We each had our regular place to sit every night. Tonight we were playing the spelling game while eating potato-hamburger hot dish. Dad would come up with words appropriate to the age level of the recipient.

"Complicated," he asked Jane which she spelled with ease. Greg was next and Dad gave him the word 'Mom.'

"M-O-M!'" He shouted with gusto.

Pat was next and with a look of chagrin, Dad gave him the word 'Viceroy.' Nonplussed, Pat rattled off the correct spelling. Viceroy was the brand of cigarettes that Dad smoked. For months now, Pat had been sneaking a number of them out of Dad's shirt pocket at night when everyone was asleep.

Finally, it was my turn. I waited in anticipation, eager to show off my recently-acquired reading skills.

"Minnesota" Dad said. My heart leapt at such a long, hard word.

"Minnesota" I repeated, and laboriously began to sound out the many syllables, creasing my brow in concentration.

Across the table from me, Marilyn was performing gyrations with her eyebrows and clutching vigorously at the front of her shirt. I tried to ignore her as I deliberated on the correct spelling of my home state. Marilyn's eyes widened to an alarming bug-like size and she started to elongate her neck thrusting her chin in my general direction all the while pulling on the front of her own shirt. I was making a muck of my word and growing more and more distracted by Marilyn's antics. I was about to finish lamely with the incorrect spelling when suddenly I looked down and realized what my wonderful sister was trying to point out to me. I was wearing one of Polly's old tee shirts with a gopher on it and the word 'Minnesota' spelled perfectly across the top of the furry creature. Reading upside down, I rapidly prattled off the accurate spelling to the applause and cheers of my supportive family.

After enjoying some of Mom's canned peaches for dessert, Greg inquired "How come Mom never gets a word to spell?" to which Mom replied: "I'll give you a word to spell: c-l-e-a-n u-p!" and she flicked her dish towel at him as we all pushed back from the table.

"All," Neil began.

"Star," Pat responded.

"Wrestling!" Greg and Danny shouted in unison as all the boys raced into the living room and began their wrestling ritual rolling around on the floor impersonating their American Wrestling Association heroes. Over the years they would masquerade as Vern Gagne, Dr. X, Mad Dog Vachon, and Nick Bockwinkel. Their favorite wrestler to mimic was The Crusher and they would roar, gnash their teeth, and grind the palms of their hands together before leaping from the couch onto their fellow wrestlers.

In the kitchen, the girls of the house undertook the clean up. Jane put everything away while Polly washed the dishes, Marilyn dried them, and I swept the floor. Mom started us off singing "You are my Sunshine," and we broke out into harmony as we completed our tasks. We sang Buck Owens songs, Buck Owens and the Buckaroos being one of Mom's favorite bands. "All ya gotta do is act naturally!" we crooned while sashaying our hips. Then I remembered to ask about Mrs. Shortpascher and how she was feeling.

"I hear she got knocked up again," Jane said.

"But with who?" Polly inquired. "There is no 'Mr. Shortpascher' and who would ever like that mop-headed. . ."

"That's enough," Mom reprimanded. "Na kazdem sprocu pravdy troche." Mom was 100% Bohemian and she often made pronouncements in Czech. "There is often a piece of truth in every piece of gossip," she translated for us.

I kept quiet and stopped moving the broom around the floor. Mom was deep in thought and I was hoping she would forget I was there while she discussed the Shortpascher's situation. "Poor Agnes," she said thoughtfully. "All those children with no support whatsoever. Imagine having to leave home to try to earn some kind of a living knowing that your kids are left completely unsupervised. I don't think I could do it. And those boys of hers are getting more and more out of hand every day. They have never been disciplined and have no respect for authority. Living absolutely hand to mouth, you should have seen how bare their fridge was. Agnes has been on her own for years. No wonder she's susceptible to taking a little comfort now and again if someone is willing to pay her the least bit of attention. Now, of course, she's the one left to handle the consequences."

"So, she's gonna have another baby," Marilyn clarified.

"Heaven help her and the poor little soul taking shape inside of her," Mom nodded.

"And the father is..."

"None of your business," Mom concluded as she slammed shut the oven door with the clean frying pan inside.

Chapter 12

The next morning, we girls hurried through our Saturday chores because we had a game to get to. Typically, our weekly chores were to clean our rooms as well as to vacuum, dust, and clean the bathroom. We loved to play our 45 vinyl records while we cleaned, singing at the top of our voices to Chubby Checkers' *The Twist*, flinging our dust cloths behind our bottoms and twisting away to the music. We took turns vacuuming the stairs, dusting underneath the dining room table, and the least favorite job, cleaning the bathroom fixtures.

Tessa Cordero stood at the backdoor asking if I could come out to play. When Mom said no because I was cleaning the fixtures, Tessa started to walk away but then turned back to ask with wonderment "What are fixtures anyway?"

The fixtures, of course, were just a polite way of saying the sink, tub, and toilet. I actually quite enjoyed my turn at the fixtures. Polishing the chrome faucets till I could see my distorted facial features ogling back at me was always entertaining. Picking up Mom's different lotions and wiping them down, sampling a little Jergens here, some Pond's Cold Cream there, always made my

Saturday cleaning take much longer than it should have. I loved to polish the bottle of Tabu by Dana and unscrew the top to smell the heavenly scent, then to dab the tiniest drop onto my finger and wipe it carefully behind my ears. I arranged the yellow rubber ducky and the other bath toys along the edge of the tub to be ready for the weekly Saturday evening bath event.

Seeing that the toilet paper roll was empty, I pried open the cupboard door across from the toilet where the extra tissue was kept. Reaching for the toilet paper, I was distracted by the stack of reading material we kept in there for longer stints on the loo. Most if it was Dad's well-worn Reader's Digest copies, Mom's church bulletins dating back years, and Archie comics that all of us kids loved to read. I shuffled through, pausing to reread my favorite Betty & Veronica comic about Betty's blazer that made her really popular and well-liked whenever she wore it. Veronica, the wealthy, spoiled friend was jealous so she took the blazer and realized that she, too, was greeted and admired by all when she put the blazer on. I daydreamed for a moment about how it would feel to own an article of clothing like that, and to be popular and admired by all.

Breaking my reverie, I shoved the stack of comic books back into the cupboard unwittingly dislodging something stuck way in the back of the shelf. It was a magazine with a plain brown cover. I opened the cover and a bare-chested woman was staring out at me with sultry eyes. Her large breasts were as big as watermelons and she was hoisting them up with her hands and touching the dark brown nipples with the tip of each finger. Her thin shoulders looked too small to be holding up such monstrous orbs and her wet lips were curved into a playful smile as if she were holding onto a couple of basketballs that she wanted to play with and was looking for a playmate. Shocked, I realized that this must be one of the magazines Dad told me about from O'Dhoul's Drugstore. I understood why they needed to cover them up now or none of their customers would ever leave the store, they would be mesmerized by the nakedness of the malformed girl on the cover.

Dad shouted up the stairs then "Ten minute warning! The Ashcroft bus to Met Stadium is leaving in ten minutes! I repeat: this is your official ten minute warning!" I stuffed the magazine under the comic book pile and shut the cupboard door before hastily wiping down the rest of the fixtures to join the rest of the family on our way to the game.

Dad did not want to have to park the car all the way in Farmington so he always insisted on leaving early for the Twins' game to get a good spot in the parking lot. He had been known to drive off with only half of the family on board because he refused to be late. The station wagon was full, and we all shouted and waved good-bye to Mom as we pulled away from the curb. Baby Chris was napping but the rest of us were on our way to the see the Minnesota Twins play the Cleveland Indians. "Are you sure you don't want to come with us, Mom?" Pat had inquired.

"This is my chance to scrub the kitchen floor," Mom said sounding so pleased to do housework you would have thought she hardly ever got the chance.

Mickey was with us, too. When Dad had heard that he had never been to a Twins' game before, he worked it out with Doc so that Mickey could join us. He had finished his chores of the day with utmost haste and had been waiting in our backyard with an old Twins' cap he'd found pulled down low onto his head. Neil had found an old baseball glove for him to take to the game. "We're sitting in homerun alley and you don't want to be caught with a grand slam ball coming straight at you and no glove to complete the catch!"

"And no reaching over into anyone else's lap to catch the ball neither," Greg piped in. "You can only catch the ball if it's coming right at you." He acted out his fantasy of a ball hit by Tony Oliva coming straight at him in the stands and catching it in his worn glove, holding both arms high into the air and taking bows while shouting "And the crowd went crazy, roar," as he imitated the sound of a stadium full of fans cheering him on.

We got to Met Stadium in Bloomington with plenty of time to spare. The parking lot was practically empty, and Dad parked where he always did, right next to the exit. We all got out and started the long walk across the cavernous, empty lot.

"I thought your Dad liked to get here early to get a good parking spot," Mickey commented reasonably.

"That's right. He considers this the best parking spot. When it's time to leave, we won't be stuck behind hundreds of cars waiting to get out the lot. We'll just pop right out the exit," I explained.

"Yeah, except by the time we walk the 25 miles through the parking lot to get to our car, everyone else will be home in bed already," Pat shouted while Dad swatted him on the back of the head with his glove.

I loved ambling companionably up the steel ramps with all of the thousands of other fans and listening to the friendly chatter about the upcoming game and the Twins' season so far. This year the stadium was always packed because last year the Twins had such a great season. They had won the American League pennant with ease and went on to play the Los Angeles Dodgers in the World Series. It was only the second time in the history of baseball that both teams playing in the World Series were from West of the Mississippi. Dad said it was satisfying to beat those well-established teams from the East. The Twins had won the first two games of the series at Met Stadium but went on to lose to the Dodgers four games to three in the end. We were hoping this year would bring more of the same.

We walked past the reserved seats and headed for the general admission benches way out in left field. Taking over a couple of rows, we settled in to watch the players warm up. Mickey couldn't take his eyes off the field and he was full of questions about who was who. Finally, it was time for the game to start and we all stood up to sing the National Anthem. Dad took off his Twins' cap and each of the boys followed his example, holding their caps proudly over their hearts. We began "Oh, say can you see," and Pat squeaked in my ear "Not very well," in reference to a joke Dad had told us about a man with bad eyesight named Jose who thinks everyone is asking him "Jose, can you see?" I struggled not to give in to a fit of giggles I felt coming on and instead concentrated on the words of the song "...the rocket's red glare, the bombs bursting in air, gave proof through the night, that our flag was still there...."

At school last year, we had learned about Francis Scott Key's long night on the ship in Chesapeake Bay during the Battle of Baltimore in the War of 1812 and how he wrote this poem about it afterwards. The poem was set to the tune of a well-known British drinking song already popular in the states at the time. I looked around at all of the fans struggling to keep up with the one and a half octaves' range singing their hearts out. "Play ball!" we shouted at the song's end and settled down to watch the game.

As the slow-moving game wore on, we were getting hot sitting in the baking sun, so Mickey and I wandered off to find a drinking fountain. We loved the freedom of being out with Dad compared with the extreme caution always exercised when Mom was with us. Dad never worried nor cared what we were up to as long as we didn't distract him from watching the game. Mom never would have let me go off by myself without one of the older kids tagging along. Therefore, I was always coming up with some excuse or other to relish the independence we rarely had when Mom was around. Dad hardly even listened to our request, and he never said no.

"Dad, I have to go borrow that gun from Lee Harvey Oswald, I'll be right back, okay?" Dad would nod his head and say "Okay, but come right back."

Mickey and I took turns slurping at the lukewarm water of the drinking fountain. "Want some ABC gum?" I asked Mickey.

"What's that?"

"Already Been Chewed!" I laughed, referring to the four or five pieces of various colored chewing gum that had obviously fallen out of thirsty mouths at the drinking fountain.

The smell of hot dogs made my mouth water and I reminded Mickey that he was going to love the hot dogs Mom would have ready for us at home after the game. It was a tradition that we would be rewarded for sitting through five hours of watching many of those around us at the ballgame gobbling the delicious-smelling but unaffordable hot dogs by eating as many hot dogs as we desired once we got home. One or two hot dogs were usually plenty but there was the time Neil had eaten twelve hot dogs in one sitting. Later that night, he was lying on the couch not feeling so well when he suddenly leapt up and sprinted towards the kitchen. He started puking as he ran turning his head to the left and right spewing hot dog chunks all over the walls from the living room, through the dining room, into the kitchen. Months later when Mom was taking down the dining room curtains to wash, she found a bit of Neil's upchucking. "I do still hold the record," Neil bragged.

"Not if eleven out of the twelve wieners ended up on our walls!" Mom had said wryly.

When Mickey and I arrived back at our seats, it was time for the seventh-inning stretch. We all stood up and stretched our arms over our heads. Over the loudspeakers, the familiar tune started up and we all began to sway and sing along: "Take me out to the ballgame, take me out to the crowd. Buy me some peanuts and Cracker Jacks, I don't care if I ever get back, for its root, root, root for the home team, if they don't win it's a shame. For its one, two, three strikes you're out at the ol' ballgame!" We raised our fists holding up our fingers as we finished the song.

"That was cool!" Mickey said. "Do they play that at every game?" We assured him that they did.

In the top of the eighth inning, the Minnesota Twins scored against the Cleveland Indians tying the game at two to two. The crowd was going crazy.

"Scalp those Indians!"

"Back to your reservations, Injuns!"

"Whites rule over redskins every time!"

I sensed Mickey stiffening beside me and turned to see him scowling in his seat. I started to ask him what was wrong when Dad suddenly announced he was heading to the car. Cries of protest erupted till Dad conceded, "You can stay until the top of the ninth inning is over but no later! And you'll have to run to the car! I don't want to get stuck in post-game traffic! Ginny and Mickey, why don't you two come with me?"

While we were skipping down the ramp, I explained to Mickey how Dad always listened to the last couple of innings of the game on the radio in his car. "He's not so keen on the crowds at the end of the game so he'd rather be in the car ready to get out of the parking lot before the rest of the horde." I didn't bother telling him how many turnovers or exciting last-inning homeruns we'd missed due to Dad's inexplicable need to beat the pack. Mickey listened without comment, a frown upon his face. I could tell something was wrong but I wasn't sure what.

As soon as we got in the car, Dad turned on the radio. So far, so good, the game was still tied up. It felt disorientating to be sitting in the parking lot listening to the game that was happening right next to us beyond the walls of the stadium. The cheers of the crowd were heard over the radio as well as outside my car window. Sometimes I could hear the crack of the ball against the bat just a hair of a second before hearing it on the radio. It gave me a sense of experiencing life while simultaneously observing it, too. Sometimes the announcers made the game sound so exciting, but I knew that just sitting there waiting for something to happen wasn't all that exhilarating at all. Were they really talking about the same game I had just attended? If we were sitting in the car already and suddenly something exciting happened such as someone stealing home, I would want to jump out of the car and race back into the stadium to see it in person; I couldn't bear to just be listening to it over the radio when I was so close to seeing it live.

During a commercial break, Dad turned around to face me and Mickey in the backseat. "Mickey," he began, "You mustn't feel bad when you hear folks saying derogatory things about Indians. They're only thinking about the sport's team you know, and not actual Indians."

Mickey nodded his head unconvincingly. "Yes sir." It hadn't occurred to me that this was what had been bothering Mickey. I had plum forgotten that he was an Indian.

"Are lots of the players on Cleveland's team Indians, Dad? Is that why their baseball team is called the Indians?"

"No, Ginny, that has nothing to do with it. It's just the name they've chosen for their team. We don't have a lot of twins on our team, do we? Baltimore doesn't have a lot of birds on their team, do they?" This got us giggling about tigers from Detroit, angels from Anaheim, and red sox from Boston.

"But Mr. Ashcroft, why do people still make so much fun of Indians? Indians haven't scalped anyone for nearly a hundred years but everyone's still talking about it like it happened yesterday."

"Because they're ignorant," Dad went on. "our country has a terrible black stain on its history that it refuses to talk about. Here in Minnesota, we committed a most atrocious crime against those who lived here before us but they aren't teaching you that at school now, are they?"

The crowd erupted in the stadium then so we paused to listen to the radio to learn what was happening. The Twins scored again and had taken the lead. Dad honked the horn in celebration and a chorus of toots of inharmonious horns replied. Apparently, we weren't the only ones sitting in our car in the parking lot. We listened to the rest of the game, caught up in the Twins' win. When the rest of the kids joined us, we headed for home. It was a raucous ride with lots of cheering, shouts, and laughter.

Mom had the picnic table set and the hot dogs, beans, and potato salad ready to serve. "You're gonna love Mom's potato salad," I told Mickey. "Make sure you put a lot on your plate because it disappears fast!" Mom puts lots of mustard on her potato salad which is just the way we like it.

After we ate, Mickey thanked Mom for supper. He went over to Neil to give him back the baseball glove.

"Keep it," Neil said. "We've got plenty, and we're always glad to have a new player on the block. Next time you see us playing in the street, be sure to come on and join us."

Then Mickey went over to Dad and told him that today had been the best day of his life. Dad assured him that we would do it again soon.

That night before going up to bed, I crawled on to Dad's lap on the recliner. He told me a little about the book he was currently reading, Alan Paton's *Cry, the Beloved Country*. I listened politely for a while before interrupting.

"Dad, what atrocious crime did we commit against the Indians?"

"I was talking about the way the white man treated the Sioux Indian when we first arrived on this land and, in fact the way we're still treating them today." Dad explained. "You see, Ginny, before the white man arrived, the Indians were here living peacefully off of the land. We came and started buying their land and signing treaties with them."

"What's a treaty?"

"It's a legal agreement, like a pact. Both sides have to agree to it and sign it. We forced them to sign many treaties starting in 1805 until about 1890. The trouble is, we never honored those treaties. We downright lied to the Indians over and over again. Finally, when the

Indians were starving and they couldn't take it anymore, they started to fight back. We kept taking more and more of their land and forcing them to live on the least productive terrain around. We made them live on rocky, sandy soil where nothing would grow nor graze. They tried to negotiate reasonably with us but when no one would listen to them, they rose up to fight. We quickly put an end to that and arrested and sentenced 303 Sioux Indians to death by hanging. Luckily, President Lincoln pardoned all but 38 of the Indians."

Two Shoes had climbed onto my lap so we both cuddled into Dad when I asked, "What happened to the 38 Sioux who didn't get pardoned?"

Dad took a deep breath and began, "on December 26, 1862, the largest mass hanging in our country's history took place right here in Minnesota, not that you'll learn about it at school. It was tragic. They built a huge platform so they would all be hung at once. The braves marched to their death singing songs and praying. Twenty-four hours later, Doctor Mayo, founder of the world-famous Mayo Clinic, Minnesota's source of pride and claim to fame, dug up those 38 corpses and sold them to medical schools for research. Those poor souls were not even allowed to rest in peace after death. And the worst was yet to come.

 After the 'conflict', for god's sake they should at least have the decency to call it a war, nearly 1000 people lost their lives, but they insist on describing it as a mere 'conflict'. Well, afterwards, all the rest of the Indians were expelled from Minnesota. Every single last Indian was rounded up, babies, grandmothers, children, women, and boys, who surely had nothing to do with the uprising, were shipped off to Crow Creek, South Dakota, the most desolate site on earth you can possibly imagine where disease and starvation killed many outright and alcohol and depression continue to kill those that remain to this day. It was an excuse, is what it was, to get rid of a problem and put it out of sight, the problem being the Indians who were here first but who were in our way and therefore had to be disposed of."

I thought about Mickey's face and how he'd looked at the game when everyone was hollering such mean things about Indians and I felt terrible. I kept forgetting Mickey was an Indian. I wanted to be a better friend to Mickey so I knew I would have to start seeing things from his point of view more often.

"This book I'm reading, Ginny, takes place in a country on the other side of the world from us called South Africa." Dad held up the book for me to see. "They've installed a most odious system of government called apartheid which is a means of keeping the wealth of their country into the hands of a few whites and cruelly forcing the majority of the population who are colored, mind you, to live barely above the poverty line with no freedom whatsoever. Our government condemns South Africa for their treatment of black Africans but we should really step back and take a good, hard look in the mirror at ourselves." The long day and the soothing tone of Dad's voice caused my eyelids to start feeling very heavy and I leaned into Dad. His chest rumbled as he spoke.

"But Indians don't have to live on reservations anymore, do they Dad? Crazy Caroline doesn't."

"No, of course not, but for tax purposes and," Dad looked down at me, "oh, this is too complicated to explain to a six-year-old, especially at bedtime. And stop calling Caroline crazy."

"She is crazy, though. And she scares me! Anyway, I'm seven, not six."

"You know calling someone crazy is not polite. She has problems, it's true, but now that you know more about her history, can't you try to be a little more sympathetic towards her?" He pushed Two Shoes off of his lap.

"I'll try, Dad," I tried to think of Caroline as someone who wasn't crazy or scary with little success.

With a hug and a kiss, Dad sent me off to bed. Just before heading up the stairs, I turned to ask another question, but Mom had come into the living room by then and Dad had pulled her onto his lap. She was laughing and scolding him that they'd wake the baby if they weren't careful. Scooping up Two Shoes, I ran upstairs to bed.

Chapter 13

"Is too!"
"Is not!"
"Is too!"
"Is not!"
"Is too!"

"Okay, that's enough!" Mom said. "What has gotten into you girls? What are you arguing about anyway?"

Polly stuck her tongue out at me behind Mom's back, secure in the knowledge that I wouldn't enlighten Mom on the cause of our squabble.

The girls and I were upstairs making the beds, putting on clean sheets and tucking all of the corners in tightly. We were going away for two weeks and a large part of our preparation was to be sure the house we were leaving behind was tidy. This was to a certain extent in case some tragedy happened and none of us ever came home alive, Mom could rest assured that her reputation would remain intact as a competent, hygienic homemaker, and partly because Mom wanted to come home after being away to a sparkling, welcoming home.

While we were putting fresh pillowcases on the pillows, Polly was explaining to Marilyn the meaning of the f-word. They were snickering and whispering under their breath till finally I insisted that they tell me what they were talking about. They refused at first, insisting that I was too young to understand, but by pestering them relentlessly they finally conceded to tell me.

"...and the guy sticks it inside where your pee comes out and that's how babies are made!" Polly finished triumphantly.

'Nuh-uh." I was aghast at the unwelcome picture this created in my mind's eye and refused to believe it.

"It's true. And furthermore that means that Mom and Dad did it nine times. Nine times!!!"

"That is so not true!" I bellowed! That I absolutely would not believe. Not Mom and Dad. Not nine times! And we bickered until Mom put an end to it.

The car-top carrier was fully loaded, and we were finally ready to leave. I was giving Mrs. Agneau final instructions on the care and keeping of Two Shoes.

"Don't worry, dear," she reassured me for the umpteenth time. "Two Shoes and I are old friends and she will be fed and fondled sufficiently while you are away." Indeed, she was sitting on Mrs. Agneau's front stoop looking bored and totally unimpressed with the tears I was beginning to shed at the thought of leaving her for 14 whole days. She rather looked as if she belonged there on Mrs. Agneau's porch. This wasn't surprising, actually, as I'd long been under the impression that Two Shoes thought the entire neighborhood was her domicile and she often graced many of the houses in our neighborhood with her presence.

"Did I show you how she likes to be scratched under her chin like so?" I demonstrated. Dad beeped the car horn and with a final hug to Mrs. Agneau and Two Shoes, who turned her head with impatience at my excessive show of emotion, I ran to the car.

Dad whistled cheerfully as he pulled away from the curb while Mom counted off on her fingertips the last-minute jobs she needed to reassure herself she had completed.

"Locked all the windows, took out the garbage, and unplugged the toaster. I do believe I remembered it all!" she exclaimed jubilantly.

One auspicious night during the previous year, our kitchen had filled with thick, black smoke and the smell of fire filled our nostrils with an acrid, fearsome odor. Unable to locate the source of the ever-increasing smolder, the fire department was called and posthaste they arrived.

Each fireman who walked into the house sniffed and said, "Food."

"Smells like food."

"Foodstuff."

"Chow.'

"Victuals."

They didn't even bother to check out the dining or living rooms which were also filled with smoke by then but instead concentrated in the kitchen where before long they identified the culprit. The well-used toaster that browned entire loaves of bread each morning had gotten stuck with the lever in the down position all day long until the wires had heated up so much they were melting the entire unit with its multitude of crumbs at the bottom along with it. Multiple rosaries and prayers of gratitude for the affirmative outcome of what could have been a veritable tragedy went on for months and resulted in Mom's unplugging of the toaster and practically every other appliance at every outing.

The drive to our destination was about two hours long. We entertained ourselves by searching for out-of-state license plates, slugging each other's upper arms and proclaiming 'Slug Bug' every time a Volkswagen Beetle was spotted, singing, and playing the alphabet game. The alphabet game required enormous concentration. We would choose a topic like boys' names, girls' names, place names, or foods. Today we chose animal names, always a favorite. Someone started: A, anteater. The next person repeated A, anteater and continued with B, bear. The next person said: A, anteater, B, bear, C, cheetah. Obviously, the further along we went in the alphabet, the harder it got to remember every animal. Some of us rattled off the names faster and faster as the game progressed, some liked to take their time and think about every letter before reciting. The younger kids got help from the bigger ones and we always made allowances for impossible letters like Q and X. Today, Greg was insisting that koala bear started with a Q as in qoala bear. We were all cracking up and refusing to let him get away with it. Too late, we realized we were getting too noisy for the mature people up front and soon Mom jingled the dreaded beads from out of her purse.

"Settle down, kids, and let's say the rosary for a safe trip." After our protestations to at least allow us to finish the game went unheeded, we settled in for five decades of the Glorious Mysteries. After the first 20 or so Hail Mary's, most of us were either asleep or feigning sleep. The comforting sound of Mom's "Hail Mary full of grace" followed by Dad's response of "Holy Mary Mother of God" lulled me into a contented state of security and happiness. Placing my head on Polly's shoulder next to me, I drifted off with the rhythmic melody of my parents' voices settling over us like a soothing blanket.

I woke up to the sound of Dad's door shutting. "We're here, we're here!" we shouted as we scrambled over one another to get out of the car to go into the Ranger's office to register. The smell of pine accosted me as I stepped out of the car beneath tall coniferous trees. The songs of the birds filled the otherwise quiet wilderness. White birch trees stood out in the sea of green surrounding us. We traipsed into the office following Dad after he'd enjoyed a good long stretch exiting the car.

We were greeted by a woman in tan khaki trousers with a collared shirt of the same color saying "Welcome to Sibley State Park." Dad recognized her from previous years so they spent some time chatting until they were interrupted by another park ranger.

"You're just in time for my introductory presentation to the park," said the ranger with the nametag 'Kevin'. "Follow me." Looking to Dad for permission, at his nod we stepped back outside and around to the back of the ranger station. There were a dozen log benches three and four deep in a semi-circular pattern where a handful of vacationers were already seated. We filled in the empty spots and sat down. Kevin went and stood in front of us looking very official in his ranger uniform, his felt ranger hat giving him a look of authority.

"Sibley State Park," he began, "was established in 1919 in Kandiyohi County on the shores of Lake Andrew, a glacial lake that was formed in a depression as the ice passed over and then melted. Four times in Minnesota's history, glaciers advanced from the north and then covered the state with a sheet of ice up to two miles thick. The last time, as recently as 10,000 years ago, most of the features of the Minnesota landscape were formed." He stepped over to a map carved out of wood and pointed. "Lake Andrew, an 815 acre lake, is only 26 feet at its deepest, but it is full of walleye, Northern Pike, bluegill, crappie, sunfish and bass. It's a magnet for those who like to fish. The park itself is a handsome example of labor-intensive rustic-style construction and master planning, thanks to the hard work of the Civilian Conservation Corps. Any questions so far?"

When no one answered, Kevin went on. "The Civilian Conservation Corps, or CCC, as it came to be known, was a public relief program for unemployed men established as part of the New Deal legislation set up by FDR. Designed to aid relief of the unemployed resulting from the Great Depression, the CCC provided vocational training through useful work related to conservation and development of natural resources in the US from 1933-1942. Many state parks were built during this time. CCC Camp SP-7, responsible for creating

Sibley, was a camp for Veterans of World War 1. They set up in the park on April 30, 1935."

The ranger Kevin held up an old picture frame with a large group of men posing in front of what looked like army barracks. "200 men passed through building roads, granite buildings, and trails. In 1938, Sibley State Park was the most complete and extensive state-owned recreational facility in all of central Minnesota. When the park was finished, the CCC camp then picked up and moved further North to establish the equally successful Itasca State Park at the headwaters of the Mississippi. Have any of you camped there before?" An elderly couple sitting in the front row enthusiastically raised their hands. "Beautiful, isn't it? Well, by the time government funding was halted in 1942, the CCC had successfully trained 3 million men. If anyone has any questions for me, I'm available. If not, I suggest you get out there and enjoy the park!" We clapped our hands along with everyone else while Pat attempted to whistle, and then we went back inside the ranger station to finish registering.

Specifying that we'd need a camping spot near enough to walk to the beach and the bathrooms but that was still next to the woods, Dad got our State Park sticker and stuck it on the lower right corner of the front windshield of the car. We piled back in and went searching for number E-30's campsite. Dad obeyed the 5 mile per hour speed limit posted throughout the campground so that when Neil saw the wooden post with E-30 painted gold carved into it, he opened the car door and jumped out without injury. He raced down the trail into the woods, his favorite place to be while camping. Dad skillfully backed the overloaded station wagon into our designated parking spot on the gravel so as not to harm the thick green grass covering the rest of our campsite.

"This is perfect!" Mom exclaimed as we admired our spacious corner lot tucked into the woods. There was plenty of grass on which to set up the tent as well as a built-in fire pit and large cedar picnic table. "I'll set up Chris' playpen right here where I can keep an eye on him."

"This way to the beach!" Jane hollered and we set off to explore.

Exhausted from hours of swimming in the lake, that night we sat around the campfire roasting marshmallows. We had successfully put up our massive new tent complete with three separate rooms divided by heavy flaps. The girls would sleep on one side of the tent, the boys on the other, and Mom, Dad, and baby Chris in his playpen would sleep in the 'entrance hallway' between the two rooms. Dad assured us it would be easier to put up the tent in the future now that we got the difficult 'first attempt' over with. Sleeping bags covered the floor of the entire tent. We each used our pillowcase full of clothes as our pillows. We had unloaded the beautiful cupboard Dad had built out of pine with enough food to last the week inside and set it on the aluminum folding table. "My portable pantry," Mom had christened it. Dad had even installed a hook with a padlock so the pesky raccoons couldn't get inside of it.

We had fried chicken for dinner complete with boiled potatoes, gravy, and green beans. We'd boiled a kettle of hot water over the fire to do the dishes. Then we'd set off into the woods to find campfire sticks to roast marshmallows. It was just getting dark when Dad used his pocket knife to whittle Danny's stick to a point reminding him that it wasn't a weapon and that he would need to exercise extreme caution while using the stick to cook over the fire. The look on Danny's face was one of extreme concentration and pleasure as he acknowledged Dad's words, hardly able to believe that he was being allowed the responsibility of possessing his very own marshmallow-roasting stick.

Fresh sunburns prevented us from standing too close to the fire that night, so we each roasted our token marshmallow and sat back at a distance far enough away not to inflame our sun burnt skin but close enough to ward off the mosquitoes and the coolness of the late evening air. In response to Marilyn's question as to why the state park we were camping in was called Sibley, Dad was explaining: "The Park is named after Henry Hastings Sibley who has the distinguished honor of being Minnesota's first governor. Can anyone tell me when that would have been?" Dad loved history. He always had a rotating stack of history books on the coffee table at home which he took back and forth to the library. There was nothing he enjoyed more than reading about history except maybe teaching it to us afterwards.

"That's easy," Polly replied. "That would have to be in 1858."

When Dad agreed, I couldn't resist asking, "Wow, Polly, how did you know that?" I tried to keep the admiration out of my voice being that I was still disgusted with her for that terrible 'making babies' explanation.

"That's the year Minnesota became a state, so it figures that would be when our first governor served, too." She explained matter-of-factly.

Dad continued, "Sibley actually built the first stone house in Minnesota. It is still standing to this day. He built it right next to Fort Snelling, for safety's sake I imagine, and then he got married in 1843. He and his wife had lots of children. They were born in Michigan, Wisconsin, Iowa, the Minnesota Territory, and finally in the state of Minnesota itself. Now, here's a riddle for you," Dad leaned back in his lawn chair, and rubbed his hands together with anticipation. "Governor Sibley's kids were born in all of those different places, but they were all born in the stone house Sibley built. How can you explain that?"

We couldn't explain it and we refused to believe it, either. Dad insisted on the accuracy of his statement, laughing as none of us could come up with a viable explanation. Finally he felt Greg tugging on his sleeve and he bent down to hear his thoughtful elucidation.

"Did he pull the house around on a trailer and drive it to all those places where his kids could be born?"

"No, Greg, but that's about the most logical explanation I've heard so far! Actually, it's because the political boundaries changed so much during that period that even though all the Sibley children were born in the same house sitting in the same spot, they were all born in a differently-named place."

We pondered over that. I tried to comprehend that I actually could have been from the state of Michigan, of all places, when Dad carried on, "Actually, Ginny, Henry Sibley played quite a role in the Sioux Uprising I was telling you about earlier. At the time of the uprising, he was appointed colonel of the Minnesota state militia and then Brigadier General. He's the one who went up the Minnesota River to teach those Indians a lesson. When would that have been, Ginny?"

"1862." I replied without hesitation. Knowing Dad, I had listened intently the first time he'd mentioned the date because I knew he would find an opportunity to bring it up again just to test me. I flushed with pleasure at his next words.

"Clever girl! So, in 1862 Sibley fought in many battles: the Battle of New Ulm, Fort Ridgley, Birch Coulee, and Wood Lake. In fact, he fought in every single battle that mattered in that short-lived war. The Indians never stood a chance against the weapons of the state militia," he shook his head sadly at the thought of the Indians fighting with so few guns.

"Sibley was responsible for arresting those 300 Indians. Even after the Mankato hanging, he carried on fighting, leading a second successful expedition out West. He chased those Sioux Indians all over the Dakota Territory, not satisfied till they were all rounded up onto reservations. His responsibility was to defend the Western frontier. In gratitude, I guess, we have a beautiful state park named after him."

Dad might well have carried on with the history lesson if there had not been a thump followed by a cry. Danny had fallen asleep by the warmth of the fire and off the log he was perched on. We all trooped to the bathroom once more before unzipping 'ol' Blue', as the tent came to be known, so we could climb in to sleep in the fresh air of the magnificent North woods.

The rest of the week flew by. Long summer days were far too short for all we wanted to pack into them at Sibley. At first light, we awakened and headed straight down to the lake. After some early morning fishing and swimming, we headed back to our campsite for the unique experience of breakfast-while-camping. The Kellogg Company produced 18-pack units of a variety of breakfast cereal which we only purchased when going on our camping trips. The ritual of painstakingly choosing which cereal box you would get to eat that morning was a remarkably exciting part of the camping experience. Frosted Flakes always went first, followed closely by Apple Jacks and Corn Pops. Late risers were always stuck with Raisin Bran or the unremarkable Corn Flakes. The originality of these variety packs of cereal was that each little box could be unwrapped on its side by running your fingernail along the serrated lines, opening the two flaps, and then tearing open the wax paper to reveal the glorious little handful of the chosen cereal inside. By adding milk to the little carton, the cereal was consumed in its own handy, self-contained cardboard bowl. If the milk wasn't always the coldest, or even the freshest anymore by the end of the week, we didn't mind at all as the novelty of each of us sitting with our own selection of cereal and eating out of the bowl we had fashioned ourselves made up for any amount of rancid dairy product we might consume.

Often after breakfast, we headed to the ball field to play a marathon game of baseball. No one was ever turned away from playing if they showed up at the field. There's no such thing as too many outfielders when playing ball at camp. At the end of each inning, the incoming outfielders passed their glove to the outgoing outfielders, and the same exchange occurred on the bases. That way, almost everyone had a glove to wear. If we were ever short, Dad would play without one. I was always impressed with his ability to catch the leather-covered ball with a smack into his bare hands without showing any pain. We played ball barefoot in bathing suits so that when the hot game finally ended, we would race each other straight into the refreshing waters of Lake Andrew. We divided the teams as evenly as possible. The older players never took advantage of the younger ones nor were so unsportsmanlike as to purposefully hit the ball at a young outfielder. When a good player came up to bat, everyone in the outfield would fan out to the furthest edges of the prairie grass at the far end of the field. The player would likely point in the direction he intended to place the ball so more outfielders would gather at that area. The ball would be hit, hopefully not over my head so I wouldn't have to be the one to run further into the tall grass where any number of sneaky ticks or unpredictable grasshoppers hid. The ball would be thrown in, sometimes through as many as seven different hands before it finally made it all the way in to the catcher. By this time, the player had run the bases in a leisurely fashion or goofed off as he did so, postponing the moment of crossing home plate until the ball was closer at hand to make the play that much more exciting.

When a young player came up to bat, the opposite occurred, and all the infielders took giant steps forward. The pitcher took a couple of huge steps to get closer to the batter and pitched the ball with a gentle little toss. There was no such thing as striking out a youngster. At times, the game was held up for ages as the little ones would swing and swing at nothing but air. Finally, when the ball was hit, the infielders chased after it, kicking it in front of them to stall for time, throwing it to each other and dropping it until the player was safely on first base. It's no wonder we all looked forward to these family ballgames. Not that the games weren't competitive. Each team was more or less balanced with good and bad players. Many an evening was spent with ice on an ankle or ointment on skinned knees as the race to be safe on base superseded caution. Heated arguments cropped up occasionally whether or not a ball was fair or a player safe, but the majority always ruled and there was no arguing with that.

Hiking to Mount Tom, the highest peak within a 50-mile radius, was an annual event when we camped at Sibley. The beautiful trails through the oak, red cedar, ironwood, green ash, maple, and basswood trees were always full of beauty. Many forest creatures were spotted along the way. Chipmunks, red and gray squirrels, mink, striped skunks, badger, and woodchucks were often seen while hiking. Common birds like the great blue herons, egrets, wood ducks, Canadian geese, loons and bluebirds were frequently sighted. More often than not we would also witness white-tailed deer as well, if we were quiet enough. The magic of seeing the surprisingly large animals move with barely a whisper of sound was unforgettable. We were always on the lookout for red and gray fox and coyote, too, which we knew also inhabited the forest around us.

It took a few hours to hike all the way up Mount Tom but the view from the top made it all worthwhile. Long, horizontal maps facing north, south, east, and west showed what we were viewing. The towns of Spicer and New London could be seen far off in the distance as well as more of the over 10,000 lakes dotting the Minnesota horizon. The granite structure at the top of Mount Tom was built to last so we took the time to carve our initials into the wooden beams of the building with Dad's pocket knife.

In the evening, we might go listen to the ranger talk if it was a subject of interest to us. At one of these talks, we learned that the man responsible for getting the Minnesota legislature to provide funds to purchase the land which was to become Sibley State Park was named Peter Broberg. We learned that his family had been massacred by the Indians in the 1862 uprising. Peter was the only Broberg to survive.

Around the campfire that night, we tried to imagine what it would be like to be the only surviving member of your family while the rest were all viciously attacked and died in all sorts of horrible ways. We speculated as to how Peter Broberg came to survive. Had he heard the Indians coming and hid in the cellar or the apple tree? Was he fortuitously off fishing in the nearby stream only to come home to find his family scattered around the farm with the tops of their heads missing? Was he at home when they were attacked but a kind-hearted Indian who disagreed with the killing of children spared him his life? Could he have run fast enough to escape the Indians?

Dad explained that the Brobergs, like most of the settler families in Minnesota territory at the time, were likely not very wealthy people. They had come to the Minnesota wilderness precisely because they needed a place to make a living. Their lives were difficult ones as they cleared the land, built their homes and barns, and raised a few crops and livestock to provide for their families. Neighbors were all a good distance away. Except for church on Sundays and the weekly shopping trip into town, it was a lonely existence with little social interaction and precious little free time. Looking around at my family in the soft light of the campfire, I felt a sudden ache at the thought of losing them like Peter Broberg had lost his family. I felt a fierce hatred of the Indians I had never experienced before. "Indians are savages!" I burst out passionately. Dad tried to explain again that the Indians were treated pretty savagely themselves at that time and in fact since then, too, but I didn't want to listen.

Curled up in my sleeping bag that night, my sleep was slow in coming. When it did arrive, I still tossed and turned. Every noise in the surrounding woods made me think of Indians sneaking up on the settlers. The hoot of an owl was surely a war cry. The lonely call of a loon on a distant lake was so mournful, I finally fell asleep dreaming I heard the cry of Peter Broberg's little sister from the woods where they once had lived.

We didn't see much of Jane up at Sibley because she was befriended early on by the Lobo brothers. They were slightly older than Jane but she managed to flirt with them equally enough so that each thought he was the preferred brother and she was ensured to have the attention of both of them all week long. The Lobos had a speedboat and often we'd be in the lake when Jane would zip by on water-skis, confidently letting go of the ski rope with one hand to give us a royal wave. We'd stop what we were doing and jump up and down shouting for a turn on the boat but to no avail. Polly joined Jane from time to time as if on a double date but the rest of us were more often than not treated as if we were no relations at all to Jane when she was with her newfound friends.

The lifeguard on the beach at Sibley was a broad-shouldered, bronze-colored young man wearing nothing but red swimming trunks. He stood for hours at a time with his feet widely planted and his hands behind his back while he stared out at the lake ready to rescue the next swimmer in distress. His nose was always covered in thick, white sun cream but the rest of his body he lathered in baby oil to enhance his deep tan. He wore aviator sunglasses with mirrors for lenses. His stoic face never once gave way to emotion. We learned his name was Tom and the goal was to distract him when he was on duty. "Hi Tom!" we greeted him with enthusiasm every time we went to the beach. He would say hello without ever taking his eyes off of the lake but we would never get any more conversation out of him than that. No matter how much we screamed or splashed or hollered, we never got so much as a grunt from Tom.

One afternoon the ranger came by to show Tom a driver's license they'd found to see if Tom recognized the picture. Tom took off his sunglasses to have a look. Behind the glasses we saw the beadiest little black eyes looking way too tiny in his otherwise handsome face. We took off running and collapsed when we were too far for him to hear, laughing and telling Polly that she could have him! He was all hers! But best to never come in out of the sun with him because the handsome lifeguard lost his looks when his sunglasses came off.

The best part about Sibley was playing in the woods around our campsite. There was a huge pit carved in the middle of a hill near our campsite. We spent hours running down into the steep bottom of the pit hoping to retain enough momentum to run back up the precipitous other side. After a few days when the excitement of running in and out of the pit subsided, Neil managed to throw a rope over the branch of the elm tree hanging over the pit.

We stood in line to take turns hanging on to the rope for dear life as the next in line would give a big shove to send one flying over the pit while screaming in terror. The trick was to remember to let go on the other side when you were relatively close to the ground so you could land with a more or less gentle thud. Many times we would forget to let go in the sheer excitement of the moment, only to find ourselves dangling from the rope hanging motionless over the gapingly deep pit. Purposely letting go of the rope knowing a ten-foot fall awaited was an experience that often required long episodes of encouragement, cajoling, and threats by the bystanders who wanted a turn at the rope before night fell and Mom called us to gather round the campfire. By the time we left Sibley, not one of us had avoided incurring at least one skinned knee or elbow and every one of us had chafed hands resulting from clinging onto the pit rope.

Taking down the tent wasn't nearly as much fun as putting it up had been and except for Mom, a blanket of melancholy settled over us. Dad promised that we would come back again next summer and every summer thereafter for the rest of our lives if we wanted to. We assured him that of course we did. We had made lots of friends throughout the week so we went around the campground saying our good-byes, hoping that we would all see each other again the following year.

 Walking back to our campsite, I marveled at how differently it looked now that ol' Blue had been taken down and packed away back in the car top carrier on the roof of the station wagon. Except for the flattened-down grass, there would be no way at all of knowing that we had ever actually been there. All the meals we'd eaten, the games of catch, the stories around the campfire, and the giggles from our sleeping bags were gone. It was as if they had never happened at all. I felt an overwhelming sense of sadness and went over to talk to Mom about it.

"Endings are always sad, honey," she explained. "But the week we spent at Sibley is now a part of your memory so it will never really go away. Our memories are some of our greatest treasures. They allow us to relive over and over again our favorite experiences. Look around you now and etch this vision into your mind to take out again and look at any time you want to in the future. It's a blessed thing that we tend to remember mostly the good things about our past and forget all about the ugly things. Each time you remember something, you're reinforcing it in your mind so that it will be as fresh and vivid a memory as when it first happened. Do me a favor now," Mom's practical side took over. "Walk around the campsite and pick up any little scrap of garbage or pop top. We want to leave the site as spotless as when we arrived so the next campers feel as welcome here as we did. We'll head down to the store at the beach when you're done for one last frozen candy bar before we go."

I spent the rest of the time picking up bits of paper and whatnot from around the campsite, deep in thought as to whether my last candy bar at camp would be a frozen Snickers Bar or Three Musketeer.

Chapter 14

As we drove from Kandiyohi to Renville County, Dad told us to think about how the countryside must have looked when Peter Broberg and his family settled here. The endless rows of corn, soybeans, and sugar beets wouldn't have been here as most of the area would have been covered in woods. The smooth, direct highway we were traveling on at a comfortable 60 miles an hour would have been no more than a dirt track wide enough for the wooden wheels of a covered wagon to amble along at 5 miles an hour. The Indians who had lived for centuries hunting and living off of the land leaving scarcely a trace as to their having been there would have been watching their entire way of life disappear as the settlers methodically removed the trees and with it the environment for the wildlife thereby preventing the Indians from living in their traditional manner any longer.

Grandpa and Grandma lived on 160 acres of fertile farmland in southwest Renville County. They were born of Czechoslovakian stock at the dawn of the 20th century in the state of Minnesota. Nonetheless, their first language was Czech. Their English was never spoken without a foreigner's lilt. Their grandparents had been born in the historical region of Bohemia in Central Europe, the

Western part of land currently in the Czech Republic. Bohemia's borders were marked with the mountain ranges of Giant and Ore, and by the Bohemian Forest.

While we drove, Mom told us the story of how our ancestors came to be here. In the poor region of the Sumava foothills, Honza Mariska was born in 1845. During the Revolution of 1848, his parents were among the many Czech nationalists calling for autonomy for Bohemia from Hapsburg Austria. After having been defeated and the old Bohemian Diet dissolved, they were a part of the first group of Bohemians to immigrate to Chicago in 1851.

The voyage to the new world lasted 3 months by boat, by which time the Mariska's supply of food was nearly depleted and the straw mattresses so filled with bugs that they threw them overboard and slept on the dingy wooden floors of the filthy below-decks of the decrepit vessel. More than 350,000 citizens of Czech origin streamed to the U.S. between 1850 and 1914. Most of them found their way to Chicago, St. Louis, and Racine, Wisconsin. Honza's family settled in Chicago at first, but after a few years, they moved further west, stopping for a while in Lonsdale and eventually staying in Bechyn, Minnesota.

In 1865, Honza married Zuza Kalina. They took advantage of the Homestead Act to settle 160 acres of fine, tillable land in Renville County. Ten years of thorny living later, Vilem was born, the sixth to be born in the family but only the second to survive the difficult frontier setting. Vilem eventually married Ivana Prochaska who gave birth to Grandpa Risa.

Grandpa married Franchesqa Prbl in the spring of 1917. They came home from church, took off their fine wedding clothes, put on their familiar work clothes, and went out to plant potatoes. All of the land around Bechyn was spoken for, so they moved 300 miles north to Thief River Falls to try to make a go of it there.

Perched on the junction of the Red Lake River to the East and the Thief River from the North, the town of Thief River Falls was founded in 1896. In the late 1800's, the combination of abundant forests and ready-made shipping by water made Thief River Falls, TRF as it came to be called, an ideal logging town. With much of the forest immediately surrounding the town destroyed by this time, Risa hoped to acquire enough property to provide for his growing family. Passing through Bemidji on their way north, Risa and Franchesqa continued on to Lower Red Lake, the biggest lake in Minnesota. Here, the Red Lake Band of Ojibwa Indians gave up much land over the years through treaties starting in 1863 and carrying on through 1905, but they never completely ceded the main reservation surrounding the lake. Though much diminished, the reservation is still nearly 408,000 acres, about the size of Rhode Island. Each July 6th, the Ojibwa celebrate their Independence Day to honor the wisdom and courage of their chiefs in resisting allotment during the 1889 Nelson Act negotiations.

At the time that Risa and Franchesqa passed through Lower Red Lake, the Ojibwa of Minnesota were about to bring a lawsuit against the federal government for theft in the selling of their lands and fraud in the handling of the proceeds. These claims were rejected by the first court to hear them, but eighty years later the Red Lake Nation would receive nearly 27 million dollars in settlement for wrongs committed against them by the ever-expanding United States.

Seventy miles west of Red Lake, Risa and Franchesqa tried for five years to establish themselves, but the harshness of the land and the stiff reserve of the Norwegians left them hungry for the boisterous ways of their fellow Czechs. They hopped on the Soo Line en route from Winnipeg to St. Paul, and eventually ended up back in Renville County. With Vilem ready to retire, Risa took over their 160 acres raising a family of eight and enough crops to provide for them.

The Great Depression of the 1930's brought hardship and poverty to many, but for the Mariska's, the difficulties were heightened due to the stroke Franchesqa suffered. Coming in from the field for lunch one day, Risa walked into the kitchen and stumbled over Franchesqa's outstretched legs. He was momentarily confused and almost started to laugh and tease his adored wife for her foolishness when his eyes met her frantic ones. He saw the little line of drool falling from the side of her mouth and realized with horror that she couldn't move any of her limbs to wipe it off.

Mom was 13 years old at the time, the fourth child of a family of eight. As the oldest girl, it fell upon her shoulders to take care of her three older brothers and four younger siblings. She dutifully dropped out of school and overnight went from being a silly little girl to a responsible homemaker and caretaker. Once the doctors in Minneapolis said nothing more could be done for Franchesqa's recovery after her stroke, Risa brought her home but still insisted on taking her to a physical therapist in Willmar weekly to try to help her to regain the use of her limbs. The right half of her body would never move well again.

Through determination and hard work, Franchesqa learned how to drag her right leg around and accomplish many household chores using only her left hand. Mom helped immensely, of course, making all of the meals, washing the clothes, cleaning the house, and ensuring that all of the kids got off to school on time. The baby of the family had been born with Downs' syndrome ten years after Mom had been born, so she needed extra care and attention, too. Risa carried on working hard with good humor and optimism.

After staying home for a year, Mom had gone back to school the following autumn. She was miserable in the class now a year behind all of her friends and felt like a big buffoon in the class of kids she used to consider beneath her. She continued to work hard and take care of the family. When she spied that worldly city boy passing through her town one Saturday night, she left 'Popcorn,' her previous boyfriend, in the dust. She married Dad in 1949 and moved to Minneapolis to live surrounded by concrete instead of pastures. While she loved her life in the cities, she always missed her rural roots. We spent as much time as we could visiting Grandpa Risa and Grandma Franchesqa back on the farm. Every harvest season, Dad used a week's vacation to help Grandpa bring in the beans or the corn.

Driving straight from Sibley to Grandma and Grandpa's farm, the miles flew by under the tires of the station wagon. Mom got more and more excited the closer she got to her girlhood home. She sounded like a tour guide as she began pointing out places from her youth: the ballroom where they went for weekend dances, the farms where her friends lived, the school she attended, and finally the spot where she and Dad had first met. She was just a school girl at the time, he was fresh out of the Navy from Hawaii as the Japs had surrendered at last and the world was at peace when they met. It had been a typical Saturday night in a small town. Mom and her girlfriends were on Main Street enjoying feeling young and pretty on a balmy summer's evening. Dad drove by with his brother and a friend from the service and noticed Mom right away driving the old Ford. He called dibbs on the driver, describing her as 'the brown-haired beauty with kissable lips'.

"And here's St. Aloysius Church where we were married in 1949," Mom pointed out. "We'll come to mass here this week-end," Mom promised as we stopped at the grocery store to load up on groceries before descending upon my grandparents, increasing their house size from two to thirteen.

Traveling on gravel roads the last few miles of the trip was the worst. Dad made us close the windows so we wouldn't suffocate from the dust, so we almost expired from heat exhaustion instead. Turning left into the driveway, Dad slowed down even more to admire Grandpa's crops on either side of the quarter-mile length driveway. "There's Grandpa!" Neil shouted, and before he could be stopped, he'd opened the car door and was running through the field to join Grandpa on the tractor.

Dad pulled up to the house and the rest of us poured out of the car like ants from an anthill. Grandma was standing at the window where she'd likely been all morning waiting for her oldest daughter to come home. We lined up to hug and kiss her while she exclaimed loudly over how tall we'd grown. I suffered through the wet kiss before heading straight to the outside of the house where the most recent batch of semi-wild kittens was most likely to be found.

We loved spending time in the country. Many of the games we played in the alley back home worked equally well and sometimes even better out in the country. The days flew by quickly when even the chores we had to do felt like fun and games. We loved to work in the chicken coop making a game of luring the nesting hens away to steal their eggs. Feeding slop to the pigs was a never-ending source of pleasure as we got to know the pigs by name and delighted in their quirky characters. Going out to the pea field with empty buckets in tow, we would plunk down in the dirt and gather all the peas within arms' reach to put into our buckets, then get up and move, sit down, and repeat the process. Digging up potatoes, carefully picking cucumbers so the nubs wouldn't prick, plucking feathers off of the chicken beheaded for supper, everything was more fun on the farm. Even helping Mom do our laundry was entertaining as the old wringer washing machine required feeding each piece of clothing into the washer by hand. The excitement of carefully maneuvering the item into the machine without losing fingers in the process was an endless thrill.

Taking snacks out to the field for Grandpa and Dad, and later the older brothers, was also a much-coveted responsibility. Ice cold lemonade would be poured into the thermos, and fresh-baked kolackies or warm apple pie would be carried out in pie tins to the edge of the field. There we would wait for the tractor to make its return trip. When it got close enough, we would begin to wave our arms around like workers on the runway at the airport guiding the planes. The tractor would sputter and cough as it shut down, the smell of fuel strong in the air. We would lay out the blanket in the shade of the tractor and sit down to enjoy the lunch.

Grandpa's farm consisted of the house, barn, chicken coop, pigpen, two grain storage bins, tool shed, and Quonset hut on 160 acres of rich black soil with a creek running through it,. The Quonset hut was a massive tin enclosure with a dusty dirt floor where all of grandpa's tractors, farm machinery, and vehicles were stored. On a hot summer afternoon when the temperature was nearing triple digits, it was magical to squeeze through the giant sliding doors to escape the sun and be enveloped in the shade and silence of the imposing temporarily-silent farm equipment. The smell of gas permeated the air while swallows dive bombed unwelcome visitors.

Each 160 acre homesteaded section had a nice grove of trees left to serve as a windbreak on the northwest corner of the house. On Grandpa's farm, this grove of trees was an endless treasure trove of old antique tractors and farm implements where my siblings and I amused ourselves incessantly. We staked out rooms in the dirt where we would play house for hours, going to the garbage heap first and gathering old tin cans, bottles, and anything else to help us carry on our fantasies. We pretended to make tasty concoctions by pouring grain and corn from the storage bins into our cans and adding water, dirt, bits of grass and anything else we could come up with to mimic a delicious stew. We climbed aboard the abandoned car or tractor and pretended to drive, shaking our shoulders up and down over the bumpy roads of our imaginations.

There were stacks of cages used to haul chickens around which we climbed into and played at being chickens ourselves. One time when Jane was in charge, she got annoyed with us for arguing too much and she left us locked in the cages for hours. Luckily, the cages were in the shade or she would have had a lot of explaining to do had we succumbed to heat stroke.

There was a small building in the woods with a rounded green roof and a sturdy broad apple tree next to it. Climbing the tree was easy as the lowest branch was just near enough to the ground to reach on tiptoes and grab onto. A multitude of robust branches grew from the tree so it was easy to clamber within it. It became a cherished game to take the leap from the tree onto the sloping roof of the little green house. We would sit munching apples we picked while discussing all manner of subjects under the sun. No matter how many times we did it, it was never easy to push oneself off of the safety and security of the apple tree to the moment of terror freefalling through the air to land on the sticky tar of the curved roof. It was necessary to immediately run up the roof to where the surface was flat enough to collapse onto in exhilarating relief. Perhaps it was the risk of the leap and the relief of the landing that caused us to open up and talk so intimately while at last sitting on top of the little green house nestled in the wood. We shared many confidences under the shade of the apple tree, revealing secrets we knew would never be brought up again away from the nurturing security of those woods.

We were inspired by the arrival of Morey, a friend of Grandpa's, who arrived in the rain in his Ford pickup with a work glove rhythmically waving back and forth over the windshield. Seems Morey's windshield wiper was broken and being low in funds as well as not very mechanically minded, he used what he had on hand and slipped the glove off of his hand and onto the bladeless wiper. Arriving at the farm, he joined Grandpa in the kitchen for a cup of coffee, leaving his truck running in the driveway with the glove continuing to wipe the rain off the windshield in a jauntily friendly fashion. Unable to resist, we took turns going to the window to wave back at the truck till Mom had enough and sent us all outside, drizzle or not.

We headed straight for the green house. More Morey stories followed, like the time we made a cake for his birthday, Morey being unmarried with no family to speak of. When it came time to blow out the candles, toothless Morey not only successfully blew out all of the candles but managed to spray the cake with enough spittle to put out an entire house fire. We had all looked at one another, horrified, knowing Mom would make us each take a piece of cake, spew or not, just to be polite. "Dodamn it all to hell!" was a favorite Moreyism we liked to quote when Mom wasn't within hearing distance. For some reason, Grandpa was Morey's barber. We loved to watch the sharpened razor as it whisked away the foamy cream leaving behind Morey's bald and lumpy skull. I never saw Grandpa cut anyone else's hair and he certainly didn't cut his own, that was Mom's job, but often Morey would be seated in the kitchen with shaving cream on regaling Grandpa with stories from town.

"Morey scares me," Greg said while lying back on the greenhouse roof. Neil, Pat, Polly, Marilyn and I were there, too, munching apples and sprawling around the rooftop. The rain had stopped and the sky was beginning to lighten in the distance.

"Not me," Polly replied. "I just kind of feel sorry for him. Imagine being all alone like he is, without anyone waiting for you to come home or to worry about you. He just lives in that old worn-down hotel in downtown Olivia and gets work where he can in farmer's fields. He has no clue how to behave in company. Why, he's probably never even been in love!" This, to romantic Polly, would be a fate worse than death itself!

"And when he dies," added Greg, "Nobody might even notice for days. His body will lay there getting stiffer and stiffer and then it'll start to smell and," he started to sing, "the worms crawl in, the worms crawl out, in your stomach and out your mouth!"

"Stop!" I put my hands over my ears so as not to hear anymore.

"Actually," Pat said gazing up at the blue sky trying to push its way through the thinning clouds, "it's not the scary-looking ones that you should actually be frightened of. Morey's odd because he doesn't have any teeth and he doesn't feel the need to get some just to be more readily accepted into society. He talks funny and he looks weird but he's just a regular guy trying to get through life the best he can without hurting anyone or doing any harm and maybe enjoying a laugh or two with friends along the way."

"It's true," Neil agreed. "Watch the way the dog acts around Morey. He's almost as loyal to him as he is to Grandpa. To my way of thinking, animals always know best because they recognize the genuine article and there's no fooling' the animals. They don't care if you're ugly or out of style or rich or popular. If you've got a kind soul, an animal will take to you no matter how bad you smell. On the other hand," he continued, "have you noticed Two Shoes when Doc Olson comes around? If you ask me, Doc is scarier than Morey any day of the week."

We thought about this for a moment or two before Marilyn asked, "Are you scared of Doc?"

"I hate Doc!" Neil said with such vehemence in his voice we all turned to look at him. Pat paused in the middle of throwing his apple core to listen. "He's a sick man. I hate him!! Oh, he's got lots of money and a beautiful wife and the biggest house in the neighborhood. He does nice things for people and doesn't charge for house calls, and he even took in a poor little Indian boy to give him a proper home. Ha! Has anyone else noticed how he treats that poor kid? Haven't any of you ever been creeped out by Doc in his office before?"

The silence which greeted the question caused Neil to keep his eyes downcast. None of us knew what to say. Finally, Pat asked in a low voice and in a tone rarely heard, "What are you saying, Neil?" I felt a strong urge to cover my ears with both hands again. Whatever Neil had to say, I didn't want to hear. The clouds above us had separated and patches of brilliant blue appeared. Sunlight shone through in blotches as it was filtered by the leaves on the branches above us. The beautiful setting was in stark contrast to the conversation as we awaited Neil's response.

Neil was quiet for so long I thought maybe he hadn't heard the question. Finally he said without lifting his eyes from his lap, "There's something wrong with Doc is all I'm saying. Something not right." We waited for him to find the right words. After a time he blew air loudly and forcefully through his nose causing his nostrils to flare and he finished angrily, "He touched me wrong, okay? One time in his office he started doing stuff that he shouldn't have and I wish I would've stuffed his stethoscope down his throat. But I didn't, alright? And I'm only telling you this so you guys be careful around him. He's a creep. Don't let yourself be caught alone with him. I don't care where, home, office, just be aware, that's all I'm saying. Alright?"

No one said anything for a while as the horror of what Neil had confessed sank in. I suddenly remembered the night I'd gone to the Olson's looking for Mickey and Doc had come to the door with his belt unbuckled. If he treated Neil badly the brief time Neil happened to be in his office alone, what might poor Mickey be enduring living like a prisoner under Doc's roof? I was distracted by a fly buzzing around me. It landed on my nearly-finished apple. I decided I'd had enough and I threw the apple, which ricocheted off the tree trunk and boomeranged back to hit me on my head.

"Dodamn it!" I said in my best Morey imitation rubbing my sticky forehead while the rest of the kids laughed uproariously, harder than the situation warranted but needing the comic relief.

"You couldn't do that again if you tried!" Greg hooted.

"Oh, yeah?" I accepted the challenge and we all began throwing apples at the tree hoping to get one to bounce back. Through the woods we heard Mom hollering at us to come in to help with supper. For me, getting down from the greenhouse was almost worse than getting onto it. I had to take little baby steps vertically down the curved side of the roof until the momentum forced me to abandon the house and jump to the ground which by this time hopefully would be much closer to me then when I had started the descent. If I waited too long to leap, gravity might cause me to fall head first. Not this time, however, and with Greg challenging us to race to the house, we took off, leaving all thoughts of fearsome grownups behind us.

We called our favorite activity at the farm 'tilting the trailer'. There was no limit to the number or age of participants. At any time during those long summer days, the thump of the trailer hitting the ground indicated that the game was on. It was equally exciting whether one of us played or twenty, and if the outcome must be described in the traditional manner, then we'd have to say we all won or we all lost together. Grandma loved to have a folding chair set outside under the shade of the locust tree where she could watch the action. When she was particularly impressed, she would take her good hand and slap it against her leg demonstrating her own manner of applause. The game incorporated exercise, skill, timing, and above all cooperation. When it was over, we'd collapse on the grass and discuss the previous maneuver play by play. Today was our last day on the farm, so everyone was on the trailer enjoying the final match.

The trailer was a large wooden platform resting on two center wheels which were positioned directly in the middle of the trailer. It was used to transport any number of things around the farm and except for in the dead of winter, it was never put inside the shed, but instead sat ever ready on the grassy patch between the buildings. In its stationary position, one end of the platform rested on the ground. The game was simply to put enough weight on the opposite side to leverage the platform off the ground. Back and forth we ran on the trailer letting our heaviness weigh one side down almost to touching the ground when we'd bolt to the other end to bring the other side down. The littler kids stood safely over the axel in the middle and very cautiously added their weight to one side and the other. The bigger kids would run from side to side causing the trailer to lilt and wave like the ocean during a storm. Finally, we would all start to spread out onto both sides of the trailer until our weight was evenly distributed and the trailer stood the way it was meant to when hauling. For long seconds we stood motionless, our feet planted widely apart listening to our rapid heartbeats through shallow breaths, our faces wreathed in grins. In cooperation and camaraderie we accomplished the perfect balance. "Blahopreji!" Grandma congratulated us, clapping her hand against her leg enthusiastically.

Twilight was falling. The car was packed and ready for the two-hour drive back to the Twin Cities. Mom had left her parents the gift of the entire house sparkling: windows, curtains, floors, rugs. The pantry was stocked with canned goods and the freezer with pies. Dad and Grandpa were boasting of the weight of the harvest they'd brought in and Greg was pulling on Grandpa's pant leg.

"Please, Grandpa, please, can we hear Happy sing before we leave?" We all chimed in to encourage Grandpa until he relented. Happy was Grandpa's dog, a most loyal and capable little mutt. Grandpa always named his dogs Happy and this one certainly fit the epithet. He was smallish, black, short-haired, and in the manner of most little canines he acted as though he were much larger and tougher than he actually was. He helped Grandpa on the farm to round up the pigs and catch chickens for dinner. He wasn't afraid of anything, not even the big wheels of the tractor, and he would run and jump on the tractor to ride along whenever Grandpa worked the fields. He never barked without reason and even then he conserved his yips to a minimum.

The only time we heard more than a peep out of Happy was when Grandpa would sing "My Wild, Irish Rose." Actually, all Grandpa had to sing was the word 'my'. Suddenly, Happy would start howling away, his little head tipped back and his eyes closed in ecstasy or concentration, his mouth wide open, the volume emanating from it belying his small dimensions. Accompanying Grandpa in the singing of this romantic Celtic melody changed Happy from a working farm dog into a romantic artist worthy of the applause we bestowed upon him as he continued to hold on to the final note.

Our week at the farm had passed by quickly and soon it was time to go home. "Vsude dobre, doma nejlepe, Mom." Mom said as she kissed Grandma good-bye. As we drove away, Mom wiped the familiar tears from her eyes that always fell when we departed the farm. We asked her again what she'd said in Czech.

"Literally, it's 'Everywhere is well, at home its best.' But we would say 'East or west, home is best.'" Facing backwards from the rear seat of the station wagon, the farm receded from view while we watched the colors of the sky turn from pink to purple as the sun continued its journey down to lighten the other side of the earth while we headed east. With all of the fresh air and physical activity, my heavy eyes soon got the best of me. I was nearly asleep when I heard the soothing murmur of Mom and Dad beginning the First Sorrowful Mystery of the Rosary.

Chapter 15

The final weeks of summer flew by after we got back from Grandpa's farm. Soon, we were following Pete the postman around again to find out our room assignments for the upcoming school year. Mrs. Agneau's son was visiting from California for a few days. Mrs. Agneau had been looking forward to his coming all summer long and she talked about it all the time. It seemed he was barely here and then he turned around and left. They had a terrific row when he left. After a respectable amount of time, Mom told me to bring a plate of freshly-baked molasses crackle-top cookies over to cheer Mrs. Agneau up with a visit. Mrs. Agneau's face was all swollen from crying when I got there. When she answered the door, I don't think it was me she was expecting because she looked so happy and then her face fell when she looked down and saw it was me. I thought maybe she had something against molasses cookies but she assured me that wasn't it.

We sat in our usual spot at the kitchen table, but Mrs. Agneau was so listless and sad, I barely recognized her. I tried to keep up my end of the conversation, telling her all about my night at the hotel with Lexie, the play that Polly and her friends were directing which we were going to perform in the Stidger's garage, the new dog that

Mickey had found, and Jane's new boots, but Mrs. Agneau just kept staring out not seeming to see anything. Twice I turned around to see what she was looking at, but it seemed to be just the bare wall that was holding her attention. I stood up and kept trying.

"So, Jane's boots are white and super shiny and they practically come all the way up to her knees. She wears them even on the hottest days going around the house singing like she's Nancy Sinatra, 'These boots are made for walking, that's just what they'll do, one of these days these boots are gonna walk all over you. Come on boots, start walking." With my hand on my hip, I imitated Jane and swung my bottom as I strutted around Mrs. Agneau's little kitchen. Laughing, I fell back into my chair, but Mrs. Agneau only gave me a fraction of her usual smile.

"That's nice, dear," she murmured distractedly.

As Mom tucked me in that night, I asked if she knew what was wrong. She explained that Mrs. Agneau's son thinks his mother is getting too old to live on her own anymore. He came here to try to talk her into moving into an old folk's home in California so he doesn't have to come such a long way to visit her. Mrs. Agneau has lived on Pleasant Avenue for the past sixty years. She doesn't want to leave and that's making her son angry. I thought about Mrs. Agneau's beautiful home full of so many things precious to her. I pictured her garden of tomatoes, squash, and peppers ripe for picking and the abundance of flowers perfuming the neighborhood. I thought about how special she made me feel when she had me over.

"I don't want her to go, either. He can't make her go, can he?"

"Let's hope not," Mom said as she kissed me goodnight.

I couldn't wait to head over to Mickey's the next morning to play with Geronimo, his new-found dog. "Don't forget to take Chris with you!" Mom hollered from the other room. Sitting in his high chair with oatmeal smeared all over his head, Chris looked at me happily and slapped both hands down on his tray, further spreading the sticky oatmeal. After cleaning him up, I carried him outside with his bottle and strapped him into the stroller. Armed with a Chinese jump rope under my arm, I pushed Chris across the alley to Mickey's. He was teaching the mangy-looking mutt to fetch a stick. Sure enough, it looked like he was already successful.

"Wow, he's smarter than he looks!" I observed.

"You better believe it. Look what else he can do." Mickey proceeded to show me how Geronimo could shake hands and speak already.

"Maybe we can teach him how to play dead," I suggested, and Geronimo immediately collapsed onto his back, his four legs rigidly pointing upwards. "Hey," I began while Mickey burst out laughing and bent down to scratch Geronimo vigorously on his stomach causing him to thump his back leg appreciatively.

"Okay, I guess someone else might have taught him already, but he's still a smart dog!" Mickey bragged.

We had been camping when Mickey had found Geronimo hanging out in the alley. He started feeding him scraps and Geronimo decided Mickey could use a dog so they'd been inseparable ever since. Doc didn't like dogs and it seemed he especially loathed this one. He wouldn't allow Geronimo into the house, so for the past week, Mickey was sleeping outside in a little orange pup tent he'd found in the garage. In all the time I'd known Mickey, I'd never seen him so happy.

"What are you gonna do when winter comes and it's too cold for you to sleep outside?"

"It won't be too cold. Geronimo keeps me warm, and I keep him warm. Isn't that right boy?" He scratched behind his ears while Geronimo looked to be smiling back at him, tongue hanging sideways out of his mouth. I was glad to see Mickey so cheerful. So often he seemed to be doing some chore or other that the Olsons kept him busy doing, or else he was worrying about the life he'd left behind on the reservation. Now that he had Geronimo to take care of, he was always in great spirits.

"Chinese jump rope?" I proposed, holding out the striped toy which looked like a super large elastic hair band.

"It takes three to play," Mickey observed. "There are only two of us."

"Nuh-uh," I said, pointing at Chris in the stroller who was holding his bottle upside down letting Geronimo suck on the nipple in a noisily effective manner. Granting that Chris was too young to play, I proceeded to stretch one end of the jump rope underneath the two front wheels of the stroller. Placing my two feet in a wide stance across from the stroller, I gestured to Mickey to begin to play. We spent the next hour contentedly taking turns on the Chinese jump rope with each of us completing the series twice. Geronimo entertained Chris the whole time we were playing and fetched every single toy from the stroller a zillion times.

"Thanks for babysitting, Geronimo," I laughed as the dog held out his paw for me to shake. That was one clever dog. "Are you coming to play practice?" I asked Mickey as Polly was hollering that it was time for rehearsal. I began to push Chris home.

"No, I'd better not. Doc left a list of some things he wants me to do. Me and Geronimo don't mind though." Mickey scratched the top of the dog's head lovingly.

Ever since I got to spend the night in downtown Minneapolis at a hotel with Lexie and her Mom, the rest of my family was so green with envy that they were doing everything they could to treat me badly. What had happened was that Stella wanted Lexie to have at least one fun thing to say about her summer when they asked, like they always did on the first day of school, for us to tell about how we'd spent our summer. On account of her agora fear disease, they couldn't go camping or anything like that, but a hotel would be okay as long as there weren't too many people around or anything. I got invited to go with them because it wouldn't be much fun for Lexie if it was just her and her Mom.

Getting picked up by the same taxi that took Stella to work every day, they came to my house to pick me up. I was so proud when the taxi pulled up. I walked down the sidewalk with the little green suitcase Mom let me borrow in my hand. There was a miniature round seat in the taxi facing the rear seat so I got to sit there, and I saw all the kids looking out the window at me to watch us drive away. I felt a momentary sense of panic that they were all there and the taxi was pulling me inexorably away from them. Lexie chose that moment to slip her hand into mine and start pointing out the window at all of the sites on our way downtown.

Stella had arranged for the driver to drive us around Minneapolis for a bit before taking us to the hotel. We went past Minnehaha Falls, Lake Nokomis, Lake Harriet (where we stopped for an ice cream and watched the ducks), Lake Calhoun, Lake of the Isles, and finally, downtown. Stella went straight to the hotel room but Lexie and I spent hours at the pool before Stella called the front desk and sent them to come and get us out of the water. Room service had already delivered our supper. The corn dogs and french fries were cold but we finished them off anyway. All of that swimming had made us hungry.

We thought the little bars of soap and tiny bottles of shampoo in the bathroom were adorable. I asked Stella if I could bring some home to show my Mom. Stella called housekeeping then and asked for three more bottles of shampoo. "I have much, much hair," she emphasized with her hands to show how much hair even though she was speaking on the phone and couldn't be seen. "Leetle bottle too leetle." She said in her strong Russian accent. She let me take all four bottles home, one for each sister and one for Mom.

Although I couldn't sleep at all in the unfamiliar surroundings and I was really happy to get home and see my family again, none of the kids acted happy to see me. I was the first in the family to get to stay overnight at a hotel and they didn't think it was fair at all.

The play Polly was organizing for us to put on was called *The Sound of Music*. It was a new musical that year and we loved singing

"Do-re-mi", "My Favorite Things", and "Sixteen Going on Seventeen". The kids with the best voices got the main parts. I usually got a singing part because my voice is pretty good, but this year on account of the hotel with Lexie, I got the part of Hitler. I don't even think Hitler is supposed to be in the play with it set in Austria where the von Trapp family lived, but they probably added Hitler just so I could play the role of a very unpopular person.

A couple days before school was to start, we walked around to all the neighbors' houses and invited them to come see the performance being held that evening in the Stidger's garage. Peeking between the cracks in the blanket temporarily serving as a curtain, I saw Mr. Finkelstein come in with Mrs. Agneau. The play started on time, and everyone seemed to be enjoying themselves immensely except for me.

My lip itched like crazy owing to the paste made up of flour and water which we used to hold the coffee grounds in place under my nose to look like Hitler's renowned moustache. Pouting my lips and wrinkling my noise, I did everything I could to relieve the itch without actually touching my lip and ruining the bogus facial hair. At last it was my cue to come on stage. I marched on stiffly, clicked my heels together loudly, and the next thing I knew I was being pelted by rotten vegetables. Regrettably falling completely out of character while the audience burst out laughing, I screamed and ran as fast as I could off the stage which unfortunately was not fast enough to avoid a tomato that struck me right above my eye. Blood was mixed with the tomato pulp, so Doc was called from the audience to come backstage, well, behind the garage actually, to see how bad the cut was and whether I needed stitches or not.

Sniffling in self-pity and vowing to find out who the tomato-tossing culprits were, I let Doc wash my wound. Suddenly I remembered Neil's advice about not being alone with Doc. We were the only two sitting outside in the dark, but as practically the entire neighborhood was on the other side of the wall, I didn't think I had too much to worry about. Nonetheless, I was relieved to hear footsteps coming down the alley. I tried to turn my head to see who was approaching.

"Hold still" Doc said harshly and he dabbed my eye with one hand while holding my chin roughly with the other. "Ow" I started to murmur when unexpectedly I saw a hand placed on Doc's arm and heard a voice hiss.

"Careful now, Mr. Doctor, this one has a Daddy to protect her." I was startled to see Crazy Caroline's leering eyes locked onto Docs. That was the second time she had come to my rescue and I didn't like it one bit. Neither did Doc, apparently, because he threw off her hand and backed up, snarling.

"Keep away from me you meddling old squaw. Stay away from me, I said!" He put up both hands as if to keep her at bay but she just kept coming toward him. Doc made as if he were going to hit her and I gasped in fright which caused him to still his fist midflight.

"I am watching you, Mr. Doctor. Don't you forget it for one instant. I am watching you," Crazy Caroline said and she stood there resolutely. Doc's breathing was hard and furious. He stomped angrily back into the garage. Caroline looked at me a moment longer before slipping back out into the dark night.

I watched her go, realizing too late that I should have thanked her. I had to admit that I was glad she had stuck up for me. I sat there for a moment examining my swollen eye with my fingers, not wanting to go back inside in case I got laughed at again. Finally, I slowly got back up and went inside to see the Edelweiss finale. That was my favorite song in the whole play but Polly said it wouldn't be appropriate for Hitler to sing it. After a moment, I decided I didn't care, and I joined the actors playing the Von Trapp family onstage to sing gustily along with them.

The following night, we had an early supper and everyone took a bath before bed. The next morning was the first day of school and Mom wanted to be sure we all got a good night's sleep. It felt so strange to be wearing pajamas while the sun hadn't set yet and lying in bed when I didn't feel the least bit tired. When Mom came to tuck us in, I asked her if time had gone by faster this summer than last because it sure felt like it had. She sat down at the end of my bed rubbing my back while she spoke.

"No, Ginny, time is made up of exactly sixty seconds in every minute, sixty minutes in every hour, twenty-four hours in every day, three hundred sixty-five days in every year. Well, except for Leap Year, of course. The older you get, the faster time does seem to go by. But as you're only seven, I don't think that pertains to you yet.

Knowing every moment is the same, it would be wise to fill those moments well and not waste them with idleness or worse, cruelty. Day in, day out, time marches on and we can't stop it. The best we can do is to try to make every moment count, to be kind to one another, and to appreciate all the beauty and the love that there is in this world. Then, when you're old and you look back on your life, you can know that you lived your life well and to the best of your ability. And maybe you'll be leaving the world a little bit better off than when you joined it. Wouldn't that be a good feeling?"

Kissing me goodnight, Mom made me promise not to read but to go straight to sleep. I went to kneel by the window to look outside not feeling the least bit sleepy. I rested my head on my forearms on the window sill. The backyard looked so forlorn on such a beautiful late-summer evening with no one outside to enjoy it. I was excited to be starting second grade but sad that the long carefree days of summer were behind me already. It would be nine long months before we could once again kick off our shoes and spend the majority of our time outdoors.

One by one, I heard the chorus of crickets beginning to chirp, a sure sign of the end of summer. I saw Mrs. Agneau sitting at her kitchen table with her head bowed over a book. I could hear Mr. Finkelstein whistling a tune from *A Sound of Music*. Across the alley, I saw Doc struggling with something he was putting into the back seat of his car, and I sat up on my knees to see. Hearing a little yelp, I realized it must have been Geronimo. The car door was shut so carefully almost no sound was made. Doc slid into the driver's seat, eased the car into gear and drove noiselessly away. Peering into the descending dusk, I couldn't see Mickey's pup tent in their backyard and guessed he wouldn't be allowed to sleep out there anymore now that school was starting. But where was Doc taking Geronimo? I climbed back into bed at last, closing my eyes to the last day of summer.

Chapter 16

Arriving at Incarnation the next morning, I couldn't wait to say good-bye to Mom and to find my second-grade classroom. Greg was starting first grade this year, and he looked like he needed Mom to himself for a while. He was holding onto her hand with both of his and didn't look like he would be letting go anytime soon. With a flippant farewell, I hurried in to find my room. I slipped into my desk, delighted to see Lexie saving me a spot. Her horrified expression reminded me that while the swelling had gone down somewhat on my eye, the greenish-yellow color and the way the bridge of my nose was still thicker than normal gave me a sort of Frankenstein look. I explained to Lexie my stint as Hitler resulting in the catapulted vegetables.

The second bell had just rung signifying that it was time for class to start when there was a commotion next to me. Mickey arrived and plopped down in the desk next to mine barely escaping being late. He looked harried and unhappy, so as soon as Sr. Marjorie started Morning Prayer, I asked him what was up. He whispered that Geronimo was missing and that he hadn't seen him since the previous night. Mickey had had to sleep indoors just as I'd suspected on account of school starting today. I felt a sinking feeling in the pit of my stomach remembering what I had seen from by bedroom window, but Sister called out 'Virginia Ashcroft' taking role, and I didn't get a chance to speak to Mickey again all morning.

We raced home for lunch together, Wayne 'light bulb-head' Schmitt chasing us as far as his house, an odd ritual he carried on from that day all the way through the fifth grade. From Mickey's backyard, we heard the familiar sound of barking. Mickey hollered "Geronimo!" sprinting to rejoin his beloved companion. I was glad I hadn't said anything about the bizarre scene I had witnessed with Doc last night.

Savoring the delicious aftertaste of creamed tuna on toast, I walked back to school with Mickey after lunch. He explained that from now on he was going to tie Geronimo up at night so he wouldn't run away again. I didn't say anything to that and my chance to tell Mickey what I had seen passed. Ever afterwards I wondered, "Would it have made a difference if I had told him what I had seen Doc do? Could it have helped at all?" I said nothing.

On Saturday, four days later, Mickey's early morning screams brought us all running. Geronimo's lifeless body lay awkwardly on Mickey's lap as Mickey shouted "No, no, Geronimo, you can't die! No! Don't do it! Please, please don't die, Geronimo. Don't leave me! You can't leave me." He sobbed as he buried his face in Geronimo's coarse fur, the leash around his neck still attached to the base of the tree.

With moist eyes, we tried to comfort Mickey. Plopping down by Mickey's side, I put my hand on Geronimo's head and was surprised to find it stiff and cold already. How could that dog which had been so joyous and full of life now be this frigid, empty body left behind? Surely, this carcass was just his shell. Where had Geronimo's spirit gone? Fighting to hold back my tears, I marveled at how quickly life leaves our bodies behind.

After a while, I suggested that we should have a funeral for Geronimo fit for the warrior he was named after. The boys readily agreed and ran off to find some spades. Doc and Mrs. Olson didn't look too thrilled about the grave we dug for Geronimo under their elm tree, but they couldn't say much with almost the entire neighborhood there to console Mickey. When the hole was dug deeply enough, we wrapped the corpse in an old sheet Mom brought over and gently lowered him into the ground. Struggling not to cry, we all bowed our heads except for Mickey. His eyes were dry and his demeanor solemn as he rose to the occasion and recited the eulogy.

"You were a good friend to me Geronimo and I thank you." Mickey threw the first shovelful of dirt on top of his dog. We all took turns after him. Chris crawled over and threw a stick down into the hole which landed with a thud on top of Geronimo. Flinching with surprise, I turned to see what Mickey made of the offering. His crooked half grin assured me that, like me, he thought it seemed appropriate that Geronimo be buried with a token of his playfulness. "Da," Chris said, possibly meaning dog, "da, da, da!" I scooped him up to be sure he wouldn't try to follow the stick into the grave.

Watching Doc from the corner of my eye throughout the morning, I felt sure he had something to do with Geronimo's demise but the horror of the thought was too much for me. I was suddenly filled with such hatred for him, I was afraid of what I might do. If he was able to commit this heinous act, what else was he capable of?

No one could explain why Geronimo had died. Anyone who had seen Geronimo friskily playing with Mickey knew that old age was highly unlikely. The other explanation was that perhaps he had eaten something fatal. Thinking about Doc's easy access to all sorts of drugs which could easily poison a small creature like Geronimo, I felt more convinced than ever that Doc had had something to do with the beloved dog's death.

Later that afternoon, Mom suggested I invite Mickey along to join Dad and me on our favorite outing. When I said Doc probably wouldn't let him come, Mom wiped her hands on her apron and told me to keep an eye on the boys, that she would be right back. A few minutes later, she came through the back door with Mickey in tow, casually announcing that not only could Mickey go with Dad and I but that he was spending the night, too. I tried to imagine exactly what Mom may have said to Doc or how she had threatened him. Mickey was sleeping over! This was an unprecedented event as Mom never let anyone sleep over on a Saturday night. It might interfere with our much needed rest to assure we looked our best for church on Sunday morning.

It was clear from his puffy eyes that Mickey had been crying, so I took it upon myself to try to distract him. All the way to Hosmer, I kept up a steady stream of chatter. Dad and Mickey seemed relieved when we entered the building and they reminded me a little too enthusiastically that there was no talking allowed in the library. That reminder wasn't necessary because the hushed quiet in the attractive building was one of the things I loved most about it.

Hosmer Public Library was built in 1916 in gothic style with many-sided pillars on either side of the main entrance. Walking through those doors was like entering a magical kingdom with books lining the walls and overflowing bookshelves filling the entire main floor. Upstairs was the reference library. Dad stayed on the main floor, but Mickey and I headed down to the basement where the entire floor was crammed with children's books. We went to the picture-book section first because it was always fun to see what new books were there. We sat on the floor and read through a few of those, nostalgically re-reading some of our favorites. After a while, we proudly got up and walked to the early readers' section. Both Mickey and I were avid readers. For the next hour, we took our time choosing the six books we were each allowed to check out of the library. Then we settled down to read.

I chose two each from my favorite authors: Donald Sobol, Maud Hart Lovelace, and Laura Ingalls Wilder. I put aside *Encyclopedia Brown Keeps the Peace* and *Encyclopedia Brown Saves the Day*, *Betsy and Tacy Go over the Big Hill* and *Betsy and Tacy Go Downtown*, and *The Long Winter*. I picked up *By the Shores of Silver Lake*. I savored the moment by simply holding the book in my hands with the cover closed knowing that I had a number of hours of pleasure in store. I went back in my mind to the previous book in the Little House on the Prairie series,

On the Banks of Plum Creek. I had just returned it to the library. I settled back in the chair to join the Ingalls family back in the 1890's. A few seconds after I started reading, I clapped my hand over my mouth and felt tears spring unbidden to my eyes. Mickey whispered from across the table, "What?"

"Mary is blind!" I told him incredulously. Mickey didn't read the Little House on the Prairie series even though I kept telling him that I knew he would love them. He thought they were only for girls, plus he didn't like the way the Indians were portrayed in the books. I told him he had no right to judge as he'd never read them and from then on whenever an Indian was mentioned in the series, I marked the spot to read it to Mickey. He was always interested in having me tell him exactly what happened in each book so he could keep up with the series that way. I slid the book over to him so he could read the sentences of the book that I would memorize and repeat over and over again. "The doctor had come every day. Pa did not know how he could pay the bill. Far worst of all, the fever had settled in Mary's eyes, and Mary was blind."

"Sad." He slid the book back over to me and carried on reading his book, Jack London's *White Fang.* I questioned the wisdom of his reading a book about dogs on this fateful day but of course I understood his desire to do so. A while later I felt fresh tears spring to my eyes but this time I was careful to keep my head down so Mickey wouldn't notice. In *By the Shores of Silver Lake*, poor old, loyal Jack, the Wilders' beloved terrier is found dead under the wheels of the wagon he had spent so many hours running beneath. I didn't want to have to tell Mickey about the death of another dog.

When the lights blinked on and off, we knew the library would soon be closing so we headed back up the stairs to find Dad. He was sitting at a round, wooden table with a copy of Mary Eastman's book, *Dahcotah, or, Life and Legends of the Sioux.* Dad was reading about history again. Closing the book gingerly, he put it back on the shelf and we left the library, the librarian locking the doors behind us.

Driving home, I was surprised when Dad skipped our turn and carried on down 36th Street heading west until he came to Lake

Calhoun. Following the lake for a bit, he ventured off to join up with Lake Harriet. Parking the car, we walked to the pavilion to get ice cream cones and then walked to our favorite spot under the shade of the willow tree to enjoy our treats. It was a warm, September day so we couldn't waste time chatting but focused on finishing our cones before they melted. I concentrated on licking halfway around my cone and then quickly licking the other side. Steadily, I prevented any ice cream from dripping. I continued happily lapping away until the ice cream was gone except for what was left inside the cone, and then I knew I could relax because the pressure was over until the ice cream started melting through the base. I glanced at Mickey to see how he was doing.

Mickey was holding his forgotten cone while streaks of chocolate ice cream melted all over his hand, down his arm, and all over the leg his arm was resting on. His face was a mirror of the melting ice cream cone as tears streamed down his cheeks unchecked. Mickey was concentrating with all his might on containing his sobs, and it looked as if his head was about to burst. I opened my mouth to say something when out of the corner of my eye I caught Dad shaking his head sadly at me. I understood him to mean I should hold my tongue. He gave a quick flick of his head, so without a word I got up and moved behind the trunk of the tree, out of sight but within hearing distance.

"I'll take that cone from you, son," Dad said and it was as if those words were the keys to unlock the dam. Mickey began to let out a screech that started off quietly and eventually bellowed loudly. It reminded me of the tornado sirens that start off sounding quiet when they're facing away from you. As the revolving sirens turn your way, the volume is loud enough to force you to cover your ears with both hands. Mickey's cries were worse than that though because they came from deep inside him and carried with them inconsolable sadness. He sobbed unchecked until it seemed he had no more tears left inside him. His ragged breaths continued to empty him completely. I wiped my own tears silently, thinking of poor Geronimo. I noticed that the unimaginable had happened, and I had somehow let my ice cream melt through the bottom of my cone. Thinking how that had never happened before, I bit the cone

from the bottom up and finished it all off completely with still not a
word coming from the other side of the tree. At last, I heard the
sound of Mickey blowing his nose. I knew Dad had taken a hanky
out of his pocket and handed it to him.

"Mr. Ashcroft, why do we have to die?"

"That's just the way the way it is, Mickey. We're born, we live, and
we die. We could just as likely ask why are we born or why do we
live?" I heard the rustle of Dad leaning back against the tree to get
more comfortable, so I sat back, too. We were going to be a while.
"The fact of the matter is we **are** born, we **get** to live, and the one
thing that not one living thing has yet to avoid is death. Every
civilization that has ever existed has tried to come up with proof
that there is something beyond this life. We certainly do spend an
awful lot of time trying to convince ourselves that there is more out
there than just the world as we know it. The truth of the matter is
that all we know for sure is that we're born, we live, and we die. We
can't control the fact that we're born, and we can't avoid the
inevitableness of death. What we do have power over is the way we
choose to live. You are making good choices, Mickey. What you
gave to that poor dog was some good times, a lot of love, and
security. I hope you feel good about that. It was just Geronimo's
time to die it seems, and for that, I'm sorry."

"I'm sorry, too." Mickey interrupted. "I wish I had never found him.
I was fine before Geronimo but now I don't see how I can live
without him!" Mickey started to cry again.

Dad was quiet for a while but then he said, "It hurts to lose those we
love but you know what? That hurt is worth it because without it
we would just be empty shells going through life without feeling
anything at all. I know it feels bad right now, Mickey, but I promise
you sometime in the not too distant future you are going to think
about Geronimo, about something he did, and it's going to make you
smile. Memories of Geronimo will make you happy. Perhaps that is
all any of us will ever be in the end, just memories. Memories of who
we are and of experiences we shared. If those memories bring

pleasure and happiness to others, then that is enough. That is a life well-lived."

After a bit, Dad called me and said it was time to head home for Saturday- night burgers. We dipped our hands in the cool lake water and wiped at our chins. Mickey avoided my eyes. I assured him that he was going to love Mom's burgers. I kept chattering the rest of the way home to try to fill the void left by Mickey's loss.

After supper and baths, we played the Mouse Trap game a number of times. It was thrilling to put into motion the heavy silver ball, watch it roll down the stairs until it finally caused the trap to drop down onto the unsuspecting mouse. Holding onto Two-shoes so she couldn't ruin it by mischievously slapping the ball off of the board, we played until Mom hollered that it was time for bed. Assuring Mom that this would be the last time, I told Mickey to watch as I let go of the cat at last. As the ball made its way around the board game, Two-shoes pounced right when the cage was coming down. When it landed on her tail, she howled and shot under the couch. Mickey fell over backwards he was laughing so hard. Mom tried to sound stern as she scolded me but she was chuckling, too, as she sent us off to bed.

Lying on the floor in our sleeping bags, I wanted to ask Mickey what had happened to his family and why he had to live with the Olsons. I really wanted to ask him questions about his Mom but I didn't want to make him sad all over again. The light from the outside streetlamp shone in just enough so we could see each other. Mickey lay on his back and folded his arms underneath his head. He looked so sad staring up at the ceiling. Just then, Dad knocked gently on the half-open door and poked his head inside. "How would you two like to listen to a little of our Minnesota history before falling asleep?"

I could think of a lot more interesting stories I would rather hear, but Dad gave me a quick wink before he moved some clothes off the chair in the corner and sat down, so I knew he had something in particular he wanted to tell us. Mickey and I murmured our consent and Dad began.

"Mickey's family is the nation of Sioux Indians which at one time covered almost 24 million acres of land," Mickey abruptly yelped in pain interrupting Dad's narrative. It was just Two-shoes come out of hiding and acting as dignified as ever while purring and digging her claws contentedly into Mickey's stomach. I told Mickey to be sure to keep the sleeping bag between himself and the cat's claws. Dad carried on with his story.

"They were the largest Indian nation on the Plains. Sioux wasn't really their tribal name. The French just called them that after hearing their enemies, the Ojibwa, refer to them as Siu meaning snake. The Sioux were divided into three groups: the Lakota, Dakota, and Nakota. Mickey's people, the Dakota, loved to fish, farm, and especially to hunt buffalo. When the railroad tracks were put in, the railroads hired hunters to kill off all of the buffalo, so the Sioux were forced to trade their lands in exchange for cattle and corn. From that point on, their way of life was over and they could no longer take care of themselves. That made them dependent upon payments from the government. They were owed those payments. They were guaranteed by the treaties the Sioux had been forced to sign. Then, in 1861, there was a terrible drought. All of the crops failed. The Indians starved all through the long winter. The next year, the federal payment was late. When the Sioux complained, the agent in charge, Andrew Myrick, said that they could just eat grass. Can you believe it? He was talking to some of the finest warriors of the Sioux nation. They were starving. And he told them to eat grass."

Suddenly, Mickey sat up and said, "He was one of the first to die anyway, in the war that followed. He was found with his mouth full of grass to see how he liked it. He deserved it, too. My great, great, great, great uncle, White Dog, was there. He didn't kill anyone, but he was blamed along with the rest of them anyhow."

"White Dog, huh? Who was he?" I could hardly keep my eyes open anymore but I couldn't believe what Mickey said.

"He was my ancestor. He didn't kill anyone but that didn't matter. He was hung anyway."

"What?" I said, starting to sit up, too.

"Lie back down and listen," Dad said, "and I'll continue with the story. Your ancestor, White Dog, is a well-known figure from the war of 1862. They say he was the most handsome Santee Sioux to ever live. Not only Dakota women, but also white women couldn't keep their hands off of him. He had many lovers. I guess he was really something. During the uprising, he fell in love with one of the white women who had been captured. They were planning to get married and everything. He was only 24 years old. This white woman talked him into turning himself in to General Sibley, promising him that she would keep him safe, her testimony and love would set him free. But she was wrong."

I was wide awake again hanging onto every word of the story. Mickey was quiet for so long that I thought maybe he'd fallen asleep. "Then what happened, Dad?" I whispered.

He carried on in a low voice, "It was Christmas Eve. All the Indian prisoners were held on the ground floor of a 3-story building in Mankato. They were only allowed to see two or three family members or friends to say good-bye. Some were brave and managed not to cry as they said their final good-byes to their children and loved ones. Most of them were crying and carrying on. It was unbearably sad.

White Dog's lover came to say good-bye to him, too. When she first entered the prison, a hush descended over the room crowded with the condemned men and their loved ones. Some of them began a hissing sound meant to signify their displeasure at the presence of a white woman, but one look at the grief on her face convinced them that she was their sister in suffering and they let her be. After everything had been said and everyone was exhausted from weeping, a silence settled over the room. Those condemned to die and their visitors alike were content just to be in each other's company. When the time came for them to say good-bye, the families left quickly. That way, the men were able to maintain their dignity until they were gone.

There was a reporter there from the St. Paul newspaper who was allowed in to see the prisoners that night. He describes how the prisoners were fastened two by two to the floor by chains. Some were smoking and chatting while others were sleeping. Most of them were young men, one was only 16, and many of them had painted their faces. The reporter said they smiled at his entrance and held out their hands to be shaken.

The next day was Christmas. The prison cooks, who were all relatives of the prisoners, were allowed to come in to say good-bye. Coats, blankets, everything the prisoners owned including locks of their hair were given to the women. The prisoners were less sad today as they didn't want the women to witness their weakness.

They added fresh paint to their faces and began to sing the traditional death-song as they waited. When the irons were removed from their feet and their hands were being tied by cords instead, White Dog asked if they could leave his hands untied. Of course, they would not allow it. The singing and conversation continued and they gave each other strength by pretending to be cheerful. All of the prisoners made a point of going around the room to shake hands with the soldiers and reporters to say good-by.

Then they stood in a circle and sang loudly to their ancestors that they would be joining them soon. When the song finished, a hush came over them and the priest began to pray with them. White cloth sacks were placed on top of their heads leaving their painted faces visible. At 10:00 that morning, when they were marched across the street to the scaffold, they tried to give the impression of being ready and eager to accept their fate. White Dog, too, kept a smile on his face while he searched the crowd for his lover. As they walked up to the scaffold, they began to sing again. The sound was overwhelming, but it allowed them to keep up their courage. One by one, the noose was adjusted on each of their necks. An enormous crowd had gathered to witness the execution. The mood was somber. Suddenly, there was a rush of movement, and the crowd parted in front of White Dog. There she was, his lover, bravely inviting the wrath of the crowd who came to cheer his death, not mourn it. Tears poured down her cheeks as she locked eyes with the man whose death would be on her conscience for the rest of her days. Their eyes spoke the love which their voices could not.

Three deliberate and slow beats were heard on the drum. As the last was still echoing, the rope was cut with a flourish. The scaffold fell. As it went down with the bodies of the 38 men, the crowd cheered halfheartedly once and then all was quiet. The bodies struggled for a while. One of them, the body of Rattling Runner, fell to the ground. His rope had broken, so he had to be hung twice, can you imagine? Twenty minutes later they were all pronounced dead. They were cut down and taken to a grave under the willows where they were all buried together," Dad finished quietly.

"Is this a true story, Dad?" I asked after a moment.

"It is, Ginny. It's not one most people know about but it is part of our history, like it or not."

Mickey's voice sounded loud compared to Dad's, "Shoonkaska," he said. "That was White Dog's name. That's who I'm named after, Shoonkaska."

That was news to me. "My Dad loves history," I said unnecessarily. Dad said good-night and left the room.

Mickey and I whispered our good-nights, but I didn't feel sleepy anymore as the scene Dad had described continued to play itself out in front of my eyes. I imagined White Dog's lover standing at the gravesite weeping guiltily. I remembered what Dad had told me about Dr. Mayo sneaking back to steal the 38 Indian corpses and use them for research. Did Mickey know about that? I hoped not. It was bad enough for me to picture the beautiful face of White Dog all sliced up in the name of medicine and I wasn't even related to him. Poor Mickey, I thought. My mind kept racing. With visions of White Dog in my head, I began to formulate a plan. It could work, I thought. Mrs. Agneau would be a part of it, and Mickey, too, of course. By the time I drifted off to sleep, my plan was nearly complete.

Chapter 17

    "Uh-oh, looks like you need to rake over here again." One of the Shortpaschers said to the amusement of the others. He walked right into the middle of the pile of leaves I had already raked up on Mrs. Agneau's lawn thereby spreading them all over the yard and making my work redundant. I momentarily felt sorry for myself for being landed with such delinquent neighbors. Then I realized that they had actually helped me by giving me a reason to prolong my task.

I had gotten into trouble at school again.

Sr. Lucian had once upon a time probably been a teacher at Incarnation but by the time I got there, her teaching days were long behind her. Her job now was to sell plastic bags to all of us kids to use to carry our books to and from school to protect them from the elements. St. Lucian stationed herself at a little desk at the entrance to the school. She watched like a hawk as we traipsed by to see if we were carrying our books in a bag or not.

"You there!" she would croak, pointing her long arthritic finger at someone to your left but if her eyes were locked onto yours then you would know she was referring to you and that her crooked finger was acting of its own accord. "Where is your book bag?" she would cackle. "Don't your parents know better than to send you off to school without a book bag? Don't they know that your books belong to the school and that you are only borrowing them?" Then she would sigh heavily. "It's your responsibility to keep them looking like new. I want to see you tomorrow with a dime to pay for a book bag, do you hear? You tell your parents that Sr. Lucian said so!" Her gnarled fingers would slap down onto her desk for emphasis making us jump.

The bags cost ten cents. Sister sat with a stack of them on top of her little desk with a metal cash box on top. Taking the dime, she would carefully maneuver the clasp on the cash box to work her fingernail underneath the lid to get it open. Then she would put the coin in the proper compartment, close the lid, and set the cashbox on the floor beside her.

Sister would then surprise you by stretching out her long, wide tongue while she moistened her index finger on it and began the lengthy struggle to remove a single plastic bag from the top of the slippery pile. This could take an implausibly excessive length of time as you listened to your friends laughing, telling stories, and having fun while you waited pointedly for your sack. Separating one plastic bag from another was undoubtedly tricky, but Sister seemed to take an inordinate amount of pleasure from accomplishing this task. She certainly never hurried the job. When you finally had your requisite book bag in hand, the smell of the new plastic was immensely gratifying, bringing with it memories of new dolls to play with on Christmas morning. Before long the shininess of the plastic bag wore off and by the end of the school year the cloudy, dingy-looking carrier was scarcely recognizable as the slick sack purchased at the beginning of the school year. To Sister, the wear and tear of the bag was a worthwhile trade sacrificed for the protection of the school's books.

After successfully avoiding Sr. Lucian the first few weeks of school, Mickey and I were caught unawares one afternoon. We were busily comparing the size of our 'thinking pills' and competing, as always, to see who was making their lozenge last the longest. The best thing about second grade was that Sr. Marjorie kept a round, exquisitely painted tin in her classroom closet full of lemon drops that she called 'thinking pills.' Whenever we had to take a quiz or complete a difficult assignment, she would go to the closet to get out the tin. She walked up and down the aisles while we sat at our desks dutifully sticking out our tongues so she could lay the drop on top. Pat said she was just a wannabe priest and this was her way of acting like she's giving out communion. I didn't care. I just knew that taking quizzes and facing difficult subjects was sweetened by Sr. Marjorie's lozenges. Mickey and I could usually make our 'pills' last for hours but sometimes I would forget. The next thing I knew, I was crunching away. Sometime later, Mickey would shoot a spitball at me to get my attention and then stick out his tongue to show me the little yellow sliver he was still savoring.

That day, Sister stopped us while we were busily comparing what was left of our 'thinking pills'. After reprimanding us and our parents for being so lackadaisical, St. Lucian bade us to come back the next day with money for a book bag. Mom gave me my dime the next morning. I was about to hand it over to Sister when Mickey admitted he didn't have one. When she asked him if he'd forgotten it, he just said no but didn't offer any explanation. I could tell by the way he held his head that Doc had refused to give him any money. Sister Lucian looked at Mickey with disdain.

"You Indians, always causing trouble with your pagan beliefs and your laws. I suppose you think the rules don't apply to you, that you don't have to use a book bag if you don't want to!" Pointing her knobby finger less than an inch from his nose, she persisted, "I want to see those books covered tomorrow or else! Give me your dime!" she turned to me suddenly and I hastily closed my fist saying I didn't have one either. I crossed my toes as best as I could in my saddle shoes to avoid the punishment I would be sure to warrant in the afterlife for lying to a nun. "Tomorrow then," she sighed excessively. Mickey and I retreated with relief.

Later, after spending some time at Mrs. Agneau's, I knocked on the Olson's door and asked to see Mickey. He was doing dishes, of course, so I helped him finish up. Then I told him to get his school books. "What for?" he asked but I told him to just get them and he'd soon find out.

The next morning when Sr. Lucian scanned the hallway waiting for our arrival, she promptly called us over. We told her we didn't need one of her plastic bags because we'd already covered our books ourselves. Looking askance at the birch bark, Sister asked scornfully, "What is this?" We had fashioned bark Mrs. Agneau had allowed me to strip from her tree into extremely durable though slightly lopsided carriers.

"Oh, just something we Indians have been doing for ages." Mickey said sincerely with nary a glimmer of a smile to give himself away. Needless to say, Sister was not amused as she meted out our punishment.

Convincing Mom that I had had to stick up for Mickey because Sister had treated him incredibly rudely wasn't easy. Mom refused to think badly of anyone who was married to God.

"Sister Lucian is old and set in her ways. It wasn't right for you and Mickey to tease her that way. You upset her. She has devoted her life to God and to educating children, and she deserves respect."

"Mickey deserves respect, too," I grumbled.

"Indeed. But he's only seven years old, and Sister is probably 87. She has earned the right to be respected, and Mickey still has to prove that he's worthy of it. Now, grab a rake and go help Mrs. Agneau with her lawn. Pray a few 'Hail Mary's' to ask for forgiveness while you're at it."

Raking up the birch leaves from Mrs. Agneau's towering white-barked tree which suffered a few balding spots due to our homemade book bags, I tried to listen in on the conversation sprinkled with laughter coming from the porch. It had taken me a week to set the plan into motion. I had conceived it on the night that Mickey stayed over and we'd heard the story of White Dog, his ancestor.

Dad was sent to the post office to buy some stamps to put on the bills he and Mom had spent the previous evening going over so I offered to go with him. Once we were in the car, it was easy to convince him to stop at O'Dhoul Drug as it had been awhile since we'd visited with Mr. Prchle. Chatting with Gerald, I persuaded him that he absolutely had to come by to see the enormous eggplants growing in our neighbor's garden. Farmer that he is, Gerald loves to check out people's gardens to see how things are growing. He happily agreed to come over.

Gerald had turned up that morning with Winston in tow. He and Mrs. Agneau had hit it off right away and the next thing I knew, Gerald was helping dig onions out of the garden. Now the two of them were sitting on the porch sharing iced tea and some of Mr. Agneau's favorite apple crisp. I was raking the lawn and trying to eavesdrop to see if my plan was actually working. I had decided that Gerald and Mrs. Agneau needed to get married so that Mrs. Agneau's son would stop pestering her to move into an Old Folks' Home in California. The first part of my plan was progressing nicely, so I thought I'd instigate the second phase. I pressed my nose into the screen door.

"I think Winston needs to go out, Mr. Prchle. He's whining."

"I am getting so hard of hearing these days," Gerald said with a shake of his head. "The worst part about that is not being able to hear the birds sing anymore. There's nothing finer in the entire world than listening to the music of our aviary friends." I saw Mrs. Agneau nodding her head vigorously. She agreed wholeheartedly with that as one of her greatest joys was watching the social goings-on at the birdfeeder she kept permanently stocked. Feeling only a little guilty for fibbing about Winston whimpering, I admonished the dog for looking startled as I let him out of the porch and took him straight over to Mickey's house.

Mickey's entire face lit up as he fell all over Winston. "Hey, boy!"

"Mickey, meet Winston. Winston, Mickey." They hadn't actually needed much introduction as they were both rolling all over each other already. Mickey was laughing uncontrollably while Winston licked excessively around his face. Later, I brought Mickey over to meet Gerald. They hit it off so well that Gerald was already inviting Mickey to come over anytime to take Winston for a walk, and I knew that the second part of my plan was a success, too.

Mickey used both hands to scratch vigorously behind the dog's ears as he crooned, "Winston tastes good like a cigarette should! Yeah, you famous dog, you. Everyone already knows all about Winston."

Gerald laughed and explained once again that Winston was named after the savior of Great Britain, not the brand of tobacco he happened to smoke. Either way, Winston the dog didn't seem to care much as he accepted all of the attention Mickey lavished on him.

Mrs. Agneau wrapped the leftover apple crisp in tinfoil and slipped it into a small brown lunch bag. Gerald bowed slightly, took the bag in one hand while with the other he brought Mrs. Agneau's spotted, veined, wrinkled hand gently to his lips. He pressed them to her hand for a long still moment with his eyes closed to better savor the experience. Mrs. Agneau's intake of breath was silenced when she clapped her free hand over her mouth in delight and surprise. Then she, too, closed her eyes so that Mickey and I could look at each other with eye brows raised conspiratorially.

"My dear lady, I thank you for the unexpected but thoroughly appreciated pleasure of your company on what has turned out to be one of the best autumn days I've had in a long time."

"The pleasure is mine," Mrs. Agneau replied but Gerald wasn't finished yet. Speaking over her, he praised her garden, her baking, and her home with such eloquence and flowery speech that Winston finally stretched out and laid his chin on his paws, unmoved by the prolonged speech. I had a feeling we'd be seeing more of Gerald and Winston in the neighborhood.

Chapter 18

"Yuck!" Neil spat the coffee grounds out into the kitchen sink as he grimaced painfully. "How can anyone drink this stuff? Coffee tastes vile!"

"Not when it's brewed properly and drunk the way it's supposed to be consumed, not chewed. Now hold still." Mom continued to pat coffee grounds onto the flour made into paste spread all over Neil's cheeks. The more she pat, the more Neil squirmed until there were practically more coffee grounds on his clothes than on his face. The coffee was meant to look like stubble on 13-year-old Neil's smooth skin.

"There!" Mom exclaimed with a hearty final pat which was a tad more forceful than necessary. "Now you look like a real hobo. Try not to touch your face or you'll ruin it. Have fun and keep a good eye on your sister!"

"But it scratches!" Neil complained as he stretched his puckered lips from one side to the other attempting to alleviate the itch.

Grabbing the empty pillowcase, he raced for the door while I hastily charged after him. Neil had promised to let me go Trick or Treating with him for Halloween this year. I had noticed in previous years that Neil had a real knack for this business of making the neighbors donate lots of candy towards our supply of cavity-inducing snacks. Not only was Neil always the last one to be in possession of the candy he collected on October 31st, but he also managed to bring home the widest variety of sweets. I couldn't do anything about prolonging the supply but I was determined to get a better assortment this year.

I tended to belong to Mrs. Agneau's "Tomorrow we may be dead" school of thought, and therefore I ate most of my Halloween candy before the sun had set on All Saints Day. Neil had more willpower than any of the rest of us. He painstakingly rationed his Halloween candy to just one piece a day. While the rest of us found our stash reduced to a few undesirable candies after less than a week, Neil had been known to make his supply last until the following year's Halloween. This year, in order to increase my selection of Halloween candy, I convinced Neil to allow me to Trick or Treat with him.

We started at Mrs. Agneau's. Being on a budget, she always gave out homemade cookies instead of store-bought candy. This was before the days of razors being hidden inside of apples so there was no danger in accepting a handful of Mr. Agneau's favorite sugar cookies. They were cut out in the shape of jack-o-lanterns and sprinkled with orange sugar.

"Have fun, dears!" she shouted after we'd thanked her and hurried on our way.

In and out of the houses we hustled collecting mini Milky Way's and Smarty's. I had only gotten my wings caught in one screen door so far and had received lots of compliments on my angel costume as well as a few extra handfuls of candy after extending my hand and solemnly bowing my head while saying "Bless you" in my best angelic voice.

Neil's costume wasn't holding up nearly as well. Mrs. Agneau's cookie crumbs had mixed with the coffee grounds on his cheeks inducing such a coughing attack that Mrs. Peterson on the corner had given him a glass of water to wash it all down. When he finished drinking, he wiped his mouth with the back of his hand and took most of the coffee grounds off of his right cheek. Most of our neighbors had to ask him what he was dressed up as for Halloween this year. The grounds on only half of his face made him look rather like a dirty little boy not unlike the way he looks on all of the other 364 days of the year. Nonetheless, we carried on up and down 41st and Pleasant, Grand, Harriet, Garfield and Lyndale Avenues. Then we went all the way down to 39th and reversed the order till we ended up on Pleasant again.

We passed clowns, ghosts, and witches wandering up and down the streets. The cool autumn evening held just enough chill in the air that we could see little puffs of breath in front of our faces. The calls of "Trick or Treat!" followed by "Thank yous!" and doors slamming filled the darkening evening.

Sometimes we had to hang around outside while one group of trick or treaters finished in the porch. We waited as they filed out before heading in. At one house, I was walking out and turned to thank the boy dressed as batman who was holding open the door. It was Tim, the cutest boy in my class. His dimples flashed as he whispered, "You look like an angel!"

"Well, duh!" I replied, feeling my cheeks flush. I walked away smiling, knowing I would remember the admiration in his eyes all the days of my life.

"Are you up for some more?" Neil asked after a while.

"Is the Pope Catholic?" I retorted as we headed east to Pillsbury, Wentworth, Blaisdell, and Nicollet Avenues on 41st Street before we made our way back home again.

My pillowcase was bulging so full of candy that I had to use one hand to hold the bottom so it wouldn't tear. Thinking how this was easily twice as much candy as I normally collected on Halloween, I was so lost in the pleasure of imagining how my candy would surely outlast everyone else's in the family besides Neil of course, that I didn't hear the footsteps running behind me until they were right upon me and I felt the push in the middle of my back.

"Hey!" I bellowed as I felt myself falling in slow motion towards the sidewalk.

 Not wanting to drop the loot from our Trick or Treating, I continued holding on to the pillowcase full of candy with both hands and subsequently landed with a double thud. The first bump was my knees hitting the sidewalk and the second my chin. With the breath knocked right out of me, I couldn't even muster up a yell when I felt the pillowcase ripped out of my hands and heard the raucous shrieks of the Shortpaschers as they ran away with my candy.

"Watch out, she's got wings!" one of them hollered.

"She just might fly after us and catch us!" Harsh laughter accompanied their hastily receding footsteps.

"Just you wait!" Neil shouted as he took off after the boys, slowed down considerably by the weight of his own bagful of Halloween treats bouncing as he ran.

Blinking rapidly to try to stop the tears from coursing down my cheeks, I struggled not to cry. "I hate you, Slim Shortpascher, I hate you, Freddie!" I shouted as the enormity of my loss hit me.

 As if cued from above, a downpour of cold, hard rain began falling from the sky at that very moment adding insult to injury. I didn't even bother trying to get up but put my head in my arms and wept.

"Oh dear, just look at you. Are you hurt? Can you move your toes? Nothing broken? Right then, up you go!" Mr. Finkelstein kept up a soothing, steady stream of chatter as he picked me up with a bit of a struggle. He carried me up the stairs and along the path taking me into his house. After explaining to him what had happened, the telling of it much delayed by my hiccupping sobs, Mr. Finkelstein comforted me.

"You'll be just fine. How about a nice, hot cup of cocoa to help make things right? I may even have some teeny-tiny marshmallows to go on top!"

We heard Neil calling for me then, so Mr. Finkelstein went to the door to let him know I was there and to invite him in, too. Neil's absolute favorite drink in the world was Nesquick Chocolate Mix. This was just about the best way for his Halloween night to end.

After he cleaned up my knees and chin, Mr. Finkelstein served us huge mugs of hot chocolate. It felt strange for me to be waited on by a man. Glancing over at Neil, he waggled his eyebrows at me and I knew he was thinking the same thing. In every home I'd ever been in, the kitchen was the domain of the woman of the house. I knew that Mr. Finkelstein lived alone but hadn't really considered that meant he had to take care of himself in the kitchen and all. Looking around the large, spacious living room, I wasn't surprised to see huge plants filling up the corners and hanging baskets in front of the windows.

"Here comes Mrs. Fussbudget to check you out, all refreshed after her 23-hour nap," Mr. Finkelstein crooned as he scratched under the outrageously fluffy cat's chin. Mrs. Fussbudget sidled up against each of our ankles and tolerated our petting her half-closed eyes when suddenly she leapt effortlessly onto the back of my chair and began swatting at my tattered and forlorn-looking wings.

"Fussbudget, no!" Mr. Finkelstein chided.

"That's okay, Mr. Finkelstein, they're no good anymore anyhow," I said as I began to feel sorry for myself again. I couldn't help giggling though at Mrs. Fussbudget's determination in swatting down my wings. I slipped to the floor laughing as the cat pounced on me and tackled one of the wings with all four legs.

"That tickles!" I squealed as I rolled back and forth on my stomach trying to dislodge the indomitable feline. Neil, remembering that we were guests in Mr. Finkelstein's home, admonished me, scolding me to sit up and act my age. Looking up at him in his tattered hobo outfit even more ragged after tussling with the Shortpaschers, his fake coffee-ground stubble spread all over his face, I was suddenly overcome by laughter and was shortly joined by Mr. Finkelstein. The harder we laughed, the sterner Neil looked which of course made him look even funnier.

"Oh dear, I haven't had this much fun since Mrs. Fussbudget got stuck up in the tree, and all of those nice firemen came to help me get her down. The first fireman got hold of her and was about to carry her down the ladder when she decided she didn't need help any longer. She leapt gracefully down by herself. The fireman hadn't realized he was allergic to cats. He suddenly puffed up so quickly that his eyes were swollen shut and he couldn't get down from the tree himself. By the time he was painstakingly coaxed down step by step and we were all congratulating him, we looked up to see Mrs. Fussbudget had managed to climb back up into the tree again and was looking down at all of us with disdain. We laughed till our sides ached, well, all of us except that allergic fireman who couldn't see a thing with his eyes swollen shut!"
Mr. Finkelstein wiped the tears underneath his glasses and as our laughter subsided, we paused as the sound of someone laughing with us from the other side of the open window reached us.

"Shortpaschers!" I hissed and I was out the door in a flash running around to the side of the house to see who was laughing at us. I stopped myself just in time from falling for the second time that night as I practically ran over Bertie Shortpascher. Mr. Finkelstein was right on my heels so we both discovered that Bertie wasn't actually laughing but was trying unsuccessfully to stifle his crying.

I had been about to sarcastically inquire if he was crying because he hadn't had enough of **MY** Halloween candy when I felt Mr. Finkelstein's hand squeeze my shoulder. I looked up to see him putting his index finger to his lips to silence me. We heard the Shortpaschers back door slam then and soon heard the sound of footsteps walking away from the house towards the alley.

Bertie held his breath and we all waited in silence as Doc walked through the alley and down the path through his own backyard. We heard the slam of his back door as he went into the house.

"Bert" Mr. Finkelstein began, "Let me help you, please!" but his words went unheeded as the little boy had already slipped away and was quietly letting himself back into his house. A bad feeling came over me then and I sensed there was something far worse going on here than stolen candy.

"Is he going to be alright, Mr. Finkelstein?"

Mr. Finkelstein's eyes looked incredibly troubled as he shook his head. "Not unless there are some changes made around here. I think I need help making those changes happen."

Mr. Finkelstein walked us home and explained how I ended up with nothing to show for my long night of trick or treating. At once, each of my siblings dumped out their bags of candy, divided them into piles and donated a percentage of their treats to me.

Later, after Mom shouted 'Ta-da' and produced with a flourish my newly repaired wings which I would likely never use again anyway, I chewed on a 'Now and Later' and thought about how very lucky I was. Looking over at Neil, his cheeks shining raw and red from scrubbing off his Halloween stubble, surrounded by hundreds of pieces of candy stacked in order of favorite to least, I lobbed a piece of Double Bubble gum at him.

"Hey, thanks for taking me."

"What are you thanking me for?" he asked as he tore into the wrapper, "You lost everything."

"Not everything." I said as I leaned back to listen to him read about Bazooka Joe from the little comic wrapped around the piece of gum.

Looking around the room at my disheveled brothers and sisters each in various stages of disarray with their Halloween costumes half off, I felt grateful for their candy. Remembering Bertie Shortpascher and his dysfunctional family, I felt grateful for my siblings and their love, too.

Chapter 19

"That's okay, Mrs. Agneau, you already paid me to shovel once tonight and you shouldn't have to pay me again. Bye now!" I shouted in a much louder tone than was necessary. I wanted to be sure the Shortpaschers heard me.

"Well, thank you dear! Don't catch a chill out there!" Mrs. Agneau advised as I retreated behind a four-foot tall snow bank and waited for Mickey to join me.

In the meantime, I formed snowballs and began lining them up and then stacking them into small, pyramid-shaped piles. I was onto my fourth pile when I heard the squeaky sound of boots on snow caused by below-zero temperatures. I peeked over the top of the bank to be sure it was Mickey.

"No fair!" he moaned as he hurled himself onto his back on the ground beside me and immediately began moving his arms and legs in a rapid up and down motion.

"Our first day of Christmas vacation and we get a ton of snow. A ton! Enough to give us a free snow day for sure and it's wasted, wasted 'cause we're already off school anyway. Aargh! Why couldn't it have snowed like this last week before I bombed the spell down?" The 'spell down' was our version of a spelling bee, and Mickey had lost on his very first word, 'oval'.

"Your angel is gonna look headless" I whispered. "And keep your voice down!"

Mickey began to rock his head back and forth in the snow enunciating "Life...is....so...un...fair!" with each turn of his head as he shaped the necessary orb onto his design. I stood at his feet and held out both of my hands. He grabbed onto them and let me pull him carefully to his feet so as not to destroy the perfect snow angel he'd created.

"Now help me make more snowballs!" I instructed.

We worked quietly while the snow continued to fall softly all around us. The rhythmic scraping of Neil and Pat's nearby shoveling was muffled by the omnipresence of the snow. The snowflakes were fat and glistening, each unique fleck sparkling as it floated down from the sky. I paused to watch my breath, little puffs of steam escaping from my lips each time I exhaled. I closed my mouth and watched the puffs shoot out from my nostrils. I began to take turns, first exhaling from my nose, then my mouth till I felt dizzy from breathing so hard to create ever larger cold air balloons.

It was a perfect winter evening. I peered over at Mickey who had tipped his head back and was catching snowflakes on his tongue. His eyes were closed and he held himself so still that for a split second I imagined he'd perished in the cold until he sighed and the cloud of his warm breath appeared in the chilly air.

I held out my black mitten and watched the snowflakes land on it. It was incredible to see each individual flake with its own exclusive design etched on to it. They were so pretty. I tried to imagine each snowflake representing a person on earth, every person as unique as every snowflake. Then I heard the sound of voices off in the distance. Of course not every person is as pretty as every snowflake, I thought.

"They're coming! Quick, get ready!" I hissed as we took up our positions.

Just as the Shortpaschers started to kick the snow back onto Mrs. Agneau's newly shoveled front walk for the second time that evening, Mickey and I began firing multitudes of snowballs at them in such rapid succession they had no time to make their own snowballs to shoot back at us. Cries of pain and indignation were soon followed by "Let's get out of here!" as Mickey and I collapsed onto the snow amidst hoots of laughter and victory calls. That would teach them to stop messing with our sidewalks. Of course, the Shortpaschers never even bothered to shovel their walk. "Why should we when it's just going to melt in the spring anyway?" they said to justify their laziness. I stopped to listen for the sound of shoveling once again and realized there was none.

"Come on, Mickey, let's get our skates on! Neil and Pat must be done shoveling the ice rink!" Before I even finished speaking we heard the crisp, clear sound of metal blades gliding across the newly shoveled ice. "Hurry up! We don't want to get stuck on the same team!"

Mom helped us lace up the old black skates, hand-me-downs from the older boys, and soon we were out the door. Holding onto the railing with both hands, we gingerly made our way down the four cement stairs onto the ice.

Each winter as soon as the weather dropped below freezing, the boys would be out with the hose flooding the backyard. What served as a basketball court the rest of the year was turned into a hockey rink over the winter.

Anyone who could get their feet into a pair of skates and their hands on a hockey stick was welcome to join in. Teams were formed nightly, mixing up the big kids with the small to make for more or less even teams. Mickey and I played at just about the same ability level so we always tried to be on opposite teams. Though he was shorter and sturdier, I was a faster skater so we took great pleasure facing off just like the professional hockey players do. Back and forth across the rink we skated, filling the heavy winter night with sounds of hockey sticks clacking, exhausted skaters grunting, and frozen pucks slapping into the net.

"He shoots, he scores!" Greg shouted lifting both arms straight up into the air to demonstrate the successful goal, right at the same time a snowball appeared from nowhere and slammed into his chest. "Ow!" he yelled.

"Take cover!" Pat barked as a volley of snowballs arched over the garage roof and landed in the yard.

"Shortpaschers!"

At that moment Mickey, took a hit to the head and cried out in pain. Neil and Pat resisted the urge to hop the fence and chase after the Shortpaschers recognizing they wouldn't get very far with their skates on. Instead they dove into the snow bank they'd created when shoveling the rink and began hurdling hastily-made snowballs back over the garage hoping some of their missiles might hit their marks sight unseen.

I knelt by Mickey, surprised that the snowball had reduced him to tears. Picking up the effective weapon, I growled in recognition and stuffed it into my pocket while I tried to comfort Mickey or at least shield him from the others so they wouldn't see that he was crying. He was doubled over, kneeling with his skates spread out on either side of his legs, shedding such huge tears they were leaving dark stains on the ice. Peering more closely, I saw that the dark stains weren't tears at all and gasped. "Mickey, you're bleeding!" I awkwardly clambered back up the stairs in my skates to holler to Mom for help.

It wasn't until much later, while sitting outside the Emergency Room of General Hospital with Mr. Finkelstein that I remembered and regretted hiding the culpable snowball in my pocket. Mom had sent me over to enlist Mr. Finkelstein's help because Dad was at work and she couldn't get hold of Doc. After Mr. Finkelstein's initial look of bewilderment when he opened his front door with Mrs. Fussbudget in his arms and stared at me standing on his front porch with my ice skates on, he quickly assessed the situation. He took over quite nicely, driving me and Mickey to the hospital, badgering the staff there to let me stay with Mickey to hold his hand while the doctor on duty put in 14 stitches to close the wound on his forehead. He even insisted Mickey get looked at all over to be sure there were no other injuries.

The doctor was a petite little man with small feet and elegant, efficient hands. He spoke in a clipped, singsong accent that I couldn't help imitating until Mr. Finkelstein whispered to me to stop it, that the doctor was Indian and that is the way they talk. When I argued that Mickey was an Indian and he didn't talk like that, he explained that the doctor was from India, a country on the other side of the world, and was not a Native American Indian.

Mr. Finkelstein and the doctor continued to chat amicably and I stopped listening to the words they were saying and instead concentrated on the lovely cadence of music their voices made. The combination of the lateness of the hour, the excitement, and all of the outdoor exercise nearly sent me off to sleep.

While we waited for Mickey's exam to be over, I showed Mr. Finkelstein my sodden pocket and explained the ice inside of the snowballs which had caused Mickey's injury.

"Ah yes, the perfect weapon, Ginny, haven't you heard? An icicle is the perfect murder weapon because it will melt and disappear, effectively erasing all incriminating evidence. An ice ball is merely a variation of the theme."

"But how could they?" I demanded. "The Shortpaschers purposely coated their snowballs in water so as to turn them into ice balls! That is so cruel! They should get into so much trouble! I wanted to show the police or somebody so that they would get sent away or something but now the proof melted in my pocket and I've got nothing!" I patted the soggy circle outlining my pocket sending droplets of water splashing to the floor and felt near tears.

"You have so much more than 'nothing', Ginny can't you see that? You have brothers who leap to your defense when you need them, a Mom you can run to for help who is always there when you need her, so many people who love you and guide you so you'll stay on the straight and narrow, and a friend who's laying on the other side of that door who thinks you're pretty special, too."

"But the Shortpaschers...." I began.

"The Shortpaschers have none of the advantages you have. You owe it to them to remember that when you're judging them for their bad behavior."

The door swung open then and Mickey stood there with his crooked grin looking really tough with his head all bandaged up.

"I'm gonna keep the bloody bandages for next year's Halloween costume!" he informed us, his puffy eyes glinting with pleasure. Mr. Finkelstein tried not to look squeamish as he took Mickey's hand and we headed for home.

We managed to fit in a dozen more hockey games that Christmas vacation without any more ice ball incidents. On Christmas Eve we had to cut the game short as Mom made us lie down and try to sleep a little before church. Soon we were waking up, getting ready, putting out the Christmas cookies and milk for Santa and the carrots for the reindeer, and walking to Incarnation for Midnight Mass.

Christmas Eve's Midnight Mass couldn't compare to Easter's when we each got to hold a lit candle for a portion of the mass. It was awesome letting the wax slowly drip down the taper onto the paper circle in place to protect our hands from the hot candle wax. Christmas Eve was better because it meant we would be getting lots more presents the next day. On Easter we only got one present each and a basket full of jelly beans with a few malted milk balls thrown in. Christmas Eve Midnight mass was shorter, too, so that was a bonus. Sitting in our usual place in the middle of the church on the right hand side, Blessed Mother's side on account of the statue, I giggled at Neil as he looked toward the back of the church.

"He's not here yet," he whispered, referring to the drunk who had stumbled into last year's midnight mass to get out of the cold and created a scene when he was refused communion wine. "Ow!" Neil exclaimed loudly while Mom stared straight ahead and continued to squeeze Neil's arm. I knew he was going to get it tonight.

We walked home at 1:30 in the morning singing "Glo-o-o-o-o-o, o-o-o-o-oh, o-o-o-o-oria, in excelsis Deo!" till Danny shushed us so we could listen for sleigh bells. We paused a moment in front of our house and looked up at the star-filled sky searching for a sign of Santa. The brisk walk had warmed us enough to enable us to enjoy the novelty of being awake and outside in the middle of the night on this magical evening on one of the shortest days of the year without being chased in by the cold.

"Is that the star the three wise men followed?" Greg asked, pointing to the brightest star in the sky?

"Most likely it is." Dad replied. "Now, whose turn is it to put baby Jesus in the manger?"

We all hollered "My turn, my turn!" at once, so great was the honor of being the one to put the little ceramic Jesus into the straw filled manger that has sat empty since the first day of Advent, an oblivious Mary and Joseph gazing fondly down into the empty cradle.

Looking through the front window at the Christmas tree all lit up, I sensed goose bumps up and down my arm. I felt myself standing outside of time for a moment and looked down upon the scene as if from above. It was as if my brain was a camera and a snapshot of my life at this moment was taken, and I knew I would treasure it always. We were so happy and joyful. I could see some of my favorite ornaments on the Scotch pine illuminated in the lights: the shiny gold balls, the doves rotating above the heat of the colored bulbs, the homemade green and red paper chains.

"Don't forget to close your eyes until you get inside!" Mom reminded us so we wouldn't ruin the next morning's surprise by looking on the porch to see what Santa had left us.

Before going to bed, we stood around and marveled at all of the wrapped presents under the tree, except for Neil, of course. Neil had an uncanny ability to guess what the presents were before they were opened and we hated when he ruined the surprise. Year after year, we tried to stump him but no matter how ridiculous or difficult, he managed to guess what the present was: a pack of batteries, a box of Red Hots, a pair of socks. Neil rightly guessed the gift before removing an ounce of wrapping paper so therefore he was banned from even looking at the presents until Christmas morning. "Goodnight, Mom, I love you!" I said as she scooted me off to bed. I was reminded of Mr. Finkelstein's words the night at the hospital and I knew that he was right, I do have so much to be thankful for. Lying in bed, I thought about the Shortpaschers and realized for the first time that they didn't have a Christmas tree in their window like all of the other houses on the block did, nor did they have any Christmas lights decorating their home. I felt a twinge of sadness for our unruly neighbors who would likely find no presents from Santa the next morning, and I reminded myself to try to be nicer to them. I drifted off to sleep at last dreaming of the sound of reindeer's hooves on the rooftop.

Christmas afternoon, I turned my back to Greg as I stuck the spoon into my 'Baby's Hungry' doll's mouth and watched her lips chew vigorously on the magic spoon.

To tell the truth, she was a little scary to me with her crazed eyes and the way she wet herself as soon as I was done feeding her, but I didn't want to seem ungrateful to Santa and I vowed to take better care of this year's doll than last. The year before, Santa had brought me a Thumbelina doll that squirmed and moved when you pulled the string protruding out of her back. I loved my little Thumbelina doll so much. I cooed and sang over her until the day Greg got hold of her and colored all over her smooth pink plastic face with blue ink and I couldn't bear to look at her anymore. Mom was so disappointed in me but I just couldn't help it, she looked so unnatural to me from then on, her serene, sleepy expression incongruent with the violently etched scratches all over her pretty skin.

Marilyn's Chatty Cathy doll was already annoying me with her 18 phrases, the boys were busy with their Matchbox cars, and Dad had gotten hold of the new Etch-a-Sketch and was carefully doodling a perfect rendition of the Harley Davidson he would be driving if he hadn't ended up marrying a Catholic who blessed him with nine children. I was glad when Polly asked me to play her new Twister game with her so I could stop feeding my insatiable doll and I ran to join in on the fun.

Just as dusk was approaching, I asked Mom if I could take Mrs. Agneau's present over to her. I had made her a hot pad holder. It had taken me forever to dig through our bags of cotton loops to find the green and orange colors to match Mrs. Agneau's kitchen and I couldn't wait for her to open it! Pushing open the back door in response to her friendly "Come on in, it's open!" my 'Merry Christmas' greeting froze in my throat when I saw Crazy Caroline sitting in front of the tree sipping eggnog as if it were the most natural thing in the world.

"Why, Ginny, how very sweet of you!" Mrs. Agneau crooned, "You brought over a present for each of us!"

I shuffled my feet as I stalled for time trying to decide what to do. Mom had sent over a box of chocolate-covered cherries for Mrs. Agneau to go with my homemade pot holder.

I knew Mrs. Agneau would open the cherries right away and share one with me if I gave her the cherries but I couldn't bear for all of my hard work on the pot holder to go to Crazy Caroline who likely didn't even have a kitchen with a pot in it! Caroline was smiling at me slyly as if she were reading my mind so I thrust the box of candy at her and gave Mrs. Agneau the other haphazardly-wrapped gift.

"Thank you, dear, it's beautiful! Look how the colors match my kitchen! Fancy that! Oh, if only Mr. Agneau were here to see this. He was always so appreciative of any baking I did for him, dear man. He would have loved to have seen me using this beautiful hot pad holder. I do miss him so. But it won't be long now," she said inexplicably.

Before I knew what was happening, Crazy Caroline was out of her chair and coming towards me with her arms outstretched ready for a 'thank-you' hug. I squealed in fright and managed to bolt before she could lay a hand on me.

"Good-bye, Merry Christmas! Mom said I had to get right home to go to bed on account of we stayed up so late for midnight mass last night so, goodnight then," I gushed lamely as I fled out the door; nearly tripping over Caroline's cart which I could have sworn wasn't there when I'd first arrived.

"Merry Christmas! Thank you!" Mrs. Agneau called while Caroline cackled merrily in the background.

On December 31, 1966, we counted down from ten and threw handfuls of torn up newspaper into the air shouting "Happy New Year!" We blew our horns and hugged and kissed all around. We didn't know it was only 8:00 until it was all over and we had stumbled exhaustedly into bed, thrilled to think Mom had actually let us stay up until midnight on New Year's Eve. Marilyn noticed her Mickey Mouse bedside clock. Mom had tricked us and changed the downstairs' clock so we could have the joy bringing in the New Year without actually having to painstakingly stay up to do so.

We had worn ourselves out by then singing and dancing to Buck Owens and the Buckaroos, the Monkees, The Beach Boys, and to a new song called *Wild Thing* by The Troggs. We'd played our annual game of Tripoli using pennies we'd saved up throughout the year. Mom was the big winner this year winning the 8, 9, and 10 on the second to the last round when it hadn't been won all night! We toasted with kool-aid the events of the preceding year with Dad commenting on the election of the first black man into the U.S. Senate and the availability of colored T.V.'s as memorable events of 1966.

"Not to mention the new warnings: "Caution: Cigarette smoking may be hazardous to your health!" on your Viceroys!" Pat read off the side of the pack of Dad's cigarettes on the table next to him.

"I know exactly how many are left in there." Dad said threateningly as Pat looked innocently on. The sound of Neil's music wafting up from the basement, Simon and Garfunkel's *Sounds of Silence* lulled me to sleep on the last day of the year.

Chapter 20

"Now just sit on the front steps and wait for the rest of us to finish getting ready, and don't move! I don't want you getting dirty before we even start!" Mom pushed me out the door and I sat down carefully on the top step so as not to soil my peach-colored skort. I turned my feet this way and that admiring the shiny, white patent leather hand-me-downs I inherited from Marilyn that morning. I had used Comet to scrub off the black marks. Though they were slightly too big on me, I just loved them. They looked so much more grown up than my previous pair with the plastic bow over the toes.

"Shhhhh! Look!" Mrs. Agneau pointed to the robin pulling a long worm painstakingly from the ground near where she was kneeling uncovering her rose bushes. "She has a nest in the birch tree. Come quietly and let's watch!"

I tiptoed off the stairs and we stealthily crept closer to the tree. Sure enough, we glimpsed Mama Robin feeding the worm to a nest full of gaping little beaks which was all we could see of her little ones. "Eeew, yuck!" I whispered as I watched the squirming worm disappear into the mouth of the baby bird.

We heard the hungry chirping complaints of her nest mates begging for more. We watched as Mama Robin flew back to the lawn and hopped in her singular fashion of quick, quick, quick, stop as she lifted her head, then hunched down again to hop forward, always on the lookout for the elusive worm. "How does she know where the worms are?" I asked, following Mrs. Agneau back to the folded blanket she knelt on to protect her knees while working in her garden.

"Some things a mother just knows. That way, we're sure to continue to propagate the species. Now, hand me that garbage bag, will you?"

I picked up the big, black bag and held it while Mrs. Agneau threw in handfuls of last autumn's leaves which had been protecting her delicate roses from the freezing winter temperatures. Then I handed the bag to Mrs. Agneau. I bent to pick up the leaves to save her from bending over too much until the screen door burst open from my house and a cacophony of my siblings' voices filled the air causing Mama Robin to take off to search for worms in more tranquil territory.

"Ginny! I told you not to get yourself all dirty!" Mom scolded as I hastily dropped the armful of leaves I was holding and looked down to see flecks of dirt all over my church clothes.

"Don't blame her, Mary; she was just helping me ready my garden for the glorious blossoms we'll soon be enjoying. Isn't that right, Ginny?" Mrs. Agneau vigorously attempted to wipe the dirt off of my blouse but spread the smudges instead making me look even worse than before. "There! She looks good as new!" she gushed and I looked at her askance to see if she could possibly be serious. A long pause followed until everyone burst out laughing, Mrs. Agneau's disloyal chuckle the loudest of all. I felt a prickle of tears burning behind my eyelids and my mouth quivered. I teetered on the edge of bursting out crying or joining in the gregarious laughter at my own unfortunate expense. Mom resolved the situation by grabbing my hand and pulling me towards the car.

"It doesn't matter, honey, we don't have time to wait for you to change and you look just fine anyhow." She pushed me into the front seat of the car to sit between her and Dad, a consolation prize of sorts for once more being the reluctantly comical center of attention in our far too rambunctious family.

We drove down First Avenue to park as near to the Basilica of St. Mary as we could. Daffodils and tulips had bloomed in force and the trees were laden with buds. The Basilica looked beautiful in the spring sunshine towering from its lookout on the western edge of downtown Minneapolis. We joined in the throng of Catholics milling about in front of the Basilica looking for familiar faces from their prospective parishes.

"Look, there's the Leefy's! And Father Mertz is with them, too." Mom ushered us over to the crowd lining up behind Incarnation's banner.

"What happened to you?" Kenny sneered as he stared at my filthy frock after I'd wandered over to join the Olsons, but Mickey took my hand, eliminating my need to answer. He led me over to the curb where a girl was sitting next to a big cardboard box

"Wait'll you see these little guys!" Mickey said excitedly. "Can we hold one, please?"

"Sure, just be careful not to let him go," said the freckle-faced girl with the most extraordinary orange-colored hair springing from the top of her head.

Mickey reached into the box and pulled out a ball of soft, black fur and held it aloft. "Hello there! Aren't you just the sweetest little puppy ever? Oh yes, you are!" Mickey cooed while nuzzling noses with the squirming little lab.

"I'm selling them for $10 but today I'll actually give you one for free. I'm just trying to find good homes for them." The girl picked up a smaller puppy and held it out for me to hold.

"He's adorable," I murmured, holding him close.

"My Dad says he'll put 'em in a gunny sack and throw 'em into Lake Nokomis if I don't get rid of 'em today. I'm sure he wouldn't really do that, well, I'm almost sure. That's why I'm here, anyway," she finished lamely.

Mickey's puppy was licking his face causing him to giggle uncontrollably while mine trembled in my hands nervously.

"Hey, it's alright, little guy, don't be scared," I crooned, cuddling the tiny dog into a hug. The heat of the warm little body against my chest was soothing until I felt the warmth spreading downward growing larger than the puppy. "No! Oh, no!" I thrust the poor, quivering canine back at its owner and looked down in horror at the yellow stain on my peach blouse. Really, could this day possibly get any worse?

"Come on, Ginny, the procession is starting!" Mom called, and I crossed my arms over my chest and walked over to her side just as Monsignor began reciting the rosary.

We always marched in the May Day Parade through the streets of downtown Minneapolis. Held on the first Sunday in May, chances were good that it might be raining. This particular May Day the blue sky was clear but for a few puffs of brilliant white clouds that weren't in the least likely to threaten us with precipitation. Of course, I would have welcomed the chance to get wet today to try to camouflage my stained exterior but no such luck.

Down Hennepin Avenue and up LaSalle, we prayed the rosary to Blessed Mother with hundreds of other Catholics. I tried to think holy thoughts, but I was too miserable in my pee-stained outfit. I trudged along the sidewalks feeling sorry for myself.

"Be right back," Mickey hissed unexpectedly in my ear and he sprinted off ahead of me into the crowd.

Watching him run off, I berated myself that he probably couldn't stand the smell of me and my urine soaked shirt, when I saw Mickey turn unexpectedly into a doorway and disappear. Looking up, I saw the building he'd entered was a derelict old hotel where drunks and the homeless could stay for cheap. Puzzled, I slowed down my steps till I was barely shuffling along and waited for Mickey to come out of the building. Seconds later he burst out of the door, looked up and down the street till he saw me waving at him, then ran up holding a white tee shirt, well-worn but clean
.

"Take it. I thought you might want to put this on." He smiled and immediately joined in, "Pray for us sinners, now and at the hour of our death, Amen," while I gratefully slipped the garment over my head and pushed my arms through the holes, happy to hide the morning's debris beneath Mickey's unexpected gift. We caught up with the Incarnation crowd again. I proudly and sincerely recited Mary's prayer with gusto. The matching outfits Mom had made for us three girls, Polly's in blue, Marilyn's in purple, while mine was now peach and white, didn't match exactly anymore but that was alright with me. When I caught Mickey's eye, he winked.

That night, when I was putting on my pajamas and getting ready for bed, I stopped myself just before throwing my clothes down the laundry chute. I set aside Mickey's tee shirt to remember to give it back to him in the morning. When Mom came in to tuck me in, she picked it up and frowned, "Where did you get this filthy ol' thing?" I snatched it back out of her hands.

"It's a lot cleaner than my shirt!" I defended Mickey's property. "I don't know whose it is. Mickey ran into some building down by the Basilica and grabbed it for me to wear 'cause I had dog's pee all over me!" The indignity of the memory caused me to grimace all over again.

Mom looked thoughtful as she held the worn shirt against her chest. "Could she really be that close and never come to see him at all?" she reflected out loud.

"Who?" I demanded, "Who are you talking about?"

Despite my repeated questions, Mom refused to tell me who she was talking about, kissed my forehead, and turned out the light. I lay there thinking. She was talking about Mickey and someone not coming to visit him. Who is 'she?' My mind wandered. Listening to Marilyn and Polly's quiet voices discussing who looked cute at the parade and who didn't, I finally drifted off to sleep.

The rest of May flew by and soon it was time for the dreaded piano torture-cital. "I'm so looking forward to attending your piano recital this year!" Mrs. Agneau called out from her porch window as I was on my way to school in the morning. I'd been taking piano lessons with St. Carolita since the beginning of first grade. My sisters and I all started piano in the first grade. It was yet another unfair disadvantage of being female in our family. While we were required to sit for a half hour each day practicing our piano lessons, our brothers were outside playing hotbox or some other carefree activity.

Sister Carolita gave lessons in the convent. Every Thursday when school let out, all the kids burst through the school doors free at last to fill their remaining daylight hours in play. I watched them go and crossed the street to enter the convent. Home to a couple dozen nuns, the convent was a beautiful building as silent as a morgue. The first time I had gone there and rung the bell, and rung the bell again. I heard footsteps approaching as from a mile-long tunnel. It took forever for the sound to grow louder and louder, allowing my imagination ample time to get the best of me. By the time the heavy door creaked open, I was ready to turn tail and run as far away from the nuns as possible. As a regular piano student now, I was allowed to simply slip through the heavy front door and enter the first room on the right, sit at the beautiful grand piano and wait for Sister to arrive.

Sister Carolita wore tiny black slippers on her feet which allowed her to glide silently into the room and take her place next to me on the piano bench with only the soft rustle of her silk garment to disturb the quiet of the convent.

She wore the old-fashioned nuns' habit that covered her from head to toe showing no more than the front two-thirds of her face and hiding the rest of her for only Jesus to behold. Her forehead and the top of her head were covered in a severe black veil. The rest of her, including right up to her chin and covering both ears, was cloaked in silky, white satin.

The sleeves over her arms were so long and generous that when she walked, she tucked both hands inside the sleeves like a muff. She used the sleeves as storage. I never knew what she was going to pull out of there. She would sneeze, reach in, and come out with a Kleenex. If I played a wrong note, she would whip out a ruler and rap my knuckles with it. She always had a pencil in there to write a G. (for Good) in the bottom corner of a sheet of music I had finished, adding a V. (for Very) if I polished it up and very infrequently erasing that to write Excellent (all spelled out!) if her high expectations were met. Finally, she would pull out of her sleeve a sheet of gold and silver star-foiled stickers to stick on next to the piece's title when she thought there was no more improvement on the horizon or when she simply tired of hearing us play the same piece over and over again. (Silver stars meaning less than gold ones). I was often tempted to grab hold of one of sister's sleeves and shake it upside down to see what else she had hidden in there, but I was even more curious about what was underneath her veil.

With only the very front of her face showing, I had no clue what the top of her head looked like. Was she bald? Grey? Or, as I suspected, did she have long, golden locks falling below her waistline when she at last slipped out of her religious armor when night fell?

As Sister concentrated on Londerry Air, I found myself focusing on her eyebrows and trying to suss out her hair color that way. Week after week, I feigned interest in the piano keys while serendipitously looking askance to see if a wisp of Sister's hair may have escaped her skull cap. I was so focused on her hair that I wasn't snapping my hands up to play the staccato notes to Sister's specification, so out came the ruler from the recesses of Sister's sleeve and once again my knuckles were rapped.

"Place your hand on top of mine, come on, do! Like this!" Sister grabbed my hand and placed it on top of hers. I tried not to cringe as I rested my small hand on top of her cold, wrinkled one. I didn't want to press down too hard on the pronounced veins of her spotted hand. Slap, slap, Sister demonstrated the abruptness of the ideal staccato with my hand on top of hers smarting with pain. She certainly seemed to enjoy the exercise more than I did.

Although the Olsons didn't own a piano, Sister had agreed to give Mickey lessons after lots of encouragement from Mom. She allowed him to practice in the room adjoining the one where she gave lessons. Sister taught us lessons on a beautiful mahogany grand piano, but the practice room had only a small upright one.

This year, Mickey and I were playing a duet for the recital, so we were allowed to practice together in the practice room. This was working out extremely well for us. Whenever there was something going on at school that we wanted to avoid, we would tell the teacher that we had to go practice for the recital. One morning, we learned that we would be working on 'Pull-ups' in gym class so we excused ourselves and headed over to the convent to practice. The convent was quiet as usual when we let ourselves in the front door. We walked through Sister Carolita's vacant room to enter the practice room through its elegant double French doors. I carefully closed the doors. We practiced our duet, *The Blue Tango*, a few times, banging out the ending as we picked up speed towards the end, anxious to finish the piece as always.

While Mickey practiced his solo piece, I took out the rubber superball from my pocket and tossed it up in the air, counting to see how many times I could catch it in a row. When I dropped it, I had to start all over again. I was up to number 74 when we swapped places. Mickey threw the ball up so vigorously that he hit the ceiling with it and the ball bounced onto the piano bench and back off the ceiling before he could catch it again. We giggled and Mickey tossed the ball extra high and even harder this time and we laughed as the ball ricocheted around the room.

I tried to continue practicing while Mickey threw the ball as hard as he could and it continued to ricochet around the room hitting the ceiling, floor, walls and everything in between. I mostly just laughed and tried to avoid being hit by the errant weapon.

After one particularly powerful throw, the French doors opened with a flourish. Sister Carolita stood there with her hands on her hips and a look of astonishment on her face. She watched the little ball continue its reverberation around the room, Mickey looking ridiculous as he flailed his arms around unsuccessfully attempting to stop it. After what seemed like forever, the thumping of the little ball slowed down and Sister remembered to close her mouth. She said not a word but rather turned on her heel and quietly closed the door behind her. Mickey joined me on the bench and we began to play through *Blue Tango* again forcing ourselves to not even glance at one another lest our suppressed giggles turn into uncontrollable gales of laughter.

Naturally, it was a perfect early-summer evening when Mom called me in to get ready for the torture-cital. Already the bottoms of my feet were tough as leather. As soon as the chill of winter left the sidewalks, we stopped bothering to wear shoes except to church and school. I hastily pulled white cotton anklets over my filthy feet, remembering last year when Sister sent me home during the recital to fetch my shoes, and I put on Marilyn's hand-me-downs.

Sitting next to Mickey in the school auditorium, I kicked my legs nervously back and forth as I waited for our turn to play. Mickey kept peering behind us every time we heard the squeaky door open.

"Your mom and dad are here," He whispered loudly. I turned around to see Mom and Dad waving at me proudly as they took their seats. Finally, it was our turn.

We both stood up and walked to the center of the stage. I announced "The Blue Tango" in a slightly shaky voice while Mickey followed with "by Leroy Anderson." We awkwardly bowed simultaneously and took our seats at the piano.

Taking a moment to sit with our hands in our laps as sister had instructed us to do, our concentration was broken by a burst of commotion as the doors flew open at the back of the auditorium. I heard Mr. Finkelstein's voice jubilantly announce that they were just in time. It sounded like he'd arrived with a herd of elephants but neither Mickey nor I dared to look. Instead, we waited till the bustling settled down.

Placing our hands over the keys, I nodded and we began to play. Though we got off a little bit in the middle of the piece, I slowed down while Mickey hurriedly caught up. We managed to rally together and finish with our usual flourish exactly in sync. We loved playing the ending and had practiced that bit more than any other part of the piece. We dramatically threw our hands up in the air after banging out the final crescendo note and the applause was instantaneous and satisfyingly loud in the large auditorium. With big grins on our faces, we once again bowed together. I was pleased to see Mrs. Agneau, Gerald, and most astonishingly Caroline sitting with my parents and all clapping loudly. Mom threw me a kiss while Dad snapped a picture with the Kodak camera. Mr. Finkelstein held fingers from one hand to his lips and belted out a shrill whistle while with the other hand he waved vigorously over his head. If Mickey was concerned about Doctor and Mrs. Olson not being there, he didn't let it show.

We held hands and bowed again and again until Sister Carolita stood up and we hastily returned to our seats. I was so relieved to be done, I don't think I heard a single other piece that was performed.

Chapter 21

With the piano torture-cital behind me, I was able to concentrate on the two best things about the month of May: the last days of school and my birthday! Last year's birthday party had gotten rained out, so this year Mom was making up for it by taking me to Farrell's Ice Cream Parlor. I invited Sandy, Tessa, Lexie and Mickey to come along. At the last minute, I decided to see if Mr. Finkelstein wanted to come, too. "Why not," Mom had answered, so I raced across the lawn to Mr. Finkelstein's and stopped short when I saw Bertie Shortpascher sitting on the front stoop with Mr. Finkelstein.

"Mr. Finkelstein, Mom says you can come with us to Farrell's for my birthday! Please, please can you come?" I'd barely gotten the question out of my mouth when Bertie was shoving his snot-nose into our business and asking if he could he come, too. "Um, there's probably not room in the car, sorry," I hastily replied, thinking the last person I wanted to help me celebrate my birthday was Bertie Shortpascher.

"Oh, don't worry about that," Mr. Finkelstein said while pushing his glasses further up his nose. "I'll drive, too, and that way we can fit in Mrs. Agneau, as well. She hasn't been to Farrell's yet and you know how much she likes her ice cream!!"

I squirmed awkwardly for a bit, bending to pet Mrs. Fussbudget to stall for time. When I couldn't come up with a polite way of saying no way do I want Bertie at my party, I mumbled something noncommittal and hurried off back home.

Mom was no help at all hinting that she had a mind to cancel the whole outing if she was made to believe her youngest daughter could really be so heartless as to want to un-invite our poor disadvantaged neighbor to her birthday party. I was feeling mighty disadvantaged myself until we arrived at Farrell's. I was greeted at the door with the red & white striped waitress shouting, "Give her a pickle!"

Instead of the pickle, we ordered the Piggy Trough, an enormous vessel loaded with ice cream, toppings, and whipped cream which we all dug into with our spoons and devoured together. I had been dreaming about the Piggy Trough for months. I couldn't believe I was actually really here.

"Thank you, Mr. Farrell!" Bertie said, gesticulating with his spoon and sending smatterings of ice cream drops across the table while the rest of us looked on with amusement. "He must be the luckiest man in the world to have so much ice cream any time he wants it!"

"Lucky? I would never refer to Bob Farrell as lucky." Mr. Finkelstein began with a clearing of his throat which indicated a lecture coming on. I didn't mind this time as it was rather nice listening to him talk while we feasted at the trough.

Looking around the table at my parents, siblings, friends, Mrs. Agneau and Mr. Finkelstein, I felt a knot well up in my throat almost blocking my intake of ice cream. I felt so grateful to have them all here to help me celebrate my special day.

Mr. Finkelstein carried on, "Bob Farrell, the founder of Farrell's Ice Cream Parlor, was born in the late 1920's. When he was only 4 years old, his Dad committed suicide. His Mom was too broke to care for Bob and his sister so she put them in an orphanage."

"What's thuicide?" Bertie squeaked, his tongue too frozen to get the 's' just right.

"That's just when someone takes charge of his or her own destination," Mrs. Agneau said with a smile to Bertie and a simultaneous frown at Mr. Finkelstein for mentioning such an unpleasant topic in front of children. Bertie seemed satisfied as he continued licking his spoon this way and that. Mr. Finkelstein carried on with his story.

"Three years later, in 1934, when Bob's mom remarried, she went to the orphanage to retrieve her son and daughter and to bring them home to live with her and her new husband. They all got along really well and Bob grew up to be a success. 30 years later, he opened his first ice cream parlor. Now I think he has expanded to about six parlors!" Mr. Finkelstein dipped his spoon into the trough for some hot fudge.

"I thought to be in an orphanage meant you were born without parents," I wondered.

"Moron!" Neil slapped me on top of my head. "Everyone's got parents, else how could you come to be born?" I blushed miserably remembering the girls' explanation of the 'f' word.

"Unfortunately," Mr. Finkelstein went on, "plenty of orphans have parents but these parents simply aren't able to care for their kids due to economics, health, what have you."

Mickey dropped his spoon with a clatter and the ice cream fell from it right on to my sneaker.

"Hey!" I laughed before noticing that Mickey's face was beet red as he was clumsily trying to wipe the ice cream off of my shoe. "Don't worry about it, Mick," I began, when I was interrupted by the entire Farrell's wait staff singing happy birthday to me. The rest of the group joined the waiters singing to me with Mr. Finkelstein singing the loudest, of course. I was happy and embarrassed at the same time while I closed my eyes, made a wish, and blew out all eight candles.

After the song, Mr. Finkelstein tried to resurrect the conversation by continuing about how Bob Farrell being placed in an orphanage at the height of the depression was not at all uncommon. Kids were placed in orphanages until their parent found a job or remarried. No one was really listening anymore. Those facts, or the fact that Farrell's would go on to open 55 more stores in the next decade paled in comparison to a Lollapalooza at the table. Bertie was asking if he could bring some leftover ice cream home while Dad was explaining it would melt before we got there.

"Come on, birthday girl, we'd better get you home so you can open your presents!" Mom said while wiping the ice cream out of the corner of my mouth with a napkin she wet with her tongue first. Bertie was watching us with the entire lower half of his face smeared with a combination of chocolate, strawberry, and butterscotch. Mom took one look at him, and setting the napkin aside, she grabbed Bertie's hand to lead him to the restroom to clean him up.

Soon the last day of second grade was upon us. Sister Marjorie passed out the last of her thinking pills. This time she bent down to each one of us and smothered us with a lengthy hug before letting us take our last pill out of the round tin.

"Good-bye dear, good luck in the third grade!" She repeated over and over again. When it was my turn to give Sister a hug, I stood up so she wouldn't have to bend so far. I unwittingly stepped on the back of her veil causing her wimple to tip backwards exposing a voluminous cascade of soft, red, waist-length hair striped with grey.

The soon-to-be third graders all gasped as one as Sister dropped the tin onto my desk and frantically tried to readjust her headpiece while shoving handfuls of her unruly hair back underneath her cap. The silence was broken by unrestrained laughter, but Sister was anything but amused.

"Class dismissed!" she crowed even though we still had seven minutes left until the bell was to sound.

"I'm so sorry, Sister," I repeated over and over again while trying to help her push some wayward pieces of hair back where they belonged, mysteriously hidden under the severe nun's habit.

"I'm sure you are dear," Sister Marjorie admonished. "Just run along now and have a good summer." She practically pushed me out the door trying to get rid of me. It wasn't till I was halfway down the stairs that I realized I hadn't received my last 'thinking pill'. As I stood there trying to decide if I dare go tell Sister I still needed a thinking pill, I thought better of it and decided I wasn't planning to do much thinking in the summertime anyway. At the playground, the rest of the second graders congratulated me on revealing Sister's hair.

"That was so cool!"

"I can't believe you did that!"

"Wow, red hair, I never would have guessed it!"

"Weren't you scared you'd get into trouble?"

The comments went on and on. I tried to defend myself by saying it was an accident, but no one was listening to me. Off to my left, I saw Wayne Schmitt lingering by the fence and I used his presence to make my escape. I started to run and he chased after me. He never did catch me but I don't think he was trying very hard to do so.

"See you, Wayne, have a good summer."

"Yeah, see ya. Thanks for showing us Sister's hair." Protesting that I hadn't intended to do any such thing, I was left to run the rest of the way home hoping Mom wouldn't find out about what I'd done.

As soon as I got home, I went out to play on the porch with my favorite birthday present this year, Lite Brite. I had been saving it until school was out to start my first project. Mickey came over to help me and we spent a long time pouring over the black sheets covered with little 'x' designs to decide what our first picture was going to be. I wanted a flower but Mickey wasn't interested in that so we finally decided on a lighthouse on a cliff. We took turns finding the right color light and poking it into the designated hole. For a long time we didn't say anything as we concentrated, but as I was thinking about my fun birthday outing, I got to thinking about Bob Farrell.

"Can you imagine being dropped off at an orphanage like that even though your Ma was still alive? What kind of a Mom could do that, really? I mean, I don't care how poor she was or sick or whatever. Course her kids are gonna be better off with their own Mom! To have to live in an orphanage as if you didn't have parents. Even worse, I suspect, to know you have a Mom who has just dropped you off like a piece of old clothing she outgrew."
Mickey was quiet for a while before he finally answered. "Can you imagine what it felt like for those kids when their Ma did come back for them though? They must have been so happy to see her come through that door! Maybe they thought they would never see her again. Maybe they'd given up hope that she'd ever really come back for them. But she did come back. She said that she would and she did. And, anyway, she only left them for four years."

"Only four years, are you nuts? Four years is forever, especially when you're a kid!" I was practically shouting at him.

"But still, after the four years, then they get to have their mom back for the rest of their lives. So you see, that would be okay then." I couldn't believe Mickey was sticking up for the Mom like this but I didn't want to keep arguing with him.

"Some Mom," I muttered under my breath, unable not to have the last word on the subject.

"But 'their' Mom, Ginny, don't you see? She's their Mom. And she came back for them. Their Mom came back. What could be better than that?"

Our Lighthouse was very nearly finished when we heard the sound of sirens screaming through the neighborhood.

"That sounds close," Mickey murmured, but we didn't think anymore of it until Mom came rushing onto the porch with a frantic look on her face. She thrust Chris into my arms.

"Polly's been hit by a car! Marilyn's taking care of the boys but you need to watch Chris for me."

"What?! Are you going to the morgue? Can we come too?"

"We're going to General Hospital. Get in the car and be quick about it! Oh, my poor Polly!"

We took advantage of Mom's distraught state and Mickey climbed into the car right behind me. Mom never even noticed he was there. We slid Chris in between us and took turns practically lying on top of him with each turn the car made. His giggles grew louder and louder until we finally arrived at the hospital. We ran in behind Mom. Polly was being examined behind a curtained area. Mom rushed back there despite the receptionist's attempts to stop her. Mickey and I found some chairs to sit on while we waited to see what would happen next. We were relieved when we heard Polly's excited chatter from behind the curtain.

"Guess she's alright then," Mickey reassured me.

"Yeah, that's good news."

Chris was getting squirmy so I began to do Sheeda Buhta with him on my knees. This was a Czech game that Mom always played with babies. I didn't know the exact Czech words but I knew the sounds of all of them more or less. Chris loved it so I kept entertaining him this way. "Sheeda Buhta, doda Buhta yak se mas. Iffen udden doodoo, then udden wheeeeeeee!" I tipped Chris backwards from my knees practically touching the top of his head to the floor while his little fists held on tightly to my thumbs.

"More!" he commanded and I obliged him over and over again.

"OW!" I yelped as Mickey dug his elbow deep into my ribs. He raised his eyebrows at me and gestured with them into the direction I was meant to look. It was the Shortpaschers, looking as disheveled as ever and making a raucous noise as they barreled through the lobby.

"Let's see what they're up to!" I hissed as I hoisted Chris onto my right hip and we followed stealthily behind our neighbors. We waited behind the pillar when they asked the receptionist which floor the nursery was on. We took a separate elevator from them up to the fourth floor. From there, it was easy to follow the sound of their belligerent voices to a corner room. We stood outside in the hallway and eavesdropped on them as they talked to their Ma. They complained to her about all of the mischief each was getting into while she was away.

"So where is she then?" one of the boys finally asked. Mrs. Shortpascher's sleepy voice answered.

"In the nursery. You can peek in on her on your way out."

Mickey and I slipped away then and followed the signs to the nursery. There were about ten babies in the nursery each with a pink or a blue cap on its head. Most of the babies were sleeping peacefully, but there were a couple who were kicking around a bit. One was screaming its head off, it's little face as red as a fire hydrant.

The big-haired nurse meant to be minding the newborns paid him absolutely no mind at all and the poor tyke was getting madder and madder by the second.

"Can you tell which one's a Shortpascher?" I asked Mickey.

"Beats me" Mickey responded vaguely. I saw that he wasn't looking at the nursery at all but rather was focused on a window facing a room across the hall. Chris was banging his little fists against the glass window of the nursery at this point, so I lifted him away.

"Come on, let's see what's over here, shall we?" We walked over and saw the saddest little sight I'd ever seen. There was the tiniest baby about the size of my marred Thumbelina doll lying on top of a trolley with plastic walls. There was a paper Dixie cup taped upside down on its head with tubes coming from it. The baby was tied down real tight to a little board.

"Baby, owee!" Chris tried to slap his hands against the glass but I managed to pull him away just in time.

"That poor baby is no bigger than a pound of butter." I said to Mickey. "Oh dear, look at that one." I pointed to the left of the Dixie cup baby where there was a yellowish baby lying with a huge light hanging above him. Behind him, there was another brown baby making little jerky movements while it slept fitfully.

"What the heck's the matter with all these babies?"

Mickey didn't seem to be hear me. He was leaning his forehead against the glass staring sadly at the baby on the trolley. The door to the nursery for sick babies opened. A nurse walked in with a girl with two long pigtails hanging down on either side of her head. We couldn't hear what they were saying behind the glass but the girl was talking to the baby with the Dixie cup. She poked her hand into a little cut-out circle in the plastic side of the trolley. Using two of her fingers, she stroked the arm of the Dixie-cup baby, her mouth moving all the while as she talked to the baby.

"What about the jerking baby? Why don't they do something for him? Maybe he's got the hiccups and all's he needs is a sip of water."

"Actually," Mickey spoke up at last, "that jerking means the baby is born with a drinking problem."

"What?"

"That baby's mom is a drunk. She wouldn't stop drinking even when she knew she was pregnant. Now the baby is born, and it won't stop jerking till all of the alcohol is out of its system." Mickey spoke in a monotone voice.

"How do you know that?"

"There were some babies born on the reservation like that," Mickey said without looking at me. Mickey's life on the reservation was sounding worse and worse.

"That's terrible," I began. Just then I noticed Doc Olson coming out of the main nursery with a pink-capped baby in his arms. "Hey, Doc!" I shouted.

Doc practically dropped the baby he was so startled to see us.

"What are you two doing here?" He sounded annoyed. We started to explain about Polly when the big-haired nurse came out to tell Doc that he should take the Shortpaschers baby to its Mama right away as she needed to nurse.

"Oh, so you know about Mrs. Shortpascher having her baby then?" I asked.

"Know about it?" Big-haired nurse parroted. "He's the one that delivered this here little angel. And has been checking in on her so sweetly as if she was his own precious little one, he's taking that good care of her."

"Right, see you at home then," Doc said over his shoulder as he hurried down the hall with baby Shortpascher jiggling in his arms.

"Darn, I didn't even get a good look at the baby, did you?" I asked Mickey as we watched Doc hustle away.

"No, and I don't care if I ever do," Mickey said so vehemently I looked at him hard. "Doc doesn't deliver babies anymore," Mickey said softly. "At least, not just anybody's babies."

I couldn't think of anything to say to that. Chris was getting heavy so we found the elevators and headed back to the Emergency Room to check on Polly.

Mom was about to raise Cain as she asked us where in the world we had been when the small doctor attending to Polly recognized Mickey from the snowball incident. The doctor inquired about his health and the state of his scar. We chatted with him while Mom went to get the car.

The doctor from India gave Polly final instructions before telling us to be sure to say hello to Mr. Finkelstein for him. Polly chattered from the front seat all the way home, reliving the trip to the mailbox, the screech of the car, the ride in the ambulance, and the nice doctor. When Polly paused to take a breath, we noticed Mom was sobbing over the steering wheel.

"Mom, what's wrong? Why are you crying?"

Mom reached over to clasp Polly's hand saying, "I'm sorry. I'm so sorry I sent you out the door at just a few minutes before five. I'm sorry I told you to be sure to get to the mailbox by five to mail my letter. It was just a stupid phone bill! I almost got you killed!" She started crying even harder. The tears rolled down Mom's cheeks and her mouth was scrunched into a tiny slit as she tried to stifle her sobs.

"Don't worry about it, Mom," Polly patted Mom's hand as she tried to soothe her, "I didn't get killed; I hardly even got hurt. And it was loads of fun riding in the ambulance and everything!"

Mom's sniffles eventually subsided, but before she put the car back into gear she leaned over and gave Polly a big hug. "We will say a special rosary tonight to thank God that you're alright," Mom said while I rolled my eyes. "There is nothing worse in the entire world than for a mother to see her child hurt or lost. Oh Polly, I'm so glad you're alright."

Polly's eyes filled with tears as she hugged Mom back. I was surprised to find I had to brush away a tear myself. Mickey reached across Chris and held my hand. Leaning his head against the window, he didn't say another word all the way home.

Chapter 22

Two-Shoes, curled up in a ball, centered herself perfectly in the afternoon sun pouring into the west-facing window. "How long has that cat been there?" Marilyn inquired. "Hey," she kicked my foot with hers, "did you happen to notice when Two-shoes lay down there?"

I put my finger on the spot in my book where I was reading and sighed heavily, "No, I didn't."

"It's driving me mad! I never see the cat move but every time I turn around, she's laying right beside us. And look at her!" she nudged the catatonic creature with her toe. "She always acts like she's completely knocked out and has been asleep for hours. I know she must have just gotten there because I've been trying to keep an eye out for her." By not responding, I hoped this would end the conversation. I went back to reading my book. A few pages later, I felt my foot being kicked again.

"Hey," Marilyn said again. "You're not really reading are you? I keep hearing you turn pages like three times faster than I'm turning my pages. Are you pretending to read? Are you just skimming?"

I painstakingly poke my finger in my book to save my spot and look up at Marilyn. This isn't a new conversation for us. Marilyn can't stand the fact that I'm a faster reader than she is despite her being two years my senior.

"No, Marilyn, I'm not just skimming, I'm really reading. Do you want me to tell you everything that just happened? Nancy just discovered that her neighbor isn't really blind and she crawled under the fence to see what else she could find out."

Marilyn squinted her eyes and scowled at me. "Well, you'd better hurry up and finish then. The bookmobile will be here in less than an hour."

Exactly, this is why I was in such a hurry to finish my latest Nancy Drew book, so I could return it to the bookmobile for a new one. I wasn't planning on getting another Nancy Drew book though. She wasn't my favorite mystery girl series. I only read a Nancy Drew from time to time so I could chime in when everyone else was talking about her books. I found Nancy a bit too predictable. My all time favorite mystery books were the Trixie Beldon series. Feisty, hard-working Trixie with her beautiful, rich friend Honey and her adorable redheaded heart-throb Jim were always finding themselves in the middle of delightfully difficult scenarios that Trixie always managed to get them out of safely. I liked to pretend that I was Trixie and that Lexie was Honey and sometimes that Mickey was Jim even though he had the wrong hair color. I was just turning the last page when Polly came out on the porch shaking a beautifully etched tin given to her by Mr. Keogh.

"Who wants candy?" she asked. Polly pried the lid off of the tin and thrust it out to Marilyn.

"Why, what do you want?" Marilyn asked suspiciously.

"Don't be that way," Polly sniffed. "I've given you lots of pieces of candy and I didn't always want something from you in return."

"Right," Marilyn drawled sarcastically as she poured over the diminishing selection of sweets.

Mr. Keogh was the man driving the Chevrolet that hit Polly when she was walking to the mailbox. The day after the accident, he had come over to our house with a check for Polly for $100 and a tin of candy that meant far more to Polly than the check did. All summer long, she'd been savoring her treats and doling them out for favors.

"I don't have time to go to the Bookmobile today. Can you take my books back for me and see if you can check out a book called," she pulled a little piece of paper out of her pocket and read, "*The Valley of the Dolls* by Jacqueline Susann."

"I'll do it!" I hollered reaching for the tin full of candy.

"Too late, Marilyn already took a piece of candy for it."

"But what if she loses the piece of paper or forgets what book it is? I already have it memorized!" I showed off by repeating back the title and the author while Marilyn sucked noisily on her candy. Polly gave a noncommittal wave of her hand and sent us on our way.

The Bookmobile was a library on wheels. It was a big bus full of books taken from the Public Library and driven around to neighborhoods so people had the chance to borrow the books even if they didn't have access to a car. Our bookmobile came to 40th and Lyndale just a few blocks from home every Monday afternoon from 3-6. I always used my plastic 'book bag' from Sr. Lucia to transport my books back and forth. I always took out six books.

We loved to get there early and be standing on the corner before the bookmobile arrived. I enjoyed standing there thinking, huh, this is just an ordinary corner with not much going on. Then suddenly, this large, lumbering vehicle would come ambling down the road and that ordinary street corner would be transformed as if by magic into a castle of books. Each of us would stand there expectantly hoping that we were right at the spot where the bus would stop, and we'd jostle each other this way and that to be the first one on.

With a wheezing sound the doors would open. I would step cautiously up the three stairs until I had arrived in the hushed silence of floor to ceiling books about everything from history to gardening to cooking to mysteries to picture books. I wished I could check out every single book on that bus but I realized early on that they kept changing titles and that I would never be able to finish them all. The librarian was kind but stern. She often whispered, "Excellent choice" or "This looks like a good one!" as she checked out my books so as not to disturb the reverence demanded of such a sacred place.

I was checking out *The Wind in the Willows, Trixie Beldon and the Gatehouse Mystery, Five Little Peppers and how they Grew, Ginger Pye,* and *The Cry of the Crow.* I also added a Dr. Seuss book for the boys that we didn't have at home, *I Wish that I had Duck Feet.* I was just about finished being checked out when I remembered Polly's book.

"Oh, do you have the *Valley of the Dolls?* The librarian paused mid-stamp and looked at me incredulously, her right hand held high above the library book. "It's by Jacqueline Susann?" I supplied helpfully in case the librarian was unfamiliar with the title.

She had recovered herself sufficiently by this point and said pointedly, "No, you may not. Not only are you far too young to be requesting such a title, but I know your mother and I know she would not allow such a book into her home. *Valley of the Dolls* indeed! What will she think when I tell her what sort of book you tried to check out?"

"Er, actually, it wasn't for me....."I finished lamely while Marilyn pushed me aside with a knowing look.

"Here you go, ma'am" she said in a superior tone as she handed the librarian her respectable stack of age-appropriate books.

I was so mad at Marilyn for tricking me into getting into trouble over the stupid *Valley of the Dolls* book that I refused to walk home with her. I shuffled my feet so slowly she finally stopped calling back to me over her shoulder to hurry up.

I strolled leisurely down 40th Street stopping to admire the pictures drawn with multi-colored chalk on the sidewalks in front of the houses where kids lived. I saw Marilyn turn on Pleasant Avenue and was just about to pick up my pace when someone called.

"Girlie! Hey, girlie! Hello!"

Darn, I'd forgotten all about crossing the street before getting to the home for the retarded on 40th and Pleasant. I tried to keep my head down as if I was really deep in thought but the voice was relentless. "Hey! You in the yellow shirt and the white shorts!" Glancing down, of course I saw that I was wearing a yellow tee shirt with white cutoffs. "Hi, girlie! Can't you stop and say hi! Aw, come on!"

"Yes, please stop!" a chorus of additional voices joined in and I knew I had to stop. Adjusting my stack of books onto my other hip, I waved vigorously and shouted back greetings.

"Won't you come up and say hello, girlie? Come closer so we can see you!" By this time one of the nurses working in the home had poked her head out the screen door to see what all of the raucous was about.

"Oh good, it's you. Come sit for a spell?" she said. "Should I get the bingo wheel?" I didn't really want to play bingo now that I had a stack of new books from the bookmobile, but the excited looks on the old ladies' faces were so hopeful that I couldn't say no. Reluctantly putting down my books, I shook hands with all of the ladies. I went from one to the other saying hello and enthusiastically shaking their hands. They were dressed in faded cotton dresses with tiny little flowers on them. Some of them had knee-high nylons bunched around their ankles or positioned at different heights along their calves. Their heads were covered with matted, yellowish-grey hair. Their glasses were a bit askew and somewhat smudged. They were so giddy you'd think it was Christmas morning.

"You're Lucy, aren't you?" Dorothy always thought my name was Lucy. I corrected her and told her my name was Ginny.

"Okay, Lucy, you sit right by me." She gave me no choice as she refused to let go of my hand.

I used to get scared when the ladies did stuff like that but I'm used to it by now. Sometimes there's sticky stuff on their hands that I have to wash off when I get home, and it always stinks in the old folks' home. After Mom explained to me about the ladies who live there, I've tried to be more understanding. These are people who are not in their right minds. Their days are long and uneventful. Mom says being with young people is good for them and that I should remember to be grateful that I wasn't born retarded. I should show my gratitude by spending time at the home to cheer up the old ladies.

Dorothy and I were partners, but if it hadn't been for me she would never have gotten a single Bingo. Whenever a number was called, she started at the B and went down the line pointing at every single square, repeating the number in a singsong voice. I used to try to tell her that if 'G' is called, she didn't need to start at B but could skip right to G but she was a creature of habit and always started at the beginning of the bingo card. I marked the squares in my mind which had been called and called out Bingo when I knew we'd got one whether Dorothy had put a marker on the square or not. She squealed with delight when we got one and clapped her hands while rocking back and stomping both of her feet at the same time. "Ooohh, a Bingo!" The stocky woman leaning against the porch railing said conspiratorially. She was nodding her head as if someone getting a bingo wasn't guaranteed to be the inevitable outcome all along.

Fearing snacks were to be served, I was about to shake hands again all around and hightail it out of there. Snacks at the home were not always recognizable to me. I had been tricked into eating what I thought were chocolates once which turned out to be dried prunes. Since then, I've played it safe by leaving whenever food was brought out. Extricating my hand from Dorothy's while she was busy using her bingo card as a fan, I stepped from the porch into the house to say good-bye.

"Thanks for having me, it was fun," I said politely to the shadowy figure in the kitchen doorway. Coming from the bright sunlight into the dark house caused me to lose my sight for a moment while my eyes adjusted but I would have recognized the voice that answered me anywhere.

"You're very welcome, Virginia," followed by a chuckle belonging to none other than Crazy Caroline. Startled, I turned and tripped over the lamp trying to get back to the door.

"Here you go, Caroline," said the nurse as she handed over what looked to be a bag lunch.

"Oh dear, what happened to you?" she asked kindly while I was getting up. I shouted that it was nothing and rushed headlong out the door.

Shaking hands around the porch as I got ready to leave, I ended with Dorothy. I asked her in a low voice what Crazy Caroline was doing there. Naturally, I left off the 'crazy' part.

"Caroline helps us feel better!" Dorothy said while gazing vaguely at me through her soiled glasses. "She puts different oil and lotion on our feet if they're sore or our shoulders and necks if we've got the Arthur-itis. When Agnes couldn't stop crying, she gave her special tea to drink and told her stories to cheer her up. And," Dorothy softened her voice as if she thought she were whispering but her voice was actually louder than before, "sometimes she lets us smoke her pipe. Heeheehee!" she giggled with both hands over her mouth so gleefully that I couldn't help but join in while she continued, "That is just, just....just," she stopped speaking as though she weren't even aware that she had stopped in the middle of the sentence.

"Just life on Pleasant Avenue," I finished for her and chuckled to myself as I picked up my books and left.

When I got home, I went to help Mrs. Agneau pick up strewn branches from the willow tree. Mickey was already there helping her. We piled all of the branches into little stacks which we then carried to the burning barrel out by the alley. After what felt like ages picking up branches, I looked about and saw that we'd hardly made a dent in the amount of branches scattered across the lawn.

"Mrs. Agneau, why do you keep such a messy tree around?" I asked as I threw myself on the ground underneath the wispy canopy.

"My dear, one doesn't discard something just because it doesn't look or behave the way one wants it to," Mrs. Agneau replied, gingerly seating herself on the top step. "This lovely old willow tree is not looking her best, it's true, but goodness me, she is practically as old as I am. This tree is sixty years old this spring. I was twelve when my father planted it here on our front lawn with great ceremony. He was quite the arborist, my father, and he taught me so much about trees."

"What's an arborist?"

"Well, a tree specialist, I guess you could say. Take willow trees, for example. My father knew everything there was to know about willows. He taught me that willows are steeped in history and rich with tradition as well as the fact that they are terrific good fun to play under. They make such excellent natural caves where you can let your imagination thrive! Many afternoons I would while away under this willow pretending I was hiding out in the jungles of the Amazon or swinging through the African forest."

"My grandpa used to tell us a story about the Wisdom of the Willow Tree." Mickey had stopped to sit by Mrs. Agneau's feet and was tying fallen willow branches together.

"Oh, indeed, the famous Osage Nation's story. Do you remember what it was about?" Mrs. Agneau prompted. Mickey's hands deftly braided the willow branches while he slowly told the story.

"Little One had begun to ask questions that the elders could not answer well enough to satisfy him. Questions like 'What is the meaning of life?' and 'Why do we have to get old and die?' He went away to try to find the answers in his dreams. Each night he set up camp and slept in a different place hoping he would dream the answers to his questions. Little one walked a long way from home but no answers came to him. He was weak with hunger and finally decided he'd better head back to his village knowing his family must have been very worried about him. While he was walking, he tripped and fell over the roots of an old willow tree. He was so weak from not eating for so long, he couldn't get up. He called the willow tree 'Grandfather' and asked it to help him so he could continue on his journey." Mickey's voice was calm and low. I could tell he was repeating the story from memory. He surely must have heard the story many times before.

I looked up at the willow tree above us and said: "Hey Grandpa!" Mickey grinned at me and carried on with his story.

"The willow tree spoke to the little one. He told him to lean on him for support as he walked through life. His ancient roots held him firmly to the earth and though they were old and wrinkled, they were very strong and full of the wisdom of having lived for so long. The strength of the tree comes from the earth. When little one was strong enough to get up, he continued walking home. He was almost at his village when a vision of an old, old man came to him. The old man looked strangely familiar although the little one was sure he had never seen him before. 'Look at me', the old man said. 'What do you see?' 'I see an old man with a wrinkled face,' said the Little One. 'Look again,' said the old man. Little one looked for a long time and remembered what the willow tree had told him. 'I see you,' said Little One. 'You may be old but you are strong and rooted to the earth like the ancient willow tree.' The old man smiled and was gone. Little One got up and walked back to his village and his heart was filled with peace. He figured out that the old man he had seen was himself as an old man. He spent the rest of his days listening to his elders. He was no longer troubled by questions about the meaning of life. He became a wise old man himself, happy and full of peace. His wisdom gave strength to his people."

Mickey finished braiding the willow branches at the same time he finished his story.

Mrs. Agneau sighed. "That's a good one. Stories abound about these lovely old trees. The willow has been written about for absolutely centuries beginning, I suppose with Hippocrates writing about her medicinal properties way back in the fifth century. The Buddhists include the willow branch as one of the symbols of compassion. Why, the Willow is even mentioned as one of the nine sacred trees in WICCA." When Mickey just stared at her blankly, she continued: "You know, witchcraft."

"What medicinal properties did that Hippo guy write about?"

"The ancient Greek texts mention using the willow tree as a remedy for aches and fever. All across our own country, the Native Americans relied heavily on the willow as a staple of their medical treatments. The willow bark was steeped as a tea and the young twigs were chewed to relieve headaches. In fact, the chemical name for aspirin, salicylic acid, comes from the Willow family name, Salicaceae."

"Yuck, this tastes terrible!" I spat out the remains of the twig I was sampling.

"Maybe, but at least you won't get a headache!" Mickey grinned at me as he threw a handful of twigs my way.

"There is so much to admire about these graceful creatures." Mrs. Agneau went on. She tugged on one of the willow's dangling branches. "Their root structures are fantastic and quite aggressive actually. Why, the roots of my tree likely stretch all the way to the Shortpaschers yard. They can spread three times the distance from the trunk to the edge of the canopy. No wonder 'Little One' tripped over them in your story, Mickey. If you look over here, you can even see some of the roots at the surface." She was pointing to a spot near our lawn. Sure enough, we could see the roots scrambling up through the grass for a bit before hiding beneath the soil once again.

"Remember 'Old Man Willow?'" Mickey asked while wrapping himself round and round inside the dangling willow branches. Mr. Finkelstein had been reading *The Lord of the Rings* to us this summer and Mickey was now obsessed with Tolkien at the moment. "Help! I'm trapped, I'm trapped. I need Tom Bombadil to rescue me!" He continued to thrash in the sagging branches. "Tom! Tom! Where are you, Tom?" I pretended to be Tom and began whacking at the clinging branches with a fallen stick vowing to help.

"Hey, I just got a book from the bookmobile about a Willow. Um, the Windy Willow Tree, I think."

"Oh, sure, *The Wind in the Willow* by Ken Grahame." Mrs. Agneau said. "Willows are featured in countless works of literature. Alexander Pope wrote of the Legend of the Willow, and Hans Christian Anderson, and of course Shakespeare uses the willow in a number of his plays."

"Romeo, Romeo wherefore art thou, Romeo?" I twirled among the branches looking for Romeo. Polly had once put on a production of Romeo and Juliet.

"Hmmm, I'm not sure if the willow is in with the Capulet's and Montague's but for sure it's in Othello. In Twelfth Night it's an emblem of forsaken love. Then there's poor Ophelia who actually dies because the willow tree branch breaks in Hamlet." Mrs. Agneau looks sad bending the willow branch in her hand back and forth until it, too, cracks, making her jump and snapping her out of her reverie. "Mr. Bombadil, rescue Frodo's friend if you please and carry on cleaning up these branches." Using the branch for emphasis, she points in Mickey's direction as we laugh and carry on cleaning up until the area beneath the canopy is free of branches.

By the time we ignited the branches in Mrs. Agneau's burn barrel, it was getting dark. The smell of burning branches mingling with the fresh evening air was so delicious I could practically taste it. We stared at the fire as it crackled and burned, mesmerized by the blue and yellow flames that were leaping out of the barrel.

Mickey fed more branches into the fire, standing extremely close to do so.

"Aren't you hot?" I asked. "Get back, why don't you?"

"I was just remembering another thing willow branches are used for," Mickey answered. "Sweat lodges."

"What lodges?"

"Sweat lodges. That's when my grandpa would build these huts out of willow branches and go sit inside with a fire burning so hot it would make him sweat. Sweating is good for you because it makes you sweat all of the bad things out of you. Bad diseases, bad thoughts, everything bad so when you came out of the sweat lodge it was like you were a baby starting out fresh all over again. Everything negative about you had just been sweat out of you. They used willow branches to build the sweat lodges. I forgot about that. I'll have to tell Mrs. Agneau."

"You know a lot about Indian history, that's for sure."

Just then we heard the unlikely sound of Mrs. Agneau shouting. We stopped stirring the fire for a moment in disbelief trying to imagine who she would be yelling at in that tone when we both realized at the same time that she was on the phone. It was dark outside now and the lighted kitchen glowed in the night. It was easy to see Mrs. Agneau clearly as she stood in the middle of the room holding the phone with the spiraling cord connecting it to the wall unit. Clutching the phone with one hand, the other was pressed against her cheek as she shook her head back and forth. Her raised voice sounded shrill. "How could you? How could you do this to me? This is my home! This has been the only home I have ever known! How could you be so cruel?!"

Mickey and I fell silent. The willow wood crackled in the barrel. The sound of laughter came from somewhere far away and a car door slammed. It felt wrong eavesdropping on Mrs. Agneau that way but we couldn't make ourselves look away.

"You can't make me!" Mrs. Agneau shouted. "I won't go! I will NOT GO, do you hear me?!" and with that she slammed the phone back on the hook and collapsed in her chair with her head in her hands. The beautiful summer evening had lost its charm and a frightening premonition settled over me.

"I think I'd better go get Mom." I said, glancing at Mickey. His eyes looked as frightened as I was feeling, and he nodded his head in agreement.

"See you tomorrow," we said in unison as I headed home.

Chapter 23

The day was a scorcher with the temperatures reaching into the high 90's and the sun blazing out of a cloudless blue sky making the blacktop in the backyard blister. The house smelled of fried chicken and the kitchen was a bluster of activity as we packed up our picnic. "That water is going to feel so good I can hardly wait!" Jane said as she wiped the sweat from her brow and continued slicing the boiled potatoes for potato salad.

"Does everyone have a bathing suit on?" Mom remembered to ask. "We might not be able to park close enough to the main beach to use the changing facilities. I don't want any of you exposing yourselves while you change into your swim trunks, do you hear?"

"What trunks?" Pat asked as he patted the jeans covering his backside. "I'm swimming in my cutoffs. Not that some lucky young lady wouldn't enjoy seeing a little of me exposed!" He sashayed his hips seductively.

"Somebody grab towels and a blanket. Two blankets!" Mom shouted. "Better yet, make it three!"

Greg and Danny were chasing each other around the kitchen table, through the dining room, into the living room, and back into the kitchen chanting, "Nokomis, Nokomis, swimming at Nokomis." Pat scooped up Chris and put him on his shoulders to join with them in the chase. They continued to chant: "Nokomis, Nokomis!" while Chris squealed with delight. Even Mom got into it standing at the stove with her heavy silver saucepan popping corn. She shook the pan rhythmically to their chanting. "Swimming at Nokomis, Nokomis!" while making popcorn in her heavy saucepan.

"I'll make one more batch of popcorn and then we'll be ready to go. Did you hear that, Tom?" Mom called.

Pat grabbed Mom from behind. "Way to shake it, Mom! Shooka-shooka-shooka!" He continued to shake her as the popping corn nearly forced the lid off of the pan.

"Enough!" Mom laughed as she pushed Pat away and poured the popcorn into the paper grocery bag.

It was the fourth of July and before we went to see the fireworks, we were going to swim at Lake Nokomis. Lake Harriet was the lake closest to home, walking distance even, so we spend a lot of time there. It was a special treat to be going in the car to Lake Nokomis. We loaded up. Neil was put in charge of the picnic lunch to be sure it didn't get eaten before it was time. We all piled into the station wagon leaving room in the front for Mrs. Agneau. Mom had been with her for over an hour last night after I'd told her what Mickey and I had heard. When I asked her about it this morning she told me not to worry and definitely not to bring it up to Mrs. Agneau, who would be joining us in our patriotic celebrations.

Mom had asked the Olsons to let Mickey come along, too, of course. He was very serious about his responsibility to carry Mrs. Agneau's freshly baked sugar cookies with vanilla frosting sprinkled with red and blue sugar decorations. Soon we arrived at Lake Nokomis.

"Last one in the water's a rotten egg!" Neil hollered as he set the picnic basket down next to the bench Mom and Mrs. Agneau were settling onto.

"Go on," Mom told Dad, gesturing with her chin. "Take the swimmers out to the dock. I'll stay in the shallow end with the little ones."

With screams of excitement, we peeled off our clothes while running into the water. At just over 200 acres of water, the lake was warm enough for us to run into without causing heart palpitations but cool enough to feel refreshing on this hot summer day. Being early July, the dog days hadn't arrived yet so the water was clear with no weeds at all gathering on the sandy shoreline. Mickey and I ran in together, slowing naturally when the resistance of the water got too deep. At waist high, we both stopped running and dove in while plugging our noses.

The older kids carried on and swam out to the floating dock with Dad. Climbing up the ladder, they proceeded to play King of the Dock, pushing each other off the dock and into the water with rapid succession. The 'King's' position alternated between Dad, Jane, and Neil while Pat provided the entertainment by posing hilariously each time he was pushed off the dock. Other swimmers joined in the milieu. For a while, Mickey and I just stood in the water watching the fun. Suddenly, there was a tugging underwater on my bathing suit bottoms. I shrieked in horror as Greg emerged sputtering while laughing.

"You're it!"

I splashed after my nearest opponent in order to take the tag off of me. We stayed in the water for ages playing tag and other games.

Later, I was holding Chris in the lake while Mom went to take Mrs. Agneau to the lavatory. We had been playing "Help! I'm drowning," where the drowner flailed about in the water shouting "Help! I'm drowning" and then went under the surface for a moment before coming up and repeatedly thrashing about.

The drowner carried on like this shouting two or three more times. One of us rescuers would swim out, drag the pretending drowner out of the water, and administer our version of CPR. This ultimately included tickling to be sure the victim was still alive.

Chris was now taking his turn. He yelled "Help!" and then very cautiously touched his face to the water which was as close as he was going to come to submersing himself at this stage. Holding up one chubby little finger, he yelled 'Help!' again and repeated the face dampening. No one was paying attention anymore as this drowning wasn't very exciting so eventually Chris and I waded a little deeper to where Dad was floating.

Dad floated with his feet poking out of the water. He was proud of his buoyancy which apparently is less common in lake water than in salt water. He mused about how easy it would be for him to float in the ocean, if he ever got there, because everyone is able to float in the ocean. We made a game, for a while, of Chris trying to get a hold of Dad's big toe. Then Dad held Chris so I could practice my floating.

Last summer, when Dad had first tried to teach me how to float, I was hopeless. I wanted it so badly that I kept trying too hard, laying there stiff as a board trying to will myself to float until over and over again I would slowly sink underwater. "Relax! Just relax!" Dad had coaxed. When I still couldn't do it and he got more frustrated, his commands to relax created evermore the opposite effect. I became more and more incapable.

Finally one day up at Sibley, Tom the lifeguard had spoken to me while I was attempting to build a sandcastle. "The trick is to not think about it." Tom said. "The ability to learn to float is most possible if you're not thinking about learning to float."

I thought, "Yeah, right." But the next time I was in the water, I remembered what he'd said. It was a lot easier said than done. How do you not think about something that you're thinking about as you're trying to do it?

I kept laying back and telling myself not to think about floating which instantly made me think about how I was trying to float. It didn't help knowing that Tom, as the lifeguard, was probably watching me fail over and over again.

"How's the floating going?" He asked, the next time he caught me out of the water. When I told him it wasn't working even though I kept telling myself not to think about floating, he said I was going about it completely the wrong way. Rather than telling myself not to think about floating, I should bring something else to mind to think about.

Standing resolutely in the grayish water, I glanced around and tried to think of something to think about while I lowered myself into the water. The sun was just setting so the sky was becoming bright orange to the West. Some kids were still laughing and screaming on the beach while their parents were beginning to pack up to head back to the campground.

I noticed the resident eagle standing complacently in the tallest pine tree off shore. His beautiful white head looked a little pink in the setting sunlight. Suddenly he took off, using his strong legs to push himself while simultaneously opening his broad wings to catch the air current and soar above the lake. Sunset is always good fishing time for both humans and birds. That's when the bugs come out, so the fish swim close to the surface to eat them.

I lay back so I could watch the eagle hunt. Earlier that summer, I had checked out a book from the Bookmobile all about eagles so I felt like I knew quite a bit about them. Eagles have amazing eyes. They are as large as human eyes in their much smaller heads, and they have an extra film over them so they can blink while still keeping their eyes open. That way they won't lose sight of their prey even when they're dropping at rapid speeds out of the sky. Not only can they see forwards like we can, but they can also see sideways and even a little backwards, too. Bald Eagles belong to the fish eagle type. Their claws are curved, the bottoms of their feet are spiny pads, and they have an outer toe to help them catch and hold fish.

~ 237 ~

I was hoping to see this eagle catch a fish. When eagles soar, they hardly ever flap their wings and so it almost looks as though they're floating up there in the sky....floating! My sudden intake of breath was so forceful it almost submerged me but I forced myself to exhale slowly which helped keep me relaxed.

I acknowledged with a huge grin on my face that I was indeed floating! It was so easy! And Tom was right. I continued to watch the eagle glide through the darkening sky above me until Mom called me in out of the water. The eagle wasn't successful hunting that night but I knew eagles didn't have to eat every day, I felt sure he'd do better another time. I was the one who was successful that night.

The next day, when Tom was at his favorite spot leaning against the concession stand building dutifully watching over the beach, I didn't even look at him as I walked straight into the water, plopped backwards, and floated.

I floated effortlessly on the Fourth of July on Lake Nokomis where the chances of spotting a bald eagle were slim. One of twenty lakes in Minneapolis, Lake Nokomis is southeast of downtown. The sign plaque by the lake says that it used to be called Lake Amelia before it was bought by the city in 1907. It was dredged to ensure a constant flow of water over nearby Minnehaha Falls.
I asked Dad why they had changed the lake's name from Amelia to Nokomis. We waded slowly out of the water and plunked down on the edge of the lake so Chris could play while Dad explained that Lake Nokomis was named for the grandmother of Hiawatha in the famous poem written by Henry Wadsworth Longfellow in 1855, *The Song of Hiawatha*.

"By the shores of Gitchee Gumee, by the shining Big-Sea-Water, Stood the wigwam of Nokomis, Daughter of the Moon, Nokomis. Dark behind it rose the forest..." I had to interrupt before Dad recited the entire thing. "From the full moon fell Nokomis, fell the beautiful Nokomis."

"Who's Hiawatha?" I interjected.

To my surprise, Mickey answered that Hiawatha is the English word for Nanabozho. Mickey had been helping Chris in his fruitless effort to dig holes in the sand at the water's edge. Chris's chubby fingers dug into the sand creating a cavern which slowly filled with water from the bottom up.

Mickey continued, with Dad's encouragement, and I learned that in Anishinaabe mythology, particularly among the Ojibwa, Nanabozho was a spirit. He was an important cultural hero who was a part of their story of the creation of the earth. He was a trickster and a shape shifter who most often appeared in the shape of a rabbit but also had shown up as a skunk or a porcupine.

According to legend, he was sent to earth to teach the Ojibwa. Naming the plants and animals was one of his first tasks. They say he also invented fishing. According to Dad, there are pictures painted of Nanabozho in the form of pictographs up in Canada. They say Nanabozho saved the Ojibwa forests from Paul Bunyan after fighting him for forty days and forty nights. They finally killed him with a whack on the head from a huge walleye fish caught in Red Lake.

"Whack! Whack!" Chris cried while hitting me with a pretend fish. I marveled once again at how much Mickey knew about Indian history. Dad interjected that in fact, while Longfellow's poem is a retelling of the Ojibwa Nanabozho stories, most of it is not accurate. The most popular story about Native Americans isn't even a truthful one, in the end.

"But it's still something," Mickey said. "It's still cool that so many places and things are named after Hiawatha, Nokomis and Minnehaha, that everyone knows these are Indians and they still want to name things after them. Even if they don't have the facts exactly straight, it's better than nothing."

Dad rubbed the top of Mickey's head thoughtfully.

"Your ancestors used to have everything. You lived in perfect harmony with the land and your fellow creatures on it, taking only what you needed to survive, hunting only enough to eat, and moving around so as never to deplete or make inhabitable where you had been. You knew this instinctively. Your lovely stories illustrate your life's philosophy so well. Your people were centuries ahead of the rest of us in acknowledging that we can never 'own' the land but are simply visitors who must nurture and cherish the earth so future generations are able to survive as well.

Then 'we', the white man came and took advantage of your innocence. You were lied to and cheated out of your livelihoods. Listening to this distorted telling of your creation story, you with your few years are gracious enough to say that it's 'better than nothing'. Mickey, you have noble blood running through your veins. Don't you ever doubt it."

Mickey nodded solemnly, never taking his eyes off of Dad's. I could tell how pleased he was with the compliment.

"Come and eat!" Mom called. "We don't want to be late for the fireworks, do we?"

After polishing off the crispy fried chicken, potato salad, and watermelon, we packed up to drive north to Powderhorn Park. We parked the car and managed to find a good spot on the hill overlooking the lake where the fireworks would go off.

"Is it dark-thirty yet?" Greg asked.

Mom said no and that we had time to play before the fireworks were to start while she and Mrs. Agneau settled down to munch on popcorn and people watch. Dad and the boys grabbed their mitts and began to play catch while the girls strolled around to see if any of their friends were around.

Mickey and I skipped rocks into the lake for a while. His rocks always skipped four or five times before dwindling off rapidly into a series of little hops that Mickey kept counting to annoy me, I'm sure. I wasn't very good at rock skipping and more often than not my rocks hit the water with a plunk and sunk immediately to the bottom of the lake.

"Wanna walk a bit?" I asked. Mickey hurled one last stone which danced on top of the water skipping at least eight times. He smiled triumphantly while some of the onlookers clapped. "Where'd you learn to skip rocks so good?"

"On the rez spending time with my grandparents."

We walked along skirting the blankets and lawn chairs spread all throughout the park for fireworks viewing. The atmosphere was festive; except for the mosquitoes, it was a perfect summer evening.

"Ouch!" I said at the same time as I bent down to slap my ankle. The blood that splashed told me the mosquito had had plenty of time to fill itself and that I would have a nasty, itchy bite to show for it. "I hope you enjoyed your last meal!" I said, pointlessly wiping my hands on my shorts. "Aren't you getting bit?"

I glanced over at Mickey, but he wasn't listening to me, he was staring straight ahead as if he'd seen a ghost. Turning to see what had caught his attention, I didn't see anything in the descending dusk except a group of a dozen or so Indians standing around. Powderhorn Park is not too far from Cedar Avenue where a large Indian population lives, so it wasn't surprising to see them here.

"What is it, Mick?" I asked, but when he still didn't answer, I followed his gaze to the little toddler he was watching.

It was a little boy about two years old sitting on the ground making sputtering noises with his mouth as he pushed a rock around that in his mind was obviously a little car. Another 'rock' came from the opposite direction with his other hand. Suddenly, the boy made a screeching sound and the two rocks collided.

In his mind, the accident must not have been too serious, however, because soon the rocks became functioning cars again and he continued driving the cars around in the dirt.

There was a woman hanging on someone's arm standing near the boy who was laughing loudly, barely able to stay upright. The man whose arm she was hanging onto got annoyed and shrugged her off. She stumbled before finding someone else to latch onto, slurring incoherent words into the air. Her amusement was not shared by her companions and her cackle sounded slightly hysterical.

Just then a swooshing sound emanated from the lake and seconds later the sky filled with a circle of brilliant green lights which burst and fell gracefully downwards followed seconds later by a loud boom.

"The fireworks are starting!" Mickey and I hurried back to stretch out on our blankets and the little boy was all but forgotten by me. Mickey kept looking back in the direction we'd seen them, however, and his good mood had completely vanished. We sat on either side of Chris who was hiding his head and covering his ears.

"The fireworks are very, very loud!" he informed us between bursts.

"Yes, but they're very, very pretty, too. Come on, open your eyes and watch with us."

We lay back on the blanket and enjoyed the spectacular display. Hearing nothing from Mickey amid the oohs and aahs emanating from the crowd, I glanced over at him and was dismayed to see tears on his cheeks. By the time the show was over and the grand finale of explosion after explosion including a fantastic red, white and blue display of brilliance had ended, Mickey was cheering loudly with the rest of us. Gathering up our belongings, we joined the parade of tired and contented spectators streaming back to our cars. There was no sign of the little boy playing obliviously in the dirt or of his wanton mother either.

Chapter 24

The dog days of summer were upon us and the school year was fast approaching. I had already learned that Mr. Hanson was to be my third grade teacher, and we'd already made our annual school shopping trip to Target. I had gotten everything on the third-grade list, even the twenty four-pack of Crayola crayons. Twenty four crayons for my own personal use. Up until now, third graders were only required to have their own twelve- pack of crayons but luckily, this year it was changed to the twenty-four pack. I had already opened and reopened my crayons numerous times taking each crayon out, reading its name, smelling it, and putting it back into its own little slot in the box. I wouldn't have dreamed of using it before school started, but I did reorganize the colors in the box. Two-shoes was lying catatonically beside me with her little tongue peeking out of her mouth. I began scratching under her chin asking, "Should I put Red, Orange, Orange Red, Orange Yellow, and Yellow, or Orange, Orange Red, Red, Orange Yellow, and Yellow, or ...."
The cat's mouth opened in an enormous yawn showing off all of her tiny little teeth. Her eyes blinked slowly at me while she continued to purr.

"She's about as interested as the rest of us," Neil said knocking me on the top of my head at the same time that Mom hollered at me to hurry up and get ready because the taxi would be there in thirty minutes.

"That is so not fair!" Jane hissed for the umpteenth time. "None of the rest of us has ever gotten to ride in a taxi before and this is her second time! 'Little miss my- girlfriend- is- an- only- child whose Mom likes to spoil her' gets to do everything!"

"You know I would invite you all along to join us if I could," I said condescendingly while Pat threw a pillow at me and told me to get out already or they'd stuff me in the closet and tell the Buehlings I wasn't at home.

This was going to be an amazing day. We were spending the night at a hotel again for Lexie's birthday. This was all part of Mrs. Buehling's treatment in trying to get her to leave the house and go someplace else other than work. She was going to spend her first night away from home since we went to the hotel last summer.

I closed the moss green, hard-covered suitcase with a click, hugged Mom good-bye, and went to sit on the front step to wait for the taxi. Mr. Finkelstein was out working in his garden so I waved at him and shouted the details of my adventure to him. I was hoping Mrs. Agneau would be out so she could see me be driven off in a taxicab as well but her front door was shut and her yard was empty.

At the corner, I saw a yellow cab turn onto our street and I hollered, "They're here! Good-bye!" which elicited exactly the response I was hoping for, as everyone came out the front door to see me off. Mom even walked all the way down to the curb with me and stuck her head in the taxi's door to thank Stella for taking me and to give me final instructions on how to behave.

I climbed in and sat next to Mrs. Buehling. Lexie had pulled out the cute little round seat from behind the driver's seat to sit on so she was facing us. We examined every inch of the taxi until we looked out the window and saw that we were downtown already!

"Just drive us around downtown awhile, can you?" Mrs. Buehling leaned forward to ask the cabdriver. Lexie and I were so excited, we clapped our hands together in glee. Finally, we arrived at the Hotel Normandy where we were to spend the night. A man wearing white gloves opened the car door for us and bowed while he greeted us in a loud formal voice calling us 'young ladies.'

We checked out the hotel room until Mrs. Buehling told us it was time to head out because she had a special treat for us. She had hired her assistant from work, Miss Isaacson, to take us out to see some of the sights of the city while she was going to lay down on the bed with a cool washcloth over her eyes and try to remain in the hotel without panicking or racing for home.

Miss Isaacson was a short, sturdy young woman with ratted hair giving her inches above her God-given height and a no-nonsense attitude who always took her assignments seriously. She had long, puffy bangs that fell down upon her fake eyelashes giving her a sweet, shaggy-dog look that went well with her eager-to-please manners. Her yellow pumps accented her golden a-line miniskirt with the hot pink polka dots. Everywhere we went, Miss Isaacson was greeted with long, appreciative stares and men hastening to open doors for us, pull out chairs, and wait on us. As we walked down Nicollet Avenue, the construction workers whistled appreciatively and catcalled. Lexie nearly tripped over the orange cone alerting us of the huge hole in the ground at the edge of the sidewalk. We walked for a couple of blocks with Miss Isaacson until we stopped in front of the Foshay Tower, the tallest building in Minneapolis. "Come on. I'm taking you girls to the top of the world!"

 Lexie and I just stared at one another, our eyes getting big with excitement. This day just kept getting better and better! The elevator ride up to the 30th floor took an exceptionally long time. I was frozen stiff with fear as each clink and clank of the elevator convinced me that we would soon be plummeting back down to ground level and beyond. It was a relief when the doors opened and we were allowed to dash out of the confining space of the elevator.

While we raced from window to window taking in the expansive view of Minneapolis, Miss Isaacson filled us in on the history of the tower. It had been completed in 1929 as the first skyscraper west of the Mississippi and was certainly the tallest building to date.

"Poor Wilbur Foshay never did get to enjoy the living quarters in his beautiful building," Miss Isaacson told us. "The stock market crashed in October just after the elaborate dedication of the building. It was attended by over 250,000 guests, among them Washington politicians, and was accompanied by an orchestra conducted by John Phillips Sousa playing an original march he wrote especially for the occasion. It was called the 'Foshay-Washington Monument March' and was followed by a 19-gun military salute. Sadly, poor Wilbur was ruined in the crash of '29." Miss Isaacson carried on. "They are transforming Nicollet Avenue into a pedestrian-friendly outdoor mall to try dragging back some of the customers from the new indoor mall in Edina. See, they're making it all curvy and attractive with bricks and pretty storefronts. They'll be planting trees in these huge holes. We'll come back again next summer and see how everything has turned out, alright?"

After leaving the tower, we headed into Woolworths to sit at the counter for lunch. We twirled around on the stools until Miss Isaacson stopped us and told us we were embarrassing her. She promised us banana splits if we behaved, which naturally we agreed to do. We ate our grilled cheese sandwiches while she told us about the protest held in front of this very same Woolworths in 1960 when Woolworths was boycotted for not allowing Negroes to eat at their lunch counter.

"That's not very long ago." I leaned forward and saw an elderly colored woman pouring milk into her coffee. She glanced over feeling my eyes upon her and we smiled at one another. She picked up the metal pitcher of milk and added another dash for good measure, winking at me as she did so. I leaned back, still grinning. Miss Isaacson reminded me that just a few years ago that sweet lady wouldn't have been allowed to sit at this counter with us. I felt the past inching ever so slowly back from the present and was glad of the changes it had wrought.

After spending hours swimming and playing in the small hotel pool, Mrs. Buehling tucked Lexie and me into the double bed for the night while she planned to sleep in the rollaway bed that had been brought in for her.

"Whew, you girls sure smell like chlorine!" she exclaimed while kissing our foreheads goodnight.

When the lights were turned out, the room was so black that Lexie and I were too scared to sleep, so Mrs. Buehling agreed to open the thick curtains for us as long as we promised to stop whispering. The lights from the downtown buildings shone comfortingly into our hotel room. They were bright enough to enable Lexie and me to clearly see each other's faces, so we continued to mouth words at one another without making a sound. Not being able to discern what we were trying to say, we bored of the game and mouthed the easily understood 'goodnight' to one another and closed our eyes to sleep.

Looking out the window at the Minneapolis skyline, I felt far too excited to sleep. The sounds of the hotel elevator kept my imagination going as I wondered who was coming and going at this hour. The loud rumble of the city buses dropping off and picking up passengers was equally interesting to me. The occasional burst of voices erupting from the elevator and traveling down the hallway until they were engulfed into their own rooms prevented me from soundly dozing off. Grumbling sounds from the television next door came through the wall.

What had been exciting to me in the afternoon felt scary at night and I felt homesick in a fierce way. Pleasant Avenue seemed a lot further away than our short taxi ride and I began to be afraid that I would never make it back there again.

In my mind's eye, I traveled around our house from the basement up to the attic pausing in almost painful nostalgia at some of my favorite places, like the landing three-fourths of the way up the stairs where we liked to play or the middle chair on the radiator-side of the kitchen table where I always sat for dinner. Exhausting the house, I then began a tour of the neighborhood, again lingering longingly in my mind at my favorite haunts. I visited each of the neighbors as if they were well-known characters in my favorite books. I liked them even better that way. Even the Shortpaschers didn't seem so bad if I thought of them like Davie, Joel, and Ben Pepper of The Five Little Peppers.

In my mind, I loitered longest on Mrs. Agneau's porch, reminiscing all of the fine times we had shared together. In that weightless state between neither fully awake nor asleep, I was suddenly filled with a sense of horror and I sat up in bed with a jerk. I must have let out a yelp because Mrs. Buehling's voice came from the other side of the room asking if everything was okay. I said yes even though it didn't feel like it. It felt as though something terrible had just happened. My palms were sweating and my heart raced so that it seemed as if I would never fall asleep. Of course I eventually did, and the next thing I knew, Lexie's mom was calling out to rise and shine and telling us it was time to get ready for church.

At breakfast, Mrs. Buehling told us all about St. Olaf where we would be going to mass. Saint Olaf was the patron saint of Norway. He had lived nearly a thousand years ago as a Viking before he went to France and fell in love with the Christians there. He decided to go back to Norway to try to convert the pagan Vikings. They weren't as enamored with the Christians as he was, so he was forced to hide in Russia for a few years for his own safety. Convinced that he was on the right path, he went back to Scandinavia where he was subsequently killed by a blow from an axe. When, after a few years, a spring sprang forth from where he was buried, the Romans proclaimed him a Saint.

For all her fears of going out in public, Mrs. Buehling always seemed to feel right at home in church. So much so that she seemed to think it was her right to march all the way down the long aisle and push her way into the front pew no matter how late we were for mass. I was wishing I hadn't been a disobedient little sister and taken Marilyn's summer sandals without asking.

I figured the devil was paying me back by causing the strap to slide off of my left heel forcing me to walk without lifting that foot off the ground. I walked with a hunchback sort of sway all the way down the slippery aisle of St. Olaf Church to keep the sandal on my foot. It was with relief that I slid past Mrs. Buehling into the front pew at last. She stood out in the aisle continuing to make a spectacle of herself as she put her sweater on before finally sitting down.

I had never been in St. Olaf church before so I looked around surreptitiously during mass. Miss Isaacson had told us the history in anticipation of our visit there. The first church built on this site burned down sometime in the 1880s. In 1941, the Archdiocese of St. Paul and Minneapolis bought the second church and dedicated it to St. Olaf on account of the large Scandinavian population in the Twin Cities. Twelve years later on Ash Wednesday, the unthinkable happened again and St. Olaf Church was destroyed by fire. Two years later on Ash Wednesday, the new church was reopened. This was the most modern church I had been in. It somehow didn't seem holy enough for me. The wooden statue of St. Olaf complete with axe didn't look anything like the familiar saints Therese and Joseph that I knew and loved from Incarnation. The 5000 pound, 36 foot high steel cross didn't even have Jesus' bloody body draped across it making it look more Lutheran than Catholic. The famous frieze of the choir boys with their singed feet from the fire looked completely out of place.

My thoughts were interrupted by the awful realization that it was time for communion and as we were sitting in the front pew, we would be the first to go up. How did they take communion here?

When I had made my First Communion back in first grade, I had felt so full of the love of God that an entire week went by without Greg being able to needle me into fighting with him. No matter how many times he called me by my least favorite nickname, Peachy, as in Virginia Peach, or pulled my pigtail when he walked past me, or pointed at his butt and then pointed at my face as if they were one and the same, I would not rise to the bait. I went about with my head bowed reverently in prayer.

I had felt so special on the day of my First Communion dressing up in my very own communion dress. It was the very first dress that I had ever owned, all the rest being hand-me-downs. Even the baptismal gown I wore when I was a baby had been worn by each one of my sisters first. The plain silk First Communion dress with matching white anklets with little satin bows and shiny white patent leather shoes would have been remarkable enough, but then there was the veil. I felt like Blessed Mother herself with the stiff white taffeta veil cascading down my back, never mind the white headband with its jagged teeth gouging into my scalp to keep the veil in place. I truly felt like a bride of Jesus. Sitting in the front pew with my family, I knew just what to do when the time came. Both of my parents accompanied me to the altar and stood behind me so I would be the first to receive the holy sacrament that day.

 Feeling the cold marble beneath my bare knees as I knelt alone at the altar, my heart trembled in anticipation. I furrowed my brow as I concentrated on making myself worthy of Jesus' ultimate sacrifice. Suddenly, Fr. Goman was strolling towards me with such a happy grin on his face that I forgot my veneration and found myself smiling widely back at him.

"The body of Christ," he said somber once again as he held out the round host in his chubby little hand. He smelled good, manly, and it occurred to me he was probably wearing Old Spice just like Dad. The silk cassock he was wearing hung majestically from his short figure. I fell in love with Fr. Goman in that moment as I closed my eyes, tipped back my head, and stuck out my tongue as we had practiced numerous times in class just for this moment. I waited.

My tongue protruded for so long out of my mouth, it began to feel dry. Finally, I peeked out of one eye only to see Fr. Goman standing before me with the host still pinched between his thumb and forefinger.

"Amen!" he mouthed, his eyes twinkling, and I was aghast. I had forgotten this crucial part of the ceremony. Amen means yes and of course I had to say yes first. Blushing furiously, I hissed 'Amen' and barely had time to open my mouth before the cardboard-like disc was thrust inside.

Gagging, I found myself coughing so frantically that the wafer shot right back out onto Father's gown. We both stared frozenly at it until in slow motion the representation of Christ's body twirled end over end until it hit the marble floor with a thwack. As I hastily reached for it, the normally jovial Reverend Father bellowed 'No!' so loudly he surely woke up the most soundly dozing penitent in the church.

"Don't touch it!" Father said as one of his altar servers pompously covered the woebegone wafer with a silk handkerchief. I hung my head in shame at messing up my first big moment with Jesus, made all the worse with my entire family with front row seats to the spectacle, literally.

"Let's try this again," Fr. Goman said, more like his old self though slightly more harried. This time, I practically shouted "Amen!" to be sure I got it right.

At St. Olaf, Mrs. Buehling stepped out of the pew to let Lexie and I pass, but she herself would refrain from receiving communion due to her antisocial tendencies. We didn't know whether this was the sort of church where everyone just stood in line to receive communion in the new "time is money" fashion or whether they knelt at the communion railing one at a time or dozens at a time. Whether they stuck out their tongues or in the more recently hygienically-correct manner, took the body of Christ in their own hands first and then put it in their mouths.

Lexie and I looked at each other in mute horror for a moment having no clue what to do. The man in the pew behind us stepped gruffly around us and stood directly before Father. I sighed with relief and stepped immediately behind him. I didn't forget to say 'Amen' either.

After a delicious meal at Burger King on the way home, where even the taxi driver came in to eat so he wouldn't have to sit in the hot car waiting for us, our magical week end came to an abrupt end. We arrived home to find the street in front of my house covered with police cars.

"Sorry, m'am, I can't get any closer," the taxi driver muttered as he began to back up the car.

"Ginny, wait!" Mrs. Buehling shouted but I was already out of the car and running as fast as I could up the street. My forgotten premonition from the night before was front and center once again. Suddenly, someone grabbed my arm from behind and I was face to face with Mr. Finkelstein.

"Let me go!" I shouted as I squirmed out of his firm grasp. "I have to see what's wrong!"

"Ginny, hold still," Mr. Finkelstein said in the tone of voice that told me something terrible had happened, so I tried even harder to get out of his grip.

"I have to find out what's going on!" I shouted as I attempted to break free.

"I'll tell you what's happened, Ginny. Your family is fine, don't worry about them. It's Mrs. Agneau."

Chapter 25

Later that evening, after Mom had given her statement to the police and everyone had left, I begged her to let me accompany her over to Mrs. Agneau's house to 'put things in order' as she phrased it before Mrs. Agneau's son flew in from California on the red-eye flight. After a few half-hearted efforts to stop me, Mom gave in out of sheer exhaustion. Using the key Mrs. Agneau had given us for emergencies, Mom and I let ourselves into her kitchen through the back door.

The kitchen floor was sparkling clean as usual, though I knew it was getting harder and harder for Mrs. Agneau to get down on her hands and knees to scrub it. She refused to use a mop, claiming they simply couldn't get the job done properly. The dishes from her last meal had been washed and left out to dry, the small crystal bowl evidence that she'd ended her meal with a scoop of ice cream, perhaps Mr. Agneau's favorite black cherry flavor. Mom put the dishes away and put coffee in the percolator, filled it with water, and placed it on the stove ready for the young Mr. Agneau to make coffee when he got there the next morning. Then she sat in Mrs. Agneau's chair at the kitchen table and looked out at the view.

Our yard light hung from high up the telephone pole and cast a circular spotlight onto the basketball court which was empty now except for the ball just in the shadow of the light.

"She always loved watching you kids play," Mom's voice cracked as she put her head in her hands. She wept silently for a moment. I put my hand on her back and watched it rise and fall with Mom's soundless sobs. I couldn't say anything on account of the tears I had managed to control thus far threatening to rise to the surface.

After a while, we went to the living room. There was nothing to pick up there, so we headed up the stairs to the bedrooms. I had never been upstairs in Mrs. Agneau's bedroom without her in it before. I felt like we were trespassing here more than anywhere else in the house. The double bed was made with her purple and green floral bedspread straightened without a wrinkle in it. All of her pillows were arranged neatly against the headboard.

She had a few violet-colored phlox in a vase on the end table next to her bed. I knew it was because she loved their scent. She told me that once you pick the flowers, they don't last long, but the glorious aroma makes their messiness all worthwhile. These hadn't begun to drop their little florets at all so she must have just picked them that day. Mom surprised me by opening the little drawer in the bedside table and shuffling through it.

"Aha, I knew I'd find it!" She exclaimed while holding up a little diary in her outstretched hand. Mom found the little key for the diary in the corner of the drawer and put both items in the large pocket of her housedress. "There is no way I'm letting little Walter Agneau get his hands on these." I smiled at the misnomer, looking directly at the last family picture taken before Mr. Agneau died. Walter towered over both of his parents and was the same width as the two of them put together. Mom also picked up Mrs. Agneau's rosary and some prayer cards from the top of the table and deposited those in her other pocket.

"Ginny, I want you to wait in here for me. Just sit tight on the bed and say a prayer for your oldest friend."

I thought about how she was right to call Mrs. Agneau my oldest friend in both senses of the word. She had known me since I was a baby so that would make her my oldest friend. She also was an old lady so that would make her my oldest friend, too.

The sound of glass breaking sent me to my feet. I hurried to the bedroom next door to help, forgetting Mom's instructions to stay put. The smaller bedroom had been Walter's, of course. The masculine colors and accents were in marked contrast to the ultra feminine bedroom next door. The small desk where young Walter must have sat doing his homework stood beneath a window which directly faced into the house next door on the other side of Agneau's house. Mom was crying as she picked up the flowers amongst the broken vase on the floor.

"I'm sorry Ginny. The sight of these flowers Mrs. Agneau placed so thoughtfully on her son's bedside table for him were just the last straw. He doesn't deserve them. But it was childish of me to throw them." I knelt beside her on the floor to help. When she heard me sniffling, she put the flowers down and held me while I cried.

"How could she do this, Mom? She knew suicide was a sin! She knows now we'll never get to see her in the afterlife, up in heaven. How could she not want to stay here with us? I thought she loved me, but she didn't even care at all how I would feel knowing she didn't want to be here anymore. She didn't really care about us at all." The tears streamed down my face and the pain in my chest was like nothing I had ever experienced before. It was as if my heart were being squeezed so sharply that I couldn't catch my breath, I couldn't breathe and no matter how hard I tried I couldn't get any air into my lungs. I felt like I was suffocating. I was going to die of a broken heart. I knew I was being selfish only thinking of how I was affected by this but I couldn't help myself. I was so hurt.

Mom let me cry a while longer before she tried to explain to me why she thought Mrs. Agneau felt she had no choice other than to end her life.

When Mr. Agneau died, he had given everything they had to their son which is what they had agreed to do. This was for tax purposes only. They didn't want to have to pay taxes twice on the inheritance their son would get, so they just gave it all to him. They felt secure in the knowledge that he would take care of the surviving spouse until their death.

The problem was that Walter Agneau was tired of traveling halfway across the country to take care of his mother. He had decided it was time for her to give up her house and move into an old folks' home in California. She would be looked after and he wouldn't have to worry about her alone here anymore. In order to pay for her care, he needed to sell the house and all of the belongings in it including the family's valuable antiques. He had been threatening this for years. This time, he had actually hired a realtor to sell the house. Mrs. Agneau was scheduled to move out the end of the month.

"Ungrateful bastard," Mom muttered, and the unexpectedness of her cursing struck me so forcefully that it caused me to laugh out loud. Mom caught my eye and defended herself saying, "I'm sorry but it's true. There are times in one's life, and this is one of them, when a spade must be called a spade."

At which point I thought I might as well give it a try, too, and I agreed with her saying, "Yeah, the stinking bastard."

"Well said," Mom commended me. We finished straightening the house while I thought about my friend, Mrs. Agneau. I said a silent prayer that she would be forgiven.

The last week of summer was over before I knew it. I found myself lying in bed before the sun had set, squeaky clean from my bath with my uniform laid out ready for the morning. Having stayed up every night of the summer until much later than this, it was impossible to get to sleep at this time. Not to mention the additional excitement of the first day of school filling me with anticipation.

Marilyn and Polly chatted in bed beside me expressing their hopes and plans for fifth and seventh grades respectively. They both would be kitty corner across the street from me now in the building for fifth through eighth grades. I would be the oldest in the family in the building for kindergarten through fourth grade. I was excited about the responsibility but nervous, too. I would no longer have an older sibling in the building to defend me against class bullies and such.

"Don't worry, you'll always have Mickey," Marilyn said. I realized that that was true. There were plenty of kids who were actually afraid of Mickey because he was an Indian. Mickey, of course, took full advantage of this and played along evoking ancient Indian spells and dances whenever he felt the need to intimidate. I was glad we were going to be in Mr. Hanson's classroom together.

Mickey stopped by to pick me up for school the next morning. Though his eyes were drawn immediately to the length of my uniform skirt, he was a good enough friend to know not to say a word. Our uniforms were a scratchy, wool green plaid jumper worn over white blouses for girls and green corduroy pants with matching green polo shirts for boys. I was too tall for the jumper I'd worn last year but far too small for the hand-me-down Mom was forcing me to wear this morning. I was practically drowning in the jumper and looked like a little girl playing dress up.

Mickey looked neat as a pin in his recently purchased uniform with the crease still in the pants. The Olsons loved to keep up appearances. New uniforms every school year were a must for Mickey and Kenny. We stood on the front steps so Mom could take the obligatory 'first day of school' picture.

Walter Agneau poked his head out the screen door next door. "I remember my first days of school like they were just yesterday. Have fun kids!" He forced a laugh. I glared at him as I'd been doing all week and didn't say a word. Mickey murmured thanks and we went on our way.

"Aren't you being a little hard on the guy?"

"I have absolutely nothing to say to that man, not now, not ever!"

Blue jays called out to one another, defending their territories, high up in the elm trees above us as we walked to school. Ever after, their distinct cawing would always evoke in me the feeling of going back to school on sunny autumn days. Pairs of kids walked ahead of us and behind us as we all headed to Incarnation. Shouted greetings were heard up and down the street.

Mr. Hanson was tall and so pale that his skin was almost translucent. His dark, shiny black hair was thick with gel and combed straight back from his forehead, giving him a look of Rhett Butler. We would find out that he liked to take a small, black comb from his back pocket whenever the class was reading or taking a test. He would slide the comb through his hair while following it with his other hand pressing down upon it over and over when he thought we weren't paying attention.

Mr. Hanson was my first male teacher. Initially, I was very shy around him. He was a very kind man and a good teacher though he was also very strict and didn't allow any goofing around in his classroom at all. He wasn't afraid to get physical with boys who misbehaved. More than once we witnessed him lift a boy completely off of his feet by the collar of his shirt, calmly walk him over to the corner of the classroom and plop him down until he learned how to conduct himself. The only way we could tell when Mr. Hanson was angry was because his face would grow red.

 We learned to write cursive in the third grade and to read chapter books though I'd been doing that for years. The real goal of third grade was to be picked by Mr. Hanson to be his afterschool helper for the week. Monday after Monday, he would call someone's name to ask if they'd be willing to stay after school a little later than usual. The student would nod affirmatively and then suddenly sit up taller, unable to suppress the superior smile of the chosen one.

At last, it was my turn and I was finally blessed with the distinction of being Mr. Hanson's helper. I painstakingly washed the chalkboard with a bucket and sponge, taking care to leave no streaks, swept the floor, and clapped erasers. Mr. Hanson sat at his desk correcting papers or writing notes. Sometimes he would chat or ask questions. He reminded me of Mrs. Agneau in the way he never talked down to kids but spoke to us the same way he talked to the principal, Sr. Marie Julia or to our parents. When he asked a question, he looked you in the eye while you answered, he didn't interrupt, and he often understood exactly what you were trying to say. When I found myself telling him all about Mrs. Agneau, the story made him really sad. He told me that he still lived with his mother. I didn't tell him that I couldn't believe his mother was still alive! She must have been ancient! He said that I should try not to judge Mrs. Agneau for what she'd done.

When the work was done, he thanked me and handed me a large tootsie roll. I loved walking out of the school long after all the rest of the kids had left, greeting the janitor on my way out, knowing that he knew I had stayed after school to help Mr. Hanson. I unwrapped the tootsie roll as I walked home and chewed each designated section slowly, enjoying the gooey chocolate while reflecting on what Mr. Hanson and I had talked about.

One of the best things about third grade was playing *Stealing the Bacon*. Mr. Hanson divided us into two teams. He was very good at making the teams equal and the games usually went on and on because they were so well matched. Three players from each team lined up facing their three opponents across a rather wide expanse. A player on each team was designated as player number one, two, or three. There was a chalkboard eraser on the ground exactly centered between the two teams. Mr. Hanson would call out a number, number two for example, and both players elected as number two's would rush out and try to be the first to pick up the eraser. Then they would have to run back to their place with it before the other number two touched them. The unsuccessful player was then eliminated until the teams consisted of as few as one player per team stealing the bacon.

Mickey was just about the fastest player ever so of course everyone always wanted to be on his team.

The boys, who were always picking on Mickey, calling him redskin and chief, just hated playing opposite him. They weren't quick enough to touch his back when he sped out, picked up the eraser and sped back sometimes before they even realized that their number had been called. I loved when this happened. I always cheered Mickey on extra hard. I was punished for this sometimes since everyone knew Mickey and I were friends. Because the bullies couldn't grab Mickey, they would take extra satisfaction in catching me to ease some of their humiliation on account of Mickey's superiority in the game. Furthermore, I was terrible at *Steal the Bacon*. Acting impulsively was not my strong suit; I liked to think about things, a lot, before I took action. To rush forward the second my number was called went against every survival instinct in me. Needless to say, I rarely got my hand on the eraser before my opponent did.

One day, both George Ryan and I were number three's. When our number was called, I surprised myself by grabbing the eraser first. I was nearly back in my place when George shoved me unnecessarily hard from behind causing me to fly forward and land face first on the playground blacktop.

"You did that on purpose!" Mickey hollered in my defense.

Before Mr. Hanson could stop him, he hauled back and punched George right in the face. Having scraped both knees, the palms of my hands and my chin when I landed, I was in some physical pain. That was nothing compared with the horror and shame of having the entire third grade class witness my fall. I was rather unsuccessfully blinking back my tears, so having Mickey take the attention away from me was the best gift ever.

Later, George and I sat in the nurse's office glaring at one another as the nurse washed all of my scrapes first. Then she put ice on George's rapidly swelling nose. We were still sitting there when we heard the click of someone walking rapidly down the long hallway to the Principal's office.

We saw Doc Olson knock and enter the office. A few minutes later he left, clutching Mickey's upper arm firmly in his grasp. They walked wordlessly back down the long hallway, their footsteps echoing hollowly in the silence.

"Now look what you've done," I hissed angrily at George while he stared blankly from his wide, flat face.

"What? I'm not the one who hit him. He hit me, remember?" Nursing my aching palms and knees, I didn't deign to answer him. Poor, Mickey. I hated to think what Doc Olson would do to him now.

Chapter 26

"Help me with this gosh-darned tie, would you Ginny?" Gerald asked as his large hands awkwardly held the two ends of striped blue silk between his fingers. I tied a jauntily crooked bow for him. I proceeded to lick my fingers to pat down the stubborn trio of hairs on the top of his head that refused to stay put. After assuring him that he looked just great, Gerald, Winston and I continued our vigil in Mrs. Agneau's living room. They should have been back a half an hour ago. Neither Gerald nor I were very good at being patient. I couldn't help but worry that something had gone wrong. Unable to sit still, I jumped up again to peer out the window just as I saw Dad's station wagon pull up.

"They're here! They're here!!" I hollered as our long wait was over at last. Gerald continued to sit stiffly in his chair with a petrified look on his face. He was too frozen to move.

"Maybe I shouldn't be here," he said perplexedly.

"Of course you should, Gerald," I said, pulling him up out of his chair. "You've been the most frequent visitor of all to the hospital. Mrs. Agneau's homecoming wouldn't be right without you here!"

It had been nearly three months since Mrs. Agneau's near-fatal suicide attempt. Gerald had been visiting her often, in the hospital first and then in the nursing home where she went to recover. Luckily, the overdose of Mr. Agneau's leftover sleeping pills had left no permanent damage.

Mrs. Agneau had felt that the corner her son had forced her into gave her no acceptable way out. She thought her only recourse was to end her life. Realizing at last that putting his mother into a nursing home was a cruel and inhumane way to treat the woman who gave him life, Walter gave up the idea. After spending the first week after the suicide attempt in his childhood home waiting to see if she would be alright, he had gone back to California and agreed to let his mother make her own decisions from now on. After a slow recovery, Mrs. Agneau was finally allowed to come back home as long as she had someone giving her around the clock care.

Gerald and I had made 'Welcome Home' signs, blown up balloons, and bought flowers with which to greet Mrs. Agneau. Tears filled her eyes when she was escorted into the room and gratefully took her usual seat next to the fireplace.

"Oh Mrs. Agneau, I've missed you so! I'm so glad you're home!" I gushed as I threw myself into her arms, smelling her familiar *White Shoulders* scent. I was relieved to feel strength in her arms as she hugged me back. After she'd commented on how tall I'd grown, how much she liked the signs, and how cute my new pixie haircut was, she turned to Gerald.

"Thank you for being here, dear," she said, lovingly cupping his cheek in the palm of her hand. "What a perfect homecoming."

"These are for you, my little lamb," Gerald replied as he held out the bouquet of carnations and baby's breath. He half-bowed to her. Apparently all of those visits to the hospital had changed a few things in their relationship. Winston appeared unaffected by the goings on around him. He lay contentedly in front of the fire.

Other neighbors stopped by to welcome Mrs. Agneau home.

Most of my brothers and sisters made an appearance, too.
Mr. Finkelstein even brought Mrs. Fussbudget with him to say
hello. When Winston got up, wagging his tail all the while, to sniff
Mrs. Fussbudget's bottom in greeting, he got a wallop in return.
Mrs. Agneau laughed so hard tears streamed down her face.

There was a knock at the back door. I rushed to let in the Olsons.
Mickey ran to give Mrs. Agneau a hug. I noticed the bruise on his
arm from where Doc had hauled him out of the Principal's office was
fading to spruce green. The other marks Doc left were not visible.
Mickey handed Mrs. Agneau the dream catcher he had made for her.
He instructed her to hang it on the headboard above her head so it
would filter out all of the bad dreams and only let in the good.
Kenny and Mrs. Olson, dressed impeccably as usual, stood silently
by while Doc offered his assistance no matter what time of day or
night should she need it.

"Do I need to check your medicine cabinet to remove any excess
prescription bottles you may have around? Do we need to worry
about a repeat performance?" Mrs. Agneau paled even further and
began fluttering her hands over her face and chest as she attempted
to answer him.

"Fussbudget, no!" Mr. Finkelstein shouted as right at that instant
the belligerent feline leapt out of his arms and onto Mrs. Agneau's
lap where she proceeded to clean herself. After a moment's stunned
silence, everyone burst out laughing and the awkwardness passed.

When the Olsons had left, the party livened up again before Mom
said Mrs. Agneau needed her rest and that we should leave her now.
Gerald kissed her hand as he departed and promised to come back
again tomorrow. Mr. Finkelstein went to take his perceptive cat out
of her lap but before he could, the cat sat up and stared into Mrs.
Agneau's face for a moment. I was pleased that Mrs. Fussbudget
seemed content with what she saw there.

As I opened the door to leave, Crazy Caroline stood with her hand
raised about to knock.

I told her that now wasn't a good time as we were all leaving so Mrs. Agneau could get some much needed rest. Caroline hissed that she couldn't agree with me more, stepped past me, and practically pushed us out the door.

I stood there with my mouth agape saying I didn't think we should leave the two of them alone together. Back at home, Mom informed me that Caroline was the caretaker hired to take care of Mrs. Agneau twenty-four hours a day.

"What?" I stammered. "What does she know about taking care of someone? She can't even take care of herself!" Taking out the heavy saucepan and filling it with water, Mom poured salt into the palm of her hand then dumped it into the pan to boil. She began peeling potatoes.

"Mrs. Agneau feels especially grateful to Caroline for saving her life. If Caroline hadn't gone to visit Mrs. Agneau the day she was out of her head and took all those pills, she would have kept right on sleeping to death."

"Right, Caroline was just there looking for a hand out," I mumbled under my breath. Mom ignored me and carried on.

"Caroline had the good sense to go upstairs to investigate why Mrs. Agneau wasn't answering the door in the middle of the morning. When she found her unconscious, she called for help. If it wasn't for Caroline, Mrs. Agneau would no longer be with us."

I knew all of this but I was having a hard time feeling grateful to her. Mom explained that a registered nurse wasn't needed for Mrs. Agneau's recovery. Hiring a nurse would have been much too expensive for the Agneau's to afford. Hiring Caroline was actually the perfect solution. It was a win-win situation; Mrs. Agneau needed someone to stay with her and Caroline needed a place to stay. Personally, I couldn't imagine a more losing situation than Crazy Caroline living right next door to me.

Not long afterwards, there was another newcomer to our neighborhood whose presence was about to irrevocably change things for all of us. It was Christmas vacation and winter was upon us in all its glory. The shortest day of the year had come and gone already. By 4:30 in the afternoon, the sun had set and dusk was settling in. There was so much snow that cars were only allowed to park on one side of the street. The alleys were lined with ten-foot tall snow piles created by the snowplows when they cleared them that we kids loved to play in. After a week of unrelenting snowfall with day after day of huge, varied snowflakes drifting down from the sky, we were experiencing a week of brilliant blue skies. The dazzling sunshine made the gleaming fresh snow sparkle. The cloudless days also brought frigid temperatures. The sun was so low in the winter sky that its warmth was hardly felt, but we couldn't have been happier. We ice skated, built tunnels in the snowdrifts, and made gangs of snowmen. Today we were going sliding at Bryant Park.

The boys pulled the long, wooden toboggan and the two Flexible Flyers. The girls took turns dragging the round saucers behind us as we walked the mile to the park. The toboggan bounced along behind Neil until Greg caught up and threw himself on it to be dragged to the park. Danny and Chris then climbed onto the saucers to get free rides. Bryant Park had our nearest big sliding hill. It was very popular, especially during Christmas vacation. It was crowded when we arrived but we practically knew everyone there.

The first time, I went down on my saucer with Danny on my lap. Marilyn pushed us off. After initially going straight, we started to spin and went down the last part of the hill backwards. We screamed until the saucer came to a complete stop, our cheeks flush with cold and excitement. Getting off the saucer, we began the slow ascent back up to the top of the hill. We chose to walk safely among the huge pine trees, their boughs laden down with heavy snow, so as not to get hit by oncoming sleds.

I joined the group on the toboggan next, all five of us lined up one behind the other, youngest to oldest, our legs spread open and our arms encircling one another's waists.

We screamed and squeezed our eyes shut, crying out when we flew over a bump and landed painfully back onto the ice-packed snow before coursing the rest of the way down the hill.

I had to wait my turn to go down on the Flexible Flyer because I wanted to steer it myself. When Danny begged to come, too, I lay down on my stomach and had Marilyn lay Danny on my back. We flew down the hill while I steered us this way and that finding the steepest sections of the hill to go down. It was freezing as we sailed down the hill. Our cheeks turned to ice and our noses ran. Walking back up the hill pulling the sled behind us, however, always warmed us up so much that our hands got sweaty and we'd have to loosen our scarves around our necks.

I saw Mickey sitting upright on his sled and I ran and jumped on behind him pushing us off. Mickey steered with his feet narrowly missing a slower sled ahead of us. Then he purposely steered us straight into a tree at the bottom. We both fell off, laughing as we did so. Stretching out in the snow, we began to move our arms and legs up and down and in and out, turning our heads back and forth as we did so to create perfect snow angels.

The sky was pink on the western horizon and the entire sky was shining an unearthly rosy hue. The snow changed colors with the setting sun. Long after the sun had set, the brilliant colors lingered. We walked home pulling our sleds behind us with the sliver of the moon sparkling off of the snow. Even without a moon, the snow-covered landscape would keep the darkness at bay.

"Do you want to go ice-skating tomorrow?" I asked Mickey.

"I can't," he replied. When I asked him why not, he murmured something about responsibilities at home.

I had to wait for a seat to put on my skates in the warming hut at the ice rink the next day. Practically everyone else was outside skating already while I was still struggling to pull on my skates. Obviously, my feet had grown a lot since last year. I could hardly squeeze them into the well-worn, hand-me-down skates.

Finally, I took off my socks. Removing that thin layer of warmth allowed my feet to just fit so I quickly laced up my skates. Standing up slowly on the wooden floor of the hut, I zipped up my coat and put my gloves back on before heading for the swinging doors leading out onto the ice. Before I got there, the incoming door swung open and the rest of my family burst back in.

"It's freezing out there!"

"We need to warm up already!"

"What took you so long, slowpoke?"

I pushed past and went out by myself. I shuffled along the ice, practically walking at first, until I got used to the sensation of balancing my feet on the thin blades beneath me, and I glided along the ice.

We were skating on Lake Harriet. I loved thinking about how we went swimming at this exact same spot in the summer time. Now here I was, 'walking on water!' I remembered last spring hearing about the boy who was out walking with his dog on the lake where he shouldn't have been because the ice had already started melting. The boy heard the ice cracking underneath him so he lay flat to distribute his weight over a larger surface so the crack wouldn't open sending him underwater. Up ahead, the boy's dog was trotting happily along when his front paw landed on thin ice and his entire leg sunk, pulling the rest of his body with it. The dog held its head above water for as long as it could, never uttering a sound, conserving its energy for the frantic dog paddling he was doing in the icy water. He stared back at his owner lying flat out on the ice not 20 feet away. After what seemed like hours but in fact was minutes, the dog succumbed to the freezing cold and quietly slipped under water. The boy scooted backwards on the ice until he got back to shore and walked home without his dog.

It wasn't until late spring that the boy told his story. When all the ice was off the lake, the dog rolled up on shore.

The boy's family was contacted on account of the information found on the dog's license still attached to his collar. Only then did the boy tell what had happened. The worst part of it was that his parent's had already gotten him a new puppy thinking that his old dog had run away. They named it Maverick, the same name his other dog had. The one he watched drown.

Skating on the lake, I scared myself into thinking I saw a dog's eyes gazing up at me from beneath the frozen ice. I skated as quickly as I could back to the warming hut. Everyone else was just coming back out into the cold by this time having completely warmed up.

"Come on!" they shouted. "We're going to play *Crack the Whip!*"

I hesitated for a split second because I couldn't even feel my feet anymore, they were so cold. Then I turned around and grabbed hold of Polly's hand, hopefully near the front of the 'whip'. loved this game! Pat was the head of the whip not only because he was fast but because he was so good at skating around randomly this way and that, making the tail of the whip flail around crazily. The more kids grabbed hands and joined in the game, the longer the tail became. The longer the tail, the more speed it forced onto the last player and the tighter they had to hold on. Gales of laughter and screeches of terror sounded as Pat twisted and turned and the whip snapped in wider and more violent directions.

 Kids flew off of the tail end and continued sailing across the ice. I had already fallen off twice. I was just picking myself up from the second fall when the tail shot past me and I grabbed the hand of the one on the tail end. I felt myself instantly snapped in the opposite direction. Not being able to hold on, I spun in the reverse direction while my foot continued twisting in the converse direction. I screamed in pain as I went down again on the rock hard surface of the ice, my throbbing leg coiling unnaturally beneath me.

After some of the kids half carried, half dragged me back into the warming hut, I was surprised to see Doc Olson come in the swinging door.

"What happened to you now, Ginny?" he asked in an exasperated manner. He sent the kids back outside while he examined me. Apparently Doc had just been dropping Kenny off to skate with us. Naturally Kenny couldn't walk to the lake like the rest of us but had to be chauffeured there instead.

Doc unlaced my skates. I held onto the back of the wooden bench with both hands, tightly enough so Doc, in his haste, wouldn't pull me right off of the bench but not so tightly that I would get splinters in my now mitten-less hands. I struggled to hold on as Doc tugged the skate right off of my foot in a much rougher fashion than was necessary. My frozen feet were pink with cold but the very tips of my toes had the look of frostbite with little black dots on the end of each toe. After Doc scolded me relentlessly for having no socks on my feet in this cold weather, he began pinching my toes to get the blood circulating back through them. The rhythmic squeezing brought tears to my eyes it hurt so much. Doc pinched harder and faster. With tears starting down my face, I was begging Doc to stop, but he wouldn't quit. He had an evil twinkle in his eyes as he looked down on me, panting. I was struck by the horrible realization that he was enjoying my pain. After pinching my toes for a while longer, he suddenly stopped. Without taking his eyes off of me, he grabbed hold of my sore ankle and slowly began twisting it back and forth. My scream of terror and pain brought some of the kids back into the warming hut. When they asked what was wrong, Doc answered in his most professional voice.

"No, her ankle is not broken but she sure is being a baby about the pain. Help me get her boots back on and I'll drive her home."

After my refusal to ride home with him and my repeated resistance to having my boots put back on, Doc threw his hands up in despair and shouted at Neil to help.

"Don't worry," Neil whispered as he carried me to Doc's car, "I won't leave you alone with him."

We both slid into the back seat for the ride home and rode all the way in silence.

When we got there, Doc insisted I come in the house so he could wrap my ankle with an ace bandage and put frostbite cream on my toes. I clung onto Neil and whispered frantically in his ear not leave me alone with Doc.

 He carried me into the Olson's living room and we saw Mickey sitting on the floor with a little boy on his lap. Mickey was reading *The Firehouse Cat* to the boy who was giggling delightedly at the antics of the feisty little kitten. As the boy looked up to see who had interrupted their reading, he looked familiar to me. While Doc explained disparagingly what had happened, I wracked my brain trying to place him. Mickey kept on reading. I forced myself not to wince while Doc spread ointment on my feet. I studied the little boy, sure that I recognized him from somewhere. Then, it hit me. It was the little boy we'd seen on the fourth of July in Powderhorn Park. My pain momentarily forgotten, I stared in amazement. Mickey finished reading the book at last and looked up at me, chagrined.

 Doc said, "Well, Mickey, aren't you going to introduce your friends to your little brother?"

Chapter 27

Mickey didn't want to talk about it. Mom told me that his little brother, Richard, would be staying with him at the Olsons under the same type of arrangement he had; not adopted, just temporarily in the Olsons' custody. The Olsons had dug out Kenny's old playpen and set it up in Mickey's closet of a bedroom for Richard to sleep in. At almost three, Richard was small for his age. His huge russet eyes set far apart on his round wide face tilted up a little bit on the ends giving him a slightly Asian look. His flat nose sat low on his face above the cutest little lips that he pushed out in consternation when too much attention was paid to him.

Richard followed Mickey around everywhere. For the rest of that Christmas vacation, every time Mickey came over to play, Richard came, too. He fit right in with Greg, Danny, and Chris. The most puzzling aspect to me was the fact that we had seen Richard at Powderhorn Park and Mickey had not said a word about him being his brother. More perplexing still was the drunken woman we had seen with Richard. If she was Richard's mother, a most likely circumstance, did that make her Mickey's mother, too? If she were, why didn't Mickey say anything to her? And why were they staying at the Olson's house and not with her?

As close of friends as Mickey and I were, I couldn't bring myself to ask him and he wasn't bringing up any of it.

Christmas vacation ended. The problem of who would care for Richard while Mickey was in school came up and was quickly solved in a most surprising manner. Mrs. Agneau offered to have Richard at her house during the day. Now that Caroline was living with her full time, she felt Caroline would be able to take care of both Mrs. Agneau and little Richard. He could play with Chris and Danny right next door. Mrs. Agneau though it would be fun to have a youngster in the house again. Mrs. Olson hesitated for a millisecond before agreeing to the arrangement as she rushed out the door to work. Mickey seemed fine with the situation and Caroline was better than alright with it. Her cantankerous old face looked years younger and her entire countenance changed in the presence of that sweet little boy.

The coldest month in Minnesota is typically January, and 1968 was no exception. February came and went, not much better. March is a fickle month with hints of spring tempting us before another snowstorm hits. We had just had such a snowstorm earlier in the week when eight inches of snow dumped on us. The morning had started off bright and cheerful, but by noon heaviness had settled in and the clouds shed a weighty grey cast to the air. By mid afternoon, the clouds opened up and huge snowflakes fell down from the sky like no tomorrow. With no wind to cause mayhem, the snow fell steadily without drifting, and piled up where it landed. Earlier in the season, this snowfall would have had no consequences, but now schools had snow days to burn, so school was canceled the next day, much to our delight.

Soon the week end was upon us. With it came temperatures in the 50s causing the snow to melt so rapidly that flooding occurred in the Red River Valley. My sisters and I removed our jackets as we walked home from church and reveled in the novel feeling of the sun on our pastey winter-white skin. We were still singing the Recessional Hymn "Sent Forth by God's Blessing, our true faith confessing" as we burst through the backdoor into the kitchen.

Laughing joyously at the perfect spring day and the pleasure of each other's company, we were brought up short by the sight of Mom's face.

Her eyes were puffy and her nose was red and swollen from crying. She was holding a pretty floral handkerchief to her mouth as she struggled to gain composure. To our worried inquiries as to what was wrong, she shook her head. Then she took a deep breath before calmly stating in a voice not sounding like her own, "My mother passed away this morning."

As we rushed over to hold Mom in sympathy, I thought how odd it was to hear her call Grandma 'Mother' instead of 'Ma' as she normally did. Ever after, she never referred to her as 'Ma' again, only as 'Mother' as a way of paying her more respect.

Later, I ruminated on the phrase 'passed away'. Passed away to where? You pass a car when you're driving, pass when you're playing cards, pass a test if you've studied hard, pass the ball when you're playing basketball, pass the law, pass judgment, pass a deadline, pass gas, pass the time, drive through a mountain pass and a boy can even make a pass. But what does it mean to 'pass away?'

I thought of Grandma as I'd seen her last, standing in the doorway at the farm. There had been tears in her eyes, as always, when it came time to say good-bye to her oldest daughter and family. She was waving with her good arm while her right arm hung listlessly at her side, immovable since the stroke she'd suffered at the age of 40. "Bubye, Bubye," she had hollered in her thick bohemian accent as we waved from the station wagon windows while twilight fell in the languorously slow manner it did in the countryside. None of us had realized this would be the last time that we would see her. Why hadn't a huge sign descended from the sky saying, 'Stop! Wait! You'll never see this woman alive again! Is there any last thing you'd like to say to her? To ask her?'

I marveled that such massively important moments could slip by into the obscurity of most of life's moments. Only in hindsight are we made aware of the opportunities we have missed.

I wish I could have told Grandma to give me some sort of sign so I could know if there really was life after death or not. I was already pretty sure 'limbo' didn't exist. No God in his right mind would make babies suffer any more than they already had by dying too young and making them live out eternity in a 'neither here nor there' state just because there wasn't time to get them baptized. Purgatory, too, seemed pretty unlikely to me. I figured God did the best he could creating this world. We should be doing our best to lead good, worthwhile lives while we're in it. But then, like the most graceful old willow tree, when it was our time to die, we died. It seemed to me the idea of heaven and hell was just the nuns' way of keeping us in line, but I did want to be sure before I blew it. I wish I had thought to have Grandma give me a signal from the beyond, if there really was one.

We had to miss school to go to Grandma's funeral in Olivia. Except for seeing Grandma dead and having to kiss her, it turned out to be one of the best times ever. Mom had been so busy helping with the arrangements that she hadn't had time to pay much attention to us. Jane was the one who chose all of our outfits and helped us get ready. She put us three girls in matching dresses Mom had made. She thought it would make Mom proud to show us off this way but Mom never even noticed.

We walked into the funeral home where the wake was held. I was aware of the casket sitting at the far end of the room with Grandma in it, but I avoided looking too closely. We all took a seat while the rosary was said for the repose of Grandma's soul. All through the seemingly endless decades of the rosary, we made eye contact with one cousin after another and tried not to smile too brightly so that we wouldn't disrespect Grandma. We were so happy to see each other though; it was hard not to let our excitement show.

At last the priest said: "May her soul and all the souls of the faithful departed through the mercy of God rest in peace," and the rest of us murmured Amen. I was rising up to follow the rest of our cousins outside to play when Mom's hands were suddenly on my shoulders.

She guided me with the rest of our family towards the side of the room where Grandma lay.

We seemed to walk forever as my eyes looked everywhere but forward in an effort to avoid seeing Grandma in the casket. One by one, my siblings knelt briefly on the red velvet kneeler in front of the casket and made the sign of the cross, bowed their heads briefly in prayer, hastily made one more sign of the cross in closing, and stood up and were gone in a flash. Mom's hands never left my shoulders and through her fingertips I could feel the electric charge of her emotions as she tried valiantly to keep them in check.

Looking at Grandma as I knelt, I felt my eyebrows quiver in distaste as I saw close up what a terrible job the funeral parlorhad done in preparing her.

She was wearing a navy blue silk dress with elegant white piping and a matching belt, beige nylons and practical black old-lady shoes. Her hands looked fat and swollen though quite serene as they clutched onto a large, pink rosary. I had never seen her paralyzed hand hold anything before. It looked abnormal to me. Her face, too, was unnatural looking. She appeared to be made out of wax by an inexperienced artist. Her eyes were closed, of course, but they had neglected to put Grandma's glasses on. None of us had ever seen Grandma without them. The identical red indents on either side of her nose emphasized their absence. Her grey hair was fixed beautifully in a high beehive style that Grandma had never worn in her lifetime. Closing my eyes in repugnance at the shell in front of me that was not my Grandma, I spastically made the sign of the cross, praying to myself.

"Dear Grandma, I'm sorry they made you look so bad. I'm sorry I always held back and tried to avoid kissing you. I always loved you but I just didn't like how wet your kisses were. Amen." Making another quick sign of the cross, I started to rise when Mom's hands were on my shoulders again. She whispered in my ear.

"Go on now, and kiss Mother Good-bye."

Was she kidding me? Her strong hands on my shoulders were pushing me ever closer to Grandma's corpse and though I resisted, Mom was stronger. The next thing I knew, my face was on top of Grandma's. I felt my lips touching the coldest surface they had ever felt. I recoiled at the touch, horrified by the feeling of her dry, icy lips. As I backed away I could have sworn I saw a slight twitch of Grandma's lips, and I felt like my prayer had been heard. Grandma's revenge was to make me long for one of her soggy, wet kisses in place of her dry dead one.

After the funeral the next day where thankfully, the casket was closed so we weren't subjected to the spectacle that was no longer our grandma, we got in the station wagon to join the long parade of cars to the graveyard. It was a straight shot from St. Aloysius Catholic Church to the cemetery a fourth of a mile down the road. The funeral director must have thought Grandma deserved a longer ride, so he drove up and down the streets of Olivia for a while. It was sweet knowing the police car was up front with his lights on and that it was okay for us to run the only stoplight in town. I looked behind me and saw that all of the cars following us had their headlights on even though it was only 10 o'clock in the morning and the sun was shining brightly. We were heading west out of town now and Mom said Grandma was getting her last ride back to the farm.

Back at the cemetery, we stood among the tombstones. The brisk, spring wind whipped around us. The priest prayed over Grandma's casket as it was lowered into the ground. Grandpa looked so small standing at the edge of the freshly dug hole, almost unrecognizable in his black wool coat with no overalls or farm cap on. When the priest was done, there was a lot of sniffling heard on the part of Mom and the aunts amid the whistling of the north wind. Grandma was buried beneath the only willow tree in the cemetery. The branches jostled hauntingly in the wind while we said our final good-byes to Grandma.

The delicious funeral luncheon was served in the basement of the church. Two whole buffet tables were needed to display the variety of salads friends and neighbors had brought.

Then there was another table for the hot dishes and one more for the desserts. Mom was pouring coffee in between hugging old friends and relatives.

After eating, we kids had hours of unsupervised playing time with our cousins on the playground in the schoolyard next door. We spun each other for hours on the child-propelled carousal taking turns riding and pushing. We climbed the monkey bars and slid down the giant slide. We played tag, Red Rover, Statue maker, and Kick the Can. We lay in the warm spring sunshine sharing stories and jokes until one of the older cousins hollered from the picnic table where they were lounging, "We're here for a funeral, remember?" They thought we shouldn't be laughing or enjoying ourselves quite so much on account of Grandma's death.

When the aunts were done cleaning up, we drove back to Grandpa's farm. Grandpa promptly went into his bedroom and lay down to take a nap. Moments later, I needed to pass through the bedroom to use the bathroom. Grandpa was lying sideways on the bed with his feet on a round footstool, snoring so loudly you'd think he'd been asleep for hours instead of just minutes. After that day, I never again saw Grandpa lie in bed any other way. His sleeping companion of over 50 years was missing. It seemed he couldn't bear to lie in bed the way they used to together.

Later, we were all in the car saying our good-byes to Grandpa when it became clear that Mom was saying good-bye to us, too. Jane, aware that much of Mom's responsibilities at home would fall on her shoulders, was angrily questioning Mom about why she had to stay on the farm. The long days of preparation and social duties surrounding the funeral which had forced Mom to keep her emotions in check were over. Mom finally allowed a crack in her composure to show as she shouted back at Jane.

"Don't you think I would rather be anywhere else but here just now? I would love to climb in the car with all of you and run away from this. I...," Mom looked like she wanted to say more but instead she shook her head and waved us on.

Her tears continued to roll down her cheeks as Dad slowly put the station wagon in gear and we drove away. I pictured her going through Grandma's closets, drawers and papers, boxing it all away so Grandpa wouldn't have to. I realized what a hard job that would be for her. The rest of the world was just coming alive in this spring season of rebirth but Grandma lay cold and dead in the ground. Mom would dutifully put away all of her things and tidily clean up her life.

Nothing went right at home without Mom there. We overslept in the mornings. The creamed tuna on toast needed more milk in it. The laundry didn't get done so I had to wear the same white blouse over and over again under my uniform jumper. Someone was always being sent to the store for one thing or another, to Van's Market to buy Viceroy cigarettes for Dad, to Red Owl to buy cat food for Two-shoes, to Grand Bakery to buy bread for sandwiches, to Ben Franklin to buy thread for Jane's sewing.

Jane had started making all of her own clothes this year. With eight brothers and sisters there wasn't enough money for Jane to buy all of the short dresses she needed in the rapidly changing mini skirt revolution, so Jane began making her own. From her sweet turquoise a-line dress with the yellow polka dots to her green and blue zigzag fitted skirt, everything she made was super short. Mom would be surprised, to say the least, at Jane's new outfits when she got home.

I was sent to Ben Franklin to pick up a zipper for Jane. I pushed Chris in the stroller for company. We walked the six blocks amidst his pleasant chatter.

"Hi George," Chris greeted the tall, elderly man behind the counter as soon as we walked in the door. George smiled warmly as he greeted us and then left us alone to shop. Even though I knew right where the sewing section was, I took my time walking up and down the aisles of the musty-smelling old store. My footsteps creaked on the shiny, wooden floor as I made my way through the knickknacks. I found the sewing notions but couldn't remember if Jane needed an 8 or a 12-inch zipper.

"Mr. Franklin, may I use your phone?" I inquired.

He laughed and pointed to the corner while he waited on another customer. I used to think George was Ben Franklin because he is the owner of the store. One day when no one else was around, he explained to me who Ben Franklin was and that he'd lived 200 years earlier. He winked saying that even though he may look to be 200 years old, he wasn't quite that old yet! He told me I could call him George. We had been fast friends ever since. I was grateful to him for not correcting me in front of the other kids, so I never tried to act like a know-it-all when other kids called him Mr. Franklin either. I still called him that from time to time just to make him laugh.

I loved using the phone in the corner of the store. I tried to find an excuse to do so every time I went there. It was a huge, black, old-fashioned wall phone with the speaking part attached to the wall and the listening part shaped like a small megaphone. George kept a wooden stepstool by the phone because the phone was up too high for kids to reach. I climbed up on the stool and laboriously dialed home. The rotary dial was big and slow. I had to wait after each number I dialed for the wheel to noisily rotate back into place.

After getting my answer from Jane, Chris and I spent at least ten more minutes at our favorite pastime of choosing which sweets we would get with the change. There were four rows of glass jars filled with a variety of candy from jaw breakers to orange peanuts. George was just about to close the shop so I told Chris to hurry and make his selection.

"Oh, my God!" George said as he turned up the volume on the radio behind the counter.

The announcer was saying "We repeat the Reverend Martin Luther King has been shot. We have no further information at this time."

George made the sign of the cross. "Bless his soul."

After we settled up, I pushed Chris in his stroller out the back door of Ben Franklins to the alley. Behind the store, there was a wall which led to the alley below. We called this spot our 'secret ledge'. Chris and I sat on the ledge, ate our treats, and chatted. We shared many stories at our secret ledge. I said I thought I might not have school the next day on account of King's assassination. Chris kept talking about Richard this and Richard that. I knew he was anxious to get back to play with his new favorite friend.

We not only had school the next day but we also had mass in the middle of the day to remember the life and mourn the death of Martin Luther King, Jr. Mr. Hanson read out loud the speech "I Have a Dream." As he did so, I noticed his accent came to sound more and more like a colored man's. He even used the same singsong technique as Dr. King where he'd start talking real quiet. Just when we were leaning in trying hard to catch what he was saying, he would suddenly start shouting, waking up anyone who hadn't been paying attention.

We were a somber group walking home from school that day; even Wayne gave up chasing us home. He straggled behind us instead until it was time for him to turn off down his own street. Mickey was taking Dr. King's death especially hard. He had some harebrained idea that the government was behind the killing because they were afraid of how powerful King was becoming at uniting the colored people of America. I let him go on and on even though I didn't believe a word he was saying. Then he went on to say it was not unlike the killing of Little Crow. He began to tell the story.

"Little Crow was the Dakota Indian the U.S. government believed was the main troublemaker behind the Dakota Uprising of 1862. One day, when Little Crow was out picking raspberries with his son, a farmer outside of Hutchinson shot and killed him. The farmer didn't even know who he was killing. He was just shooting at the poor starving Indian he saw stealing from his field. To the Indian, this had nothing to do with stealing, however, as the Indians believed the raspberries belonged to everyone. There was never any question of someone owning a raspberry bush.

When the officials realized who it was the farmer had killed, he received the standard twenty-five dollar bounty for the scalp of any Dakota plus an additional five hundred dollars. Little Crow's body was dragged down the main street of town while firecrackers were placed in his ears and dogs nibbled at his head."

"That's awful!"

"That was over a hundred years ago, but do you know what? His skull is still there, sitting in the rotunda at the capital in St. Paul. Little Crow's relatives keep trying to get it back, but no one listens to them."

Deeply engrossed in Mickey's story, I didn't notice the crowd standing on our front lawn until we were practically on top of them. Mom was home! I ran into her arms while Mickey stood back with a wistful look on his face until Mom pulled him into our embrace as well.

Chapter 28

The country was suffering from back to back assassinations, first of Martin Luther King followed just two months later by Robert F. Kennedy. We had all been devastated by Dr. King's and Robert Kennedy's assassinations. Mom had set up her ironing board in the living room to watch the sad processions. Again, she cried when she watched the enormous Kennedy clan incomprehensibly mourning the loss of another of their bright young sons.

Mickey felt badly about the assassinations. He said Robert Kennedy had been even more concerned for minorities than his brother the president had been. Oddly enough, Mickey was mourning another bizarre assassination attempt that had occurred two days before Robert Kennedy's. A woman named Valerie Solanas had shot the pop artist, Andy Warhol, because she felt he somehow had too much control over her life. Warhol went on to live decades longer, but the attempt on his life affected him greatly.

Mickey really admired the artist and went about drawing remarkably good likenesses of everyday items in Warhol's honor. He drew on paper with pencil, markers, and crayons, and he drew on the sidewalk with chalk.

Everything was changing by the summer of 1968. That fateful summer, I felt my siblings getting older. They were seeking their pleasures outside of the family home and even beyond the neighborhood. It seemed everyone in the family had a job but me. Jane was working at Walker Nursing Home, Neil at the Dairy Queen, Pat as a caddy at the Minnekhada golf course, Polly at the Grand Bakery, Marilyn at a house on Harriet. She was babysitting fulltime for a family with just two kids. The kids were practically Marilyn's own age, so she was really just getting paid to enjoy herself and play all summer long without having to help out at home at all!

This year, instead of the neighborhood kids looking in, I felt as though I were looking out through our chain-linked fence longing to be on the other side of it. I felt trapped more often than not in our fenced-in backyard taking care of my three little brothers and their friends, supervising them in the pool, refereeing their basketball games, and directing this year's summer play, *Oliver*.

Danny was playing the part of Oliver. The Academy Awards had been postponed for a few days this year on account of Martin Luther King's assassination. The previous year, *In the Heat of the Night* had won the best movie Oscar starring the handsome black actor Sydney Poitier. The movie showed how blacks and whites could work together, help each other, and eventually even learn to like each other.

A few years earlier we had seen Sydney Poitier in an even better movie called *A Patch of Blue*. It was about a blind girl who falls in love with Sydney Poitier's character, but she doesn't know he's black. When they kissed in the movie, Dad had said, "Kids, you are seeing history in the making."

Down South, they didn't get to see history in the making because they took that scene out of the movie on account of they thought it would set off riots and such.

Dad thought that the movie *Oliver* won this year because it was just a 'feel good' movie. Our country needed something to feel good about instead of thinking so much about race, war and everything wrong with us. Danny got the part of Oliver not so much because he could sing well; he couldn't. It was due to the fact that he was good at memorizing. He looked so cute when he held up his bowl and said "Please, sir, may I have some more?" that we ended every rehearsal with him standing in the middle of the stage in Stidger's garage repeating it.

After rehearsal one day, I headed over to Mr. Finkelstein's house to ask him if he was still interested in playing the part of Fagin. I was surprised to see the little Indian doctor who had treated Mickey and Polly seated at the kitchen table, Mrs. Fussbudget languishing on his lap.

"Ginny, you remember Dr. Chowdbury, don't you?"

"Yes, of course." I thrust out my hand. I was amazed to see my hand was the same size as the petite doctor's as we clasped them together in greeting. They almost looked the same color, too. The long, summer days had browned my skin considerably.

"Shakespeare was just asking me about Mickey and how he's doing these days," Mr. Finkelstein said, and my eyebrows shot up in surprise while I hastily looked away and tried to hide my giggle behind a cough.

"Oh, that's quite alright," Dr. Chowdbury said in his charming voice. "I have been getting astonished reactions my entire life due to my parents' odd choice of my first name. You see, they were determined that I would receive an education outside of the village. The only book they owned was an enormous volume of the entire works of William Shakespeare. I used to sit on it as a booster chair for years. Eventually, I began to read from it. Surely the knowledge that came from that massive manuscript did help me to satisfy my parents' wishes by being able to study outside of the village. In due course, I would study outside of the country, too.

They hoped that by naming me 'Shakespeare', some of his wisdom and poetry would channel itself into me. I do not know if that has happened or not. I do know it hasn't been easy, as you may well imagine, going through life as Shakespeare Chowdbury. No, indeed not."

I was offered a bowl of fresh rhubarb crumble with vanilla ice cream on top. Mr. Finkelstein stood up to pull another chair over for me to join them at the table. He squeezed the doctor's shoulder as he walked by and said it was a noble name full of character that completely suited him. Dr. Chowdbury reached his delicate hand up to squeeze Mr. Finkelstein's in return. At that moment, Mrs. Fussbudget stretched and dug all ten of her claws deep into the doctor's legs. The doctor leapt up in agony but Mrs. Fussbudget hung on for dear life. Mr. Finkelstein extricated the cat, scolding her scathingly as he ferried her out the door.

We began to hold play practice in the evenings to rehearse the scenes requiring Mr. Finkelstein's presence as Mr. Fagin. This evening was hot and humid without even a hint of a breeze allowing the mosquitoes to languish noisily in the garage. They attacked our sweaty skin, hungrily filling themselves with our blood before drifting off to die. The heat was making everyone cranky and forgetful. I found myself reading out more of the lines from my book than the actors were reciting by memory. The thumping of someone playing basketball down the alley kept tempo with the pounding of the blood in my ears as the excessive humidity caused my head to throb. Danny began to complain about how long rehearsal was taking and how he wished he were out playing basketball himself.

"Well, you can't," I admonished. "Not till we've got this scene down."

"Who's shooting buckets anyhow?" Danny asked. "I thought everyone in the neighborhood was in the play!"

"Kenny's not," I said, glancing up and noticing the red hair through the opened garage door. With the words barely out of my mouth, Mickey looked up from the set he was painting looking worried.

"Where's Richard?" he asked.

"He went home ages ago. I guess you had gone to get the ladder when he told me he was tired and wanted to go home. Tessa took him."

Mickey dropped his brush with a clatter and ran out the door heading towards his house. I assigned some of the other kids the task of finishing up the blue paint for the sky that Mickey had left undone. We rehearsed a few more scenes before finally calling it a night. I released everyone to go on home and sit in front of a fan or something to get some relief from the muggy air. I washed and dried the paint brushes after everyone had left wondering what was going on with Mickey. It wasn't like him to leave the paintbrushes without rinsing them out first. He never treated anything so carelessly. I decided I'd drop by the Olsons on the way home to see what was up.

Kenny was still playing basketball. The warm night made his tee shirt cling to his skinny frame as it was soaked through with sweat. His shaggy, ginger hair looked slick as he tossed his head to get his unshorn bangs out of his eyes. I set down my clipboard and hip-checked Kenny as I reached in for a rebound.

We played one-on-one for a while though neither of us was really very good at it. The sound of our breathing was loud in the still August night as the game carried on. We played up to ten. When Kenny got lucky with a left-handed layup, he shouted, "That's ten!" We both collapsed onto the grass in exhaustion.

"Thanks, Ginny," Kenny said, and I responded no problem, thinking that it was rare for me to be around Kenny without Mickey around. In fact, I was never around Kenny at all.

"Hey, it's not too late for you to help out with the play this summer, you know," I was saying when the stillness of the night was pierced by the sound of someone screaming. Both Kenny and I were on our feet in an instant. Then we froze as we stared up at his house.

The screams were accompanied by shouting now and the sound of a door slamming. I looked at Kenny and saw his face drain of all color. He looked as terrified as I felt.

"I'll get Mom," I managed to eke out though my throat was almost completely closed in fear.

"Don't leave me!" Kenny shrieked as he wrapped his sweaty fingers tightly around my wrist. "Please!"

"But Mickey needs help!" I hissed as I struggled to extricate myself from his panicked grip. I knew it was true. It was Mickey who needed my help. Behind Kenny, I saw a movement in the shadow of the garage. "Help!" I bellowed.

In the light of the streetlamp, I saw the unwelcome figure of Crazy Caroline. Again, she was the one coming to rescue me. Her eyes held none of their usual jitteriness as she calmly told Kenny to let go of my arm so I could run home for help. Jerking my arm away, I fled across the alley toward home while Kenny remained motionless, paralyzed with fear, Caroline standing awkwardly by his side.

After calling the police, Mom refused to let me go with her and Pat as they ran over to the Olsons. It felt like forever before we finally heard the far-off wailing of the sirens. Marilyn was the oldest one at home. She was unrelenting in obeying Mom's instructions no matter how much I begged her to let me go to the Olsons to see what had happened and to be sure Mickey was alright.

"Mom said you have to stay here!" she insisted. I ran upstairs to look out the windows which would afford a better view as to what was going on across the alley. When I saw the paramedics carrying someone out on the stretcher, I screamed and raced back downstairs, slipping halfway down, descending the second half of the stairway on my bottom.

"Marilyn! Someone is being carried into an ambulance on a stretcher!!"

"What?! Who?" Marilyn's cool demeanor was finally cracking.

"I don't know, they were completely covered by a blanket."

"Oh, my God!" I was astonished to hear Marilyn take the Lord's name in vain. After a moment's hesitation, she was practically shoving me out the backdoor. "Go!" she commanded. At last, I was racing back over to the Olsons but stopped in my tracks when Marilyn's final warning reached my ears. "The blanket over the body means they're dead, Ginny. Someone died over there. Go find out who."

The ambulance was pulling away when I got there. Mickey was holding his arms awkwardly in front of himself. I was so relieved to see that he was alright, that I was running to him when I felt Pat's hand on my shoulder holding me back. That was when I noticed the handcuffs on Mickey's wrists. Mickey's eyes met mine. I was surprised at how calm he looked as the police officer took his arm and began leading him away to the squad car at the curb. Opening the back door, the officer helped Mickey into the back seat before getting behind the wheel. Mickey didn't turn his head to look at us at all as he was driven off, not even when Richard's screams turned hysterical as he shouted Mickey's name over and over again.
I was unaware of Pat's hand still on my shoulder until he turned toward me. I buried my head into his stomach. He held me close and kept patting my back gently while all around us havoc reigned.

Mrs. Olson was hysterical as she cried over and over that it couldn't be true, he couldn't be dead, and she wouldn't believe it. Mom tried in vain to comfort her. When I realized it was Doc Olson who was under the blanket on the stretcher, I whispered, "Doc?" for confirmation. Pat simply nodded his head. Richard was still crying. He was struggling to escape from the police officer's arms so I walked over and reached out to him.

"Hey Richard, wanna come over to our house and play with Chris?" He started squirming in my direction now and leaned as far as he could out of the officer's arms as he strained towards me.

"Go with Ginny!" he repeated again and again as he turned to rubber trying to slip out of the officer's grip. Mom finally convinced them that it would be best if I took the little boy home with us, so Pat, Richard, and I headed back across the alley.

"What about Kenny?" I asked as I held tightly on to little Richard's hand.

"His Mom's gonna need him tonight," Pat reflected. "It's time for the favorite son to pull his weight."

Chapter 29

The play, *Oliver*, went on as planned, although no one's heart seemed to be in it anymore. We had one of the biggest audience turnouts ever from the neighborhood. Greg said that was just because the neighbors all wanted to get together to gossip about Doc Olson's death. He apparently fell in the kitchen with his head hitting the corner of the stove, and he died minutes afterward. Mrs. Olson had been upstairs when she heard the commotion. By the time she got downstairs, the blood was pouring out of Doc's head. Her screams had echoed throughout the neighborhood. She barely had time to cradle Doc's head in her lap when he died. Her lime green skirt had been soaked right through. Surely that was the first time any of us had seen her looking so disheveled. Later, we found out that Doc's pants had been down at his ankles when he fell. Then, they said he hadn't actually fallen but that he'd been pushed by Mickey.

When Mickey had run in the door after leaving play practice, Doc had been holding poor little Richard so tightly that the bruises on his tiny arms lasted for weeks. At our house, when Richard concentrated on crashing the hot wheels cars into each other while playing with Chris, I would stare at those bruises.

They showed so clearly Doc's fingers, how they'd grasped onto Richard's arms. But now Doc was dead, his hands wouldn't cause any more bruising to anyone.

The police officers had come to collect Richard from us later on the night of the shooting. They wanted to examine him to see the extent of the abuse, but Mom refused to let him go. She said if he had to be examined that night before any evidence disappeared, then the doctor could come to our house. He could examine Richard in the familiarity and safety of our own home.

When the doctor arrived a while later, we were delighted to see that it was Dr. Chowdbury. He acted all business in front of the police officers, but when he crouched down to talk to Richard sitting on my lap listening to me read *Hop on Pop*, he winked at me reassuringly. Richard didn't hesitate to go to him at all. Mom was allowed to stay with Richard during Dr. Chowdbury's examination. When they finished, the door opened, and Richard ran right back to my lap and picked up the Dr. Seuss book. Dr. Chowdbury was beaming. I was surprised to see Mom crying although she, too, had a smile on her face.

"It's alright, he's fine. He hadn't been harmed yet, he is just fine!"

"Of course he's fine," I reiterated while I kissed the top of Richard's head. His pitch black hair felt silky to my lips. I felt as though he had somehow escaped some dreadful experience, though I wasn't really sure just what.

"Read!" he commanded me while he slapped the open page of the book. "Read now!"

He looked so surprised when everyone erupted into relieved laughter that he repeated himself over and over again to see if the ridiculous grownups would continue to laugh at his bad behavior. Finally, Mom told me to take Richard up to the boys' room and finish reading to him there.

I wanted to ask about Mickey and where they'd taken him but I didn't want to upset Richard by bringing up his name. Instead, I carried him slowly out of the room while Mom continued to thank God and Dr. Chowdbury over and over again.

While Richard was safe with us, Mickey had disappeared into the bowels of the juvenile delinquents' system. I was relieved, at first, because I thought he had been taken to jail. Then Neil chastised me saying jail might even be better than the homes they had for troubled boys, especially troubled Indian boys. Mom spent hours on the phone trying to find his whereabouts. Because she wasn't a blood relative, she had no legal jurisdiction over him so no one would tell her anything. She went to ask for Mrs. Olson's help because, oddly enough, Mrs. Olson was still listed as Mickey's legal guardian. Mrs. Olson apparently said no, because Mom came back home to report that Mrs. Olson had let loose with some doozies.

I was playing tic-tac-toe with Greg, Danny, and Chris out on the blacktop using chalk. Every time we finished a game, we would scoot over a little bit to a clean patch of the backyard and draw the four lines to begin another game of x's and o's. Mom began sweeping the back steps while she talked about Mickey.

"How could Mrs. Olson hold such a young boy responsible for Doc Olson's death when truth be told she carries plenty of the blame on her own shoulders? She allowed all those shenanigans to take place under her very own roof. It's unforgivable! Mickey ought to be held up as a hero for protecting his little brother like that, not be made to suffer while he's placed in a home for delinquent children," Mom fumed.

"Who are 'the Lincoln' children?" Greg asked.

"What?" Mom continued furiously sweeping the steps.

"Who are 'the Lincoln' children?" He repeated.

"The Lincoln children? What are you talking about?" She looked puzzled.

"You keep talking about 'the Lincoln' children's home. I never knew Mickey was a Lincoln but he must be if he gets to stay at their house, right?" Greg's face look puzzled as he waited for Mom to reply.

A big smile took over Mom's face. "Oh, honey, not the Lincoln children, delinquent children. A delinquent child is one who has broken the law or behaved in a way unacceptable to society."

After musing over this for a while, I asked, "But what if the delinquent breaks the law to stop someone else from 'behaving in a way unacceptable to society'" I mimicked. "Shouldn't that be okay then?"

"Ginny, I couldn't agree with you more," Mom sighed as she took her broom and went back inside.

Summer carried on with no word on Mickey or his whereabouts. I was so worried about him it practically made me sick. I had no desire to join in any of the neighborhood games. Nothing was the same without Mickey around. Even the Shortpaschers stopped tormenting me. Just before summer ended, something happened that gave us some insight into Mickey's current situation, but I almost wished that it hadn't.

We were in St. Paul for the Minnesota State Fair. We loved going to the state fair. It was an annual event that for us was a day-long affair. It ushered in the end of summer and the start of the new school year as certainly as the crickets rubbing their legs together chirped it.

Even though Minneapolis and St. Paul were twin cities side by side separated only by the Mississippi River, for eighteen years, the only time I crossed the river to go into St. Paul was during the state fair. This wasn't unusual, either. The two cities existed completely detached from one another. While Minneapolis was as familiar to me as the back of my own hand, St. Paul was as foreign as any other American city.

Early on this late August morning, we left the car in the residential area near the fairgrounds to save money on parking. We began the long walk to enter the fair. As we strolled along, we started listing all the things we were going to see and eat at the fair. Mini donuts would be first, of course, then some sweet corn. We would definitely enjoy malts in the dairy building while we admired the sculpture carved out of butter reflecting the Dairy Princess's likeness.

Mom and I had been holding hands so we let go while Mom stopped to tie Danny's shoe. As I waited, I admired the chalk drawings on the sidewalk in front of a rather dilapidated old house whose front yard was littered with toys and rusty old bicycles. The multicolored chalk was used to draw a perfect copy of a can of chicken noodle soup. An uncanny feeling came over me which made me shiver. I looked down to see goose bumps covering my arms.

When we walked on, I mulled over what was troubling me. As the day progressed, we passed through each of the barns at the fair. We admired the beautiful horses, remarked on the sad eyes of the cows, and marveled over the winner of Minnesota's Biggest Pig contest. The poor pig was too large to stand up on his little legs. We ambled through the Home Improvement Building, the Dairy Building, the Art Building, and the DNR Building. We ended up on Machinery Hill as always and had a ball clambering up into the enormous John Deere tractors, pushing the clutches into place and pretending to drive the huge combines.

We left before dark to avoid the huge crowds at the Midway. The rides at the fair were too expensive so we never even ventured into that area.

The walk back to the car seemed infinitely longer than the trip going. We were all exhausted and the little boys had to be carried as we retraced our steps through the neighborhood adjacent to the fairgrounds.

Just before we got back to the ramshackle house, it hit me what had struck me about the chalk drawings.

They looked just like Mickey's! The can of soup I had seen on the sidewalk was exactly like another I had seen of Mickey's earlier that summer when he was imitating Warhol's renditions of everyday items. Looking up at the decrepit old house just as the revelation hit me, I could have sworn I saw a face peering out of an upstairs' window.

"Mickey!" I shouted and at the same time I ran toward the house.

"What's wrong with her?" Polly asked but I was already pounding on the front door and simultaneously ringing the doorbell. Mom had caught up to me by then, and I explained as succinctly as I could in my excited state why I thought Mickey was living in this derelict old house. Mom had overseen enough of our art work over the summer to realize that what I was saying made sense. She knocked even louder on the front door. After what seemed like forever, the front door eased open. An annoyed-looking woman with long, greasy hair stood glaring at us.

"Yes, sorry to bother," Mom began in her take-charge mother tone of voice. "Are you a foster parent?"

The woman was nodding her head affirmatively when she asked what business it was of ours. Mom explained that we had lost track of a young friend of ours but that we'd recently learned he might be living "in this stately old home," Mom finished unconvincingly, and the skeptical woman let a sneer pull back her lip momentarily before she caught herself in time.

"You got the wrong house. Good night." She slammed the door in our faces.

Mom hissed, "Well, I never!" under her breath and rapped her knuckles firmly on the front door once more and continued knocking until the door was pulled open with a jerk. "Yes, now if you could hear me out..." Mom began until she was interrupted by the surly-looking man who now stood at the open door.

"No, you hear me out, lady. I don't care who you are or what snot-nosed kid you're looking for. Ain't nobody here wants to see you. What kids we got under our roof are our business and not yours. Go find your own 'wards of the state' to take care of and don't go trying to steal any of ours!"

He banged the door shut so loudly that it was followed immediately by a baby's wail. Figuring there was nothing else to do, we joined the rest of the family at the curb and carried on walking back to the car. I picked up Richard and turned back to face the house. It was dark now in the room in which I thought I had seen Mickey's face at the window but I stood there anyhow for a good minute holding Richard's face towards the house just in case. I wanted Mickey to know that his little brother was doing just fine, thanks to him, so I stood there as long as I could looking up at the house while Richard sucked contentedly on his thumb. Finally, I turned around and joined the rest of the family shuffling slowly back to our car.

There was good news and bad news that came along with starting fourth grade this year. The good news was that Incarnation School's Cleary Hall only went up to the fourth grade. That meant we were now the oldest kids in the building. All of the younger kids looked up to us and accepted all of our rules and decisions. The bad news was that Miss Pettigrew was the fourth grade teacher, and she was terrifying!

She had been teaching fourth grade at Incarnation for years and she knew every kids' trick in the book. Even the toughest kids bowed their heads and politely answered every question with "Yes, Miss Pettigrew" or "Thank you, Miss Pettigrew." Miss Pettigrew's room was always quiet and well-disciplined. Only the sound of her sensible low-heeled black shoes thumping in the aisles as she walked up and down was heard during any given school day. No one ever dared deceive Miss Pettigrew.

During Lent, we were expected to attend daily mass. My family usually went at 6:30 in the morning before school started.

It was torture sitting in the quiet church being expected to stay awake when we had barely woken up to get there and had practically sleep-walked into the church. The kids who didn't have the sort of parents who forced their kids to attend daily mass were looked down upon and penalized for not being such diligent churchgoers during Lent.

Often Miss Pettigrew would ask those who had been to mass every day during Lent to stand so they could be recognized. I had been to mass twenty nine days in a row. That particular morning, Mom decided we wouldn't go to mass but rather would wait and go to five o'clock mass that afternoon. Miss Pettigrew asked who had been to mass every day that Lent and for the first time, I didn't stand up with the rest of the regular churchgoers. Several students turned to stare at me. Lexie raised an inquisitive eye as she knew Mom made us go every day during Lent. Miss Pettigrew repeated the question. When I still didn't stand up, she came and stood over me with her heavily-lined eyebrow arched in consternation.

"I'm disappointed in you," she said disdainfully. "Have you not attended church every day this Lent?" Loathing such negative attention on me, I murmured that I had been to mass every day except that day. I tried to say that we would be going later that afternoon but Miss Pettigrew had already moved on, shaking her grey curls in a disapproving manner as she clucked her tongue and no longer judged me worthy of her high expectations.

It felt strange to be at school without Mickey. I missed seeing his big round head bent over the desk while he would work diligently on his schoolwork. I missed him even more in the neighborhood.

Sometime during the school year, Mrs. Olson had a "For Sale' sign erected on her lawn. Before the house even sold, she took Kenny and left town. Prior to leaving, she took a whole carton of eggs and threw them one by one at Mr. Finkelstein's house. She stood in the alley right up against his fence and threw each egg as hard as she could. Not all of the eggs reached the house because Mrs. Olson didn't have a very good arm. Lots of them broke on the cement path leading up to the back door.

I helped Mr. Finkelstein hose down the sticky yolks afterwards. He wasn't even that upset about it.

"She's mad because I'm defending Mickey," he said as he scraped the dried egg off the screen door, one of the few eggs that made the bulls' eye hit. "A person really can't blame her. She must be feeling guilty for a) either being unavailable or unaware of what was happening under her own roof, or b) even worse, knowing what sick deeds were being done by her husband and not doing anything about it. If the latter is true, she should be in jail herself."

"What about Kenny?" I asked.

"Yes, what about Kenny?" Mr. Finkelstein stopped scraping and came to sit beside me on the stoop. "Evidence suggests that Kenny was not being abused. Stories are now coming forth from many of Doc Olson's patients over the years who claim to have been abused in his office. When poor Mickey moved in, he was an easy target. As soon as we became suspicious, Shakespeare reported the abuse. We were trying hard to get Mickey removed from the Olson's home. Inexplicably, instead of having Mickey removed, they placed his little brother with him who was even more unable to defend himself.

Doc Olson used his influence as a member of the medical profession to convince the state that Richard would be better off living with his brother than on his own in some other foster home. You see, Mickey and Richard's mother had been arrested again, this time for disorderly conduct, so Richard had to be placed somewhere. Fortunately for us, all of that documentation is on file at the Child's Welfare office and cannot be ignored. Why Doc wanted to adopt Richard as well as Mickey, well, that's too unpleasant to think about, really. The good news is that we have the Shortpaschers helping us. It won't be long now and we should have Mickey home."

I still couldn't get over the Shortpaschers being willing to help Mickey. I always thought they hated Mickey as well as everyone else in the neighborhood who wasn't a Shortpascher. Turns out they hated Doc even more.

He had been abusing the Shortpaschers, too, as well as having an affair with their Mom. She was hooked on prescription drugs and he had been happy to keep her well-supplied as long as she continued to pay him in favors. Now the Shortpaschers were willing to testify on Mickey's behalf. I was trying to get used to this feeling of being grateful to the Shortpaschers. It was going to take a while.

Lying in bed unable to sleep, I tried to picture where Mickey might be. I pictured his face the way he looked when I last saw him with Doc's blood all over him. I relived that night over and over in my mind. Mickey had left play practice in such a hurry after he had heard Kenny playing basketball outside because he knew that meant Richard was alone with Doc. He knew exactly what that sort of opportunity would mean. He had spent the six months since Richard had arrived being sure such a situation would never present itself.

When Mickey got home that night after play practice, Doc had locked him up in his room. It took him a while, but Mickey managed to pick the lock and escape. Racing back downstairs, he walked in on Doc and Richard. That's when he gave Doc an almighty shove. Luckily, he had arrived in time and no harm was ever done to little Richard. Poor Mickey. To think that all the time he lived with the Olsons, he was being abused by Doc, and all the time since Richard had moved in, he was protecting his little brother from the same thing happening to him. I wished he had confided in me, but I could certainly understand why he hadn't. It was awful to think about.

Now Doc Olson was dead and they were saying that Mickey killed him. I wished I knew how Mickey was feeling now.

Chapter 30

I was holding Two-shoes in my arms on the front steps in front of the screen door enjoying the smell of spring in the air. The cat was purring loudly while draped over my shoulder. I scratched under her chin and behind her ears just the way she loved it. All of a sudden, a growl began in the pit of her stomach. I could feel it as well as hear it as she moaned her displeasure. Turning, I saw Mr. Finkelstein walking towards me carrying a very unhappy Mrs. Fussbudget struggling to get out of his arms. I held onto Two-shoes even tighter. "Go ahead, Mr. Finkelstein, and take Fussbudget right inside. Mrs. Agneau is expecting you."

Mr. Finkelstein started to jog a bit as he struggled to get his hissing cat inside. Just in time, too, as I was no longer able to hold onto my squirming cat that had very successfully used her sharp claws to expedite my release of her. That was alright. Two-shoes would be spending her afternoon much as usual with very little excitement going on as her tail twitched while she spied on the birds and squirrels unwittingly landing in our yard. Then there would be much longer segments of time spent sound asleep in some out of the way spot.

Mrs. Fussbudget, on the other hand, was spending her afternoon attending a wedding. I felt certain that if we were to ask her, she would have been far more content to remain in the tranquility of her own home and leave the wedding festivities to her two-legged friends. Mr. Finkelstein however, considered his cat his family. Like it or not, he was insisting on Mrs. Fussbudget's presence at the most important ceremony of his life.

Mom came out the door then and scolded me for sitting idly when I was supposed to be gathering flowers for the bouquet. She looked beautiful in her navy blue dress with her hair all ratted up on top of her head. She smelled good, too. I told her so. She thanked me briskly while repeating that I needed to go in the back and pick the prettiest flowers I could find to carry. Walking around the side of the house, I was humming the Monkees' *'I'm a Believer.'* Two-shoes took advantage of my distracted state and leapt out from under the lilac bush, latched onto my foot for a second while I squealed in surprise, then darted off in the opposite direction.

"Ow! That hurt, you horrible cat!" I shouted after her and began to pick daffodils from the backyard. I was on my knees carefully choosing the right flowers for the wedding bouquet when I heard the familiar screeching of a grocery cart. I looked up to see Crazy Caroline pulling her cart out of Mrs. Agneau's garage. She wheeled the cart right over to where I was kneeling and stopped right in front of me.

"Guess you'll be glad to see me go," she chortled.

"What do you mean? Where are you going? " I sat back on my haunches and shielded my eyes from the sun to look up at her.

"Oh, I finished what I came for and now it's time for me to go," Caroline said. "I never did care for spending so much time indoors. I hate that trapped feeling and spending all my waking hours taking care of stuff, cleaning stuff, looking after things. I like when everything I own is right here inside my cart and I don't have to worry about this or that, I can just look up and appreciate the stars over my head."

For the first time, I considered that I might have been wrong all this time, that Caroline wasn't crazy at all. What she said made sense to me especially when she sighed and said, "I come from a long line of proud Dakota Indians who survived in much harsher surroundings than this. It's in my blood, staying for a while and then moving on, still following the buffalo herds as it were. I go where the wind blows," she made a whooshing sound as if the wind were picking up to send her off right now.

After Mrs. Agneau had told me the astounding news that Caroline was actually Mickey and Richard's grandmother, I had tried not to be so afraid of her. Caroline's daughter was an alcoholic and a poor excuse for a mother. Grandma Caroline had been watching out for Mickey and Richard their whole lives as best she could. When she had heard that the Olson's were taking Mickey under their roof, she had checked around and was not happy with the rumors she heard about the doctor. The night of the shooting, Caroline had had a bad feeling and was just heading over to the Olson's house when she heard all of the commotion of Mickey pushing Doc. She had done her best to take care of her family. That's one of the reasons she had moved in with Mrs. Agneau, to keep an eye on her grandsons.

I left the flowers on the ground as I stood up to face Caroline. I looked her right in the eyes because I wanted her to see that I wasn't afraid of her anymore. Her eyes darted this way and that as usual but finally they met my own.

"Are you sure you won't stay for the wedding? I'm sure it would mean a lot...."

When Caroline adamantly shook her head negatively in response, I gave up. "I'll see you around then. And Caroline thanks. Thanks for, you know, everything." Before she could stop me, I reached up and gave her a quick hug. She stood motionless while I bent down to pick up the flowers. Before I got indoors, she was pushing her creaky cart down the alley, humming loudly as she went.

Carrying my bouquet into Mrs. Agneau's living room, I chuckled over Mrs. Fussbudget lying right in the middle of the room. She was propped up in a sitting position as she leaned forward and licked her side. She paused in her bath to eye me curiously for a moment before carrying on with her habitual cleansing.

"No, she's not shy at all. Or nervous, either, like I am!" Mr. Finkelstein said, wringing his hands. "Thank goodness the wedding is just here among friends. I can't imagine what I'd be like if we had to be out in public getting married. I don't think my nerves could take it!"

Just then Dr. Chowdbury walked in the door with Mickey right behind him. Thanks to Mr. Finkelstein, it was settled that Mickey had only acted in self-defense and he was released of all responsibility. Both of them were dressed in dark suits, white shirts, and powder blue ties.

"Don't let Mrs. Fussbudget out!" I yelled, but the cat didn't even look up from cleaning herself this time.

Mickey ran straight for her, laughing, "She's not going anywhere, are you, Mrs. F?" and he proceeded to rub her all over. As soon as Mickey stopped petting her, she lay down with her paws underneath her like a pillow and promptly closed her eyes. "You won't be able to stay in the middle of the room," Mickey laughed. "There are a couple of weddings taking place here today!"

Mickey looked so happy, and Mr. Finkelstein and Dr. Chowdbury did, too; just like one happy family, which is exactly what they were. Not only had all charges against Mickey been dropped, but Mr. Finkelstein had been appointed his legal guardian. Mickey was still holding out for his Mom; he heard she was in treatment again and he felt sure this time she would be able to kick her addiction. In the meantime, both he and Richard were moving in with Mr. Finkelstein and Dr. Chowdbury just as soon as they got back from their honeymoon visiting the Taj Mahal in India. In the meantime, they would be staying with us.

Gerald came in the door then followed by Winston who wandered right up to Mrs. Fussbudget and stuck his nose under her tail. She didn't open her eyes all the way, but she swung her big paw right at his snout. He let out a yelp and backed off, keeping clear of her for the rest of the day.

"Where's my bride?" Gerald bellowed, "No, not you, Finkelstein, even though you do look pure and virgin like today!"

"Why thank you," Mr. Finkelstein said while tapping Gerald's lapel daintily.

"I'll go find her." I raced up the stairs into Mrs. Agneau's room. Mom was standing behind her touching up her hair. I saw that they both had tears in their eyes. Seeing my concern, Mrs. Agneau assured me that they were tears of happiness, not sadness. Reaching for a tissue, she carefully patted her cheeks and sighed.

"I had given up on life and now, here I am, getting a second chance at love and happiness. If only Mr. Agneau could see me now. He would be so happy for me."

"I'm happy for you, too," I said, handing her the bouquet of flowers. "Instead of losing you for a neighbor, we get to keep you and add Gerald and Winston, too! Mr. Finkelstein said that Mickey could finally get his own dog, too, but we're not to talk about it in front of Mrs. Fussbudget. She's got enough changes to deal with at home already!"

We heard the music start. Mrs. Agneau descended the stairs and stood next to Gerald. Mr. Finkelstein stood next to Dr. Chowdbury. Mr. Darcy, the minister, cleared his throat and began the ceremony.

We knew it wasn't legal for the two men to get married, but by standing up with Gerald and Mrs. Agneau, they were going to be as close as they could get to having their own ceremony. As far as we in the neighborhood were concerned, it was a double wedding. We would ever after consider the two couples married.

As the minister began, "We are gathered here today," I smiled happily at Mickey. He grinned right back at me, the same smile he had on his face the first time I ever saw him so long ago standing on the other side of the chain link fence.

<u>Acknowledgements</u>

First and foremost, I need to thank my parents, John and Lucy Dotray, for the wonderful childhood they provided in a home truly filled with an abundance of love and laughter. Thank you to my sisters, Kathy, Jessie, and Mary, who always told me I should and could do this, and to my brothers, John, Dave, Joe, Pete, and Tom.

I am grateful for my extraordinary readers, Timothy, Jackie, my Writer's Group: Bette Traxler and Jon Megahan, Cindy Curtis, Mary Brahs, Jessie Bappe, and Lucinda, Alastair, Jacqueline, and Kareena Tulloch. I am so grateful for your thorough readings, encouragement, and support.

This book is a work of fiction. Names, characters, places, and incidents either are products of the author's imagination or are used fictitiously. Any resemblance to actual events or locales or persons, living or dead, is entirely coincidental.

Made in the USA
Charleston, SC
22 August 2012